PENGUIN BOOKS

THE PALACE GIRLS

Emma Royal is the pen name for established romance writer Katie Ginger, who also writes as Annabel French. She has always loved historical fiction and has a Master's degree in history. When not writing, she can be found running around after her two children and two dogs along with her husband.

THE PALACE GIRLS

EMMA ROYAL

PENGUIN BOOKS

PENGUIN BOOKS

UK | USA | Canada | Ireland | Australia
India | New Zealand | South Africa

Penguin Books is part of the Penguin Random House group
of companies whose addresses can be found at
global.penguinrandomhouse.com

Penguin
Random House
UK

Published in Penguin Books 2023
001

Typeset in 10.4/15pt Palatino LT Pro by Jouve (UK), Milton Keynes
Printed and bound in Great Britain by Clays Ltd, Elcograf S.p.A.

The authorised representative in the EEA
is Penguin Random House Ireland, Morrison Chambers,
32 Nassau Street, Dublin D02 YH68

A CIP catalogue record for this book is available
from the British Library

ISBN: 978–1–804–94548–3

www.greenpenguin.co.uk

To my lovely agent, Kate Nash.

Thank you.

King George VI ascended the throne in 1936 after his brother, King Edward VIII, abdicated to marry Wallis Simpson. A shy but conscientious man, he then led the country through the terrors of the Second World War.

On 23 September 1951, a few months after opening the Festival of Britain, he underwent an operation to remove his left lung. His daughter, Princess Elizabeth, took over many of his duties during his recovery.

November 1951

Chapter One

It was a strange thing for a working-class girl to call a palace home, but that's exactly what it was. Buckingham Palace, home of King George VI, with all its opulence and finery, had been home to Milly Hendry since she was ten years old.

As she stared at one of the paintings in the long, carpeted hallway, duster in hand, she contemplated the twists of fate that had brought her here and almost laughed at the ridiculousness of it all. Not many orphans ended up in a palace. If she hadn't been evacuated to a Devon farm, she might have died in the same air raid that had killed both her parents during the Blitz in 1941, and if her Aunt Edie hadn't taken her in, she might have ended up on the streets, poor and destitute like so many others.

Dear Aunt Edie.

But again, it seemed to Milly so strange that of all the places Edie could have worked, she'd found a job at Buckingham Palace and Milly had followed in her footsteps as soon as she turned fifteen. Only as a cleaner, mind, and one of hundreds at that. But it still seemed odd that she should be standing here now in one of the long crimson-carpeted corridors with gold on the ceilings and at the top of each enormous column, surrounded by paintings and statues, cleaning for a king and queen.

'Are you gawpin' at that paintin' again?' Edie's hushed voice, which couldn't be further from the plummy English accents some of the higher staff spoke with, not to mention the royal family themselves, slipped along the quiet corridor towards her.

'Shhhh!' Milly pressed a finger to her lips, smiling as she did so, and Edie lowered her voice as she drew level.

'Don't you shush me, you little terror. Now, get on with you. Caroline's lit the fires, Davey's refillin' the coal scuttles and you and I better get this corridor done and dusted in the next five minutes or we'll be behind schedule. Why do you keep gogglin' at that paintin' anyway?'

'I don't really know,' Milly replied, crossing her arms over her chest. 'I just like it, I suppose.'

It depicted a pack of hounds running in front of riders on horseback. She didn't know who it was by. Milly didn't really know anything about painting or artists apart from the fact that nearly everything in the palace cost a fortune and was by some famous person or other. All she knew was that she liked it. She liked the riders' glossy helmets and fancy jackets, their shining black boots. But most of all she liked the freedom it showed. It would be amazing to just jump on a horse and ride off without a care in the world.

'You do realise that's a hunt, don't you?' asked Edie, her rosacea-covered cheeks matching the red of the carpet. They hadn't always been this way. When Milly thought back, she remembered Edie's pale skin and thick, tawny hair. It was peppered with grey now – inch-long fingers of it reaching

4

out from the top of her head. 'You know, where they all race around after a poor little fox then the dogs tear it to shreds?'

'What?' Milly's eyes widened as she looked at her aunt.

'Oh, my girl, sometimes I think I didn't do you any favours bringin' you here.'

It was true that her life had been somewhat cloistered, living with Edie in their small staff apartments in Buckingham Palace along with all the other housekeepers. And the gardeners, cooks, footmen, kitchen staff . . . too many people to mention. With so many below-stairs staff, and the seniors who worked directly with the King and Queen, the palace was like a city within a city. It had everything they needed, and with the royal kitchen providing all their meals there wasn't any need to stray far.

So many people during the war, and in the years since, had had to buy or rent homes because theirs had been destroyed, to begin their life again after they'd lost literally everything. Milly averted her eyes from the fox she now spotted in the corner of the painting and counted her blessings. The pain of losing her parents still struck her, particularly on special occasions: birthdays, Christmas, that sort of thing, but at least she had memories of good times rather than bad.

'Sometimes,' Edie continued, brushing a strand of grey-brown hair behind her ear, 'I think I should have made you work somewhere else so you got out into the world a bit more.'

'Oh, come on, Aunt Edie. It's not like I never go into the city.'

How could she not? The bustling world of London was

right on her doorstep. She and Edie often went to Oxford Street shopping, or to Bloomsbury to visit the British Museum. She'd even been to Covent Garden to see a show with one of the under-butlers, though he'd been dismissed for thievery so the less said about him the better. It wasn't that she didn't know anything about life outside the palace walls, she just didn't know everything.

Milly nudged her aunt with her elbow. 'I'm not that naive.'

'Really.' Edie crossed her arms over her chest, resting her ample bosom on top. She was what Milly had always called sturdy, with her short, round body but was as strong as an ox and had once proved it by arm-wrestling one of the kitchen porters after too much Christmas sherry. She nearly broke his arm.

'I'll be twenty-one tomorrow. And it's not my fault I don't know what that painting is about. These poshies are always off somewhere or other on a horse. Princess Margaret and Princess Elizabeth love to ride. And why would anyone want to hunt foxes?' She adjusted one of the pins in the straw-blonde bun at the nape of her neck.

'Beats me, but there you are. Come on, what have I told you? The best servants are neither seen—'

'—nor heard,' Milly finished.

'And you'll be both if we don't get a squiggle on. You do this side and I'll do that one. I'm still tryin' to get sticky finger marks off the wall from Prince Charles's birthday party.'

The little prince had turned three just two days before and had been staying at Buckingham Palace, along with his baby sister, Princess Anne, rather than Clarence House as his mother and father, Princess Elizabeth, and Philip, the Duke of Edinburgh, were on a state visit to Canada. The eldest princess had taken on more of her father's duties since his illness back in September when he'd had a lung removed. It had been a pleasant day and a great success, but the cleanup had been awful. Cake crumbs lingered everywhere.

They worked on in silence for a few minutes, moving down the length of the corridor dusting every available surface. The palace was famous for never containing a speck of dust and all the housekeeping staff took pride in the fact that was down to them. Some of the staff had the pleasure of hobnobbing with the great and the good, but it was thanks to the cleaners they could show off the palace knowing it would always look its best.

'Aunt Edie, why can't we get one of those fancy vacuum cleaners? I saw them advertised in your *Woman & Home* magazine. They'd save us ever such a lot of time and make it easier to get this dog hair out. Those corgis really do shed.'

'And how much noise would that make? What would Queen Elizabeth say to that? Never mind the poor old King who needs as much rest as he can get. Neither seen nor heard, remember? Cartin' one of those things around, as well as the racket it'd make when we switch it on, would wake everyone.'

Out of the window, looking out on to the grounds at the back of the palace, the sun was just beginning to rise. A pale sky tinted by a watery sun was edging further out of the navy-blue dawn and climbing over the colossal trees that lined the edge of the garden. The leaves had all fallen now, swept away by cold winter winds leaving nothing but bare branches and birds' nests. Even the birds hadn't yet risen, but Milly had grown so used to the early starts she often forgot that while they worked as quickly and quietly as possible, the rest of the world was still asleep. Not just the royal family, but most of London too.

The sound of fast footsteps could be heard in the distance and Milly tried to place them. She knew the tread of King George and Queen Elizabeth, his steady and even and hers short and light. And she definitely knew the firm, military steps of Peter Townsend, the Deputy Master of the Household – one of their senior bosses. It definitely wasn't any of them.

Just then, a woman Milly had never met before came bustling along the corridor. She could see from her clothes she wasn't a member of the royal household. She wasn't wearing the same immensely impractical white dress the housekeepers wore. Whilst clean and tidy, her slightly battered tweed suit was more East End than English royalty and her black hair was falling out from under her hat.

'I say, excuse me,' the woman said. 'I don't suppose you know where the telephone exchange is? The chap at the gates pointed me in the right direction but I was in such a panic I must have taken a wrong turn and now I'm completely lost.'

'It's easy to do here, love,' said Aunt Edie gently. 'But you're in totally the wrong place. I don't quite know how you've managed it.'

The woman's cheeks coloured, and Milly stepped in, hoping to make her feel better. She was only a little older than her though a sadness seemed to weigh her down. 'It's all right for you, Aunt Edie. You've been here for – what, thirty years?'

'Give or take,' Edie replied with a slight nod.

'You know this place like the back of your hand but for some of us it's still a bit of a muddle.' She turned to the woman. 'I've been working here since I was fifteen and there are some bits even I don't know. With so many corridors and hidden stairs it's easy to get lost.'

'Gosh. I haven't even come across any hidden stairs yet, thank goodness. Who knows where I might have ended up if I had.'

'Maybe in the King's bedroom,' Milly said with a giggle and was pleased to see a smile lift the corners of the woman's mouth. 'I'm not sure that'd do his recovery any good.'

'Milly!' Edie scolded. 'Don't you go talkin' about the King like that. Though he is a very handsome gentleman, in my opinion.'

The smile faded from the woman's mouth as she checked her watch again. 'I'm so sorry but which way do I go?'

'That way,' answered Edie, pointing down the hallway they'd just cleaned. 'Follow it round, then down the steps, first left, second right and then second left. That'll take you to the staff block. The telephone exchange is in that bit. Then you need to go . . . Actually, I won't tell you any more. It'd be better to get someone to show you when you get there. Did you get what I said?'

'I think so.'

Milly wasn't convinced she had.

The woman began to straighten her jacket and as she

pulled down the hem, her elbow knocked into a vase sat on top of the side table behind her. The vase wobbled on its base and the woman spun, reaching out instinctively even though it was too late to stop it.

'No!' she cried out.

Milly watched as it fell sideways and rolled off the table and on to the ground, smashing to pieces. The sound of breaking porcelain echoed around the empty, silent hallway, the noise reaching every corner of the palace and bouncing back towards them, just like the dinner gong they used for special occasions. That thing always made Milly jump even when she was expecting it.

The woman's hands flew to her face. 'Oh no. What am I going to do? I can't afford to pay for that and it's my first day.' She shook her head as she spoke. 'I can't lose this job and I'm already late. First my father, then the bus, and then when I finally got here, I couldn't find the servants' entrance. It's all going wrong.'

'What happened to your dad?' asked Milly, wondering why she hadn't said more.

'Oh, it doesn't matter.'

Tears threatened the poor woman's eyes and Milly stepped forwards. 'Don't worry, we can clean it up and I'll tell them I did it.'

'I couldn't possibly let you do that. Won't you get into trouble?'

'No, she won't,' Edie said, 'because I'll tell them I did it. It's not one of the priceless ones. At least I don't think it is.' The woman's face paled. Clearly the idea it might have been was too much.

'It still must have cost a fortune even if it isn't priceless. Will they make you pay for it? I can't possibly let you.' Milly suddenly noticed how blue her eyes were and they shone even brighter with the glassiness of unshed tears.

'It's fine,' Edie replied soothingly. 'Accidents happen.'

'Are you sure? It's all far too kind of you. I don't want you to get into any trouble because of me.'

'I won't have to pay for it, dear. They're not monsters here. Besides, you can count the things I've broken on the fingers of one hand. If you're goin' to be a housekeeper at Buckingham Palace, you need to be careful. But you better get off, my girl, or you'll be even later and then you definitely *will* get into trouble.'

'You're right. I'm really terribly sorry but thank you. Thank you so much. You've been so kind to me.' A tear escaped her eye, and she quickly brushed it away.

'Now, now, we don't need all that. You've got first-day nerves, that's all. I'm sure you'll be fine.'

'The day can only get better, I suppose.'

'What's your name?' asked Milly before she left. 'I'm Milly Hendry and this is my Aunt Edie.' She stuck out her hand and, as she did so, saw Edie roll her eyes.

'It's Mrs Barnes to most people. Only Edie when we're off duty.'

'Helen. Helen Hill.' Helen shook Milly's hand and then Edie's. Her gloves were cream. Well, mostly cream. They too had seen better days. 'I really can't thank you enough. You really are too, too kind.'

'You said that already,' Milly replied with a smile. 'Go on, go, and good luck.'

Helen hesitated, casting her eyes once more to the fragments of vase that were scattered on the floor. 'All right then. Goodbye and thank you ever so much, both of you.'

She dashed off and Edie and Milly crouched to collect the shards of porcelain, careful not to cut themselves.

'Do you think they will mind?' Milly asked, taking the pieces she'd collected to the small cleaning trolley.

'I shouldn't think so.'

'How can you be so sure?'

A wry smile pulled at Edie's mouth. 'The King hates this vase.'

'How do you know that?'

'He told me.'

'When?'

Edie straightened and glowed with pride at the memory. 'He found me dustin' it one day and said so. Like I said, he's a gentleman and always talks to us if he can spare the time. Best to avoid him when he's in his gnashes though. Got quite a temper sometimes.'

'She seemed nice, don't you think?'

'Nice enough, but you know what some of these other departments are like. Some of them – not all, mind – but some think they're better than us housekeepers just because we clean for a livin'.'

'I don't think she seemed like that.'

'Hmm.' Edie glanced back over her shoulder. 'Anyway, I doubt we'll see her again except in passin'.'

'But you must think so too, or you wouldn't have offered to say it was you who knocked the vase over. Do you think she'll make it to the telephone exchange on time?'

'Not a chance, my lovely. Not a chance.'

Two hours later, Milly and Edie were settled around a large table in the Household Breakfast Room. The team always gathered for breakfast together, particularly if they'd had an early start and breakfast was more like lunch. Relaxing a little, they ate buttered English muffins and drank strong, sweet tea. Eggs were still rationed, even for the royal palaces, and Milly longed for one boiled that she could dip her soldiers into, but she'd already had her ration for the week. She often wondered what the King and Queen ate for breakfast and if they stuck to the rules. Edie always said they did and Robert, one of the kitchen porters, said they only had extra eggs when they were laid by the hens kept by the ground staff. King George had been sure to make everyone use ration cards and Princess Elizabeth had even used her clothing coupons for her wedding dress back in 1947. It was hard to believe that, with the war over for six years already, they were still being rationed.

One of the older footmen had once told Milly that before Princess Elizabeth's move to Clarence House with her new husband, she had often joined the family for breakfast, though Princess Margaret had a habit of being late, coming down when she wanted to even if everyone else had finished by then. Milly wasn't entirely sure what she thought of Princess Margaret. In some ways she sympathised with her. It must be awful being born into a position you didn't want to fill and to always be second best to a sister who would one day be queen. But she was lucky to have money, a family who loved her and a purpose in life – and so Milly couldn't help thinking Margaret just a tad ungrateful.

Though Milly and Princess Margaret were the same age, she felt much more of a kinship with Elizabeth. Milly had been brought up here and everyone had assumed she'd end up working at the palace just as Elizabeth would one day follow her father to the throne, whether she wanted to or not. She heard a male voice and turned, thinking it was Timothy Ranger, one of the footmen, who had dark-brown hair and eyes like melted chocolate. He only had to glance at Milly and her heart would flutter uncontrollably. But it wasn't him. He must have been on duty.

Caroline, one of their newest recruits, gave an almighty yawn, bringing Milly's mind back to the present.

'Tired, Caroline?' asked Aunt Edie.

'Knackered, Mrs Barnes. Fair done in.'

'Shame, that,' Milly replied. In the six months since she joined, the young girl had become like a little sister to her. Or, at least, what she assumed a little sister would be like if she'd had one: annoying or sweet depending on their mood. 'We've got a lot more to do after breakfast. Better eat that up to give you some energy.'

'Maybe', Edie said, eyeing the young girl over the rim of her teacup, 'you should think about goin' to bed earlier. Don't think I haven't seen a light on under your door far longer than it should be.'

'I ain't got the foggiest what you're on about, Mrs Barnes. Honestly,' Caroline replied, shifting in her chair. She had a strong cockney accent whereas Milly's had changed over time, growing up around the royal family. 'If my light was on I must have just been to the loo. Or maybe I was reading.'

'You? Reading?' Milly spluttered.

'Hey! I can read. I like books actually.'

'Oh yes, what have you got?'

'None of your beeswax, Milly Hendry. Don't be such a nosey parker.'

Just as Milly was about to tease Caroline a little more, one of the postboys approached their table.

Buckingham Palace had its own post office, which was very handy for those with family to write to. Milly's only family sat opposite her, wiping butter from the corner of her mouth. If Milly had written her a letter, Edie would have thought she'd gone mad.

'Here you are, ladies,' the postboy said. 'Thought I'd find you all here. Caroline, there's two for you.'

She took them eagerly, tearing the top letter open, her eyes scanning the words quickly. She received at least two letters every week and sent out goodness knows how many more. All her wages must go on stamps. Caroline's lips moved, forming the words as she read, and Milly felt a stab of jealousy. No one ever wrote to her. There was no one outside the palace who needed to.

'Here's one for you, Mrs Barnes.' The boy handed over another letter to her aunt. She had friends up and down the country and wrote almost as many letters as Caroline.

'And last but not least, one for you, Milly.'

'Me?' She sat up straighter, knocking her cutlery on to her plate with a clatter. 'Who's writing to me?'

'Birthday card maybe? We're all looking forward to your little party. It'll be nice to have something to celebrate. Goodness knows the mood's dark enough around here at the moment.'

Since the King's operation on his lungs in September, he'd had to rest for four weeks, and though he was up and about, and performing some of his normal duties, the mood in the palace was sombre both above and below stairs. Doctors still haunted the hallways like ghosts, appearing and disappearing without warning. Everyone loved the King after the way he'd staunchly stayed at the palace all through the war, even when London was being bombed to bits. But the war had taken its toll on him, and an unspoken fear played on everyone's minds that his recovery was taking longer than it should. No one wanted to think of exactly what that meant, and no one voiced their concerns out loud, especially in earshot of the senior staff or the royal family.

Milly turned the letter over, inspecting it as if she'd never seen one before.

Edie's brow creased in concern, and she leaned forward, eyeing the letter in Milly's hand as though someone had handed her an incendiary device. 'What's that then?'

'Don't rightly know, Aunt. I can't think of anyone who'd want to write to me. Can you?'

'Don't just play with it,' Caroline said. 'Open it and see who it's from.'

Milly carefully lifted the flap on the envelope and pulled out a letter, scanning the thin pieces of paper. The writing was so messy it was difficult to read, and her face screwed up in confusion as she studied each line, slowly and carefully deciphering the scrappily written words. As she moved further and further down the page, her heart rate sped up just as it did when she saw Timothy, but this wasn't a pleasant sensation.

'Milly?' asked Edie. There was a note of tension in her voice. A slightly strangled tone that Milly had never heard before.

'Yeah, come on,' added Caroline. 'Don't keep us guessing.'

The muscles in Milly's stomach tightened as she got to the end of the letter. Reading the signature on the bottom, her hands shook, and she had to force the words out through her tight throat.

'It's from . . . It's from my mum.'

Chapter Two

'Your mum?' Caroline asked. 'But isn't she—'

Edie launched herself to standing, rounded the end of the table and grabbed the letter from Milly's hand before she could react.

'Aunty!'

'Let me see.' Her rosy cheeks were suddenly pale, her hazel eyes wide as they darted over each sentence. 'It can't be . . .'

'Is someone playing a horrid trick on me?' Anger grew inside Milly, and she stood up, needing to move, to free the frustration fighting to get out of her muscles. Such a cruel reminder of her parents clouded her mind with a grief she'd hoped to forget.

Caroline bent her head down, staring into her teacup. The postboy began to back away. The rest of the Household Breakfast Room had fallen silent. Some stared at Milly in disbelief; others averted their gaze, embarrassed at the unseemly outburst. But Milly couldn't hold back the surge of emotion forcing the words to cascade from her mouth. Everyone knew her mother and father were dead. Everyone.

'If someone's having a laugh at my expense, it isn't funny. Not funny at all.' Milly watched her aunt, who was frantically rereading the letter, turning the pages over and over.

Her face was ashen, drained of all colour, and even her rosa-cea had paled to a blotchy dusty pink.

'I don't believe it,' she muttered. 'She—'

It felt as if the eyes of the world were on Milly and, as humiliation burned the back of her neck, chest and face, she couldn't stay standing in the silence, in front of the disap-proving looks any longer. Someone muttered, 'Well I never,' and Milly bolted from the room. The last thing she heard as she shoved open the door was chatter erupting behind her, but she didn't care what they thought. They could all mind their own business.

Milly dodged other members of staff as she darted down the corridors and pushed open another heavy door, letting the cold winter air hit her cheeks. She took three deep breaths as the wind cooled her burning face but soon goosebumps rose on her arms. The freezing air stroked her skin and the promise of sunlight she'd seen this morning had vanished behind dark grey storm clouds. Embarrass-ment mixed with hurt and anger inside her. Who would do this to her? Was this someone's idea of a joke? A twenty-first birthday prank? That would be too heartless. Her mother was gone, and everyone knew it.

Milly's mind flew to the day Edie had told her of the ter-rible bombing that had caused her parents' deaths. She'd made the trip down to the farm in Devon where Milly had been evacuated, plonked in the middle of the countryside surrounded by sheep and chickens and cows as big as horses. Some of the kids had loved it, but she hadn't. She'd missed the city, the noise, her home.

The London train had pulled into the station billowing

smoke and Edie had stepped off on to the platform. Milly, who had been standing there with Mrs Harlow, the woman who'd looked after her, had thrown herself into her aunt's arms, so happy to see her. She'd thought it was just a visit. Her aunt had been the only person to visit her while she was there. Mum and Dad had been too busy. Milly's dad had worked for the railways, in a protected occupation, and time off had been as rare as hen's teeth. But Milly hadn't known then that this particular visit was going to change everything.

From the station they'd all travelled in Mr Harlow's cart with Daisy, the draught horse, pulling the way. The Harlows didn't have a car – they couldn't afford one. In Milly's memories, Edie had smiled and everything had seemed normal but of course it couldn't have been. She would have been holding on to the dreadful news and no doubt there would have been signs if Milly had been smart enough to read them.

Seated around the large wooden table in the kitchen, Edie had taken Milly's hands and told her calmly that she was so, so sorry, but Milly's mother and father had been killed in an air raid. The house had been completely destroyed and then a fire had followed, ripping through everything, leaving nothing behind.

Milly had cried and shouted that it couldn't be true, but people died every day back then. Here one day and gone the next with no idea it was coming. Edie held her as she wept. The mother who she remembered as smiling and kind and the father who was always cracking jokes were gone.

A week later, Milly had returned to London for the

funeral though there'd been a mix-up in the timings and she'd arrived after the service had taken place. Edie hadn't wanted her to attend anyway – she'd said it would be too much for someone her age. But young girls up and the down the country were losing loved ones and attending funerals. Milly's grief wasn't unique or special. She was simply another person who had lost someone and there was bucking up to be done, stiff upper lips to be kept.

In the churchyard near her old house in Bethnal Green, the headstone named her mother and her father as lying within, resting in peace. Afterwards Milly had moved into Edie's staff apartment and lived with her at Buckingham Palace. Her new life had begun.

This letter had to be a joke. A cruel, silly joke. There wasn't any other explanation.

The door opened gently, and Milly turned to see Helen, the woman from earlier.

'Hello. Are you all right? I saw the kerfuffle in the Breakfast Room and couldn't help but come after you.'

Milly began to pace, willing her emotions to stop crashing around inside her. One minute she wanted to cry and the next she wanted to hit something. She forced herself to stand still. 'What are you doing here?' she asked, mustering a smile. 'Are you lost again?'

'No, not this time. I'm on a tea break and fancied a little something to eat. I didn't get the chance to have any breakfast this morning. Too nervous and it's such an early start. When I saw what happened in there, I thought I better check on you.'

'That's kind of you. You didn't have to. Did you make it to the exchange on time?'

'No, but I wasn't too late, thankfully. I just explained what happened – most of it, anyway – to my boss and he said it sounded like I'd had a horrid enough beginning to my first day without him telling me off too. Jolly decent of him, I think. I didn't mention the vase – I fear if I had, he may not have been so forgiving.' Helen leaned against the wall. She pulled a pack of cigarettes from her handbag and offered one to Milly, who shook her head. 'So what was all that about?'

'I got a letter.'

'Letters don't normally elicit that sort of reaction from people. What on earth did it say?'

'It's from my mum.'

'Right.' Helen hesitated, clearly unsure why that was a problem.

'And she's dead.'

'Oh.' She pushed herself upright, releasing the smoke from her lungs with a long, slow exhale, her mouth forming a pretty circle. 'Goodness. I see.' She didn't really, but there wasn't much else to say in this situation. 'That must have been terribly upsetting for you. I'm so sorry. Is it some sort of mix-up?'

'I don't think so.'

'Then who do you think—'

The door opened again, and Edie stepped out, panting as though she'd had to single-handedly clean the ballroom and had been timed doing so.

'There you are,' she puffed. 'I'm too old to be runnin' around after you, Milly Hendry. Oh, my lungs.'

'Oh, my heart,' Milly replied, pressing a hand to her chest, knowing she was being dramatic but unable to stop herself. It took a lot to make Milly cry. Sometimes she thought she'd shed all her tears years ago. Had used them all up. But they were trying their best to get out, misting her vision so she had to open her eyes wide against the cold wind to dry them. Edie often said what doesn't kill you makes you stronger but right now Milly was ready to give who ever had done this horrible thing a clip round the ear. She couldn't deny the pain it was causing. It was like reliving their deaths all over again.

'I had better go,' said Helen. 'My tea break's nearly over and I don't want to be late back.'

'Do you know your way now?' Milly asked.

'I wrote it down.' Helen stubbed out her cigarette, and unsure where to put the end, slid it back into the packet before taking a small notebook from her bag and waving it at Milly. 'Listen, I know we've only just met, but if you ever need to talk, I'm always happy to have a chat. You seem nice and . . . well, you know where to find me.'

'I might take you up on that.'

'Maybe we could have lunch?' Helen said.

'That'd be lovely.'

'And I still intend to show you both how grateful I am for this morning. In the meantime, feel free to bend my ear if you need to. I know what it's like not to have anyone to talk to.' Realising Edie was standing right there, Helen blushed, adding, 'I mean, I know you have your aunt but it's always good to have friends too, isn't it?'

Edie scowled and Helen hurried back inside.

'Actually,' Milly called, and Helen paused. 'I'm having a small party tomorrow for my birthday, if you want to come?'

'I'd love to, but . . .' She took a small step back towards them, lowering her voice. 'My father's a bit poorly at the moment so I'm not sure if I'll be able to make it. I promise I'll do my best though.'

From the forecourt the sound of the Changing of the Guard carried across the air. The regular rhythm of the drums, the slight tinny whistling, the crunch of gravel underfoot. Milly had heard it so many times and yet today, when everything was strange and undone, the notes seemed sharper, cutting through the haze.

'This has to be a joke, doesn't it, Aunt Edie? Unless someone's pretending to be my mum. But why would they do that? She didn't have much. She was a nobody, like me, and she's been dead for ten years.'

'You're not a nobody,' Edie replied sternly. 'You're Milly Hendry and there's only one Milly Hendry in the whole wide world. That makes you special.'

'You would say that.' Milly reached out, her fingers trembling, silently asking for the letter back. With a final glance, Edie handed it over and Milly took a moment to reread it. 'Who would have done this to me? Do you think it's that horrible pot wash who works the morning shift? Your friend Mrs Chadwick doesn't like him, does she? And Caroline told me he's always making trouble.'

'Possibly,' Edie replied. Mrs Chadwick, the cook, was one of Edie's closest friends and she'd moaned about him to both Edie and Milly on several occasions, but Edie didn't seem convinced. 'I reckon the best thing to do is to forget about it. If it's a horrible joke, then showin' the person you don't care is best. Don't let them know it's bothered you.'

'What?' Edie was a very calm person but still, Milly had expected her to be calling out for complaints to be made and punishments dealt. 'How can you say that? This person needs telling off, putting in their place. They can't get away with doing something so horrible to someone. It's hurt me, Aunt Edie. It really has.' She would not let the tears fall but the stinging at the back of her eyes made her sniff.

Edie stepped forwards and wrapped her arms around Milly. 'Come on back inside and we'll have a nice cuppa in the apartment.'

'I don't want a cup of tea. I want to know who'd do something like this so I can . . .'

'So you can what?'

'I don't know. Punch them on the nose—'

'You'll do no such thing. You'll lose your job.'

The fight inside Milly suddenly vanished. 'Everyone knows my parents are dead.'

Edie's grip tightened but there was a slight waver to her voice. 'If I were you, I'd burn that awful letter and forget the whole thing.'

'Burn it? Why would I do that? Surely I need it as evidence to show the Head Chef or Mrs Chadwick if it is that horrible pot wash.'

'You can't go accusin' people willy nilly, Milly.'

A tiny smile lifted the corner of Milly's mouth at the silly rhyme. Her aunt always knew how to cheer her, but why wasn't she as outraged as Milly was? She'd expected indignation, fury, even cursing, but all Edie seemed to want was to forget about it.

'Aunt Edie, why aren't you angry about this?'

'I – well . . .' She crossed her arms over her chest. 'Of course I'm angry, I just don't think—'

'You know everyone around here. And you've always said you're a good judge of character. You must have some idea who could have sent this.'

'Maybe I'm as shocked as you are, Milly, ever think of that? But whoever it is might lose their job or at the least get a warnin' if you go to the nibs. You need to calm down and think clearly before you do anythin' in case you're wrong.'

Milly lifted her chin defiantly. 'I'm going to find out who did this, and I don't care who they are, they'll not get away with it.' Her eyes dropped to the letter and Milly paused in confusion. 'It's postmarked Birmingham. I don't know anyone from Birmingham. What does it mean, Edie? There's something fishy going on here. Maybe we should tell the police.'

'No!' Edie shouted, reaching for the envelope again. She grabbed it and took a step back. 'Maybe someone in Birmingham's made a mistake and thinks they've written to the right Milly Hendry but haven't.'

'I thought you said I was the only Milly Hendry in the world,' Milly replied, aware of the petulance in her voice.

'You know what I mean, young lady.'

Milly shook her head. 'The letter says about our old house in Bethnal Green and the farm in Devon. It's signed Jean and that was my mum's name. She wants to meet. She even mentioned that it's my birthday soon. Look, I'll show you.' Milly opened her hand, but Edie held on to the letter. For some reason she couldn't quite explain, she was worried her aunt was about to tear it up. 'Can I have my letter back please?'

Edie hesitated again, finally looking up to meet Milly's eyes. 'Not until you promise not to go to the police.'

'But, Aunt Edie—'

'You have to promise.'

'Why?' Milly stared, meeting her aunt's gaze straight on. Edie's face was as serious as Milly had ever seen it, but under the frustration, there was fear. It danced over her eyes, tightening the wrinkles cut into her skin.

Her aunt's eyes dropped. She stared at the ground and let her hand fall so the letter landed in Milly's palm. She seemed beaten, dejected, and Milly's heart went out to her. She should have considered how much of a shock this would have been for her too. How horrid it must be to see a fake letter from a dead sister. The cold wind bit into Milly's skin and she shivered.

'You can't go to the police,' Edie said calmly, and Milly's sympathy gave way to a jolt of unease.

'Why not? Edie, what's happening?'

Closing her eyes, Edie sighed as if something heavy was weighing her down, pushing all the breath from her body. 'There's somethin' I need to tell you.'

Chapter Three

Seated at the small table in Edie's apartment, Milly watched as Edie brought over a tea tray. The pink crocheted pot warmer her aunt had made covered the small white pot and the cups and saucers were stacked neatly. The letter sat between them on top of its envelope.

Edie had refused to speak any more out in the freezing air at the back of the staff kitchen and, her anger abating a little, Milly had agreed to go inside. She desperately wanted to know what exactly it was her aunt needed to tell her but with people coming and going, Edie had wanted somewhere more private. After the spectacle Milly had already made of herself there didn't seem much point but she'd agreed for her aunt's sake.

On the walk back to the staff quarters, Milly's mind raced. Did Edie know more than she was letting on? Did she know who had sent the letter? If someone here had written it, which was the only option as far as Milly was concerned because she didn't know anyone in Birmingham, they could have sent it to their family to post back. But why would someone go to all that trouble just to play a birthday prank?

Whatever discussion they were going to have, they didn't have long. Both she and Edie were due back at work. In fact, they were already late, but there was no way this conversation could wait. She hoped Caroline would cover for them if the Chief Housekeeper asked where they were.

The apartment was cold. They didn't have any of those new, fancy electric fires in the staff rooms and it seemed wasteful to light a fire when they weren't normally anywhere near it. Impatiently, Milly flicked her eyes over the room, urging her aunt to begin, but Edie took her time, stirring the teapot and pouring the dark, restorative liquid into cups. As they sat in the tense atmosphere, the familiar room seemed altered. The pictures that lined the mantelshelf watched on like ghosts. There was one of her mum and dad on their wedding day, before she was born. Her mum had been beautiful, her dad handsome. In contrast, the small picture frame showing a young Edie Barnes showed a woman with a hard, angular face. Not unattractive as such, but nothing compared to her sister. Edie had grown into her features as she'd aged, and they'd softened as the lines of her body had softened too.

The dim winter light leaked in through the small windows, so different to the large panes in the main part of the palace where the light flooded in, shining off the heavy glass chandeliers. It had started to rain and, as the room darkened further, tiny drops pattered against the window.

'You should have some sugar,' Edie said, dropping a cube into a cup and handing it to Milly. 'For the shock.'

Yes, she was shocked, but she was angry too, her nerves shredded waiting for Edie to explain. It was taking every ounce of patience she had not to shout at her to hurry up. Instead, she quelled the tumbling nerves in her stomach and said, 'Edie, what's going on? What do you mean you've got something to tell me?'

Edie sat back in her chair, her cup and saucer held in front of her. 'Before I start, I need you to know I did it all for the best.'

Milly's stomach vaulted, sending up a wave of queasiness. 'All of what?'

Edie stirred her tea one more time and took a deep breath. 'Your mum didn't die in a bombin', Milly. Though God knows things would have been easier if she had.'

The muscles in Milly's body went momentarily loose as if she had no control over them, and the cup and saucer almost fell from her fingers. She tightened her grip, her body reviving after the initial shock, steadying the tea. With her eyes on Edie, she said, 'What?' She sounded stupid. Like a child at school who can't solve the simplest maths problem or get their letters right, but she had no words. Her mind wouldn't move past the sentence her aunt had just uttered. 'When *did* she die then?'

'Oh, Milly love, she didn't die. Not then and not since, as far as I know.'

'Are you telling me my mum's alive? Are you saying she really did write me this letter?'

'I think so.'

'You think so.' It was half statement, half question.

Edie took a sip of tea, but her calm demeanour riled Milly. She couldn't pretend that they were having tea and scones and a gossip about the day as they normally did. This was madness. Nonsense. It couldn't be true. Tears stung Milly's eyes and this time she couldn't hold them back.

Without the fierceness of anger to overtake them they slipped from her eyes and down her cheeks. She felt betrayed. She'd always trusted Edie implicitly, never questioned anything she said, but now the one pillar in her life, the one constant thing, was crumbling.

'But there was a funeral. A grave. Why did you lie to me?'

'My girl,' Edie said, placing her cup down and reaching for Milly's arm. She squeezed it but the familiar, reassuring warmth of her touch wasn't as powerful as it had been before. Things were different now. 'I'm so sorry. I never heard from her again and I think, in the end, I convinced myself she had died in the war.'

'I don't understand,' Milly mumbled. Her mum's eyes stared out at her from their place in the photograph and she wished she could run and turn it over. She remembered toast served for breakfast, a smiling face delivering it to her. Her dad kissing the top of her head before he left for work.

'I know it don't make any sense, and it seems it's time I told you everythin'. I'm ashamed, Milly. I am. But I thought I was doin' the right thing, so I need you to listen to me carefully. Your mum – my sister – was always very headstrong. She liked to go out and have a good time. Even the war didn't stop her like it did others. In fact, it made her worse. The idea we could be bombed any minute meant she did exactly what she wanted, when she wanted. Why do you think I looked after you so much here, even when you were little?'

'Because Mum was working. That's what you always

31

told me.' She had spent a lot of time with Edie, staying put in her room here so as not to get underfoot.

'It's what I told you and I wish to God it had been true, but it wasn't. Your dad was a fine man, always workin' to give Jean what she wanted, but it was never enough. Nothin' ever was for her. If your mum wasn't at home, she was off with some fancy man or other. She didn't care what the neighbours said or how people gossiped about her.'

'She – she didn't love Dad?' A cold tear ran down Milly's hot cheek and she swiped it away. How could this be true? She had so many memories that said otherwise. Her mum and dad had worked a lot and there had been disagreements before she was evacuated a few months into the Blitz, but it was wartime and life was difficult.

'No, my girl, I'm afraid she didn't.'

'But you always said—'

'I know what I always said,' Edie replied softly. 'I said it to spare you. You were only a child.'

'What happened?' Frustration mounted. She wanted the truth. All of it. Now.

The rain had grown harder, and the drops raced down the panes, obscuring the view.

'I don't know how to tell you this.' Her voice was small and unfamiliar. Edie had always been the type of woman to be certain of everything – everything she did, everything she said – and to hear her hesitant and doubtful rocked Milly's already shaken world anew. 'When your mum found out she was pregnant our father – your grandfather – almost threw her out. The only reason he didn't was because your dad agreed to marry her. A shotgun weddin'.'

Milly's head swung back to the photograph. Was there any hint in that old, faded picture it hadn't been a fairy-tale romance? To her their smiles had always looked genuine, but was there a tightness to her mum's mouth? A slightly trapped look to her eyes?

'I don't think my mother ever recovered from the shock, though it wasn't a shock to me. I could see the writin' on the wall even before then. From the minute your mum turned eighteen she was out on the tiles every night. I hoped being a mum would change her. It changed me the day I saw your little face. I thought: how could anyone not love this tiny precious thing? You were beautiful. Like a little china doll. So beautiful.'

She studied Milly's face, tears forming in her hazel eyes, and Milly could see the pain written in the lines on her brow and the turn of her mouth. She wanted to wind the clock back to before this dreadful letter arrived and carry on as they always had. But her aunt had lied to her and right now she still didn't know why.

'Jean didn't like being a mum. At first, when she struggled, I thought she just had the baby blues. Hoped it would fade and she'd see how lucky she was to have you and a man who loved her – because your dad did love her, though she never really loved him, and he loved you more than anythin'. But Jean was never one for bein' grateful for what she had. She missed bein' free and single and before long, she was out most nights havin' affairs.'

'Affairs? No, she couldn't have. I was there.'

'I know you don't want to believe it, my girl, but it's the truth. She didn't always bring the fellas back to your house.

33

She'd go to theirs and come home at ridiculous times of the night. But there were times she brought some of them back, especially when your dad was workin' nights. She was careful to get them out before you woke though. It was disgraceful and it broke your dad's heart.'

A searing pain ripped through Milly. She couldn't believe any of this was true. Surely she'd have remembered it? She'd only been a child, but she had memories of other things that had happened: hiding in the underground until the all clear sounded, the destruction in the streets, being evacuated. This couldn't be right.

'Anyway.' Edie brushed her skirt, clearly not wanting to linger on the subject. 'When you were evacuated, she took up with a right villain called Billy Venables. Said she met him at the bus stop but I know she was goin' out to clubs at all hours of the night. He was a piano player – how many of those do you meet at the bus stop? – and a conman.'

'How do you know?' Milly hadn't meant to sound accusatory but the story she was hearing was harrowing and she wanted to find some shred of evidence within it. 'Maybe they were in love.'

'In lust more like.' Edie's words cut Milly and she cast her eyes down. 'I'm sorry. I know this is hard for you, but if I'm goin' to tell you the truth I might as well tell you all of it.'

'You better go on then.' Milly's defiant, angry tone rang around the silent room. She didn't want to hurt Edie, but Edie had hurt her by lying to her for so many years, and now she was shattering the memories she had of her mum. And memories had been the only thing she had left.

'When I heard the house had been bombed, I ran straight

there.' Edie took a deep breath. 'Your dad's body had been laid out on a stretcher. God, I wept for him. He was such a good man, God rest his soul, but your mum's weren't there. I was relieved. She was my sister, after all. Then she appeared on the arm of this Billy, tellin' me they were off. I said, "What do you mean, 'off'? Off to get Milly?" She looked at me like I'd gone mad. Like she'd forgotten about you until I said your name.'

Milly's chest exploded in pain. She felt her lip quiver and bit down hard to force it to stop.

'She says, "No, we need to leave London." This Billy had arranged for a death certificate to be signed by a doctor he knew. No doubt some shady sort like himself. They were goin' to take the life insurance on your dad and start again up north. A new life for the two of them. I said, "What about the body? You need a woman's body, not just a man's," and Jean says to me the doc's got one. An unclaimed body he can use. She said they didn't have a choice. Billy owed money to some East End gangster and needed to do a midnight flit. She said it was the safest thing for everyone, you included. So that's what they did. I had to arrange the funeral – we couldn't do anythin' else – and when the money came through, she told me to send it to a boardin' house in Birmingham.' Edie shook her head. 'They had it all sorted out. All planned.' She lifted her head to meet Milly's gaze.

Milly's mind raced. 'Did you give me the wrong time for the funeral on purpose?'

Edie toyed with the small gold cross hanging from a chain around her neck. 'I couldn't watch you cry, buryin' a mum who wasn't there. I never wanted you to go in the first place, but you insisted. It was the only thing I could think of.'

'How could you? How could you do that to me? I had a right to say goodbye to them. But when I arrived it was all over. The coffins were already in the ground.'

'I know, and I'm sorry. I'm so sorry.' She shifted forwards about to hug Milly then stopped, as if unsure if it was what Milly wanted. Milly wasn't sure herself. 'Believe me, I'm not proud of any of this, but she begged me. I didn't keep a penny of that money. Didn't want it. And to think your poor dad's buried with some woman he'd never met in his life. No, I'm not proud of it, Milly. But I did it for you. She was never goin' to get you from Devon, and I couldn't let you stay with the Harlows. They were nice enough but you're my niece. Family.' She took another breath. 'I'd get the sack if anyone here ever found out what I've done.'

Milly stared at Edie, her eyes unseeing. Where the aunt she knew and loved sat was a vague shape – someone she didn't recognise. It was as if her life had been turned upside down. Everything Milly knew, or thought she knew, was a lie. Were her memories even real? Over the years it had become hard enough to picture her parents' faces and to remember the things they'd done, the times they'd spent together, but now she couldn't trust any of it.

Her mum hadn't wanted her.

Hadn't ever wanted her.

Her heart broke: a piece that had always belonged to her parents falling away inside, disintegrating to nothing. Tears were stinging the back of her eyes and nose again and she pulled the handkerchief Edie insisted she carry from her apron pocket, pressing it hard into her eyes as if the pressure would force the tears away. 'Why did you agree to it?' she asked, stifling a sob.

''Cause your mum was goin' to leave anyway. There was no stoppin' Jean once she'd decided on somethin'. But I made her promise that if she went, I got to look after you and she was never, ever to come back. I thought you'd be better off without her. I never got the chance to be a mum. Never found a man I loved or who loved me back, but I'd loved you since the day you were born. Since the first time I held you in my arms and rocked you to sleep. You could fit in the crook of my arm. Just here.' She ran her hand over her soft skin from elbow to wrist as if imagining Milly as a baby once more. 'I thought I could be the mum you never had, and I could bring you up here with people who'd look out for you.'

Milly sobbed, a great, heart-wrenching moan escaping from her mouth. She covered it with her hand, as if trying to press the sound back inside. Edie flew to her, crouching down beside her chair and wrapping her arms around Milly.

'I'm so sorry, my girl. I'm so, so sorry.'

'You've lied to me for ten years,' Milly cried, anger pushing her tears away. 'Ten years, Aunt Edie. Half my life. You let me believe—'

Edie squeezed her tighter. 'I let you think you had a good mum who died. I thought it better to tell you that than the truth. If your mum hadn't broken our agreement, it's what you'd still believe now and you'd still be happy.'

Milly's eyes went to the letter she'd assumed was a tasteless joke. It lay on the table between them; one of the pages lifted in the draught coming through the old windowpane. The rain battered the glass now and the watery sun that had started the day was completely obscured by dark grey clouds.

'So this letter *is* from my mum?'

'I think so. But why she's written to you now I don't know.'

Milly tried to unscramble her thoughts. She was angry at Edie and a part of her hated her aunt for lying to her for so long. Could she trust anything she said now? On the other hand, her mum had abandoned her. Yet the words in her letter had been so heartfelt. So genuinely sorry. Another surge of fury overtook Milly and she stood, grabbing the letter and waving it at her aunt.

'Maybe she's telling the truth. Maybe because it's my twenty-first birthday she wants to see her daughter.' Edie shook her head in disbelief and something inside Milly snapped. 'Maybe she's changed, Aunt Edie. Maybe she wishes she'd been here for these last ten years and wants to make up for lost time. That's what she said in the letter. You read it. Why don't you believe her? Maybe there's more to it than even you know.'

'I understand why you want to think that, Milly, but I know your mum better than you do.' In the silence, her voice echoed off the walls and faded to nothing. Edie paced, stopping at the window and looking out into the gloom. 'I hate to say it but sometimes you have to call a spade a spade: she's a selfish creature and always has been.'

'You don't know that. She might have been selfish when she was young but that doesn't mean she is now. She said she's realised how much she loves me and doesn't want to miss any more of my life.'

Edie spun, her eyes wide and fearful. 'You will burn that letter, won't you? Or write back and say you don't want to see her? I know what she's like, Milly, she'll want somethin' from you. She doesn't deserve your forgiveness.'

'And you do?' The words clearly struck Edie hard as her face creased in pain. Milly regretted them immediately and repressed her anger, softening her voice. 'What about giving people a second chance? When Caroline first started and couldn't tell one end of a broom from another you kept telling me to give her chances.'

'That was different.'

'Why?'

'Because that didn't mean gettin' your heart broken.'

'You've also been lying to me and you want me to forgive you.' How could she judge her sister so harshly when she'd deceived Milly too? Edie wasn't innocent in all of this. It had hurt Milly to hear what Edie had said but maybe there was more to the story than she was telling her.

'I know my sister, Milly.' Edie lifted her chin in defiance. 'And nothin' good ever happens when she's around. I know it's a hard thing to believe but it's true. We're both better off without her in our lives.'

'Are you just worried the palace might find out? Is it me you're thinking of, Aunt Edie, or yourself?'

Edie's mouth fell open. Milly knew her aunt had never been selfish. She'd always done everything she could for her niece. Talking about how much she'd loved her as a baby had moved Milly, but she couldn't stop the pain roiling inside her belly, pushing its way out. Edie had lied to her face every day for the last ten years, keeping from her a truth that made her who she was.

'I am worried about losin' my job, Milly. I won't lie. Where will I go if I get sacked and what will I do if this all comes out? This has been my home for thirty years. But I'm not lyin' either. Not now. If you get in touch with her, it won't end well.'

'You don't know that.'

'I do. Haven't I always done right by you?'

Before, Milly would have said yes without any doubt, but Edie had lied to her face every day of their life together. It was all based on deceit.

'Will you go and see her?' Edie's voice was strained.

'How can I not, Aunt Edie? She's my mum.'

'Only by birth. Did she even wish you happy birthday in that letter?'

Milly looked at the pages still fluttering lightly in the draught. She hadn't, but Milly couldn't turn down this chance to see her mum's face.

'Don't go, Milly. Please.'

Edie's pleading tone struck her heart. She couldn't ignore it. Not many orphans got a second chance at seeing their parents and Edie must be wrong. Her mum must have changed.

'Please don't ask me that,' Milly begged in return. 'She wants to make things right. Why else would she get in touch now?'

Chapter Four

'Happy birthday, Milly!' Edie's friend Mrs Chadwick called out, carrying another plate of food to the buffet.

'Yes,' the Chief Housekeeper added. Mrs Fernsby was a wiry woman with severe grey hair and a hook nose, and she didn't sound all that pleased about the party. 'Happy birthday.'

Milly stood in a pink party hat, the elastic tight under her chin, as various people strolled past, tea plates full of party food, wishing her well. Along one wall of the Household Dining Room, the venue for her birthday party, plates of crustless finger sandwiches sat alongside cubes of cheddar cheese and tiny Victoria sponges, snowy with icing sugar, so dainty they could have belonged upstairs on the King's table. Normal sugar was still rationed but her small palace family had clubbed together to save enough for Mrs Chadwick to make her an actual birthday cake. It wasn't huge, but it meant the world to Milly. It all did. The cooks had made the buffet, mostly in their own time, but on palace time when they could get away with it. She stared at the Union Jack bunting hanging from the walls left over from the opening of the Festival of Britain and possibly even VE Day. It was a little worn and tattered, just as Britain itself was, but the thought that someone had put it up for her made Milly smile.

Still, she wished she felt happier. She'd been so excited for today before the letter had arrived, before Edie had admitted lying to her.

'Happy birthday, Milly love,' fellow cleaner Mrs Atkins said, planting a kiss on her cheek and breaking into her thoughts. Startled, Milly responded by squeezing her arm partly as a thank you and partly to steady herself.

Chairs had been moved from their normal places and tiny groups clustered together, chatting and laughing. The noise was almost deafening and behind it all, a jazzy version of 'When the Saints Go Marching In' played on a gramophone someone had brought in from the Household Lounge.

'Are you having a nice time?'

'Yes, lovely. Thank you so much for coming.'

Mrs Atkins left for the buffet and Milly peered around, worried that people were talking about her display of yesterday. It would be only natural, she supposed. This was the first time most people had seen her since. She hadn't bothered with lunch yesterday, preferring to work and make up for the time they'd lost talking, and Edie had let her have dinner in her room away from prying eyes and wagging tongues. She hadn't eaten much. Couldn't face it with her stomach tied in such a tight knot.

She could see Edie at the side of the room, speaking to Leonard Newington, a senior clerk, while keeping a watchful eye on her niece. Milly was sure the kind and still handsome gentleman would much rather Edie kept her eyes on him rather than glancing over at Milly whenever she

42

possibly could. She'd been different since their chat, almost shy, as if she needed reassurance that everything was fine. Normally Milly would have fired back a wide grin. A part of her wanted to give Aunt Edie that peace of mind, but the truth was that she couldn't when only yesterday she'd found out the aunt she loved had watched her sister abandon her only daughter and had even helped her do it.

Old Bill, another of the cleaners, but who worked on Mrs Nelson's team, nudged Milly's arm. 'Cheer up, young 'un, it's your birthday!'

'It's all a bit overwhelming.' She cast her hand out towards the balloons, the bunting. 'All this.'

'I guess it might be, but you should enjoy it. It'll only happen once.'

She smiled instinctively as sadness flashed across the old man's eyes. Old Bill's son had died during the war, never reaching his twenty-first birthday. As Milly regarded the people around her, she knew many of them were still feeling the effects of the conflict. Six years might have passed since the war had ended, but the country and everyone in it were still recovering.

Adjusting the elastic of the party hat, she thanked him for coming. He couldn't have heard about it all yet: the drama of the letter. How anyone could have missed it was beyond her. Though they were in many ways a family, gossip swept through the palace like a gale-force wind both above and below stairs. Even if you didn't want to hear it, you would. Everyone knew about Princess Margaret and the attention Peter Townsend, the Deputy Master of the Household, often paid her, even though he was married with two children and she was half his age. They'd all discussed the outrage and sheer sense of betrayal felt by Princess Elizabeth last year when her governess, Marion Crawford, published her book *The Little Princesses*. And some even still spoke in whispers of the Duke of Windsor, the abdication, and That Woman. There was no escaping rumour and chatter in such a closed, small world.

Milly's eyes followed Old Bill as one of the older ladies took him to one side. Heads bowed together, sly glances in Milly's direction: now he knew. Milly went to the buffet and removed her party hat before picking up a ham sandwich and taking a bite. The bread stuck to the roof of her mouth, and she forced it down with her tongue, swallowing though it gave her no pleasure. She put the sandwich down and edged her way through the crowd to the darkest corner of the room. She wouldn't be able to hide for long, but perhaps one of the birthday balloons would give her enough cover for two minutes to get her head straight. No amount of time would be enough given how confusing everything was, but a brief break might help her push it all down so she could enjoy the party. She'd been looking forward to it for months and everyone had gone to such great lengths she didn't want to ruin it by walking around po-faced and miserable.

'P-penny for them.'

Robert, one of the kitchen porters, took the seat next to her, pushing the balloon out of the way. He was only a year older than Milly, but his brow had creased like an old man's. As usual, his short, walnut-brown hair was ruffled and his cheeks were turning pink, hiding the freckles that dotted the bridge of his nose.

'I was just thinking about ham sandwiches.'

'N-no you weren't,' he stuttered. Robert's stammer meant he didn't talk to many people, but he always spoke to Milly, and they'd become friends almost instantly. Some of the chaps in the kitchen teased him, but the cooks never stood for it if they were around and neither would Edie, come to think of it. They'd always be reminded the King had a stutter and you wouldn't catch them taking the mickey out of him. 'You were thinking about your mum, I'll bet. I don't blame you. I'd give anything to see my mum again.' Robert's mum had died when he was fifteen though he rarely spoke of her. All Milly knew was that it had hit his family hard. His dad in particular. 'And look at what upstairs are going through. Family's important.'

The King had been due to open parliament, but his speech had been read for him by the Lord Chancellor as he was still too sick to do it himself. A chill ran over Milly's arms despite the heat from the bodies in the room. Not for the first time she said a silent prayer that his health would begin to improve properly.

'He did have a lung taken out,' Milly replied, more to convince herself than Robert. 'It's going to take a long time to recover from that, isn't it?'

Robert agreed. 'I suppose so. Did you see everyone went to meet Princess Elizabeth at the station today? Everyone but the King and you know how much he wanted to be there.' It had been another much-discussed topic. 'How do you f-feel now you've got used to the news about your mum?'

Milly and Edie hadn't sat and agreed what they'd tell people, but both knew they'd have to say something, and

45

soon, or people would start to make up their own stories, which would no doubt be much more fantastical than the truth. Though the truth itself was pretty hard to believe. It would embarrass her aunt too much to admit that she'd been in on the deceit, and she might lose her job too. No matter how angry and distant Milly felt from Edie right now, she couldn't do that to her. This was the only home her aunt had ever really known and though Milly was angry she wouldn't take that away. It was best for everyone that they pretend Edie hadn't known anything about it either and that her mum had somehow done a runner leaving Edie and Milly to assume she'd died in the bombing.

'I wish I knew how I felt,' she confided. 'Sometimes I'm happy, sometimes sad, sometimes I'm so angry I could scream. It changes from one moment to the next. All I do know is that I need to understand why from her own mouth. I can't pretend this hasn't happened and carry on like before.'

'There's that old saying, isn't there, curiosity—'

'—killed the cat. Yes, I know.' Milly sighed, worried he thought she should steer clear of her mum and ignore the letter.

'But satisfaction brought it back. That's the bit people forget.'

Milly raised her head, staring into Robert's pale green eyes and relaxed into her chair. He was the first person to offer her some sensible advice. She'd hoped to speak to Helen but without her here there was only really Caroline to talk to and she wasn't sure Caroline would understand. Her own family were so tight-knit, so close, she couldn't possibly appreciate how Milly's loyalties were torn.

'Look.' Robert reached into his jacket, taking something from the inside pocket. 'I got you something.'

'You did?'

For what felt like the first time since the letter arrived, genuine happiness filled Milly, pushing aside some of the hurt and pain that had weighed on her bones. Robert handed over a small box wrapped in red tissue paper. A bow had been tied around it with string and she pulled it loose. Flicking her eyes to Robert's, she unwrapped the gift to see a small, pale blue Bakelite brooch in the shape of a swallow.

'Robert! It's beautiful. Wherever did you get it? It must have cost you your month's wages.' Being a kitchen porter, he didn't earn much, though Mrs Chadwick had promised she'd start training him as a cook for the staff kitchens.

'It's only from Spitalfields and I had to get you something for your twenty-first birthday, didn't I?' Milly took it out and pinned it to her jumper. The light shone off it and she beamed at Robert. 'It m-matches your eyes.' He blushed furiously and turned aside. 'Happy birthday, Milly.'

'Thank you, Robert.' She gave him a gentle kiss on the cheek and Robert's face flamed an even deeper red. 'It's such a wonderful present. You're such a good friend.'

Something flashed across his features and dulled the shine in his eyes, but before she could figure out what was wrong, a deep voice forced Milly's attention away.

'Not interrupting, am I?'

The tall, rakish figure of Timothy Ranger hovered over them. His almost-black hair flopped slightly on to his forehead, and he pushed it back with a flick of his wrist. Milly's heart skipped as she shot to her feet. He was even more handsome in his uniform. The polished buttons of his red tailcoat caught the light as he slipped his hands into his trouser pockets. Something they weren't allowed to do upstairs on duty.

'Timothy, I didn't know you were coming. I thought you were working.'

'I am. Sneaked downstairs for some cake, didn't I? You look nice.'

Edie had been knitting her a new twinset in a striking dark green wool and had presented it to her this morning. Milly thanked her with genuine affection but the hug that had followed had been awkward. She'd paired it with a skirt that flared out and as she turned on the spot, aware of Timothy's attention, it swayed around her calves.

'That's pretty.' He pointed to the brooch. 'Edie get you that?'

Milly shook her head. 'It's from Robert. Isn't it lovely?'

'Very nice.' He eyed Robert admiringly. 'Very thoughtful, Robert, ain't you? Bit jealous I didn't think of that meself. Next time I need advice with the ladies, I'm coming to you.' Timothy was from the East End of London and, though he was trying to speak more like the Royals and senior staff, there were times when his accent came through.

Mrs Chadwick called for Robert to come and join her conversation.

'I'd b-better go,' he said. 'Don't want to get in trouble.'

Milly frowned. 'I thought you were off duty tonight?'

'That's never stopped her before,' he replied with a grin.

After Robert had left, Timothy said, 'You really do look nice, Milly. Listen, I was thinking, instead of a present, I thought maybe I could take you to the pictures, next week?' He looked up shyly from under dark eyelashes. '*Green Grow the Rushes* with Honor Blackman is on. It looks pretty good. What d'you reckon?'

'I'd love to,' she gushed. Most of the women who were the same age as her longed for Timothy to ask them to step out and he'd picked *her*. She brushed down her jumper and reined in her joy while she regained control of her voice; she didn't want to seem too keen. For a moment, Milly felt her life was slightly less of a mess. A glimmer of hope that a romance might fill the emptiness Edie's lies had left gave her something to hold on to.

Timothy laughed and the wide smile made his eyes shine. 'Brilliant. Friday week OK?'

'Perfect.'

'Good.' He leaned in towards her, speaking softly. 'One thing, I hate to ask but . . . well, here goes. Your aunt ain't me biggest fan, so can we keep this just between us? From the sounds of it you're having a hard enough time as it is and don't need me making it worse.'

It was true Edie didn't really approve of Timothy Ranger. His cheekiness often rubbed her up the wrong way, especially when it was something to do with work. Edie was proud to work at the palace and was easily annoyed by those who didn't take it as seriously as she did. Not that Timothy didn't do his job well. Edie was in no place to judge though. Not only because of how deceitful she'd been with Milly, but she'd also once encouraged Milly to step out with a boy who turned out to be a raging tea leaf. Whatever Aunt Edie might think, her judgement wasn't always as good as she thought it was.

'You're probably right,' she agreed, glancing at Edie to see her still watching while Mr Newington did his best to distract her. Though she'd never thought of it before, she wondered if Mr Newington's interest was more than just professional.

'Where's this cake then? Have you cut it yet? Given a speech?' He gently nudged Milly's arm and her skin almost stung where he'd touched it. She savoured the feeling.

'It's not a wedding and I'm not giving a speech. Not after yesterday. I bet everyone's laughing at me for making a spectacle of myself already.'

'No one's laughing at you. We care about you.' Timothy gave her another nudge and this time, his eyes seemed to stay locked with hers for an eternity.

'Milly?' Her aunt bustled over, and Milly reluctantly gave up Timothy's gaze. 'We should say thank you to everyone and give them a piece of cake, it's gettin' late and we're up early again tomorrow.'

'We were just talking about that, Mrs Barnes,' Timothy replied, rocking on to his heels.

'Call that uniform pressed, Mr Ranger? I'm surprised they let you get away with it.'

'What's wrong with it, Mrs B.?'

Edie bristled. 'That'll be Mrs Barnes to you and there's too much to mention in one sittin'. Now, get away. You must be due back upstairs in a minute.'

'Right you are.' Timothy gave Milly a mischievous grin and winked as he stepped away.

'Wait!' Milly's hand shot out, grabbing his sleeve as she leapt forward. 'You need some cake.'

Racing over to the table, she spotted the large knife beside it. The cake had been iced in white royal icing and decorated with winter flowers from the gardens. It was beautiful and heart-warming to know it had been made for her. As much as she didn't want to draw any more attention to herself, she couldn't just cut it up and hand out pieces without speaking to everyone first.

'Excuse me, everyone,' she shouted over the hubbub. When no one heard she grabbed one of the chairs and stood on it, raising her head above the din. 'Hello! Oi, you lot!' Everyone turned and from the corner of her eye she saw Edie lower her head and rub her temples as her neck went pink. 'Thanks for your attention, everyone. I just wanted to say thank you so much for this lovely party. And thank you to everyone that's given me a gift.' She hadn't expected anything from anyone and the tokens of affection people had given filled her heart with love. 'Even if you didn't, don't worry, we all know times are still tough. I'm just so happy you could all join me this evening. Most of you have seen me grow up so it's really special to me that you're all here.' Her previous birthdays had been small affairs with more people joining her as she'd grown and made friends of her own. The effort everyone had gone to to mark her birthday this year had been overwhelming. Fond glances met her, and she wished she'd never thought of them gossiping about her. It felt disloyal. 'Umm, that's it really. Thanks again and I'm going to cut the cake now so if you want some do come and get it.'

She hopped off the chair and Edie strode over, dusting the seat with her hand before putting it back and helping Milly slice the cake.

'Make sure you get some,' Edie said. 'You're the birthday girl, after all. Here, let's put this bit to the back just to make sure.' She was trying to catch her eye. They hadn't exchanged more than a few words since the truth had come tumbling out yesterday. 'Are you not talkin' to me any more then?' Her tone was both a joke and an earnest question, said low so only they could hear.

Only when I have to, Milly thought and turned as if distancing herself from the sentence. She wished the angry part of her that wanted to punish her aunt would disappear. It wasn't like her. 'Of course I am.' Milly managed a smile that she feared would do nothing to convince Edie. She wrapped a piece of cake in a napkin and took it to Timothy. 'Here you go. This should see you through your shift. What time do you finish?'

He flicked open the corners of the napkin and tore off a large piece. 'Midnight.' He popped the piece of sponge into his mouth. 'Scrummy. Happy birthday, Milly.' He bent down and placed a kiss on her cheek just as she'd done for Robert, but this wasn't a friendly peck. As soon as his lips touched her skin a fire began in her belly and spread throughout her body. She said goodbye in a daze and went back to help Edie, who was beginning to tidy up.

'Have I missed the party?'

Milly spun, happy to see Helen. She was wearing a blue dress under the same suit jacket she'd worn yesterday but she looked pretty, nonetheless. 'I'm sorry I'm late. I needed to settle my father.'

'Is he still unwell?'

'I'm afraid so. But let's not talk about that. I want to know how your party has been. Happy birthday!' She presented a card and Milly opened it. A tiny bunch of dried flowers had been stuck to the front. Helen had made it herself and that made it all the more special to Milly. She had a feeling money was scarce for her new friend and was just grateful Helen was here.

'It's beautiful. Thank you. Come on, come and have some punch.'

Milly led Helen to the remains of the buffet and, using the ladle, drew two glasses of dark red liquid. 'I'm not really sure what's in it, but it tastes pretty good. There isn't much food left but help yourself to whatever you fancy. Better than it going to waste.'

'Thank you, I will. It all looks scrumptious.' She loaded up a plate and the two women went to find a seat in the corner. 'Do you mind if I ask what happened yesterday? I mean, I know you received a letter from a mother who was supposed to be dead but . . .' She paused, a sandwich half-way to her mouth. 'I never thought I'd say a sentence like that.'

Milly laughed. 'It is a bit odd, isn't it?' After a sip of punch, she outlined everything she'd said to Robert. 'And that's all there is to say right now.'

'Bit of a tight spot for you, isn't it?'

Before Milly could answer Caroline slumped into the chair next to them.

'Ain't it been a lovely party, Milly? Have you enjoyed it?' Caroline's cockney twang was so different to Helen's more refined way of speaking but both women were already smiling at each other as Helen nodded her agreement.

'I have. Very much. I'm very lucky to have everyone here.' She introduced Caroline and Helen to each other and after sharing the usual pleased-to-meet-yous, Helen said:

'I don't suppose anyone has mentioned the vase? I've been worrying myself silly over it.'

'What vase?' asked Caroline.

'I accidentally broke one yesterday. I was up all last night worrying.'

'It doesn't matter,' Milly replied. 'Honestly, things get broken all the time, please don't fret about it.'

'I broke a pill box of the Queen's once. Probably cost more than my ma and pa's house,' Caroline said. 'I started crying I was so scared, but she was ever so lovely about it.'

'Who was?' asked Helen, her eyes widening. 'The Queen?'

Caroline nodded. 'She told me not to worry. Said she couldn't even remember where it came from. Then she gave me a handkerchief to wipe my eyes with. I've still got it in my room. I wasn't really sure what to do with it after I'd used it.'

As she finished speaking, Timothy walked past on his way to the door.

'I say,' said Helen. 'He's rather handsome.'

Caroline blushed and turned away to face the opposite direction. Did she like Timothy too? Milly understood if she did: Timothy was the most good-looking and affable footman in the palace. Feeling awkward as she'd just agreed to go to the pictures with him, she changed the subject. She didn't want to rub Caroline's nose in it.

'That's just Timothy, one of the footmen.'

'I'm rather jealous,' Helen said after finishing a bite of her sandwich. 'It's all women in the exchange and our supervisor looks rather like an unhappy toad.'

Caroline giggled and the three of them went on chatting about life in the palace and the various people they knew.

After their conversation ended, Caroline headed off to bed. Most of the household staff, especially ones who were needed day and night like footmen and housekeepers, slept in rooms in the main part of the palace in an area specifically for staff, though some more senior people had larger apartments on a higher floor. Helen, working in the telephone exchange, lived off site and left to get the bus back home. The crowd continued to thin until just one or two people were left in the large living room. The record player stopped, the deafening chatter became a few quiet whispers and the only food that remained were pieces trodden into the carpet. Edie eyed the room with her hands on her hips.

'We'll have some cleanin' to do later, my girl.'

Milly wanted to ask her aunt not to call her that. It hurt too much, but what good would it do to pour salt on to the wounds?

Edie went on: 'Never mind though. You only turn twenty-one once. Did you enjoy your party?'

Genuine happiness filled Milly and lifted the corners of her mouth as she thought of Timothy's offer, Robert's beautiful gift, and her conversation with Helen and Caroline. 'I did, very much. Thank you, Aunt Edie.'

Edie's hands fell from her hips, seemingly overcome with emotion. 'It's what you deserve. You're a good girl, you always have been.' Milly waited for her to say something about her mum, but she didn't. 'You can go to bed if you like. You shouldn't have to clear up after your own party. I'll make a start now and finish off in the mornin'.'

Milly's right foot moved to do as she was told, but she couldn't leave it all to her aunt. Edie was tired enough as it was. Her eyes were puffy, and though she'd tried to cover the dark shadows they were still visible under her make-up. After bidding the last few stragglers goodnight, Milly said, 'I don't mind helping. It'll be quicker if we do it together.'

She began to tidy the plates, piling them along the table that only hours before had been full of food. Milly could sense Edie was silently pleading for everything to be the way it was before, but there was no going back now. Milly took a deep breath.

'Aunt Edie, I'm going to write to Mum tomorrow and ask her to meet me. I know you don't want me to, but—'

Edie turned. 'It's not that I don't want you to, my girl.'

'But yesterday you said—'

'Yesterday I was angry. Angry at myself, mind, not you. I've been tossin' and turnin' all night thinkin' about this.' She took in a breath that lifted her chest and then let it out slowly. 'I do understand you want to see your mum. It's only natural. I just can't help worryin' you're goin' to get hurt.'

Milly ran to her, hugging her tightly. Edie's understanding was the best present she could have received. 'I don't think I will, Aunty, but I promise I'll be careful. You've always looked after me and I'm ever so grateful for that.' Edie sniffed and Milly could hear she was as choked as Milly was. An idea suddenly occurred to her. 'Do you want to come with me? We could go and see her together?'

Edie gently eased Milly away, wiping her eyes. 'I don't think so, my girl.'

'Maybe one day?'

'Maybe.'

Milly could tell from Edie's tight jaw she was unsure she'd ever be ready to see her sister, but she hugged her aunt again anyway. 'Thank you,' she said.

'That's enough now. Come on, this place won't clean itself.'

'And we can't leave it to Mrs Nelson's team.'

'How that woman still has a job, I've no idea. You stack the plates and I'll give the floor a quick once-over. The night staff said they'd do a bit for us, but I don't want to push my luck.' Milly moved away to get started when, after a moment, her aunt's quiet voice halted her. 'Milly . . .'

'Yes, Aunt Edie?'

'Please be careful with Jean. Sometimes, as much as we want them to be, things aren't always what they seem.'

Milly kept her gaze on the plates in her hand and didn't reply, not wanting to shatter the fragile peace woven between them. The exchange had given her a glimmer of hope that things might be all right again one day. Not immediately. It would take time for both of them, but at some point in the future there was a chance they'd be as close as they had once been, before her life had been turned on its head.

Chapter Five

Within an hour of starting, the letter was written, sealed and delivered to the post office in the palace. Known as the Court Post Office, it was run by a small team of staff led by the Court Postmaster. It was only small, on one of the strange jutting arms of the palace that came out from the main building, but near the front so the bags of mail could be delivered easily. It always astounded Milly how much post the palace actually received. It seemed like the world and his wife were writing to the King and Queen about one thing or another.

It had been as difficult for Milly to pen the letter as her conversation with Edie had been to endure. Anger mixed with sorrow, love with hurt. Milly had thought it would be full of emotion, her wish to reconnect and get to know her mum flowing through the words, yet she'd found herself holding back. Maybe it was Edie's warning circling in her mind that had stopped her pen, or maybe it was her own instinct not to give too much of herself before she'd even seen her mum's face. Perhaps it was the anger that bubbled just beneath the surface because she'd been left behind like an old unwanted suitcase. Whatever it was, the tone of the letter had ended up formal and businesslike.

Taking into account the time it would take for the letter to be delivered and a response received, Milly had suggested that they meet in just over a week's time, on her day off, which would give her mum plenty of time to travel down from Birmingham. Within a few days, she'd replied, and the date had been set.

The days passed slowly, each one full with the normal routine: early starts, a break for breakfast, then working on till lunch. Or if they were working the afternoon shift, a lazier start, lunch all together and then working into the evening. But as time went on, anxiety and doubt crept in. What if her mum really was as cold and hard as Edie said? What if she was disappointed in Milly? Until now, Milly hadn't ever considered the possibility she wouldn't be *enough*. She always had been for Edie. Yet, her mum had left her once. What if, despite her words to the contrary, she found Milly lacking in some way? Not pretty enough, not smart enough, not funny enough. In her own little world, Milly had always been sure of who and what she was, but that all changed as the date grew nearer.

Soon, she was no longer the subject of gossip, her behaviour overtaken by the news of a lady-in-waiting having an affair, and an ill-fated assignation between a coffee room maid and a junior clerk. Milly wondered if her meeting today would come up, but at breakfast Caroline had been full of the rumour that a postboy was getting the sack for trying to open the King's mail, so there was every chance she'd get away with it.

Milly buttoned her coat, ready to leave to meet her mum – to see the woman who she thought had died ten years ago. Edie watched her from the armchair of Milly's own apartment. She'd knocked just moments before, her actions jittery and nervous.

'Good luck then,' she said, toying with the sleeves of her cardigan. 'I hope it goes well.'

Milly smiled, grateful for her support though the tension in her aunt's muscles and the chewing of her lip told Milly the effort was costing her. She was hurting and Milly meeting her mum was the cause.

'Right.' Milly flattened her lapels one more time. 'I'm off then, Aunty.'

Edie stood. 'I'll be here when you get back.'

Out of nowhere, words tumbled from Milly's mouth. 'I – I'm not doing this to hurt you, Aunt Edie. You know that, don't you?'

'Course I do. Just—'

'I know, be careful.'

Edie gently touched Milly's cheek before closing the door quietly behind her. Milly rolled her shoulders back, marched to the door and out into the city.

Another Changing of the Guard was taking place and though she could leave through the side entrance, she listened to the music coming from the front of the building. The short regular ceremony happened every Sunday, Monday, Wednesday and Friday and the city stopped as the Old Guard left Buckingham Palace on the arrival of the New Guard from Wellington Barracks just down the road. Milly had soon grown used to the brass and drums and particularly enjoyed them playing more modern music, though the King didn't always like it. It was rumoured that King George VI's father, King George V, had once sent a note to the Director of Music, saying, 'His Majesty does not know what the Band has just played but it is never to be played again.' Milly smiled to herself at the idea of the King doing that now. At least it would show he was getting better.

After leaving Buckingham Palace, the cold winter wind scratching at her face, Milly made for Green Park. She'd decided to walk rather than spend money on the tube and she liked roaming through the city, remembering that she was part of this busy, sprawling place and the big, wide world that existed outside the palace gates.

The skeletal trees appeared black against the pale blue sky, but Milly was just thankful it wasn't raining. When she'd looked out of the window this morning, a thin, silvery layer of frost had covered the ground; it had since evaporated in the sun, and the grass now sparkled in the sunshine. Women pushed prams over the wide expanse of green which soon gave way to the busy, bustling street of Piccadilly and, with each step, trepidation built in her stomach.

Buses and cars sped past, shoppers in head scarves or hats bustled to the next store, and businessmen barged through with briefcases. Life was so much busier here in the centre of town. There were still the occasional empty plots where buildings had been destroyed, or piles of rubble that hadn't yet been cleared. The rebuilding of Britain was taking far longer than anyone had anticipated but the Festival of Britain earlier in the year had given them all hope. Milly allowed herself to be swept up in it as she joined the busy-looking people with their heads down against the wind, charging along.

Before long, she was at the central hub of Piccadilly Circus. The giant billboards glared down and the weight of traffic grew to a frenzy. Milly edged and dodged her way around cars, buses and crowds as she crossed the main thoroughfare and hurried on until she arrived at the junction of Coventry Street and Rupert Street where she and Jean had agreed to meet at the Lyons' Corner House.

She wondered how she would recognise her mother after all this time. She had no current picture to go on, nothing except the old photographs in her and Aunt Edie's apartments and her own imaginings. Would Jean have aged much? What would she be wearing? Milly imagined her in smart, modern clothes, happy and successful, something that would make the abandonment worth it. Would she be round and matronly from having more children? It was a thought that had only just occurred to her: she might have half-siblings, a new family Jean had started with this other man. An icy shudder ran down her spine.

Further down the shop front, Milly spotted a woman standing on her own. She had blonde hair, lighter than Milly's. Unnaturally so. Platinum blonde from a bottle. It shone almost white as she turned her head. She wore a shabby red coat, buttoned down to show off her slim figure and tiny waist. When she lifted her head, cornflower-blue eyes, the same colour as Milly's, met hers. A nervous smile lifted the corners of the woman's mouth and in politeness Milly replied with one of her own.

A sudden surge of such strong mixed emotions rose within Milly that she placed a hand on her stomach to quell it. Queasiness climbed from her belly while both fear and anger tightened her muscles. She had an unexpected urge to run away, back to Edie and the safety and comfort she had always known. Until now she had never considered that the truth could be even worse than Edie had said.

The woman opened her mouth as if to speak, but no sound came out. Her mum had begged to meet her and had come all this way. Milly couldn't back out now. She took a step forward and the woman copied, moving closer. Their footsteps were tentative, uneasy, but soon they were face to face.

'Milly?' the woman asked, her voice weak and uncertain.

'Mum?'

The word came unbidden. She could have said mother or called her Jean, but the title had flown from her mouth before she could think.

'Hello, darling.'

Jean's smile grew wider, and Milly realised how much she resembled her mum. Though her hair was dyed brighter and gentle wrinkles emerged from the corners of her eyes, it was as if her own face was reflected back at her. Where Edie's had been angular, Jean's was rounder with cheeks that lifted as she grinned.

'Shall we go inside?' Jean motioned to the door as the wind whipped her hair on to her face.

'Yes, it's freezing today, but at least it's not raining.'

When they were sitting at a table and had ordered tea and buns from the waitress in her black and white uniform, an uncomfortable silence fell between them. Anger and pain kept Milly's mouth closed. She wanted Jean to be the first to speak. Besides, she had too many questions buzzing in her mind to arrange them in any kind of order. How did you start a conversation with the mother you hadn't seen in ten years? Jean, too, seemed lost for words and kept her eyes down, watching her fingers as they spiralled around each other. Her nails were long and painted red to match her coat and lipstick. By comparison, Milly's were short and stubby, unable to stand up against her manual work. She placed her hands in her lap.

Eventually, as the silence lengthened between them, Jean spoke. 'Thank you for writing back to me. I wasn't sure you would.'

'I wasn't sure either. At first.'

'You're angry,' Jean said, placing her hands flat on the table. 'I understand why but I can explain it more now we're together. There's only so much you can write in a letter.'

Milly stared into her mum's blue eyes, wondering what she could see there. Guilt? Regret? Jean seemed to be waiting for a response, but Milly gave none. Anger gave way to hurt as memories of the funeral and the reality of her mum's abandonment rushed back. Milly wasn't a spiteful person, but she didn't want to make it too easy for Jean either. Her pain needed to be recognised. Apologised for. Her mother needed to know she couldn't just walk back into her life as though she'd always been there. There was so much she'd missed. Edie had been the one to mop her brow when she'd been sick, to badger her into doing her homework, to buy her treats when she needed cheering up. Her mother hadn't.

The waitress arrived, delivering a small pot of tea for each of them, milk jugs and a sugar bowl. She placed them on the table and added the teaspoons and rock buns. When she'd left, Jean looked down at her teacup and said, 'What did Edie tell you?'

'About why you left?'

Jean sipped her tea, placing it back in the saucer with a quiet tinkling sound. Though the café was busy with chittering voices and the clamour of cutlery scraping plates, Milly could hear little above the pounding of blood in her ears and the thumping of her heart. Only Jean's sigh was audible, and the world contained only the two of them.

'She told me you'd never really wanted a child. That you hadn't loved Dad and wanted your own life. A single life.' The apples of Jean's cheeks coloured but she kept her eyes lowered. Milly continued. 'She said you had affairs and met a man called Billy Venables, and when he had to do a midnight flit you went with him, faking your own death so you could start again somewhere else. She said it was like you'd forgotten about me until she mentioned my name and then you said it wasn't safe to take me with you. Edie didn't believe you.'

The words were tumbling out yet, apart from the pinkness to her cheeks, there was no other evidence of Jean's feelings. She didn't move. Her fingers rested either side of her teacup, one hand on the handle, the other on the rim. Her face was expressionless, her brow uncreased. Milly's words hung in the air and when Jean didn't answer, she added, 'I didn't think people faked their own deaths except in films.'

Jean looked up at last, a flash of amusement lighting her eyes, which faded as quickly as it came. 'Milly – I – I don't want to call your aunt a liar. She's my sister, after all. But that's not quite what happened.'

Milly felt a protectiveness towards her aunt flare at Jean's accusation, which was surprising considering she'd lied to her too, but it didn't make sense that she'd have made up what happened, especially knowing how much pain it would cause Milly to hear it. Edie's words of warning had formed a wariness inside her when it came to her mum and she didn't know whether to be angry or grateful to her aunt.

'What did happen then?' she asked, keeping her voice level.

'We better drink this before it gets cold.' Jean stared down at her cup. She took a sip and, a second later, began. 'It's not true to say I never wanted you. I did. Of course I did and I loved your father too. Do you remember much about him?'

Milly shook her head. He was more like a ghost than a memory now.

'Well, he wasn't always an easy man to get on with, your pa, and he could be jealous. If I so much as spoke to another man he'd question me about it for days. Do you remember I used to work in a hotel?'

'A bit.'

'Well, of course I used to meet all sorts of people there: families, couples, single men *and* women. Your father could get jealous just because I said good afternoon to someone.' Jean's eyes, rimmed with kohl and with lashes darkened with mascara, met Milly's.

She hadn't remembered him being like that at all. All she remembered was a broad smile and him sometimes reading her bedtime stories if she woke in the night. 'But you did run away with someone and you must have been seeing him while you were still married to Dad.'

The challenge was clear in Milly's voice: *Don't lie to me*. She might have been duped at ten years old, but she wouldn't be deceived now.

Jean tilted her head and conceded. 'No, you're right. I won't lie. I did meet someone else, but it wasn't because I had affairs like Edie said. It was because I wasn't happy with your father, and I fell in love with someone else. Have you ever been in love, Milly?'

Milly thought of Timothy and their trip to the pictures in a few days' time. She could easily imagine falling in love with him, but she wasn't in love yet. Her silence answered Jean's question.

'When you fall in love, you'll know how powerful it is.'

'More powerful than a mum's love for her child?' Though her voice was firm, the stinging at the back of Milly's nose betrayed her true feelings. She took a sip of tea, forcing the tears back before Jean noticed them.

'I didn't abandon you like your aunt Edie says,' Jean replied, her voice stronger than Milly had heard it so far.

'So you're calling her a liar? Why would she do that?'

'I'm not exactly—' Jean laid her hands on the table and leaned forward. 'I love my sister, but Edie was always a bit jealous. She'd always had a bit of a thing for your father. He was a neighbour of ours when we were growing up, and she was cross when he married me, not showing any interest in her. She was never— Well, she took after our dad in the looks department, and I took after our mum. I think she hated me for that.'

Hate seemed a strong word but her own anger towards Edie's lies left Milly unsure how to feel about this new information. She knew from photographs that Edie had never been as attractive as Jean but Edie had never struck her as the jealous type. 'Edie said Billy Venables was a piano-playing conman.'

Jean tutted and shook her head. 'I don't know why she'd say that. He was a piano player – ever so talented – but he wasn't a conman. Whyever would she think that?' She laughed as though the notion was absurd.

'So you're saying Edie just lied. Again.'

'No.' Jean calmly sipped her tea. 'I'm saying she's mistaken. Billy got into debt, like a lot of us did during the war. You won't remember how tough times were back then, but they were hard. Desperately hard. He took a loan from the wrong people, that was all. He thought he could trust them, but they turned out to be loan sharks and when the debts spiralled, he couldn't pay. The next minute they were threatening him and when they found out about me and you, they were threatening us too. That's why I couldn't take you with me, you see. It wasn't that I didn't want to. I just couldn't.'

A pleading look entered Jean's eyes, willing Milly to understand. But that didn't explain such a long absence.

'So why has it taken you so long to get back in touch?'

'I had to know the coast was clear and I didn't for a long time.'

'How do you know it is now?'

'I suppose I don't for sure, but it's been ten years, and everything happened in the East End. I doubt anyone would remember us now. We were nobodies. But I'm tired of moving around and being away from you. We had to keep moving at first to keep safe. I went from working in hotels to singing in them and then singing in nightclubs with Billy's band – moving all the time. It wouldn't have been fair to drag you with us. You had your schooling to do and when I knew the coast was clear I just—' Jean stumbled, fumbling in her pockets to retrieve a small white handkerchief, pressing it to her nose and then dabbing under her eyes. They were shining with unshed tears. 'It didn't feel right to turn back up and take you away from your aunt. From your home. Every time I thought about it, I knew you'd be happy at the palace with her. I mean, how many kids get to grow up in Buckingham Palace?'

Jean looked at Milly expectantly, but now didn't feel the right time to talk about that part of her life. There was so much Milly needed to know before she could open up and she still wasn't sure she wanted to.

'I just thought it was better you were there and settled than living hand to mouth with me. I couldn't have given you half the things you've had. And as painful as it was for me, my job as your mother was to put you first.'

The remains of Milly's tea had gone cold, and the rock bun sat uneaten. Jean shifted in the prickly silence, but again Milly made no move to break it. Though she wasn't sure jealousy would have been a reason for Edie to do anything, it was possible that she'd misremembered things. What Jean was saying did make sense and if Milly had been threatened by this gangster, she'd done the right thing to protect her. Milly needed a reason that justified her pain and Jean had provided it, though she didn't know where they went from here.

'So where's this Billy now?' Milly asked, finally tearing off a piece of her rock bun and eating it. 'Did you marry him?'

'I used to call myself Mrs Venables and we pretty much were married, but it was never official. I'd have liked to and so would he, but you need documents and things for stuff like that and we didn't want to risk it.'

'And children?' Milly asked, the words sticking in her fear-ridden throat.

'We never had any.' Milly hoped the relief wouldn't show on her face. 'Billy died a few months ago.' Jean pressed the handkerchief to her eyes again. 'He had a heart attack. Dropped down dead one night. He'd been playing the piano and then – he just went.'

'I'm sorry,' Milly said, not really sure how to feel about this man who had helped take her mum away.

'He would have loved to have met you.'

Would she have wanted to meet him? A tiredness that made her bones ache and her eyelids heavy swept over her. She was exhausted. Wrung out by the day's meeting. Milly checked her watch. 'What time is your train back to Birmingham?'

Jean wiped her nose and put her handkerchief back in her pocket. 'That's partly why I wrote to you. With Billy gone, I thought I'd come back to London. Stay here.'

'Here?'

'Yes. I've got a job in a club and a little flat. Well, a room anyway. I thought if we were going to start again it'd be easier if I was down here and not travelling back and forth all the time.'

The ground suddenly shifted under Milly. This was all too much, and far, far too soon. She hadn't thought beyond this single meeting. She hadn't even known if there'd be more.

'You don't seem too pleased.' Jean's voice was edged with something sharp, and Milly glowered at her. 'Oh, I'm sorry, darling. I know you're still angry at me, and I do understand. It's all been such a shock to you and I shouldn't have expected so much. I'm sorry. Perhaps I should go.' Jean rose and put on her coat. She took a small piece of paper from her coat pocket and handed it to her. 'I really would like to keep in touch, to get to know you and make up for lost time. Here's where I'm working. I'm there most nights. And I'll write to you again, if you won't mind? If you'd still like to see me.'

Panic forced Milly from her seat. The risk of losing her mum again was suddenly too great. Perhaps now she'd heard her side of the story, heard of the misunderstandings between her and Edie, she could begin to forgive her. She just needed some time to deal with this meeting before throwing herself into the next one. Milly took the piece of paper and gave a placatory smile. 'I do want to see you again. Perhaps I could have your home address to write to? Maybe come for tea sometime?'

'Where I'm staying?' Jean shook her head. 'Not yet. It's only temporary until I get somewhere nicer. I wouldn't want you to see me there.' She wrapped her untouched rock bun in the napkin and put it in her pocket. 'Goodbye, Milly. I can't believe you've turned into such a lovely young woman. For what it's worth, I'm very proud of you.'

The words shouldn't have meant so much to her, but she coloured, warmed by the compliment.

'Goodbye then. I'll see you soon.'

Jean left and Milly sat back down. Could it be as easy as

a misunderstanding? Her mum's account was so different to Edie's that right now she had no idea who to believe. She'd walk back through Green Park on the way home and give herself time to think. The wide-open space always made that easier than the walls of her small room.

The waitress approached and it was then Milly realised that with their last heated exchange her mum had forgotten to pay her share. There was no use chasing after her now and it was probably Milly's fault too; they hadn't decided to go halves – with other, more important things to discuss, the subject hadn't come up. Milly found the money in her wallet and paid before standing up again, tearing a piece from her rock bun and hoping the fresh air outside would help her think more clearly.

Chapter Six

Opposite Green Park, Buckingham Palace stood proud and stately. Milly took in the detail she never saw from the inside looking out. The gold tops of the cast-iron gates and railings glinted in the sun. The windows reflected the light and the balcony on which the King and his family often stood drew her attention along with the columns on either wing. It was a wonder of the world. So much had been restored since the bombings that had destroyed the chapel and other parts of the palace during the war. That it had survived at all was a miracle, but remembering the bombings only led her back to her own wildly differing thoughts about her mum and Edie and the lies both of them had told. She took a deep breath and dodged her way through the crowds to the servants' entrance.

Edie was cleaning one of the State Rooms and Milly entered the White Drawing Room quietly, knowing that on this level of the palace the royal family might be nearby. The ceiling and walls were so ornate it almost hurt her eyes to look at them, and she dropped her gaze to the deep red, patterned carpet as she closed the door with a quiet click.

'What are you doin' here?' Edie stage-whispered. 'You're not supposed to be up here unless you're workin'. You'll get in trouble.'

'Only if I get caught.'

'And what will you do if someone comes in?'

'Hide behind a curtain. Or that vase of flowers.' She pointed to the enormous floral display on a marble-topped table next to Edie. 'There's pretty much a whole bush in there.'

Edie paused, dusting cloth in hand. 'I suppose it's been done before.' They shared a look and a second later, Milly was surprised to find Edie in front of her, arms outstretched. Milly returned the hug, nestling into Edie's shoulder. She'd missed their closeness and the moment's respite comforted her.

'What's all this for?' she asked, her voice muffled.

'I've been a silly old fool,' Edie murmured as Milly sank into her aunt's tenderness. 'A part of me worried you wouldn't come back afterwards. That you'd – I don't know – run off with her or somethin'.'

'I was always going to come back, Aunt Edie. This is my home.'

The thin red veins in her face were even brighter with emotion as she broke away, cupping Milly's cheeks. Her hands were warm and smelled of beeswax. 'You're right, and I should've trusted you. I was just worried. I shouldn't have got so upset about one meetin'. Even if you do see her again it's not as if it'll be every day. You'll still be my Milly, won't you?'

Milly's stomach knotted like someone tightening a screw. 'Of course I will, Aunt Edie.'

'Good. Go and stand by the windowsill. You can dart behind the curtain if need be.' Edie began dusting again, moving methodically around the room, the pale winter sunlight dancing off the giant chandeliers. After a second and without turning back to look at her, Edie asked, 'Did you see her on to the train?'

'No. No, I didn't.'

'I suppose that Billy was there to take her home.

'Umm . . . Billy died.'

'Well, I'm sorry for that,' Edie said earnestly. 'Truly. If they were together all this time, she must have felt somethin' for him. Maybe more than I gave her credit for. Did she say what she's doin' for work in Birmingham?'

'She's singing.' A yawn overtook Milly and she pressed her hand to her mouth.

Edie glanced back over her shoulder and bent to dust the legs of the marble table that held the enormous vase of flowers. 'Is she? And that pays enough to make ends meet?'

'Maybe they pay more in London.'

'London?' Edie stood upright, her worn knees clicking with the effort. 'What does it matter if they pay more in London?'

As soon as the words were spoken, Milly realised her mistake.

'She's movin' back?' Edie's voice had risen. She wasn't shouting, but it was clear the news had been more than unexpected, just as it had been for Milly. This wasn't how Milly had hoped to tell her. She'd intended to keep quiet about it until they were alone in either her or Edie's apartment. Safe in familiar surroundings. Milly searched for a way to soften the blow as the door flew open, and the King strode in.

Seen and not heard, that was the rule.

Milly considered the curtain, but it was too far away. There was no hiding now. Edie would have her guts for garters, that was for sure. Her aunt froze for a moment, but gathered herself enough to curtsey. Milly dropped her head and then dipped into a curtsey too.

'Your Majesty,' Edie mumbled. Milly echoed a second later.

He was pale and thinner than normal, though it was wonderful to see him up and about. His face broke into a friendly smile.

'I thought I heard voices in here.'

'I was just dustin', Your Majesty. Milly here was ... was—'

What was she doing? Edie's neck had mottled, and Milly leapt in to save her. 'I know I'm not supposed to be here if I'm not working, Your Majesty, but I just needed the key to my aunt's room. I'm sorry, Your Majesty. It won't happen again.'

He tapped the side of his nose. 'Ah, your secret is safe with me. Where would we be without you lot keeping this place so spick and span, hmm? Carry on, won't you.'

There was no hint of the stammer that had caused him so many problems when he'd first come to the throne and as he left the room, relief slowed Milly's rapidly beating heart.

'We just lied to the King.' Edie leaned on the marble-topped table for support. 'I just told porkies to the King of England. Oh, my life.' She pressed a hand to her chest. 'I should've known he'd come in. It's been like Piccadilly bleedin' Circus in here today. Lords-in-waitin', equerries, even the Prime Minister's popped by for a quick chat. Though how he's still runnin' a country, I don't know. Ancient, that Mr Churchill is. And if you ask me, the King's seein' too many people. He needs to rest until he's back to full health.'

The door opened a second time, and this time Milly was able to dart behind the curtain.

'I say, Mrs Barnes, did the King come this way?'

Edie curtseyed again. The Queen always made an effort to remember everyone's names and it was appreciated by all below stairs. 'Yes, Your Majesty. He left a minute or so ago. I'm afraid I don't know where to as he closed the door behind him.'

Queen Elizabeth, in her old-fashioned but perfectly tailored dress, smiled warmly. There was a wonderful bubbliness about her that complemented the King's rather serious manner. 'No matter. Carry on. Splendid job, by the way.' She left with her normal brisk pace that reminded Milly of a foxtrot.

'I think I'm havin' a heart attack. Do you think she heard me?' Her wide, fearful eyes pinned on Milly who had stuck her head out from behind the curtain.

'No, I don't think so. I don't think she'd have held back in saying something if she had.'

'Oh Lord. And if all that weren't bad enough, you say my sister's movin' down to London. When?'

'She's already here. She thought if we were going to make up, she should be nearby so we could see each other more easily.'

'I see.' Edie went quiet. She stared at Milly, obviously thinking; then she began dusting again with more force than was strictly necessary.

The door opened for a third time and Mr Newington walked in, his back as straight as always, his salt and pepper hair slicked down but a warm smile on his face as he saw Edie. He must have been in his mid-fifties but was still handsome. Being a clerk, he didn't have to wear a uniform and instead wore a smart charcoal suit that set off his features.

'Ah, Edie, are you—' He noticed Milly for the first time, half of her hidden by the curtain. He gave a slight double take as she edged out, pushing the bulk of the curtain behind her. 'Oh, Milly. Good afternoon.'

'Afternoon, Mr Newington.'

Her presence seemed to have knocked him off course and he gaped helplessly around.

'Was there somethin' you needed, Mr Newington?' Edie asked formally.

'No, not at all. Well, I was just wondering about – well – are you having dinner with the rest of us this evening, Mrs Barnes, or had you planned to eat in your room? I know you said it was going to be a—' His gaze flicked to Milly, reddening. 'Well, a . . . a long day.'

Milly hadn't missed the quick switch from Edie to Mrs Barnes, nor the fact that Edie must have confided in him about today. Though Edie's cheeks were always red with the rosacea, they flared even brighter.

'I'm not sure, Mr Newington. We'll have to see how the rest of the day goes. I can't say more than that at the minute.'

'Of course.' He gave a single sharp nod and quick-marched out of the room.

Milly grinned. 'I think he likes you, Aunt Edie.'

'Don't you even think it. I've got enough on my plate

right now without you sayin' silly things about Mr Newington. He's a senior clerk, for heaven's sake. And don't think that smile on your face will stop me askin' more about your mum.' She placed her hands on her hips. 'So she's here to stay and you'll be seein' her again?'

'I think so.'

Edie started work again, slowly at first and then faster as if she was working through a problem in her head. Milly knew she was hurting. Normally they could chat for hours about anything, but any conversation about Jean was short and carried an undertone of words unspoken. Yet, Milly had been telling the truth: she thought she'd see her mum again, but she didn't know when or where.

'Do you want some help?' Milly asked.

'You run along. You're in your nice coat.' She tossed her arm out to gesture at Milly, the cloth duster flying like a flag.

'I can change and come back. I don't mind.'

'No, no. I'll be done soon.' Edie turned back, the conversation finished. She'd always let Milly help before, but it was clear she was hiding. Hiding from Milly and the pain Jean's return was causing.

Milly left, sneaking back to the staff quarters. Despite the comfort of her normal routines her palace world now seemed unfamiliar. All the relationships she'd known were changing, shifting around her, and she was lost in a sea of emotion, fearful that if she didn't cling to something, she may very well drown.

Chapter Seven

If London was busy during the day, it was nothing compared to Covent Garden at night.

On the last day of November, Milly strode around town, gripping tightly on to Timothy's arm, beaming with pride. She wasn't oblivious to the looks he received from women passing by. Some would giggle, others would catch his eye and look away coyly as if Milly wasn't even there, but she had no fear. Timothy was out with her, and she was the one he was smiling at.

'Fancy a quick drink before the film starts?'

'That'd be lovely.'

'Here?' He signalled to a pub called the Sword and Shield to their left. The lettering on the front of the building was slightly drab but the warm orange glow welcomed them out of the cold, dark night.

They made their way across the busy street. She adored Covent Garden market, the stalls and shops, the theatres and pubs. Yet, at night, it turned into something completely different. She'd come to the flower show in June to watch the traders race with stacks of baskets on their heads and it had reminded her of Aunt Edie teaching her perfect posture with a book on her head, but the traders had baskets six feet high and somehow were still able to run. Milly had never managed more than a slow stroll across her aunt's room. During the day this section of London was friendly and cheerful but at night it was alive with an electricity that singed the air. Like the palace, it was its own little world: another city within a city.

She studied the women dressed up for the evening, their hair expertly set, red lips pouting. Normally, she'd have gone to Edie for advice on what to wear, but adhering to Timothy's warning, she hadn't said anything to her. Helen had been her excuse, saying they were meeting for a drink. Milly had taken far more care with her make-up than she normally would. A swipe of powder across her nose wouldn't have been nearly enough. Eyebrows had been plucked, eyeshadow carefully applied and lipstick a shade or two darker than her normal pale pink had been swept over her lips. She'd even worn her best dress, careful to hide it under her coat so Edie didn't see. As she'd stepped outside in her highest pair of shoes, she'd felt confident, transformed from Milly the servant into a young lady.

Timothy held the door of the pub open for her and she edged into a sea of people crammed in like sardines. Cigarette smoke floated above their heads in wispy clouds and filled her lungs in a single breath. She tried to make her way to the bar, wriggling between customers and eventually found a spot against the wall. She was glad to have something to lean against: there were no tables or chairs available.

It was six thirty and the evening performances at the theatres would soon be starting, meaning most people would file out to take their seats. At least, that's what she hoped.

With so many people, the pub was hot and next to the bar the smell of beer was so strong she could almost taste it.

'What d'you fancy then?' Timothy unbuttoned his coat to reveal a grey suit and navy-blue tie. He was handsome and the attraction she felt towards him drew her closer. There was a hint of stubble on his jaw as he lit the cigarette between his lips.

'I didn't know you smoked,' Milly said.

'Didn't you? Seems there's a lot you don't know about me, which is why we're out for a drink first. But I want to know about you, Milly Hendry. Starting with what you'd like to drink.' He flashed straight white teeth.

'Gin and bitter lemon, please.'

He turned to the barmaid, his voice loud amid the din of those clamouring for her attention. She ignored the gnome-like man in front of her and came to serve him, and a few minutes later delivered their drinks with a lingering look; but again, Milly refused to feel jealous. Not least because of the smudge of lipstick on the woman's teeth, but mainly because Timothy hadn't seemed to notice her glances at all.

In the stifling heat, Milly unbuttoned her coat and Timothy flicked cigarette ash into the metal ashtray on the counter.

'You look cracking tonight.'

'Thank you.' Robert's birthday gift was pinned to her dress and Timothy signalled towards it.

'I'm still worried I should be jealous.'

'Of Robert?' Milly laughed at the idea. 'No. He's just a friend.'

'You sure?'

'Certain.'

'Glad to hear it.'

'Anyway, if anyone should be jealous it should be me.'

'What d'you mean?'

At his wide-eyed astonishment Milly laughed again. 'Oh, come on. I've seen all these ladies gawping at you.'

He looked around comically. 'What ladies?'

'You know full well what ladies.'

'I don't. Honest.'

Milly took a sip of her gin and bitter lemon. 'All the ones who smile and giggle at you as you go past, or stare at you like the barmaid did.'

'I thought I must've had gravy on me chin.'

'Hmm.' She met his eyes and the intensity sent a fizz of excitement through her. She was enjoying their conversation: the flirting. He leaned forwards and she mirrored him. The lingering tobacco smelled sweet on his breath.

'Maybe I only have eyes for you.'

'Is that so?'

'It is.'

She hoped he was going to kiss her, but after watching her face for a moment, he pulled back. Timothy drank his beer and flicked more ash into the overflowing ashtray littered with lipstick-rimmed cigarette butts. 'So, what don't I know about you, Milly Hendry?'

'I don't know. Why don't you ask me a question?'

'All right then.' He thought for a moment. 'OK, I've got one. Seeing as you've always been at the palace, didn't you ever want to go and do something else?'

'I never really thought about it. I suppose working there was just what was always going to happen.'

'So what's the plan? Work with Edie 'til you get married and start a family?'

It sounded so boring she almost laughed but Timothy's expression was earnest. 'I hadn't even thought about marriage and a family. I've only just turned twenty-one.' She hadn't thought about ever doing anything else either. She knew she'd have to leave when she did marry and have children, but it seemed so far away it was almost as if it would happen in another lifetime. That was the unwritten rule: you couldn't work there if your husband also did. One of you had to go and that was invariably the woman. Children weren't permitted at the palace either, not for staff – it was only because of Edie's long service and Milly being an orphan that Milly had been allowed to stay.

'What are your plans then?' she asked Timothy.

He took another sip and ran his finger round the collar of his shirt. 'You'd think I'd be used to starchy collars from our uniforms.'

'Don't avoid the question.'

He laughed and shyly dropped his eyes to his drink. 'Honestly? What I really want is to make senior footman one day.'

'You want Mr Dankworth's job? You'll be waiting a long time. He's been here since he was a nipper and doesn't show any signs of slowing down yet.'

There were a few senior footmen, but Mr Dankworth was the one most connected with Timothy. He'd been training him up since he started and was his supervisor.

'It might not happen right away but it's good to be ambitious and I don't mind hard work.'

He was right. It was impressive.

'It's definitely hard work at the palace no matter what you do,' Milly said. 'Even the royal family are always darting off here, there and everywhere to open scout huts or a new Co-op or—'

'Summer fairs.'

They both laughed.

'And then?' she asked, eyeing him over the rim of her glass. 'What will you do when you make senior footman?'

'When I've got enough for a decent place of me own, I'll find a nice girl to settle down with.'

'And what will she be like?'

Though she hadn't much experience of flirting, Milly thought she was doing pretty well. Her night out with the man she'd come to know as the palace thief had been difficult and conversation stilted. This was very different.

Timothy's eyes sparkled. 'She'll be beautiful, like you. Funny, like you. Clever, like you and . . .' He reached out and tucked a few strands of her hair behind her ear. She was wearing it down tonight and it curled past her shoulders. Milly's heart beat fast against her ribs. 'She'll want for nothing.'

They stared at each other until the noise of the pub intruded.

'Shall we go?' he asked after clearing his throat. 'Get some fresh air before the film starts?'

Milly finished her drink and rebuttoned her coat before they headed outside. The cold winter wind refreshed her skin, and though a light drizzle had begun to fall, snuggled into Timothy's arm she didn't care.

They made it to the cinema with time to spare and settled into seats near the back. As the film started, Timothy's arm wrapped around her shoulders, and she had to force herself to stop smiling. When he leaned over and made comments on the film, his breath tickling the hairs on her neck, her heart skipped and her stomach tightened. Once or twice she turned back to him and saw his dark eyes sparkle in the glow of the screen. His lips were close to hers and she was more than ready for him to lean forward and kiss her. A couple next to them had barely come up for air since the film started, but Timothy was obviously more of a gentleman than that.

Afterwards they wandered back through town to the front gates of the palace. The drizzle of earlier had stopped and the pavements glistened in the light of the streetlamps. The hustle and bustle receded, leaving the air quiet. Timothy stopped, holding the bars tightly in his hands and pressing his face through a gap.

'What d'you see when you look at this place, Milly?'

'I don't know. Home, I suppose. What do you see?' She joined him, looking through the space next to him.

'Success. D'you know what people say when you tell them you work at the palace?' She shook her head. She didn't have any friends outside the palace walls. 'Their mouths just drop open, like you've said you work on the moon. They can't believe it of someone like me.' She tilted her head quizzically. His voice grew quieter. 'Poor as church mice, my family. My brother died in the war. He was older than me. Signed up as soon as he could. Didn't last more than a month. Killed as soon as he'd learned to hold his gun.'

'I'm sorry, Timothy. I didn't know.'

'I'm going to make something of meself, Milly. And what better place than here.'

'I'm sure you'll achieve the things you want, Timothy. All of them.'

He turned to her, their fingers touching on the railings, and he stroked her skin before dropping his hand, drawing her towards him. He pressed his mouth to hers in a gentle kiss and the feel of his lips, soft and firm against hers, sent tremors through her heart. Her hands moved naturally around his neck, stroking the soft skin where his hair met his collar.

When he drew back, he whispered breathlessly, 'D'you know, I've wanted to do that ever since I started working at the palace.'

'A year? You've wanted to do that for a year?'

He smiled. 'Since the moment I saw you. I thought you was the prettiest girl in the whole place.'

'Prettier than Princess Margaret?' she teased.

'Even her. Can I – can I do it again? Just one more time?'

She lifted her head, inviting him. His lips met hers as if appreciating the soft curve of her mouth. They seemed to fit together so perfectly.

''Ere, what're you two up to?'

A harsh voice shook them apart and Milly turned to see a heavyset policeman lumbering towards them.

'Nothing, Constable,' Timothy said. 'Just seeing this young lady home.'

'Is that what you call it? Well, see that you do. Come on, chop, chop.'

Timothy took Milly's hand and they made their way to the servants' entrance, giggling at the untimely interruption.

'You know,' Milly said, filling the silence though it had sat comfortably between them. 'There is one thing you're going to need to change before you become senior footman.'

'Oh yeah, and what's that?'

She fingered the lapel of his suit jacket. 'You'll have to press your uniform better or Aunt Edie will have your guts.'

Timothy laughed and the happy sound filled Milly's ears as they fell into step with each other. All those women looking at Timothy tonight and she was the one he'd kissed, the one he was telling his hopes and dreams to.

The men's and women's rooms were in separate areas of the staff quarters and Timothy bid her goodnight with a gentle kiss on the hand before heading off to his corridor. Milly walked in the opposite direction, floating on air. All her troubles seemed to have disappeared. She'd never dreamed her first date with Timothy would have involved two such romantic kisses. The first had been like Clark Gable kissing Vivien Leigh in *Gone with the Wind*. She'd been to watch it at the cinema with Aunt Edie and had hoped that one day she'd be on the receiving end of something like that, but had never expected it. Milly wasn't the swooning type – Aunt Edie would never stand for swooning – but if she was, she would have fallen into Timothy's arms.

She needed to tell someone what had happened, or she was going to burst, but Timothy was right, she couldn't tell Edie. Caroline's crush put her out of the picture so that left Helen and she just knew Helen would be as happy as she was.

December 1951

Chapter Eight

With the royal family away, Edie deemed it the perfect time to deep clean the King's private rooms. The family had left for Windsor Lodge the day before and it had been the first time he'd left the palace since his lung operation in September. He'd appeared better than expected, according to the papers Mr Dankworth had shown them. A selection were delivered daily and one of the junior footmen – generally the newest – had the job of ironing them to remove creases and dry the ink before they were sent up to the Royals. It meant the juiciest bits of gossip were shared below stairs first.

Milly had just returned to the King's bedroom, having run back to the storeroom for a new pot of beeswax polish. She was out of breath. It took a good fifteen minutes to get from one side of the palace to the other and back again.

'I'll have that, thank you, Milly,' Edie said. 'And I'll leave you to get on while I do the sittin' room.' She marched away into the adjoining room, though it was really quite far away. The two footmen who had shunted the bed over leaned against a windowsill, waiting to move it back, their arms folded, gossiping like old ladies about the latest football results.

'It always surprises me how small this room is,' Milly said. 'I mean, it's the King's bedroom. You'd think it'd be bigger than this. When you compare it to the Music Room or the White Dining Room it's tiny.'

'You'd get the whole of our downstairs in it though,' Caroline replied. 'And it has a huge bathroom and a massive sitting room. It's not like he has to live in just this little bit. In my house there was me, my sister and brother all in one room and my ma and pa in the other. I think they were secretly glad me and my sister moved out. My brother was anyway. It was all a bit of a squeeze.'

'I bet your house is lovely,' Milly said timidly, nervous of speaking about her family too much, knowing how much Caroline missed them. 'Cosy. Like a real home. Here's nice but it's so grand I wonder if it can ever feel like home, even to the royal family.'

'Don't you reckon it feels like home to the Princesses? Maybe not Elizabeth, she was older when they moved here, wasn't she? But definitely for Margaret. I dunno what they'd make of my two up two down.' She giggled to herself. 'And they wouldn't like to see my brother's smalls blown about on the line which is what I went home to yesterday.'

Milly laughed. 'What's your brother like?

'Trouble and no mistake. Ma says he's turned her grey.'

'And your sister?'

'Nancy? She's . . . well she's bloody bossy. She takes after Ma.'

'Does she look like you?'

'Sort of. She has Ma's eyes but she got Pa's ginger hair, like me.'

'I love the colour of your hair,' Milly said honestly. 'It's beautiful.' She'd been envious of Caroline's deep red hair ever since she'd arrived. Caroline looked exotic even though she came from Whitechapel.

After a second of sweeping the dust from the carpet, Caroline said, 'Milly, can I ask you summat?'

'Of course.'

She paused, resweeping the same patch of carpet though Milly was sure there was no more dust to gather. 'Is there anything going on between you and Timothy?'

From the corner of her eye, Milly checked the footmen weren't listening, but they were still busy assessing Liverpool's odds against Tottenham Hotspur that day. Caroline was blushing again, her cheeks matching the red of her hair.

'What do you mean?' Milly asked to buy herself some time. A direct question like that was hard to avoid.

'Are you two . . . you know—' She cocked her head to the side. 'Stepping out?'

'Has he said something?'

'No, it's just . . . well, people have been talking.'

So the gossips had been at work again. Milly didn't want to lie to Caroline, but with her crush on Timothy and the fact she was so honest she might blurt it all out to Aunt Edie, Milly couldn't risk telling the truth. The memory of Timothy's kiss burned on her lips. 'No, we haven't been seeing each other.'

'Right.'

She seemed relieved and though guilt prickled Milly's skin, she felt the need to continue denying it and ensure Caroline was convinced. 'I'm just not sure he's right for me,' she added with a shrug. 'Does Edie know about the gossip?'

'I dunno. Possibly. She ain't said nothing to me if that's what you're worried about.'

That at least was reassuring. 'Are you looking forward to going out tonight? I am. I can't wait to see my mum perform.'

She brightened at the idea. 'Too right, I am. I ain't never been to a club before.'

'Are you sure you're all right to meet us there?'

'Course. I have to nip home when we finish today. Ma's got my dress ready for me. I'll go straight from there.'

Milly was looking forward to having Helen and Caroline join her tonight. Not only did it mean she didn't have to go to a club on her own, but they could spend some time together away from the palace. She didn't know why she and Caroline hadn't done it before. Sometimes she felt that the palace walls were often more akin to prison bars trapping her in her routine.

'Come on, Aunt Edie will be through to check on us soon so we better get cracking. That bathroom's going to take ages and she wants it done today.'

'Are you two finished yet?' asked one of the footmen. 'We do have other things to do, you know.'

'Sorry,' Milly replied, shuffling backwards on her knees and drawing the little pile of dust into her dustpan. 'There. All done. How about you, Caroline?'

'Hang on, I just spotted a bit back here.' She moved to the wall and brushed some dust from the skirting board, which was far grander than in any other house in London, into her own dustpan. 'There. Perfect. Even Mrs Barnes can't argue with that.'

'She certainly can't. I'll tell her you paid particular

attention to the skirting. You know what she's like for remind-ing us about that. She'll be pleased you remembered.'

Caroline turned and gave it one last glance. 'Hang on a sec. There's summat stuck behind the bed. It's been caught between the bedframe and the wall.' She reached behind the bed, squeezing her arm into the narrow gap.

'What is it?' Milly asked.

Caroline pulled it out using the tips of her fingers, only just able to get hold of it. It was a piece of fabric, bright white but with patches of rusty red. She handed it to Milly, but before she could even look at it herself, Caroline flashed her eyes and shook her head.

For a second, Milly wasn't sure what she was getting at, then it hit her: secrecy. She hid the piece of fabric behind her back, out of sight of the footmen. 'We're finally done, you two. Off you go.' They hauled the bed back into place.

As they left, the girls took a moment to correct the sheets and pillows, Milly smoothing them down with one hand, the other hiding the object from view. 'I know another team will change the beds, but we don't want them looking untidy, do we, Caroline? You never know if the Royals will pop back unexpectedly. It's happened before when plans have been changed at the last minute.'

One of the footmen gave her a strange look. She didn't usually talk so much. Normally it was Caroline, but their roles were reversed as Milly's nerves overtook her mind. The footmen left, resuming their conversation, having decided that Tottenham had a better chance of winning after all.

As soon as they were alone, Milly laid the piece of fabric out on top of the bed. Her eyes were immediately drawn to the initials embroidered in fine royal blue thread in the top corner. The royal cipher: G VI R. 'King George VI, R for rex. It's the King's handkerchief,' she exclaimed.

'What's all that brownish stuff? Tobacco?'

Milly shook her head, her stomach coiling into a knot. 'It's blood.'

Caroline's hands flew to her mouth. 'Oh, crikey. Should we tell Mrs Barnes? Or someone else – the Queen or—'

'Let me think for a second.'

'Oh Lord. This ain't good. He must have been coughing into it in bed and dropped it down the back. Is he still poorly? I mean, really poorly.'

'We don't know how long it's been there,' Milly replied calmly, sitting on the edge of the bed. 'It could have been there for ages, since before his surgery. We don't get to clean behind the bed every week – not even every month because it's one of the biggest bits of furniture to move and because the King's been here so much. Normally we'd have done it while he's away, but this is the first chance we've had for months.'

'Let's hope they see it like that,' Caroline said, biting her nails. 'But what if they don't?'

Milly's eyes dropped to the handkerchief again and her stomach turned. 'I don't want Edie to get into trouble for not doing her job properly. And what if the King doesn't even know it's there himself? It could have been there for a bit, couldn't it? It could have been dropped right after his operation.'

'It might not mean he's getting worse. But should we tell Mrs Barnes?'

'She won't be happy and not just because she loves the King. She'll be cross with herself for not finding it sooner and I don't want her feeling any more unhappy than she is right now. She's struggling with me seeing my mum and it's December. Christmas soon. That always gives us more work. Let's leave it between us for now and I'll get rid of it somehow.'

'So we're not telling her? Or anyone?'

'Not yet. I need to think about what's best to do.'

'Milly, I really think we should.' Caroline leaned in, whispering even more forcefully than before. 'If it's new it means he's getting worse and—'

Fear was written on both of their faces. 'Like I said, it could have been there for ages. We just don't know.' Milly screwed it up and stuffed it into her apron pocket. 'Come on, we better get the rest of the floor swept.'

'I hate this carpet,' Caroline replied, clearly trying to distract herself from the difficult thoughts haring through both their minds. 'It's so thick it makes my arms ache.'

'Me too,' Milly replied.

But the bloody handkerchief was already weighing down her apron, almost burning a hole in her clothes.

Chapter Nine

'He *kissed* you?' Helen asked, aghast, as she and Milly trooped down the street. She spoke with a hairpin between her teeth before removing it and repinning an errant curl.

Having met at Oxford Circus, they'd walked to Soho and were nearing the club where Milly's mother worked. Helen had run home first to check on her dad and had just managed to catch the bus to bring her here. Caroline would be joining them shortly. Milly envied them their hurried trips home to family, but she was after all off to see her mum.

Jean had written and Milly had replied, agreeing to meet again. She was still wary, guarding her heart, but the more she thought about Jean's version of events the more she could see where misunderstandings could have taken place.

The streets were busy even on a weekday evening, but then, London was always busy. There wasn't a day went by where hustle and bustle didn't drift on the air, and crowds surrounded the palace. Only yesterday people had gathered to watch the King leave, waving and cheering as the car left the palace grounds. She pushed thoughts of the King's handkerchief aside. Tonight wasn't the night to think about that.

The ferocious wind buffeted women with their hair wrapped in headscarves, heads bent, their arms threaded through a gentleman's. Drinkers spilled out of pubs and into the streets. Some were respectable, talking amongst themselves of busy days, deals done and telephone calls taken, others were not, whistling or calling out.

''Ey, darlin', fancy a drink?' one shouted to Helen. She ignored him. Others were cruder, making Milly blush.

In a narrow Soho street, the smell of a jellied-eel stall turned her stomach. She'd never liked jellied eels. Never been to the seaside either. Perhaps one day she would, when her life took her outside of the palace just as it was starting to now. She and Timothy could get the train down to the coast. Spend a day in Margate, maybe, and eat fish and chips on the beach.

The salty, vinegary scent of the eels assaulted her as she passed. Mixed with the smog and exhaust fumes from the cars, Milly screwed up her nose. Sometimes she forgot how beautiful the palace smelled. There were fresh flowers in almost every room. She'd once heard a delivery man joke the Queen must think the world smelled of roses and in some respects he was right. But if the Queen thought the world smelled of anything, it would be of thick beeswax polish: honey-scented and sweet.

She pointed over her shoulder to the stall. 'How can people eat those? They smell awful.'

'I don't like them either,' Helen replied as they hurried on. 'So? He kissed you *twice*?'

'He did. It was . . .' She searched for the right word. 'Heavenly.'

'Gosh, it sounds it. Where are we going, by the way?'

'I think it's down here.'

They turned down a dark and dingy side street. Rain pooled in the potholes in the road, and in the throng the girls were unable to avoid them, the dirty water splashing their shoes. The odd cigarette butt, tossed aside when finished, floated on the water's surface. Holding the piece of paper Jean had given her close so it didn't get wet, Milly read it again.

'It's called the Sunrise Club.'

'There it is.' Helen pointed to a pink neon sign glowing in the darkness, illuminating a small doorway. It resembled a door to a house more than the entrance to a club, but the echoey sounds of a trumpet and the deep humming notes of a double bass drifted towards them. The girls exchanged glances as they reached the threshold, each trying to read the other's reaction. The stairway walls were a dark, crimson red, and the floorboards were painted black. They followed the curve of the stairs down into a basement bar, but as Milly entered, expecting something dank and dingy, she gasped.

The cellar club had a high, vaulted brick ceiling that seemed to go on forever. Along one wall, a bar set with bottles of bright-coloured liquid was busy with customers all clamouring for a drink, and at the other end, a jazz band played on a small wooden stage. Though it was only eight o'clock, the evening was already in full swing. The bass vibrated in Milly's ears, the trumpet and saxophones sang, and the continual thump of the drum matched that of her heart. This was another world; one that couldn't be further away from the *Woman & Home* magazine her aunt read in the evenings and the quiet of the palace. This was infinitely more exciting.

A dancer, draped in front of the drums in the splits position, suddenly jumped up, gyrating and wiggling her hips provocatively. She wore a grass skirt and a bikini top revealing so much of her bare, pale skin Milly felt herself blush. Next to her, another dancer with rich, dark skin swayed from side to side, jiving on her own.

Milly couldn't understand people who were racist. Considering the country had been happy for anyone of any colour to fight and die for them during the war, it seemed more than a little hypocritical to discriminate against them now it was over. Yet she was aware of the hate in the newspapers, and that sometimes filled the faces of some of the people she knew.

The dancer's eyes were closed, and her body moved as if she were swaying in her bedroom, not in front of a room full of strangers.

'Goodness me,' Helen replied. 'I haven't been in a club like this for ages. Oh, I've missed this music. Doesn't it make you want to dance, Milly?'

'You've been to a club like this before?'

'Of course. Haven't you?' Milly shook her head. 'Shall we sit over there?' Helen pointed to a table in the corner and Milly agreed. 'I'll get us some drinks first.'

They made their way to the table and Milly squeezed into the tiny space, leaning forwards so her shoulder didn't hit the shell-shaped wall light sticking out. The ashtray was already overflowing, and her bag stuck to the surface of the table where someone had spilled their drink. It made an unpleasant noise as she lifted it away and placed it by her feet. The metal chairs were hard and uncomfortable but at least they'd managed to bag a seat. A couple who'd arrived shortly after them were having to stand at the bar, hoping a table would become free, but everyone was having such a good time they weren't going anywhere soon. Helen joined her a moment later.

'Here we are. I got us gin fizzes. I hope that's OK.'

'It's perfect, thank you.' She sipped it, the sharp lemon taste pricking her tastebuds.

'What time is your mum on?'

'I don't know. I just wanted to get here before Caroline joined us. I don't want to talk about Timothy in front of her.'

Helen frowned. 'Why not?'

'Firstly, Timothy wanted to keep things secret because Edie doesn't like him. Secondly, I think Caroline might have a bit of a thing for him and thirdly—' She hesitated. 'Because I might have lied and told Edie I was seeing you rather than him.'

'Oh, Milly. That puts me in a bit of a spot.'

'I know,' Milly replied. 'I'm sorry. I panicked.'

'You'd best tell me everything before Caroline arrives then. Start at the beginning.'

'Well, we went to the pictures and—'

'Oh yes,' Helen said, raising her eyebrows. 'Snuggling in the back row?'

'He was a perfect gentleman actually.'

'It doesn't sound like it to me – you said he kissed you twice.'

'He didn't kiss me until we were back at the palace. Oh, Helen, it was wonderful. We were pressed up against the gates, and then, all of a sudden, he turned towards me and . . .' She replayed the moment in her mind.

'And then? Come on, I have no love life and doubt I will for some time. I'm living vicariously through you.'

'It was the most amazing kiss I've ever had and then he said he'd wanted to do that since he started working at the palace and asked if he could do it again.'

'I do love it when men ask if they can kiss you. It's rather sweet. And then?'

'Then it was over, but he kissed my hand before he left.'

'So he *is* a gentleman. And when are you seeing him next?'

'I'm not sure. We haven't sorted anything out yet and I didn't want to seem too keen by asking.'

Helen replied with a firm nod. 'Quite right too. Make him do all the work.'

'There's Caroline.' Milly stood and began waving. Caroline raised her hand and made her way over. 'Don't forget, it's a secret.'

'I won't. Oh, and no one has asked about the vase, have they? I still come out in a cold sweat whenever I think about it.'

'I'll tell you if they do.'

'Shall I get you a drink?' Helen asked Caroline as she arrived at the table.

'I can get one in a minute.' She pulled her coat down from her shoulders, tucked it on the back of her chair and sat down.

'What a beautiful dress,' Helen said, admiring the deep green frock with short cap sleeves, matching belt and flared skirt.

'It's lovely,' Milly agreed. 'Is that the one you picked up today?'

Caroline beamed with pride. 'Believe it or not, it's about ten years old but after Ma did a bit of a nip and tuck and changed the buttons, it's much more fashionable. I know they say redheads shouldn't wear green, but I like it.'

'It suits you,' Helen said. 'And all that nonsense is wrong. It's very striking. I wish I had skills like your mother's though.' Turning her arm to show the darning she'd done on the sleeve of her dress, she added, 'Look at this. I'm absolutely terrible.'

'She can help if you need anything mended.'

'That's very kind. Is that what she does for a living?'

'Her and my older sister. Nancy works at a dressmaker's not far from here and Ma for one in Bloomsbury. What were you two just talking about? I didn't interrupt, did I?'

Milly was quick to answer. 'No, we were saying about the club that it's not quite what I expected.'

'Me neither,' Caroline replied. 'I was a bit scared before I came in.'

'It does look quite intimidating from street level,' Helen added.

'But I like the music. Thanks for inviting me.'

Caroline glanced at Milly from under her eyelashes and Milly smiled. Caroline was only twenty. A year younger than Milly, but it seemed like an age. Perhaps it was just that so much had happened in Milly's life compared to Caroline's. Caroline had struggled moving into the palace and away from her family but she'd never really suffered losses like Milly. Even with the war she'd been one of the lucky ones with an entire family pretty much intact. She hadn't been evacuated either. Her parents had insisted they all stay together.

'Helen was saying she's been to a club like this before,' Milly said, leaning forwards, speaking louder as the music swelled. 'When was the last time and who was it with? That's what we want to know.'

'Rather,' said Caroline.

Helen dropped her eyes to her glass and gently ran her fingers over the rim. 'Yes, but not for a long time and not quite like this either. This is a bit more, umm . . . daring.' She took a sip of her drink. 'I'm only three years older than you, Milly. It's not like I'm ancient. And I've only been out with a couple of chaps. Besides, it was before my father became ill. I've barely left the house since then.'

'What's wrong with him?' Milly asked. 'If you don't mind my asking.'

'He has Parkinson's disease. It wasn't too bad at first, apart from the shaking in his hands. But it's been gradually getting worse. That's why I was late to your party,' she said, glancing at Milly. 'His balance is all off and he had a fall. I had to make sure he was comfortable in bed before I left.'

'That must be hard on you.'

'And your ma,' Caroline added.

'Oh, she's dead.' Helen drained the last of her gin fizz. 'She died a long time ago. It's been just me and him for most of my life, really. That lemon's very sharp, isn't it?'

Caroline blushed. 'Sorry.'

Milly had learned a long time ago, from her own bitter experience, that it was better not to assume that someone had parents, children or siblings. After the war, whoever you spoke to had lost someone and it was often wiser not to enquire in case it dragged up difficult memories.

Helen raised her head and gave a placatory smile. 'That's all right. You weren't to know, and I really am fine about it.'

'If there's one thing you should know about me, Helen,' Caroline replied cheerily, 'it's that I can put my foot in it at a moment's notice. Just ask my family or Mrs Barnes.'

'Does Mrs Barnes know we're here tonight?' Helen asked Milly.

'Sort of.' Milly shifted uncomfortably and raised her head to expectant expressions. 'I told her we were all going to meet my mum, but I didn't say it was here exactly.'

'What did you say?'

'That it was a nice, respectable club.' Milly observed the scandalous sight of a white woman kissing a black man in a darkened corner, at the couples dancing dangerously close together, at the so-called rules being broken. 'Somewhere with tablecloths and waiters.'

'Don't worry, we'll keep your secret,' Helen said.

Caroline nodded firmly, as if convincing herself she could. 'I bet Princess Margaret's trip to Paris weren't nearly as exciting as this.'

'She did get to go to a ball and dance with a prince though,' Milly replied. 'Several of them from what I've read in the papers. Shall I get us another round of drinks? We were having gin fizzes, Caroline. Is that all right with you?'

'Lovely.'

Milly wasn't sure Caroline had ever tasted one before, but they'd be travelling home together so she could make sure she was OK if she got tipsy. As she sat back down with the drinks, the song finished and a man with a pencil-thin moustache and navy pinstripe suit danced on to the stage.

'And now, ladies and gentlemen, let me introduce you to the fabulous, undeniably talented, Jean 'the Queen' Beaumont.'

Milly clapped as her mum sauntered on in an elegant evening dress. Her shoulders and most of her back were completely bare, pale against the deep black of the dress.

'Speaking of Princess Margaret' – Helen leaned in keeping her voice low – 'I don't think she'd have got away with a dress like that.'

The bodice was tightly cut, accentuating Jean's small waist. It hugged her hips, flaring out in a fishtail to the floor. Her arms were encased in black velvet gloves that finished above her elbow. Jean sauntered slowly with a confidence Milly felt she would never possess.

From one of the windows, she'd seen the royal family leave the palace on visits to the Royal Opera House and had marvelled at Princess Margaret and Princess Elizabeth in their beautiful frocks. Queen Elizabeth's were always a little more old-fashioned, but her children, Margaret especially, chose dresses that were up-to-the-minute; this was more daring than even she would wear. Jean's gown was nothing near the same quality with their acres of lace, pearls or diamonds, but was stunning none the less.

Jean stood in front of the microphone, her eyes dark with kohl and her lips prettily pink. After a few seconds' silence, the band started playing a slower number. Jean's hips swayed in time to the music and her left hand rose, gently reaching around and caressing the microphone stand. Her mouth opened and the voice that rang out was velvety and smooth – she sounded like a singer you'd hear on the radio, someone famous. Not a normal person. Milly glanced at her friends, who were as rapt as she was. A strange feeling grew inside her and she realised it was pride. Of course she was proud of Edie too. Edie worked at Buckingham Palace and was one of the longest-serving members of staff, well respected by everyone. But this was different. Her mum had talent. A God-given natural talent for something extraordinary.

When the slow number finished, the tempo picked up and Jean sang songs that got the crowd up and dancing, jiving and lindy-bopping, legs and arms flailing around. How they all didn't crash into each other was a miracle. Milly's heart raced just watching them, then a voice approaching their table drew her attention from the stage.

'Milly? What are you d-doing here?'

'Robert! I could say the same about you.'

'My friend works behind the bar. It's his b-birthday. Why are you here?'

'That's my mum.' Milly pointed to the stage, her smile wide and her eyes flashing.

'Gosh. She's very talented.'

'Isn't she?'

Robert noticed Caroline and Helen and lifted a hand in greeting.

'Look at you out of your uniform,' Caroline teased. 'In your Sunday best.'

It was true. His hair was slicked down in the latest style

and his trousers were smart. The sleeves of his white shirt were folded up at the elbow. He was almost handsome. It certainly made a change from the kitchen whites he normally wore. Had he been dancing? Milly wondered who with and looked over his shoulder to where a young woman in the centre of his group of friends was watching them.

'Do you want to dance, Milly?'

'Like that?' She pointed to the floor. 'I'm not sure I can.'

'Of course you can. I'll show you. I might st-stutter when I talk but not when I dance. Come on.'

'OK, but I warn you I won't be any good.'

Robert led her to the floor and within seconds she was spinning out, pulling back in, changing hands, all with Robert leading her through the moves. Her nerves disappeared replaced with elation as she enjoyed the music, the cooling air on her face as she spun, but most of all having Robert teach her. Learning now, with her friend, would come in handy if she ever brought Timothy here. Helen was soon dancing too, though Caroline refused the offer.

When the dance finished, they all clapped, turning to face the band. Jean left the stage and Robert led her back to their table.

'Robert, that was wonderful. Thank you for asking me. Though I'm not sure your friend's very happy about it.'

The girl who'd been watching them earlier still had her eyes pinned on Milly.

'She's probably just hoping I don't embarrass her. I better get back to my friends. Maybe we can dance again later?'

'I'd like that. I can't be too late tonight though. You know how early we start work.'

'Too early!' Caroline interjected.

Helen dismissed her dance partner with a practised air. 'Why didn't you dance, Caroline?'

'Oh, I—' She toyed with her fingers. 'I'm happy to watch.'

Given how outgoing Caroline was most of the time, Milly thought it odd she'd sat out, but perhaps she didn't know how and had been worried about making a mistake.

Helen sipped her drink. 'I wish we could stay here all night.'

'Me too,' Milly replied. 'Oh, Robert, I need to ask. Please don't tell anyone you saw us here.'

'L-let me guess, you've told Edie you're at a respectable, quiet pub?'

'Something like that.'

He mimed zipping his mouth closed. 'I won't tell.'

Robert left as Jean approached their table. When she stopped in front of Milly, a man in the group beside them pulled out his chair and offered it to her.

'Oh, I couldn't possibly, but thank you so much. You're such a gentleman.' She lowered herself on to the edge of the chair. It couldn't be easy in a dress like that. All the while the man watched on lasciviously, but Jean turned her back on him and gave them her full attention.

'Mum, that was—'

'Jean. Call me Jean when we're in the club, won't you, darling?' She leaned in conspiratorially, taking hold of Milly's hands. 'I might have told a tiny white lie about my age. Clubs don't want singers over the age of thirty these days, no matter how good you are.'

'It's lucky you look so young,' Helen said.

'You look even younger than me,' Caroline added, gazing at Jean as if she were meeting a film star.

A warm smile spread over her face. 'And who are these lovely ladies?'

'These are my friends Helen and Caroline.' Milly gestured to each one as she introduced them.

'And do you all work at the palace?' They bobbed their heads. 'How fascinating.'

'Caroline works with me and Helen works on the telephone exchange.'

'That must be exciting. I haven't had chance to visit Milly there yet but I'm hoping to soon.'

A sudden chill flew over Milly's skin. She would far prefer to keep these two parts of her life separate for the time being.

'I can't even imagine being surrounded by such fine things all the time. Do you get used to it after a while?'

Caroline shook her head. 'Not really.'

Helen added, 'I've only just started working at the telephone exchange and it isn't like the rest of the house. We're lucky if we get to see daylight.'

Caroline suddenly sat up straighter. 'Milly, you should bring your ma to the palace. We could all have tea.'

Milly froze, trying to find a way to put it off. It was too soon. Too soon for her, too soon for Edie, but her mum was nodding.

'Yes, that would be lovely, darling.'

'Soon,' Milly replied, hoping that would be enough.

'Have you been singing long?' asked Helen, changing the subject. Milly shot her friend a grateful look. 'You're really very good.'

Jean adjusted one of her gloves. 'Thank you. Yes, I've been singing for ages. In all sorts of clubs. Mostly up north but it's lovely to be back in the city again.'

'Who's that man?' asked Caroline, pointing to a young chap in the corner. He was in his late twenties and his fair hair seemed darker where it had been slicked back. His features were pointed, like a rat's. As they turned, he began to make his way towards them. 'He's been staring at you for ages.'

'I don't know. I've not seen him before, but I think he's something to do with the club. His drink was free, I know that much.'

'Good evenin', ladies,' the man said, pulling up a chair and sliding in between Jean and Helen. The acrid smell of too much cologne stung Milly's nostrils. ''Avin' a nice time?'

'Yes, thank you,' Jean replied. 'Are you going to introduce yourself?'

He laughed at her forwardness. There was something about this man Milly didn't like. She couldn't put her finger on it, but the way he kept glancing at them all with his small, black eyes made her uncomfortable. Caroline could see it too and had shrunk in her chair. 'Call me Jack. Everyone does.'

'And what do you do, Jack?' Jean pulled out a cigarette and Jack took a lighter from his pocket, snapping down the shiny metal lid and igniting the flame. She leaned in, keeping her eyes on him as the end of her cigarette glowed orange in the dim light.

'I'm the owner 'ere. So yer should be very nice to me.'

'Should I?' Jean threw her head back, laughing. 'Aren't I working hard enough as it is?'

'I s'pose so. That was quite a show. You got a good voice.' He leaned in closer to Jean. ''Ere, don't I know yer from somewhere?'

Milly stiffened as she saw worry flash across Jean's eyes, though no one else would have noticed it. Then her mum calmly replied, 'No, I don't think so. I've only just come to London.'

'Is that right? Where'd yer come from?'

'Southampton.'

The man sat back, and Milly relaxed a little.

A second burly gentleman appeared behind Jack and put a hand on his shoulder. 'Boss?' He whispered something and the young man stood.

'Business to attend to, I'm afraid, ladies. I 'ope you 'ave a nice evenin'.' He winked at Jean and she pouted as she watched him make his way back through the crowd and out of a side door near the stage.

Caroline blew out a deep breath, puffing her cheeks. 'Crikey, Jean, you knew just how to handle him.'

'You have to show these young men you won't be pushed around. You'll get the hang of it as you get older.'

A look that Milly couldn't read clouded Helen's eyes. Perhaps she hadn't liked Jack either.

'Milly?' Jean turned to her daughter, reached out and took her hands. 'Thank you so much for coming tonight. It means so much to me. I have to go and get a drink then I'm back on in a minute. Would you like to meet for a walk soon?'

To her surprise, disappointment consumed Milly at the short time they'd had to talk. She wanted to know more about her mum and understand this other London she inhabited. The anger from that first meeting was slowly receding and the idea of seeing her again was welcome. A piece of her that had been missing since her parents died was slotting back into place. She couldn't let that go. 'How about Thursday afternoon? I finish work at three.'

'Fabulous. Let's say three thirty and I'll meet you in Green Park. It was lovely to meet you girls,' Jean called as she weaved her way through the crowd back towards the stage.

'Milly, your ma's – well, I dunno what she is exactly,' Caroline said. 'Not like any ma I know.'

'What did you think of her, Helen?' Milly asked, eager for her opinion.

'She seems nice. I understand what Caroline means, she isn't your average mum working in a typing pool, but she obviously wants to continue to get to know you, and that's good, isn't it?'

'Yes,' she replied. Then repeated the word again to give it more weight. 'Yes, definitely. I just wish Edie would give her a chance too.'

'I'm sure she will in time.' Helen checked her watch. 'I should head off. I need to get back for my father.'

'And we're up so early we probably should too. Is Robert still here?' Milly asked, looking around. 'I can't see him.'

'They all left,' Caroline said. 'He gave a bit of a wave while your ma was talking but you didn't see.'

'Oh, right. Shall we head off then? We can walk you to the bus stop, Helen.'

They made their way through the crowd and back up the staircase to street level. Soho was even busier than when they'd arrived earlier that evening. Smokers leaned against walls, couples canoodled in doorways and young ladies danced down the street. The night was young for many of them, but for Milly, Caroline and Helen, responsibilities encouraged them home.

Chapter Ten

'Come on, my girl, put some elbow grease into it or you'll be there all day.' Edie's voice echoed around the empty Marble Hall even though she'd spoken in barely more than a murmur.

Over the last few days, the palace had been a hive of activity. The three huge Christmas trees that adorned the Grand Hall every year, brought over from Windsor, had been put in place and decorated by a special team – it wasn't left to just anyone – and now the trees glittered with lights. Someone had to come and check the tiny bulbs every day and replace them if they broke. Milly was grateful to be staring at the tree rather than doing that. She didn't fancy that job much. Yet, even with so much happening, the King's handkerchief weighed on her mind day and night, like a spectre. It sat folded in brown paper at the back of her underwear drawer, hidden from view yet constantly in her thoughts. She and Caroline had had private conversations about it, but both were still undecided on the best course of action. Why had it been them who found it?

'These bloody pine needles get everywhere,' muttered Edie. 'And there's a tree in nearly every room. You lot know how much I love the royal family, but do they need this many trees? The blimmin' garlands are sheddin' as well.'

The Grand Staircase had been decorated with fir garlands that ran in swags up the banisters and along the landing. If there wasn't an actual Christmas tree in every room, huge floral arrangements in deep reds and greens were popping up everywhere. It made the palace feel wonderfully festive, but also made cleaning even more of a task.

'And I might normally love it,' Edie continued. 'But if I hear that bleedin' parp parp parp of the Changing of the Guard again, I'll go barmy. We've just got too much to do.'

'We'll get there, Aunt Edie.' Milly wiped the sweat from her brow and went back to polishing the marble floor. The large red carpet that covered most of the bright white stone was too heavy to move, but Edie had rolled the edge back so she could sweep underneath it while Milly polished the remains of the visible floor.

The rest of the team had already gone through, gently dusting the enormous chandeliers with a large feather duster and cleaning the white marble columns. They weren't to touch the sculptures or any of the paintings: that was the job of the conservators. When the sun shone, the white marble reflected the sun and when it caught the gilded tops of the columns and cornicing, Milly had to look away so she didn't get a headache. Each room like this one took hours just to maintain. They were never allowed to get dirty, and the Chief Housekeeper would not be happy if she found even a pine needle that had been missed. Milly thought of her bed.

Was Jean sleeping in this morning? It was only just after ten and Milly had been up since five and at work from six. After Jean's set had finished, Helen had said she'd have been expected to hang around and act as hostess. She wondered if that sleazy man Jack had reappeared. Thinking about him made the hairs on the back of her neck stand on end. As she rubbed the floor, feeling the muscles in her arms ache with tension, Milly retreated into her imagination and pictured what the rest of Jean's evening had been like: floating from table to table being chatted up by handsome men, knowing they'd love to buy her a drink. She thought of the topsy-turvy life so different to her own: living at night while most of the world was asleep, then sleeping through the day while everyone else worked. The idea of showing Jean the splendour of the palace, her own little room, proving that she'd done all right, was growing in her mind, her initial reticence fading.

'There's a smear there,' Edie said, pausing to sweep the tiny pile of dust into a dustpan. 'And blimmin' paw prints over there.'

'I spotted them too,' Milly replied, once more mopping her brow. 'Marble's always a bugger when it comes to getting the smears out.' She should have been cold, given the rain battering the window and the lack of fires in the room, but her back was wet with sweat and the fabric of her ridiculous white uniform clung unpleasantly under her armpits, chafing her skin. White. Who'd decided they should wear white?

They'd left the club at midnight, but she hadn't been able to sleep after climbing into bed. The music still pulsed in her veins and the memory of dancing with Robert had played repeatedly in her mind. He'd looked so different in his civvies, but not as handsome as Timothy.

Edie went off to empty the dustpan and when she came back a few minutes later said, 'That's lookin' much better.' It wasn't really. Milly still needed to buff out the smears, but Edie was always encouraging. That's why everyone liked her. 'Those corgis can be little villains though. Do you know, they nipped poor old Mr Parker the other day. Not that I mind that too much, he does nothin' but gossip. You girls have a nice time last night?'

The question took Milly by surprise. Knowing how difficult Edie was finding things, she'd assumed she'd prefer not to talk about it. They'd avoided talking about her mum most evenings when they'd sat together either in the Household Lounge or in Edie's apartment.

'It was lovely, thanks, Aunt Edie. I didn't stop in when I got back because I didn't want to wake you.'

Edie was now on her knees helping to polish a section of floor. 'Jean lookin' well, is she?' The simple query gave Milly hope.

'She looked beautiful last night. Her dress was lovely, Aunt Edie, and she had these long gloves on that went all the way over her elbow.'

'Very fancy.'

'Was Mum always such a good singer?'

The hand holding the polish cloth slowed, and then picked up speed again. 'She was always singin'. Even as a little 'un.'

'Did you think she had talent? Did she ever have singing lessons? Like the choir here does.'

Some of the staff from all different departments sang in a choir, just for fun, and they sometimes got special teachers in to help with particular songs.

'Singin' lessons?' Edie laughed. 'How would we have afforded those? There were times we barely had enough food on the table. And who would we have asked? There weren't many singin' teachers on our street in Bethnal Green.'

'Shame. She could have made a career out of it. When I heard her last night, I thought she could have been making records.'

'Dreams are all well and good for sleepin' but they don't pay bills in the real world, my girl. They don't replace clothes when you grow out of 'em or buy new shoes.'

'Did you ever dream of doing something else, Aunt Edie?'

'Me?' Her face was so shocked Milly could tell the idea had never occurred to her. 'What would I have done? I can't sing. You know that well enough. My dad once said I sounded like someone playin' the trumpet the wrong way round.'

Milly giggled. 'No, you don't. You've got quite a sweet voice actually.'

'You'll get blisters on your tongue you tell such lies, Milly Hendry.' Edie went back to polishing the floor. She shuffled backwards on her knees, her bones moaning and creaking in protest.

'Didn't you ever have a dream of going somewhere or doing something?'

'Not really. I needed to work and when this job came up,

that was enough for me. I remember—' She sat back on her haunches, a faraway look in her eye. 'When I came to see if I was suitable the Chief Housekeeper was terrifyin'. She had glasses on the end of her nose, and she'd stare down at me and I was sure she could read my mind. When I was fourteen she seemed about ten feet tall, but she can't have been more than five foot four if she was an inch. She gave me a tour – well, it was more of a route march really – tellin' me what my duties would be, how I'd be expected to behave, and as soon as I walked up those servants' stairs and came in here, I thought I'd stepped into a dream. It was like nothin' I'd ever seen and I knew then if I was lucky enough to get this job, which came with somewhere to live – and not a dormitory neither: my own room – I'd be happy for the rest of my life.'

Milly saw the palace as Edie had as a young girl and remembered her own first encounter with the main part of the house. After she'd come to live with Edie, she was supposed to stay in the staff quarters, but once she'd crept in after her aunt and run straight into the King. Her knees had almost buckled with fright. She'd thought he'd tell her off. His face could be stern and forbidding, but he'd grinned and made a joke about the little fairies living in the palace who did such amazing work but weren't supposed to go roaming around and encouraged her back to Edie's room. A footman had escorted her and as soon as they were out of earshot, gave her the telling-off of her life.

Brisk, light footsteps sounded on the marble and Milly was suddenly aware of Princess Elizabeth and Princess Margaret walking towards them.

'Aunty,' she whispered.

'I'm just saying, Lilibet,' Princess Margaret said, 'that you could speak to Papa and ask him to allow me to do more than just float around at silly functions.'

'They are not silly, Margaret. They are important.'

'Quick,' Edie said. 'On your feet.'

She and Edie stood, Milly helping Edie as she was a little slower to push herself up from the floor. They waited for the princesses to walk past with their heads dipped. Elizabeth's pace didn't slow as they dropped into a curtsey.

'You would say that,' Princess Margaret grumbled. 'You get to do more exciting things.'

'You have just been to Paris, Margaret.'

'Yes, and I got told off for that picture of me sitting next to Prince Nicky. It wasn't even my fault. I can never do anything right—'

'Nonsense. Oh, I say, ladies,' Princess Elizabeth interrupted her sister with a gentle touch of her hand. 'Jolly good work. You are doing an absolutely smashing job. Well done.' She smiled her wide, friendly grin and her eyes were bright with intelligence. Princess Margaret sparkled too, the public mask coming down.

'Rather. Thank you so much.'

'Thank you, Your Royal Highnesses.'

The Princesses carried on. Two short, round corgis followed behind and, as surreptitiously as possible, Milly kept a watch on them until they had left and weren't likely to nip back and bite them. Edie beamed with pride before she dropped back down to work.

'You mustn't forget we all had responsibilities to our

families back then. I sent most of my money back to my folks. Every one of us needed to work for us to get by and there was a war on.' Edie's face darkened. 'Don't forget what I said, Milly, about Jean. You can't always believe everythin' she says.'

'She didn't say anything bad about you or your family.'

'I'm glad to hear it.'

Feeling the conversation had ended, Milly focused on the floor, turning her head so the light reflected and caught the smudges on the marble. How was she to bring these two strands of her family together? It would take a long time to be as close a family as Caroline's, but they had to start somewhere. Surely if she was doing her best to forgive her mum her aunt could too?

Jean and Edie needed to talk and to see things from each other's points of view.

Suddenly, Milly had an idea. She was meeting her mum for a walk in the park on Thursday when she finished work. If she took Edie along with her, she'd have no choice but to speak with Jean. She was sure that if her aunt saw her, spoke to her, she'd be able to put the past behind her. Jean too. Jean was her sister after all. And Thursday afternoon would be the perfect opportunity. She just knew that if they could sit and talk, they could work out their problems and Milly would then be one step closer to having a family again.

'Aunt Edie, do you fancy going for a walk on Thursday after we finish? We could just nip out and get some fresh air.'

'A walk?' She indicated the rain battering the glass. 'In this weather?'

'It's meant to be nicer on Thursday.'

'I suppose we could as long as it's better than this. It'll be nice to spend some time together away from here.'

A prickle of guilt swept over Milly's skin, but she pushed it aside. This was for Edie's own good and Milly would be there to make sure things didn't go wrong. Three grown women were meeting in a park. How wrong could things go?

Chapter Eleven

The sun shone through the leafless branches of the trees making dancing shadows on the ground. They were bundled up in coats with headscarves tied under their chins. Other women were chatting in pairs or chasing after children. One mother ran after her son flying a kite. Good job he hadn't tried that yesterday; he'd have taken off and landed in France.

Her coat thin against the chill breeze, Milly shivered, but the day was brighter, the world more colourful, and she was grateful she hadn't had to traipse out in a gale or sleeting rain to wait for Jean. Pigeons huddled in little troops, feathers ruffled, pecking through the soft soil for worms. Guilt closed her throat, but she took a deep breath to calm her nerves and reminded herself the deception would be worth it. It would be like pulling off a plaster: a shock at first but better after.

'It's lovely to be out of the palace for a bit,' Edie said. 'Especially after that fire the other day and all the hubbub that caused.'

Two days before, a small fire had broken out in the rafters of Buckingham Palace where some men were working. The alarm had been raised and all hell had broken loose. Fire trucks had arrived, and the blaze put out within minutes without much damage, but it had been terrifying to see. Fires could rip through buildings reducing them to nothing but ash. Milly knew that all too well.

'Where shall we stop then?' Edie asked. She was hobbling a little today and Milly had noticed her left knee was swollen. She'd have to get her something from the palace pharmacy. Like the post office, it wasn't more than a small room, but they were able to dispense most medicines any of the Royals or palace staff needed. After days of sweeping up pine needles on top of their normal cleaning duties, and the consequences of the fire, both Milly and Edie were glad of a day off and some time to rest.

'There's a bench down there. Shall we sit for a bit?' Milly pointed, sure this would be the route Jean took. It was the most direct path from the tube station to the gates nearest the palace and where they'd most likely come across each other. They hadn't arranged an actual meeting place, but everything had seemed so strange and other-worldly in the club that night. A world filled with excitement that she longed to see again.

'All right then,' Edie replied. 'There's somethin' I wanted to ask you about anyway.' They sat on the cold bench, thankful their long coats protected the backs of their legs from the damp wood. The mossy green trunks of the trees shone brighter after the rain of the last few days, and a dog chased a stick before settling down beside a particularly large trunk to chew it. The sky beyond was virtually white, the clouds merging to create one giant, colourless blanket.

'It's about Caroline,' her aunt began again.

Milly's heart rate spiked, worried Caroline had told Edie

about the gossip over Timothy. Had she let something slip about the club the other night or had she mentioned the handkerchief? Milly coughed to release the tension in her throat and tucked her straw-blonde hair back under her scarf. 'What about her?'

'I think she's doin' much better, don't you?'

A tiny laugh escaped Milly's mouth. Her nerves were so on edge this afternoon. 'Oh, yes, I'd say so. I think she's not so scared of dropping or damaging things.'

'That's what I thought. I'm not quite ready to let her near anythin' too important yet but she's definitely less skittish. I think she enjoyed meetin' you and that Helen the other night. It was good for her. The poor love's struggled bein' away from her family. I think she's the apple of their eye.'

'I do too, and she is very sweet. When she first started, she was like an annoying little sister, but we get on well now.' The word 'sister' floated like a wisp of cigarette smoke taken on the breeze. Milly waited for her aunt to say something about Jean, and when she didn't, Milly continued: 'And Helen's lovely too. We had a nice chat. Did you know her dad's poorly?'

'I thought somethin' must be up, but I didn't know what.'

'There's only her looking after him. It must be terribly hard for her.' Milly wondered once more about mentioning the handkerchief. On any other day, this would have been the perfect opportunity. Being away from the palace would have given Edie time to react without fear of being overheard but Milly couldn't risk upsetting her. She peered around again, watching for Jean.

'What are you gawpin' at?' Edie laughed. 'It's like your neck's made of elastic, pingin' this way and that.'

'I'm just looking around, that's all.'

'For Robert or Timothy?' A wry smile pulled up the corner of Edie's mouth.

'Neither, actually.'

'They're both sweet on you, you know. But you watch that Timothy. I wouldn't trust him as far I as could throw him.'

'I don't see why not.'

'Robert's much nicer. Respectful. Less cocky. He has kind eyes. You can tell a lot from a man's eyes.'

'Robert's a friend. Like Mr Newington.' A sudden flash of them dancing together and his hand on her waist raced through Milly's mind, causing a feeling she couldn't pinpoint. She'd have to find out when Timothy wanted to go out again. Then she could show him how good she was at dancing.

Edie chuckled. 'It'll take more than that to embarrass me, my girl. You've gone all pink.'

'It's the wind.'

'Righty-ho.'

In the distance she saw Jean, her platinum-blonde hair curling out from under a red hat. It appeared to be new, the colour more vibrant than the faded crimson of her coat. Though she couldn't wave, she caught Jean's eye and surreptitiously lifted her hand in greeting. Milly turned slightly to block Edie's view. She didn't want either one seeing the other and having time to escape. Within a few minutes, Jean was beside the bench.

'I'm so glad to see you. I was worried we'd miss each other.'

The weight of the bench shifted and she turned back to see Edie glowering at Jean as she pushed herself up to standing.

'Blimey, Milly, what have you done?' Edie asked, her voice ringing with hurt. She backed away, taking short, unstable steps.

'Aunt Edie, don't go. Please. I just thought—'

'Edie?' Jean sounded amazed the woman in front of her was her sister. She couldn't be that unrecognisable, surely. Jean's gaze shifted to Milly. The friendliness she'd seen over their last two meetings vanished and in its place was a cold, hard glare. 'Milly—'

'I just thought you two should meet and talk about things. I thought—'

'That's not your decision to make,' Edie snapped.

'Oh, don't be so hard on her, Edie,' Jean said, softening. 'She's trying to make things right.'

'Make things right? By forcin' us together?' She snatched her bag off the bench. 'Milly Hendry, I can't believe you'd do this to me. I said maybe when I was ready. Was this the only reason for our walk?'

Milly leapt forward and grabbed hold of Edie's arm, her ears ringing with the thrum of guilt. 'I'm sorry, Aunt Edie. I just thought if you could hear Mum out you might be able to understand why she didn't come back and then we can—'

'I told you why she didn't come back.' Her angry eyes were pinned on Jean.

'Edie, please,' Jean said. 'I didn't come back because I

didn't know it was safe and when I did, I didn't think it was right to wrench Milly away from you and here' – she motioned to the palace – 'where she was settled.'

'Oh, is that right?' Edie scowled, clearly not believing a word. Jean crossed her arms over her chest.

'Yes, it is actually.'

'You could've fooled me.'

'Shush!' Milly pressed her finger to her lips. 'People are looking.'

The boy with the kite was openly watching, the mother doing her best to drag him away. The dog was happily chewing a stick, but the owner kept glancing over, while a couple passing watched the drama unfold from the corner of their eyes.

'What are you looking at?' Jean shouted at a woman, who tutted as she hurried past towards the tube station.

'Jean, stop it,' Edie hissed. 'You'll make even more of a scene.'

'Me? You started it.'

Edie turned to Milly, her eyes dimmed with sadness. 'How could you, Milly?'

Jean stepped in before Milly could answer. 'You should give her a break. She's just trying to help.'

The fire in Edie's eyes frightened Milly. She'd never seen her aunt so angry and upset. While she hadn't expected hugs and sobs, she hadn't imagined they'd end up shouting at each other. Milly searched for some way to bring things round.

'Please, both of you.' She held a hand out to each of them. 'Edie, you're my aunt and you've raised me since I was ten.

You're so important to me. And, Jean, you're my mum. You're both sisters. It shouldn't be like this, and it doesn't have to be. If you two could just talk.'

Hurt had hardened Edie's features. 'The past is done and gone.'

'Please stay, Aunt Edie.' Milly hated that she was having to plead so hard, but she wasn't prepared to give up. She looked between the two older women, wondering why she, the youngest of them all, was playing referee.

Jean studied Milly for a second; then she turned to her sister. 'If you're willing to stay, Edie, then I am too. I have missed you, you know.'

'I find that hard to believe. You always hated me. Making comments about my weight, my looks.'

'Fine. If not for me, then Milly. We should talk for Milly's sake.'

A heavy silence descended. It felt almost damp as it lay on Milly's skin, covering her like the smog that often filled the London streets. But Edie didn't move. Milly had never seen her aunt like this. There was normally a kindness to her. Everyone knew it. But it was as if she'd closed the gates and wasn't prepared to let anyone in.

'Please, Aunt Edie. Just five minutes.'

Edie checked her watch. It seemed five minutes, to the exact second, was all they were going to get. She sat back down, her handbag perched on her lap. Milly sat too, making room for Jean, who fitted into the space to her right. They all stared forwards in silence, watching the boy with the kite. It would have been comical if Milly's heart hadn't been straining under the tension.

'Someone needs to speak first,' Milly said when the still-ness became unbearable.

'I'll go,' Jean said calmly. 'I want you to know, Edie, that I never stopped thinking about you or Milly. Leaving was harder than you realise.'

'Was it now?'

'It really was. I always wanted to come and see you but as a visitor you can't get further than the front gate of the palace. They don't let just anybody in.'

'That they don't,' Edie replied.

Were the waters smoothing just a little? It was too much to hope for.

Jean went on, 'I'd always hoped that one day I'd come back. It just took longer than I was expecting.'

'Let me ask you this then, Jean. In all those years, when you knew exactly where I was and exactly where Milly was, why didn't you write, hey? Not one letter in all that time. You never asked me anythin' about her. Not once in ten years.'

Edie turned to stare at Jean and Milly couldn't help but do the same. It was a good question. One that Milly hadn't thought of. Her mind raced, thinking of everything both Jean and Edie had said. The pendulum swung towards Edie. It was fair that Jean hadn't wanted to drop a letter on Milly as a child. It had been hard enough to receive news of her at twenty-one. Any younger and she might not have been able to cope at all. But why hadn't she written to Edie?

'You never asked me what she'd got for Christmas or for her birthday. You never sent a penny for her. Not that I'd have taken it anyway, but I'd have put it in savin's for her.

You could have asked if she was doin' well at school or had any friends. You never once wrote just to say I'm thinkin' of you both. So how am I supposed to believe that it was all for Milly's sake that you never wrote?'

'I – Well . . .' Jean stuttered and after glowering at her for a second, Edie checked her watch again. The seconds dropped away like water from a leaky tap. There was a blankness to Jean's face that worried Milly. Her cheeks were growing pinker, and the colour seeped down her neck, under the scarf wrapped around her throat.

'I didn't think you'd have an answer for that.' Though Milly hated to admit it, there was a triumphant note to Edie's voice. She'd proved a point, but while Jean didn't have an answer, Milly found herself hoping there was an explanation.

Jean shot to standing. 'Milly, darling—'

'Darling?' Edie rigidly pronounced the 'g'. 'Since when did you talk like that?'

'Some of us have changed, Edie, that's all. It's not a bad thing.'

'Just stop it, Jean, please. Stop lyin'. I don't care about what happened before or how you've hurt me, but I won't let you hurt Milly. You need to be honest with her. You can't mess her around again.'

'I'm old enough to stand up for myself, Aunt Edie.'

Milly had meant to try and calm the situation. To show Edie she didn't need to get upset on her behalf, but Edie grimaced as if she'd betrayed her and began to walk away.

'I didn't write to you,' Jean shouted, ''cause I could never say anything that'd be good enough.'

Edie's steps faltered but she didn't stop or turn around and instead kept on towards the palace.

When it was clear she wasn't coming back, Jean collapsed on to the bench. 'I was never good enough for your aunt, or for any of my family. I was always the one who got things wrong, made the wrong choices. Always a disappointment.'

'I'm sure you weren't,' Milly said, reaching out for her arm, though she had no proof either way.

'I could never be what they wanted me to be. That was the problem.' She sighed, defeated. 'The dutiful daughter living in drudgery to help pay the bills. I see she's as bossy as ever though. Does she still cross her arms over her chest like this?' Jean mimicked the exact way Edie did it, even pursing her lips comically. 'She did that when she was telling on me at home. She always thought she was in charge.'

Milly giggled. 'Yes, she still does that. And she does this little wiggle of her shoulders. Like this.' She copied the gesture and was pleased to see her mum laugh.

'I better go. Do you remember Jack from the Sunrise Club? He's been talking about me singing on more nights.'

'Has he been asking more questions?' Concern tightened Milly's stomach. 'About you?'

'Yes, but nothing to worry about, darling. And he's not the loan shark Billy ran away from. He's far too young. Anyway, like I said before, that was in the East End not the West End. To be honest, I think he has a slight crush on me. Silly, really.'

Jean stood and Milly squeezed her hand. 'I'm sorry today didn't go well, Mum. I didn't think any of this would happen.'

'You did what you thought was right, darling. I don't blame you.' Jean cupped her cheeks, and it was such a maternal gesture Milly's eyes filled with tears. 'And you mustn't blame Edie either. Your aunt's always been stubborn but she'll come around.' It was a kind thing to say. 'I'm not going anywhere so she'll have to get used to things eventually. Listen, I'm singing at a hotel next Thursday night. Not the same club as last time. Do you know the Mason Hotel in Poland Street?'

'No, but I'm sure I can find it.'

'Why don't you come along with your pals, and we'll catch up again then.'

'All right. Aren't you singing anywhere this weekend?'

'Yes, but . . . it'll be busy, so I won't be able to spend much time with you. It'd be better if we could meet next week.'

'OK. I'd better get back to the palace.'

'Do you like working there, Milly?'

The question seemed to come out of nowhere. Did she? The work was physically demanding, but she knew how lucky she was to have a job and a nice place to live, good food to eat, friendly people around her. 'Yes. Yes, I do.' Her mum's face was unreadable. 'I like your hat, by the way. Is it new?'

Jean adjusted it, running her fingers over the thick, luxurious fabric. 'Yes. Just a little treat to myself for working so hard. Every woman should treat herself, Milly. Otherwise, what's the point?'

'Have you had any luck finding a new place to live? I'd love to be able to visit you at home rather than in windy old parks.'

'Not yet, darling, but things take time, don't they?' She stepped forwards and placed a hand over Milly's. 'Edie will come round, eventually. We won't give up until she does.' The affection in her expression was almost overpowering. 'Right, I better be off.'

She left, and Milly took a moment to sit on the bench alone with her thoughts. The boy's kite was still dancing, directionless on the wind. She felt the same way. Torn one way then another. Why couldn't Edie have stayed calmer? Stayed for longer? Given the meeting a chance? Her mum had. The sun slowly dipped behind the trees as dusk drew near. She didn't want to be in the park alone after dark but back in the palace she'd have to face Edie. She'd have tried not to make too much of a scene in public but in her room, in the safety of those four sturdy walls, Milly was going to face both barrels and after how badly this meeting had gone, she didn't much fancy her chances of survival.

Chapter Twelve

'Milly.' Caroline's overly loud whisper halted her as she made her way to Edie's room. She took a breath, her heart still calming from the way the meeting between her aunt and mum had ended. Caroline gripped her elbow. 'Milly, we've gotta talk about the handkerchief and what we're gonna do.'

Though she'd lost some of her cockney accent since she started working at the palace, it was clear as she spoke earnestly of her concerns.

'I haven't decided yet,' Milly said. 'And this isn't really a good time.' Her eyes darted down the corridor to Edie's door. She couldn't tell her aunt now, or anytime soon by the looks of it.

'There ain't never a good time – we're always so busy – but it's tying me up in knots. I can't sleep properly.' She rung her hands together. 'I've been thinking about it, and I think we need to tell someone. Mrs Barnes or one of the head housekeepers.'

'But what if Edie gets into trouble? She's miserable enough as it is.'

'But if we don't and it ain't old it means the King's not as well as we thought. We have to think about him too.'

'You're right,' Milly conceded, pressing her hand to her forehead. 'But I'm scared for Edie.'

'Why don't we ask Helen what she thinks? She has her head screwed on and might think of summat we can do.'

'Good idea.' They needed another opinion. Milly's brain was too full of other problems to think straight. 'I'll speak to her and find a way for us all to meet.'

'Good.' The relief on Caroline's face was clear and she dashed off, leaving Milly to walk the few remaining steps to her aunt's door. She tapped lightly.

'Come in.'

'I'm sorry, Aunt Edie,' she said, popping her head around the gap as if to make sure there weren't going to be any missiles thrown at her.

Edie stood by her armchair, her hands on her hips. Milly could tell she'd been pacing, trying to wear off her annoyance. A piece of embroidery sat half done on the table. Having always put things away as soon as they were finished with, the fact that it sat there, left out, showed her aunt had tried to settle to it but couldn't.

'How can you do that to me, Milly? Play a trick on me like that.'

'It wasn't a trick, Aunt Edie.' She came further into the room, closing the door softly behind her. She unbuttoned her coat and laid it over the back of a chair. 'I just thought if you could speak to Mum face to face you might be able to sort some things out.'

'Sort what out?' Edie placed her hands on the back of the armchair, leaning forwards. 'I know exactly what happened ten years ago. I was there. She made her choices, and I can't believe you're just lettin' her walk back into your life like nothin's happened.'

'That's not what I'm doing.'

'Isn't it?'

'I just thought it might help you start to forgive her. I think there might have been misunderstandings.'

'Misunderstandin's? Don't you see she's lyin' about it all? Even down to the way she talks. She never talked like that when we was younger. It's all an act.' Milly dropped her eyes and Edie's tone became a little softer, though it was clear she was a long way from forgiving her niece. 'Ambushin' me is not the way to make me forgive my sister for all that she's done.'

Edie turned on the wireless. Whether it was to drown out their own raised voices so the other staff couldn't hear or to fill the thick silence that crept in whenever one of them stopped talking, Milly didn't know, but the reedy voices of actors performing a radio play filled the room.

'I didn't mean to ambush you. But I'm trying to move on. I hoped you would too.'

Edie crumpled as the words left Milly's mouth, folding in on herself. 'You didn't have to deal with it all. You didn't have to sort a funeral for a sister who'd broken the law and abandoned her only child, all because she wanted to run off with some bloke and pretend her old life never happened. You didn't have to bury a good man – a kind man – who'd never get to see his daughter grow up. I'm only glad he didn't live to see Jean leave him for that no-good—'

'That's not what happened.' Milly stood her ground,

keeping her voice calm and level. Edie pinned her eyes on Milly.

She'd thought long and hard about everything Jean and Edie had said and had come to the conclusion that for whatever reason, one had misunderstood the other. Maybe Jean hadn't told Edie everything at the time. They clearly hadn't been close. Maybe in her anger Edie had read something different into Jean's actions. Neither of them were perfect and given Edie had lied to her for ten years she couldn't sit in judgement on Jean. But more than anything Milly needed to believe her mum. She had to believe that her leaving had been for something important. Something that meant it wasn't a case of her not being enough to stay. Couldn't Edie understand that?

Edie once more returned her hands to her hips. 'So you believe her? You really believe she never wrote 'cause she was puttin' you first?'

'Yes, I do. I don't much like it, and it hurts like hell, but what else am I supposed to do?' Milly's voice was rising, and she tried to pull it back down, yet the anger inside couldn't be stemmed. She was angry at everyone: her mum, Edie, the palace-prison. Everyone and everything.

'And you believe she didn't write to *me* 'cause I was always horrible to her?'

Milly's voice was brittle. 'That's not what she said.'

'It's as good as. And I can tell you that's a load of old twaddle.'

'Well, I do believe that,' she shouted, regretting it instantly when Edie's face contorted with pain as if struck by a physical blow. 'Mum told me how she was always a disappointment to your family. Always the one who was never good enough. And when you told me about the letter, it was obvious you never liked your sister. Maybe Mum's right and you were jealous of her.'

Edie didn't answer, clearly still stung by the knock Milly had dealt. When she did, her voice had dropped to barely more than a whisper. 'She's turnin' you against me.'

'No, she's not, Aunt Edie,' Milly replied, taking a step forward. 'But you not even giving her a chance is.' Edie's hazel eyes were swimming with tears. 'If you just got to know her again—'

'I thought you were smarter than this, Milly. I'm beggin' you, don't be taken in by her. It's not that she out-and-out lies all the time but she twists the truth, she always did. Even as kids she'd make out things were everyone else's fault. She did it to your dad, convincin' him she wasn't havin' those affairs, that he was the one bein' jealous over nothin', but I knew the truth. Don't get sucked in like your dad did.'

'Mum didn't have lots of affairs. She had one. And it wasn't an affair, exactly. She fell in love. She said Dad was jealous and difficult to live with.'

'What?' Edie stalked towards Milly. 'Your dad was a gentle soul. Kindness itself. Don't you remember him at all?'

That was what was so hard – she didn't really. Just vague moments of them together. They could have been from a film she'd seen once, or a book she'd once read. They could have been anybody and the realisation made her wretched. Her dad was gone. Even her memories of him were fading. She couldn't let go of the chance to get to know her mum.

'Did you love Dad?' she asked, her voice quivering.

Edie's brow crinkled in confusion until the penny dropped. 'He was my sister's husband. Jean may never have cared about things like that, but it mattered to me.'

'So you did love him.'

'I thought he was a fine man.' Something in Edie's eyes shifted.

'Mum said you were angry at her that Dad liked her and not you. Is that why you don't believe her? Because Dad loved her and they had me and—'

'And what?' Edie's cheeks were flaming. The little veins caused by the rosacea burning across her cheeks. 'And no one else loved me? Is that what you were goin' to say? No one else wanted to marry me?' She shook her head incredulously. 'I am sorry I never met anyone I liked enough to marry, but that was my choice. Believe it or not, Milly, I had offers and I turned them down. I wasn't goin' to settle for someone I didn't love with every bit of my heart. I've always been happy with my lot. I've always had you and this place. Sometimes we don't get the things we want in life and need to be happy with the things we have. You might want to think about that, Milly Hendry. It's a lesson you could do with learnin'.'

Milly didn't know what to say and the single tear that ran down her aunt's face caused such a wave of guilt to roll over her she thought she'd die of shame. She grabbed her coat and left as quickly as she could before either of them could hurt the other any more.

Out in the hall, Milly took a deep breath. Her hands were shaking. Her legs were unsteady as if someone had replaced all her bones with string. Leaning on the wall for support she stumbled along the corridors, outside into the fresh air. As if by some wonderful stroke of fortune, Timothy was outside, smoking a cigarette. His back was against the wall, one leg crossed over the other at the ankles. He blew out a long stream of smoke, taken by the breeze.

'Blimey, Milly, what's happened to you? You're white as a sheet.' He threw the stub of his cigarette away and embraced her, rubbing her back. 'Your teeth are chattering. Are you ill?'

'No, I'm fine. I just—' She tried to control her body, wrapping her arms over her chest for warmth. 'I just had a row with Edie, that's all.'

'Must have been a whopper if you're feeling like this. Want to talk about it?'

'No. Not yet.' She went to let her head rest against his chest and noticed him checking around before she did. A second later, she felt the warmth of his body through his shirt and turned her head up, relaxing under his gaze.

'Fair enough. You're having a right old time of it lately. You can always talk to me, you know. People say I'm a good listener.'

'Who says that?' she asked, a smile lifting her mood.

'Anyone and everyone. I know what'll cheer you up.'

'Oh yes, what's that?'

'A play.'

'A play?' The tension in her throat eased and Milly breathed more easily.

'Well, a musical. I thought we could go and see *Kiss Me, Kate* at the Coliseum. It's supposed to be good. A chap I know took his girlfriend last week and she loved it. As it happens, I have two tickets for Saturday week.'

'Oh, you do, do you?' He'd planned to see her again already. The peace of being wanted swept away a little of the pain. 'Well, in that case, I'd love to go. I haven't seen a show in ages.'

'You'll come?' His eyes were bright but his tone uncertain. That he seemed worried she'd say no made her heart feel light.

'I'd love to.'

'Brilliant.' He studied her for a second. 'Will you tell Mrs B. this time? She'll have to know we're courting sooner or later.'

Courting. The word chased away the gloom of the previous hours. 'I will eventually,' Milly replied, tightening her arms around her. 'Just not yet. You don't mind, do you?' She didn't need anything else to argue about at the moment. The conversation earlier had proved that.

'Not if that's what you want.'

'I'll tell her soon. I promise.'

He gave her a peck on the cheek and bid her goodbye as he returned to work. She was sorry to see him go, but at least something in her life was going right for once.

Chapter Thirteen

The kitchen of Helen's small but tidy house was about the same size as Milly's room. The table was just big enough to sit the three of them for Sunday lunch and she, Caroline and Helen were finishing up what had been a delicious meal.

'That was smashing, Helen. Thank you ever so much,' Caroline said, resting her knife and fork on the plate.

'You're welcome. Thank *you* for the delicious pudding.' The apple crumble Caroline had brought, courtesy of her ma, was heating in the oven, the scent of apples and cinnamon heavy on the air. 'Father's really looking forward to some.'

'Are you sure he doesn't mind us being here?' asked Milly, raising her eyes to the ceiling as he was in bed upstairs.

'Of course he doesn't. He's pleased I'm actually seeing people and not pottering about all on my own. I told him a bit about going out to the club the other night. Not everything, of course, but that I'd danced and had a lot of fun.'

'I'm sure he was happy to hear it.'

'Why didn't you dance, Caroline?'

'Oh – I . . .' Caroline adjusted the cutlery on her plate. 'I just didn't fancy it. People are still talking about you and Timothy, Milly.'

'There's nothing to talk about,' she replied with a chuckle, her eyes darting to Helen's. 'You should have danced with Robert. He's a good teacher and you won't learn the steps if you don't try them.'

'Oh no, I know how to dance. Ma and Pa taught me. She's a brilliant dancer, my ma.'

'So what was it then?'

Caroline's pale skin began to redden as she dropped her eyes. When she spoke, the words came out in short, indecisive bursts. 'I . . . like to be careful around fellas, that's all.'

Helen and Milly shot each other a worried glance before Helen rested her hand on top of Caroline's. 'Did something happen?' For a moment, Caroline didn't move at all; then she nodded. 'Did someone take advantage of you?'

Seeing the colour drain from Caroline's face, bile rose into Milly's throat.

'No one knows about it,' Caroline suddenly blurted out. 'Please don't tell.'

'Of course not.' Helen gripped Caroline's hand tighter, and Milly reached for the other. That explained her behaviour around creepy Jack the club owner.

'It was a while ago. A man I thought liked me, he – he went too far.'

'Oh, Caroline,' Milly moved closer, draping an arm over her. 'Did he . . .?'

'No.' She shook her head vigorously. 'It ain't as bad as that, but . . . it wasn't very nice either.' Whatever happened sounded awful enough and had clearly left its scars. This must have been before she'd started at the palace. Milly wanted to find the man and punch him on the nose or report him to the police. Caroline folded her arms across herself. 'I've gone and ruined a nice meal now, ain't I?'

'Of course you haven't,' Helen replied.

'Not at all,' Milly added. 'We're your friends, Caroline. You can always talk to us. Did you never tell your parents?'

'God, no. Pa would kill him, and it'd break Ma's heart. Better to just forget about it. I know it could've been a lot worse. Let's talk about summat else.'

Helen and Milly looked at each other in concern. 'If you're sure,' Helen said. 'But promise you'll speak to us if you need to.'

She gave a thin smile. 'Promise.'

'I'll just nip some crumble up to Dad. It smells ready.' She took it from the oven and served up portions for them all. 'Back in a tick.'

They waited for her to return before tucking in.

'Your mum's a wonderful cook, Caroline,' Milly said, as soon as she'd tasted the first spoonful. 'This is delicious. As good as anything we've had at the palace.'

Helen closed her eyes and savoured the taste too. 'Dad was very excited when I brought it in. This will really lift his spirits.'

'Good,' Caroline replied, keeping her eyes on her bowl. After a moment, she lifted them. 'Shall we talk about the handkerchief now?'

'Handkerchief?' Helen enquired.

Milly took a sip of water. Nerves churned in her stomach. It had already been a week since they'd found it and after Caroline's horrific revelation she felt sick enough. 'Caroline and me, we need your advice.' She outlined how they'd

147

found it, their fears over telling the truth and that it was still wrapped in brown paper at the back of Milly's underwear drawer.

'Goodness,' Helen exclaimed, taking a sip of water herself. 'What a difficult position you're in. So Edie doesn't know you found it?'

'No. I didn't know when or how to tell her. You know how difficult things have been between us, especially since our walk in the park.'

Helen cast Milly a sympathetic look before straightening. 'Unhappy or not, this is quite serious, Milly. What if the King isn't being honest about his health? I mean, I know it could have been there for ages like you said, especially if the blood's brownish by now, but neither you nor I are doctors.'

'So you think we should tell?'

The kitchen door opened, and Helen's father edged unsteadily inside. 'Hello, ladies.'

He was thinner than Milly had expected, his skin pallid and his hair lank, pressed against his scalp. Yet she could see the resemblance between the two and could well imagine Mr Hill having been dangerously handsome in his day. After Helen had told her he suffered from Parkinson's disease, she'd grabbed a medical book from the staff library and tried to learn more about it. She knew it was a degenerative disease that caused shaking, but she hadn't expected him to be so ill-looking.

'What are you doing out of bed?' Helen stood to give him her chair.

'I just wanted to come down and meet your friends. I'll go back up in a minute.' He spoke softly but with the same well-spoken English as Helen. From their speech and the house, they weren't working class, but neither were they particularly middle class either.

'Oh, Dad, you shouldn't have. We could have come up to you if you really wanted to meet them.'

'And see me in my dressing gown and pyjamas? Nonsense.' He'd managed to get dressed but his shirt buttons were fastened incorrectly and the knitted cardigan that had probably once fitted him well hung off his thin frame. Thinking of the King's illness and their discussion of moments before, Milly's chest tightened.

'Sit down then and I'll introduce you.' She gave him Milly and Caroline's names and they shook his hand when he offered it. His grip was weak; his fingers had barely any strength.

'Thank you for the crumble, Caroline. I can't remember the last time we had one. It's one of my favourites.'

'Ma insisted I bring you summat nice and she's a good cook is my ma.'

'I'm not good with sweets,' Helen admitted. 'But I'm pretty good with savoury things.'

'Oh yes,' her dad replied. 'She makes a rather fabulous minced-beef pie. Good, flaky pastry.'

'And Milly's brought us some chocolate, so we can have a square of that later with our cocoa.'

'What a treat. Well, I'll leave you ladies to your gossiping, but it's lovely to meet you. I'm glad to know Helen has such lovely friends.'

It could scarcely be called a conversation, but it seemed to have tired him out already. With Helen's help he made his way slowly from the room. As they got to the door, Helen said, 'I'll be back in a minute. I'll just help Dad upstairs.'

'What do you think she's gonna say?' Caroline asked when the creaking stairs indicated they were out of earshot.

'I don't know. I hope she tells us to burn it and forget about it. I just want it all to go away, don't you?'

Caroline hugged her arms over her chest, both knowing that wasn't really possible. They remained silent until Helen returned.

'So, where were we?'

'What do we do, Helen?' Caroline asked. 'It's worrying me to death. Oh Lord, what a stupid thing to say. See, I always put my foot in it.' She buried her head in her hands and Helen rubbed her arms.

'It's all right, Caroline, but I do think you should tell a senior person as soon as possible. I understand you don't want to worry your aunt, Milly, so perhaps you could tell someone above her and see what they say? My belief is that they'll want to keep this quiet. The last thing they'll want are rumours flying about below stairs. The fact you haven't told Edie might work in your favour.'

'Do you really think so?'

'I do. But you can't keep this to yourselves any longer. It might mean the King needs more treatment or give them a clue to something else that's going on. Medical things can't be hidden.'

Her words hung in the air, clearly loaded with her own unhappy struggles.

'All right,' Milly said, nodding at Caroline. Deep down she'd known that was the answer. She suspected Caroline did as well but hearing it from Helen's sensible mouth meant there was no putting it off any longer. 'First thing tomorrow we'll go and see the Master or Deputy Master and tell them.'

'The Master?' Caroline gasped. 'Not the Chief Housekeeper?'

'I'd rather face the Master of the Household than Mrs Fernsby, wouldn't you?'

Caroline slumped down, resting her head in her hand. 'Don't suppose it matters,' she replied. 'I'm terrified of both of them.'

The next day, Caroline and Milly stood in front of the Master of the Household's door, both trembling slightly. They should have been having breakfast in the Household Breakfast Room, but neither could face anything and had made separate excuses, leaving Edie finishing her toast and tea with the rest of the team.

'I feel sick,' Caroline mumbled.

'Me too.' Milly took her hand, squeezing it gently. 'But we're here now. Let's get it over with.' She knocked on the door and a deep, formal voice sounded from the other side.

'Come in.' They stepped through and were greeted by Lieutenant Colonel the Honourable Sir Piers Legh sitting behind his large mahogany desk. 'Ah, Milly, Caroline. What can I do for you?'

Milly cleared her throat and took the lead. 'Good morning, sir. I – we—' She took a breath. She might as well just come straight out with it. 'I'm afraid we found this when we were cleaning the King's bedroom on the first of December.'

She pulled the small parcel from her apron pocket and unfurled the paper revealing the handkerchief. The sight of it made her stomach turn over. The dried blood was flaking away from the fabric and though it couldn't be anything more than her imagination, she was sure a rust-like scent drifted into the air. She didn't want to hold it any more and offered it to the Master, who rose out of his chair, cautiously leaning over the desk.

'You found this in the King's bedroom? Where?'

'Behind his bed. It had fallen between the bedframe and the skirting board and because we haven't been able to move the furniture in his room since before his operation we only just found it.'

He took it from her, examining it. 'First of December, you say?'

From the corner of her eye, she glanced at Caroline. 'That's right, sir.'

When he looked up, there was a hint of fear in his normally inscrutable face. Milly's stomach contracted. 'Does anyone else know about this? Mrs Barnes perhaps?'

'No. No one.' He eyed her suspiciously. He knew Edie was her aunt, and that they were normally very close – everyone in the palace knew that. What he couldn't know was how a chasm seemed to have opened up between them since she'd stupidly brought her mum and aunt together. 'I swear, sir. I haven't told anyone and neither has Caroline, have you?'

'No, sir, not no one.'

'You're sure?'

'Absolutely. We've not breathed a word to anyone.'

'Good.' He paused, staring at the handkerchief, which now sat in the middle of his desk.

'What should we do, sir?'

'Do? There's nothing for you to do. Nothing.' The words were spoken sharply as he moved around his desk to stand in front of them. 'Absolutely nothing. You never saw this. You never found anything behind the King's bed, do you understand?'

'Of course, sir,' Milly and Caroline both agreed.

'Why has it taken you so long to come to me?' Neither of them answered. 'Speak, girl,' he shouted at Milly. 'I should sack you both for this.'

'It's my fault,' Milly said, wanting to protect Caroline as much as possible. 'I wasn't sure what to do, sir. I was worried you might think we hadn't been cleaning properly. But we all love the King and knew we had to say something.'

'You should have come to me straight away. I'm very disappointed in you both.' He stalked back around to his chair and collapsed into it, drawing his fingers along his jaw. 'And by rights you should both lose your jobs.'

Caroline stared at Milly, tears clear in her eyes.

'Please, sir.' Milly bowed her head, hoping his anger would abate if it was clear she understood.

He folded the paper back over the handkerchief. 'I'll decide what to do with you two later but for now, if either of you breathe a word of this to anyone you'll find yourselves out of the palace before you can say His Majesty. Have I made myself clear?'

'Absolutely, sir.' Milly gave her response more strength than she felt.

'Yes, sir,' Caroline answered, her voice, in contrast, weak and wavering.

'To reiterate: whatever happens, do not mention this to anyone. Now get out of my sight.'

Milly closed the door softly behind them and they traipsed down the corridor, away from the senior staff's rooms and back to the areas they were both used to. Her legs were shaking and putting one foot in front of the other took all the energy she had.

'Well, that didn't go well, did it?' said Caroline.

'Not really.'

'I can't afford to lose this job, Milly.'

'I know. I don't want to lose mine either.'

Caroline stared at her, wide-eyed and fearful, and Milly wished she could say something to help, but the words wouldn't come. Knowing the gossip mill as she did, she feared there was every chance someone had seen or heard something, like Milly and Caroline going to the Master's office, and once the mill began to work, there was no telling what might be said. She just had to pray that once he'd calmed down the Master of the Household would change his mind.

Chapter Fourteen

The days passed with their normal monotony, the only excitement being Mr Churchill spilling tea on to the carpet of the White Drawing Room while meeting the King. By Thursday night they'd heard nothing more from the Master of the Household and both Milly and Caroline were doing their best to keep it from their minds.

That evening, the Household Lounge was full. Edie, who had been chatting to Mr Newington in a quiet corner, came over to join Caroline and Milly, who were sitting in comfortable armchairs reading. Caroline had a book, Edie opened a copy of *Good Housekeeping* magazine Mrs Chadwick had given her, and Milly was deep in the latest issue of *Tatler*. The day had been busy, cleaning the State Rooms and Milly had been looking forward to sitting and relaxing. She quite fancied a long hot soak in the bath but with a communal bathroom at the end of their hall, it wasn't always possible, and she needed to be ready to visit her mum in Poland Street. She hadn't mentioned it to Edie after their last conversation about Jean had been so heated and planned to simply slip out later, she hoped without anyone knowing.

Conversation had been frosty with her aunt so when Edie snorted at something she'd read, then leaned over to

Milly, showing her the page and saying, 'Look at this: "Be Your Own Masseuse". As if after cleaning all day I've got the energy to go squelchin' and rubbin' my neck and back,' Milly took it as a peace offering.

'What's that machine they're using?'

'Somethin' to wallop your muscles till they give up, I think.'

'That doesn't sound very nice.'

'Doesn't, does it?'

Milly savoured the moment of harmony until raised voices carried down the corridor and instinctively all three stood up, moving towards the sounds. The rest of the staff, who'd been seated chatting or listening to the wireless, followed.

'What's going on?' Milly asked Robert, who was edging out of the fray.

'O-one of the chefs burned the Royals' dinner and now they're all having a row about it. They've kicked us cooks out of our side of the kitchen and all hell's b-breaking lose. We were trying to prep for the morning and Mrs Chadwick's having none of it. They're three people down with the flu and it's causing all sorts of problems.'

While the royal family had chefs, the palace staff had cooks – and the rivalry between the two sides was fierce. The cooks were proud to serve everyday food, which was, of course, excellent, but some of the chefs thought themselves higher in the pecking order because they made fancy food for the royal family and all the important guests. Milly wasn't jealous of the food the Royals had. Though the chefs were very talented, the dishes that went upstairs were often tiny and wouldn't fill up the footmen and cleaners who'd been on their feet all day.

'What's happenin' now?' Edie asked, pointing to where Mrs Chadwick, surrounded by men in chef's whites and silly hats, was giving as good as she got. Probably better, if her body language was anything to go by.

'I'm not sure but apparently the Queen's hungry, the King's already in a mood and everyone's blaming every-body else in case they get the sack.'

The scrabbling voices suddenly dimmed, and Mrs Chadwick stomped over to them. 'Robert, come on. I need your help. I've agreed we'll give them a hand to sort out their mess as long as they help us prep for the morning. I know we're not normally allowed to touch their fancy ingredients but it's all hands on deck. I'll need you to help me in the kitchen.'

Robert beamed at his temporary promotion from kit-chen porter, which generally meant washing up and peeling potatoes. Milly smiled, not only at Robert but at the way, when all was said and done, they pulled together if need be.

'Do you need us, Flora?' Edie asked and Mrs Chadwick's round, angry face immediately softened.

'Oh, that's kind, Edie love, but no, we've got it all under control, or will have soon enough.'

'Wish me luck,' Robert said as he left, and Milly obliged.

Everyone returned to the lounge and took up whatever they'd been doing again, though at times loud voices could still be heard echoing through the ground floor of the palace. They hadn't long sat down when a bell rang on the wall. It was the bell to summon the housekeepers. This was why they lived at the palace. Some of the staff's jobs were day-time only, but there was no telling when someone might need something clearing up.

'That's us,' Edie said with a sigh. 'I wonder what's hap-pened now. I better go and change.' She attempted to push herself out of her chair but as she put weight on her knee it gave way and she fell back into the seat with a thump. 'Bloody knee,' she scolded. 'It's makin' me feel about a hun-dred years old, this blimmin' thing.'

'Why don't I go, Aunty? I think Timothy's working so I can send him down if I need any help and it won't take me a minute to run and change.'

Caroline reddened and hid behind her book but not before Milly had spotted her reaction. Perhaps the reason she hadn't acted on her feelings for Timothy was because of everything she'd told them at Helen's house. If that was the case, the last thing she needed was Milly flaunting her bud-ding relationship in front of her.

'Are you sure?' Edie said, a look of grateful acceptance pushing away her frown. 'Go on then. Just this once.'

After a quick change into her uniform, Milly made her way upstairs to the family dining room, leaving her small trolley of supplies outside the door. All the Royals were seated around a large dining table, including Princess Eliza-beth and her husband the Duke of Edinburgh, and Queen Mary, the King's mother. Little Charles and baby Anne must be with their nanny at Clarence House. Unlike the public rooms, this dining room was cosy. It still had enormous can-delabras on the formally laid table, but the mantelshelf was adorned with family pictures and the room felt far less stuffy.

After all the problems downstairs, the first course had now been delivered but the atmosphere in the room was tense. Surely a burned dinner hadn't caused this much unhappiness?

Timothy stood bolt upright in the corner, his hands behind his back. Though he couldn't respond to her arrival, she was pleased to see his eyes flick towards her and the corner of his mouth lift slightly. Next to him one of the butlers in their black trousers and tailcoat waited to retrieve the dishes. Milly bobbed a curtsey as Queen Elizabeth spoke to her.

'Oh, Milly, I'm so sorry but one of the corgis has widdled on the rug. Peters' – she signalled to the butler – 'saw it happen; he'll show you.' The Queen's voice had its usual cheerful tone and carried no hint of the tension evident on the family's faces. 'Now, darling, what were we saying?'

The last remark was directed at the King, but Milly still curtseyed and followed Peters to the corner of the room where the edge of a beautiful rug that covered most of the floor was damp and smelling unpleasantly of urine.

'We were saying', the King began, his voice firm, 'that you simply cannot continue to go around with this Mayfair set, Margaret.'

'Papa, you're such a snob,' Margaret responded, giggling and sipping her wine.

'I am not a snob. And perhaps you should drink some water.'

Peters whispered to Milly, 'If I were you, I'd sort this out as quickly as you can. Then get out.'

'Your father is not a snob, darling.'

'I just need some bits from my trolley,' Milly whispered back and moved towards the door.

'You really are, Papa.'

'Margaret,' the Duke of Edinburgh interjected. 'Stop this nonsense.'

Mr Dankworth, the senior footman, opened the door for her, closing it and waiting on the other side while she found a cloth.

'Are you all right, Mr Dankworth? You look quite shaken.'

'There've been some words tonight, Milly, I can tell you, and I don't think they're finished yet. Got everything you need?' She grabbed an extra cloth just to be on the safe side and Mr Dankworth let her back in, resuming his place by the door with his hands behind his back. Milly caught Timothy's eye again as she kneeled down to work on the mark.

'I believe Papa was speaking to me, Philip, not you.' Margaret turned her attention to her father. 'They're all perfectly well bred, and why shouldn't I say hello to them when I'm out. I cannot exactly ignore them, can I? What would the dreadful papers make of that? "Princess Margaret snubs so-and-so." I can just see it now, can't you? That would not do the family reputation any good at all, which is all anyone here seems to care about.'

'Our reputation is p-paramount, Margaret,' the King replied angrily, a hint of his stutter creeping in. Though he was clearly angry, his face was still pale. 'Do you know how long it has taken to win the country back after my brother's abdication, not to mention the war?'

'Oh Papa, please, don't start on about the war again.'

Queen Mary watched the antics of her family from the end of the table. Milly couldn't see her face, only the turning of her head depending on who was speaking.

'Margaret,' Princess Elizabeth said calmly. 'You know perfectly well what Papa means. The people of Britain are facing terrible austerity and you're seen out every night enjoying yourself and some of your friends are rather risqué. You are being tainted by association.'

'Lilibet, do you always have to take his side?'

'This isn't about sides,' the Queen interjected. 'Margaret, darling, you must realise that you have to act in a way that is appropriate for a member of the royal family.'

'Am I not doing that already?'

'No,' the King boomed. 'No, you are not.'

The Duke of Edinburgh slugged back some wine. 'In fact, Margaret, you really are acting like a child.'

Milly rubbed at the stain, trying to get as much liquid out of the carpet as possible. Whichever dog it was clearly hadn't been let out for a while as the clean-up was taking much longer than Milly would have wished. One of the little rascals came over and sniffed at her hand as she worked. A slight fear rose it was going to nip her as it had Mr Parker.

'Perhaps if you let me do something other than attend all the meaningless functions none of you wish to go to—'

'That is not fair, Margaret,' Princess Elizabeth said while

her father tried to calm down. His breathing was ragged, and Milly could hear the effort each breath was taking. She could sympathise with Elizabeth and her attempts at keeping the peace, at being reasonable. She'd felt exactly the same when she was trying to get her mum and Aunt Edie to talk. The royal family were like any other, with ups and downs, but that didn't stop it being a shock to hear them fighting like this. 'Everyone must do their bit while Papa is recovering.'

'I know that,' Margaret shouted, her voice rising. 'And I am, but I should be able to see whom I like. Next you'll say I can't speak to Peter either.'

At the mention of the Deputy Master's name, the atmosphere in the room suddenly shifted. Even Milly's muscles stiffened. She could hear the tightness in the King's jaw as he spoke.

'We will speak about that later.'

Milly rubbed harder until she was sure she'd removed as much as she could. It would need another going-over tomorrow, just to make sure there was no stain, but it would be fine for now. She just wanted to leave.

'You say I'm acting like a child, Philip, but is it any wonder when I always get treated like one?'

'You never behaved this badly when you were a child.'

'She did sometimes,' the Queen added cheerily. 'Poor old Alah had quite a lot to deal with at times. But we love you anyway, darling.'

Milly had heard of Alah: the Princesses' nanny. A formidable woman named Mrs Knight. Alah had been her nickname. Milly noticed Marion Crawford, or Crawfie as she had been known to them, wasn't mentioned.

The King ignored his wife's remark, concentrating on his daughter. 'Would a child be sent to Paris?'

Without speaking, Milly walked towards the door just as Princess Margaret stood, her chair flying back from the table. Peters and Timothy both reached forward to grab it as Princess Margaret flounced away, barging past her grandmother, who had jumped at the sound of the chair clattering to the ground, and giving Mr Dankworth only seconds to open the door before she was ready to walk through it. Her glass, which had been knocked to the edge of the table, fell to the floor. Shards of crystal glinted in the puddle of dark red wine as it soaked into the rug.

The Queen, who had forgone red wine in favour of champagne, sipped delicately from the flute in her hand. 'Oh dear. But at least Milly is already here to clean it.'

Half an hour later and with the help of Caroline, the red wine had been mopped up. She'd never heard the royal family argue like that. She'd never really heard them argue at all. If they did it was normally done behind closed doors and news would reach them below stairs via the butlers and footmen. Everyone would have to guess what was true and what had been exaggerated, only considering details to be facts when one or more people said the same thing. To be there first hand had made her feel incredibly uncomfortable, not least because it reminded Milly of her own family troubles.

Later that evening, Milly yawned as she changed back

into her own clothes, wishing she was visiting her mum at her flat rather than in a hotel. A place where she could kick off her shoes and relax. She was dog tired from a much longer day than usual and her bones ached. Yet, she reminded herself that she was, at least, seeing her mum. Something she had longed for. With a quick glance at the clock and throwing her hand in front of her mouth to suppress another yawn, she made her way out of the palace, glad to step away from the tension and drama surrounding them all at the moment, both above and below stairs.

Chapter Fifteen

The next morning, Milly rolled over and rubbed her tired, gritty eyes before stretching her limbs. Her head was groggy as if someone had filled it with cotton wool. There was a slightly sour taste in her mouth and her teeth were fuzzy. In fact, her whole mouth felt downy and thick. She sat up, looking for her clock. At this time of year when she woke it was normally dark, but today a muted light seeped around the curtains. She leaned over the side of the bed to find her alarm clock on the floor still ticking. She focused on the time. It was nearly eight o'clock and she'd been due at work an hour ago.

'Oh crumbs,' Milly muttered as she jumped out of bed. The icy air in her bedroom bit at her skin, making her shiver as she quickly changed into her uniform. Thankfully she'd left it folded on the chair when she'd taken it off yesterday, just as she normally did. Her fingers fumbled over the buttons, not because they were cold but because Edie would be furious. Milly pressed a hand to her head. She shouldn't have had that second gin fizz. Or had it been three in the end?

The Mason Hotel in Poland Street had been dark and dingy with a metal sign hanging from one hook. The scruffy brick building definitely wasn't the Ritz and inside the patterned tiles of the floor were dirty under a large thread-bare rug. The Sunrise Club couldn't be called top class, but it had been exciting. The Mason – a second-, possibly third-rate hotel – wasn't what she'd pictured before she arrived last night. Remembering the place now, she felt suddenly sorry for her mum. Her dreams had never been fulfilled, even after all these years.

There hadn't been a band, just a rusty piano player, but her mum's singing had still been wonderful, as had the blue cocktail dress she'd worn, with its three-quarter-length sleeves and skirt held up by a large petticoat. A gold band had reflected in the light, bright against her white wrist-length gloves. Milly had commented on it: apparently it had been a gift from Billy bought years ago. Their quick chat had been cut short by a gentleman's admiration of her voice and though Milly had stayed through the second set, Jean had been so busy acting as hostess that when the clock struck two, Milly had given up any hopes of another conversation, put on her coat and made her way out, back to the palace. Surrounded by compliments, Jean hadn't even noticed.

Once dressed, Milly splashed some water on her face and brushed her teeth before slipping stockinged feet into her shoes. Even they seemed to pinch, her body rebelling against any constriction, trying to force her back into bed.

Edie didn't tolerate lateness from anyone; indeed, no one at the palace did. Milly had known people to be sacked on the spot for less. Not by Edie but by senior butlers and foot-men. Milly calmed. She'd get away with it this time. After all, she'd never in all her life been late and that had to count for something. She raced through the staff areas into the main part of the palace.

'Don't run, Milly,' chided Old Bill, one of the other cleaners, who was working outside in the corridor.

'Sorry, Bill,' she whispered, calming to a quick trot.

'Edie was asking after you earlier. She won't be happy with you turning up late.'

'I know. I didn't mean to.'

Why hadn't anyone woken her? She'd have called in on Caroline if she hadn't arrived on time. She couldn't believe Edie hadn't knocked for her.

'Tell her you're poorly.'

She hurried past and saw him wink. It brought a smile to her face but one that faded as her stomach roiled. She didn't feel well at all. Her forehead and top lip were clammy, the sour taste in her mouth remained even though she'd thoroughly brushed her teeth and given her tongue a scrub. The fuzziness in her head was easing a little but in its place grew a stabbing in her temples. She hadn't drunk too much, had she? She didn't think so. She hadn't been unsteady on her feet and she'd known exactly where she was going on her way home. Though, now she came to think of it, she had giggled when a man had whistled at her outside a busy Soho pub and normally that would've scared her half to death. No, she hadn't been drunk exactly, but clearly while waiting for her mum she'd drunk more than she should.

At least they were working on the principal floor and not up a hundred flights of stairs. That should save her some time and stop her from dying on the climb up. She hurried on, bursting into the room to find Edie, Caroline and other members of the team hard at work along with footmen, equerries and other palace staff all ensuring the room was ready for the day's events.

Edie was standing on the top of a step ladder, polishing a large mirror over one of the marble fireplaces. She paused, whispering, 'I was gettin' worried about you. Where the bleedin' hell have you been? It's the King's birthday lunch-eon in here today. This room needs to be spick and span.'

That explained why no one had come to get her. Milly remembered they were to be up and at it before break-fast. Nobody could be spared, even for a second, and after last night's tensions during the family dinner, which she'd reported back to Edie after leaving the family dining room, Edie obviously didn't want to risk anything being wrong.

In her befuddled state Milly couldn't help but think that no one would even notice if they didn't clean today – there was never a speck of dust anywhere in Buckingham Palace; but as she peered around at the hustle and bustle, some pine needles that had fallen from the Christmas tree in the corner caught her eye. 'I'm sorry, Aunt Edie. I over-slept. I don't know what happened. I set my alarm like I normally do.'

She replayed the night in her head and found she couldn't quite remember if she had. She could see herself doing it, but that might be nothing more than a memory of a previous night, her replaying an action she'd taken a million times before and putting it in last night's place.

Edie climbed down the ladder and stood in front of her. 'Overslept?' She crossed her arms over her chest. 'Someone said you went out last night.'

'Who did?' Heat ran up her back, prickling her skin.

'Doesn't matter. Did you?' Milly hesitated and it was her undoing. Edie could always read her like a book. Her hands went to her hips. 'I see. They said you smelled of alcohol too. Was it Jean? Were you off to some club or other like before?'

'It was a hotel.'

Edie rubbed her forehead. 'Oh, Milly, this won't do. I know you want to see your mum, but you can't let it affect your work—'

'It hasn't, Aunt Edie. It was an accident. I'm sure I set my alarm. I—'

'But it has happened, Milly, hasn't it? And today of all days. What will His Majesty think if he comes in here and finds it grubby, hey? On his birthday. His actual, proper birthday, not the official one.'

Milly bowed her head under Edie's disappointed gaze, though she wanted to point out not a single thing in Buckingham Palace could be considered grubby.

'I am very sorry. Really.'

Edie said nothing but crossed her arms over her chest. Milly felt everyone's eyes on her, watching her. Her neck reddened, the blush flooding on to her cheeks. Her eyes stung with tears. She'd never been so humiliated in her life.

'I've never been so disappointed in you as I am right now, Milly. What kind of example is this to set to the newer ones like Caroline? Thank God she was here. She's been doin' her own work and yours too.' Edie's eyes burned into Milly as she studied her, but Milly kept her eyes cast down to the floor. 'Lord knows I wish I didn't have to do this but you haven't given me much choice. I'm givin' you your first warnin'.'

'What?' The Master's recent threat resounded in Milly's ears. If he heard about this, there wasn't just a possibility she'd lose her job, she definitely would. It was the perfect excuse for him to get rid of her.

'What else can I do, Milly?'

'But I've never been late before.' Milly lowered her voice so only her aunt could hear. 'This isn't fair, Aunt Edie.'

'Fair? I wouldn't put up with this from anyone else, would I? If Caroline or Davey waltzed in an hour late, they'd face the same. I've always said lateness, especially when you live here, is unacceptable. It's one thing if you travel in and the bus is late, but you only have to walk through a few corridors. I don't like it either, but I have to treat you the same way I would everyone else and you decided to go out last night, even though you didn't finish till late. This is Buckingham Palace. The home of the King. If we don't have the highest standards, then where should? He's knightin' his doctors today. For all they've done for him, for this country, they deserve to see the place at its best.'

'But . . .' Milly struggled to justify herself. She knew her aunt was technically right, but it still felt unfair. She'd always been a perfect member of staff. Didn't that count for anything? 'It's the first time and I always work hard.'

'I hate to say it now, Milly, but I might as well. Lately your standards have been slippin'. You're missin' surfaces, forgettin' to check for cobwebs. I was goin' to mention it later when it was just the two of us but now's as good a time as any.'

Was that true? Her attention had been wandering lately but there was a lot on her mind. She gave a final plea. 'But I'm your niece, Aunt Edie.'

'There'll be no favouritism here. Maybe you should stick to seein' Jean on your days off. She's a bad influence. I told you she would be.'

'That's not true.' There was a steely edge in Milly's voice now, and Edie flinched. 'She didn't make me late. I'm the one who overslept. You can't blame her for that, even though you like to blame her for everything else.'

'What's that supposed to mean?'

'Nothing.'

'I'll not discuss my private life in front of everyone. You'd better get to work. You can start in the corner and work round and meet us at the end.'

Milly took a duster and made her way to the corner. The room was wide and long with high ceilings and four startling chandeliers. The walls were covered in the most beautiful silk coverings. Milly had once called it wallpaper and been corrected by a footman. It was a wall covering, not like wallpaper normal people had. It reminded Milly of a theatre foyer in some strange way. Perhaps it was the plaster swags, reminiscent of a stage curtain, that ran around the top of the room, or maybe it was the expectant feel of the place. The King and all the royal family would be here shortly to celebrate his birthday, something intimate and personal. She hoped they had a nicer time than they had last night.

Milly moved to the end of the room and began dusting a windowsill. Another large vase of flowers sat in the middle, blooms reaching out and filling the space. Though she tried to avoid knocking one, the sun appeared from behind a cloud and the flash of blinding sunlight sent her off balance. The whole vase wobbled, and everyone looked at her as she cried out, steadying it before it fell.

'Be careful, Milly,' Edie hissed.

'Sorry. It was an accident.' She carried on, even more gently this time.

After they'd worked around the room, it was time to sweep the carpets and floor. Each using a soft bristled brush, Milly and Caroline, and two others, began in the centre of the rug, all sweeping out towards the edges. They took a quarter each because the room was so big and this way no one ended up trampling over the already cleaned sections. While she swept, Milly replayed Edie's dressing-down over in her head. It seemed the closer she moved towards her mum, the further away she got from Edie, all because Edie wouldn't give her sister a chance, wouldn't believe that she'd changed. Milly's contented, quiet life of just a few weeks ago seemed miles away, as though it belonged to someone else or had existed in another lifetime. She'd come to look on the palace as an opulent prison and today it seemed even more so.

'Psst,' whispered Caroline. 'Milly?'

'Yes?' She looked up as Caroline checked over her shoulder, wary of Edie's presence.

'You missed a bit.'

'Where?'

Edie appeared between them. 'There.' She pointed at the spot. 'This isn't good enough, Milly. You're gettin' sloppy. Caroline, make sure she does it properly, please.'

Milly paused, holding her broom tightly. 'I don't need Caroline to check my work.'

'Yes, you do. Things need to change, Milly. I don't want to give you a second warning 'cause . . . well . . . you know what happens after that.'

Surely Edie wouldn't sack her own niece. If Milly lost her job she'd have to move out of the palace. Out of her home. Edie wouldn't take all that away from her. Yet uncertainty swirled inside her. Buckingham Palace had been Edie's life. She wasn't a senior housekeeper in title, but she was treated like one and Milly couldn't be sure she'd jeopardise her own reputation by letting standards slip. A ball of fire sat in her stomach: she had never been so angry with her aunt.

'Caroline,' Edie continued, 'I want you to make sure Milly's work is up to scratch and report back to me at the end of each day.'

Caroline dropped her head, refusing to meet Milly's eye. 'Yes, Mrs Barnes.'

As Edie passed Milly she whispered, 'I wish I didn't have to do this, Milly. I really do.'

But before Milly could think of a response, she was gone.

Chapter Sixteen

'Honestly, Timothy I am absolutely furious. I know I was late and that's entirely my own fault, but don't you think it's just too much giving me a warning?'

'Over the top, definitely, but don't tell your aunt I said so or she'll give me a thick ear.'

Milly laughed as they strolled about in the foyer of the Coliseum. She sipped her drink, having opted for water instead of anything alcoholic. She hadn't been able to get to the telephone exchange to talk to Helen and as Caroline was now acting as her superior, albeit unwillingly, Milly hadn't dared talk to her either. She'd bottled up her feelings all yesterday and today, and though she'd already given Timothy a rundown of what happened on their walk into the city, she didn't quite feel she'd said everything she needed to in order to get it out of her system.

'She said it was because it was the King's birthday party, but . . . Oh, I don't know. I feel like she's punishing me for seeing my mum.'

'Or rewarding Caroline.'

'For what?' Milly turned to him, and he averted his eyes.

'Nothing. Nothing. It doesn't matter.'

'Go on,' she prompted. 'Tell me.'

He hesitated, until her steely tone convinced him. 'Now,

it could be nothing, but . . . well, I hate to say it, but maybe Caroline wants to impress her. Maybe she wants to . . . I don't know . . . rise up through the ranks?'

Or protect her job. After all, Milly had been the one to take the blame for everything when they'd spoken to the Master. Maybe Caroline hoped that if he did decide to sack someone the blame would fall solely on Milly.

'It's not uncommon,' Timothy continued. ''Specially at the palace. Just sometimes, getting ahead means stepping on people on the way up.'

He was right. She'd seen it happen. Not so much in their department, but in others certainly – the more prestigious posts with the most access to the royal family were known for it. Rumours were always flying about that someone had been undermined or dropped in it accidentally on purpose. The butlers were the best source of information, and you could learn a lot from cleaning the ladies-in-waiting's rooms, but she'd never have thought Caroline would do something like that. She'd seemed embarrassed when Edie had asked her to check on Milly's work.

'I don't think Caroline would do that. She's my friend.'

Timothy hugged her close. 'I'm not saying she is. Just, you know, be careful. If I'm honest, I've never really liked that Caroline.'

'Why not?'

'I don't think she's as sweet and innocent as she makes out. Underneath it all I think she's quite wily. She was yacking to your aunt a few days ago and they both stopped when I went past as if whatever they was talking about was top secret. Come on, they're opening the doors. Let's find our seats.' They made their way up several flights of stairs to the top tier of the theatre. 'It's a bit high, but these were the best seats I could get.'

'It's wonderful,' Milly replied, secretly glad she didn't suffer from vertigo. 'And we've got a great view of the stage.' She peered over from their seats in the balcony.

'As long as no one tall sits in front.'

Timothy had managed to get them seats a couple of rows back, and she studied the stage, the ornate plasterwork covering every surface, the cherubs on the walls and the giant domed ceiling. It was a match for the palace in its way, the seats and the stage curtain mirroring the dark red of the carpets in Buckingham Palace.

Seats were beginning to fill and, before long, the lights went down. Milly snuggled next to Timothy as the play began. The comforting warmth of his arm on her shoulders seeped through the thin fabric of her blouse.

Though she tried to concentrate on the play, Timothy's words rang around her head. She wasn't sure he was right, but what could Edie and Caroline have been talking about so secretly? The only thing she could come up with was her. The ball of fire began to burn in her stomach once more. Edie's lies had proved she couldn't truly trust anyone. If Caroline was hoping Milly would get the sack so she could take her place she had another think coming.

At the end of the play Milly applauded. She couldn't remember a lot of it and felt guilty at the money Timothy had spent on the tickets only for her to be too preoccupied to watch it properly. She had, however, enjoyed the songs. 'Too Darn Hot' still buzzed around her head as they left, and she had a feeling she'd be singing it at work over the coming week.

'What d'you think then?' asked Timothy as they descended the stairs back to the foyer. 'I thought it was pretty good.'

'I enjoyed it,' Milly replied. 'The songs were terribly good, weren't they? I wonder how they do it. Do they write the lyrics first and then find some music to fit, or do they do the music first and fit the lyrics to that?'

'No idea. Good question. What shall we do now? Seems a shame to go home just yet. Fancy walking around for a bit? Stroll along the Thames?'

'Yes, I'd like that.'

They walked down to Trafalgar Square, past the beauty of the National Gallery and the majesty of Nelson's Column. The fountains and lions stood sentry at night, ancient keepers of the city. On they went down Northumberland Avenue until the murky waters of the Thames rose before them. These were all places she'd seen hundreds of times in her life but seeing them with Timothy was like looking at the world through fresh eyes.

The crowd had thinned, and the street was almost deserted. Frost crept on to the surface of the pavement, glittering in the lamplight, and Milly's breath clouded as she strolled alongside Timothy, who had lit a cigarette and blew out clouds of his own. They chatted companionably, looking at the view across the dark expanse of water, brilliant in its dazzling brightness. The world had been so dark during the war and the blackout lit only by bombs and fire, but now lights punctured the black, illuminating the city.

When Timothy had finished his cigarette, he paused before he threw it away. 'Milly, have I told you how beautiful you look tonight?'

'Hmm.' She pressed a finger to her lips. 'Do you know, I can't quite remember.'

He smiled shyly. 'Well, you do. You look absolutely smashing. Makes a chap proud as punch to have you on his arm.'

She drew closer to thank him and as she did, he took her hand and pulled her in for a kiss. He cupped her face, his fingertips brushing against the pins in her hair, and she fell into him, holding him tightly. She wanted him to like her, to know that she had strong feelings for him too.

In the coldness of the night, the warmth of his mouth made her stomach flutter and her heart thrum against her ribs. She kissed him back, enjoying being so alone with him. At first, she was only vaguely aware of his other hand moving from her back, around her body, to the neckline of her coat. She thought he was going to gently touch her chin, but instead of moving up, his fingers followed the neckline down to her cleavage. The passion inside her began to cool, replaced by a nervousness that heightened her senses. She wasn't quite ready for this, and especially not here in the middle of the street. Her stomach roiled. She felt grubby. He kissed her harder, the heel of his hand pressing into her breast, and instinctively she pulled away.

'No, Timothy. No.'

'What?'

'What do you think you're doing?'

He backed away from her, mortified. 'I thought—'

'It's too soon. I—'

'Oh blimey, Milly. I – I'm sorry,' he stumbled. 'Shit.' She'd never heard him swear before and he turned away, running a hand through his hair. 'I'm so embarrassed. Stupid. I thought – I thought that's what I was supposed to do.' He'd always been so assured, but even in the dark she could see how confused and embarrassed he was. 'You must think I'm scum.'

'Supposed to do?' she asked angrily, adjusting her coat, ensuring the buttons were tightly fastened. Though she felt sorry for him, she couldn't control her agitation.

He was pacing around now but without any direction, going round in circles and doubling back on himself. 'You know . . . second time out and all that. All me friends keep telling me I should be doing that sort of thing. They say it's what a girl wants.'

'Well, it's not what I want.'

'I – I shouldn't have listened to them. Blimey, Milly, can you forgive me?'

She pushed her cold hands inside her pockets, her evening bag bashing into her thigh from the force of the movement. Seeing his genuine regret, she didn't want him to feel worse, but remembering what Caroline had gone through, she needed to make clear what she would and wouldn't put up with. 'I like you, Timothy, and I want to get to know you. A kiss is one thing, but you don't need to go grabbing at me like I'm a prize ham.'

He laughed, relaxing a little. 'You're right. Totally right. The chaps are idiots. They say a girl should take it as a compliment but—'

'Well, if you want to pay me a compliment, tell me my hair looks nice or that you think I'm clever. I'd much rather that.'

'You're right.' He stepped towards her, offering his arm, and after a second, she placed hers through his. They began walking again, strolling slowly, and silence stretched between them. 'Sorry for being an idiot.'

'I should think so.' His eyes darted away from hers and his jaw was set with shame. She went on: 'Let's just forget about it, shall we?'

'Y-you—' He was floundering again. 'Please don't tell anyone about this, will you, Milly? I'm so embarrassed I could throw meself in the Thames.'

'You don't need to go that far.'

They continued on and though neither of them spoke, with each step the horrible exchange moved further and further behind them. He still seemed embarrassed, unable to look at her.

When they finally made it back to the palace, he said, 'I've no right to ask after earlier but . . . can I kiss you?' He sneaked a glance at her from the corner of his eye. 'Only if you want me too though.'

She turned to him, and his lips barely brushed hers.

'You really are the best of them, Milly Hendry.'

Was she? It didn't feel that way. Her loyalty to everyone was being tested as her life tied itself in knots, distancing her from those around her. Caroline was after her job, her aunt could barely look at her any more and Helen wasn't happy being used as an excuse for Milly to see Timothy. The only person she could speak to – the only person who seemed to understand her – was her mum and as they hadn't yet arranged another time to meet, it felt like a long time till she'd get to see her again.

Chapter Seventeen

For some occasions, the Royal Household were required to change out of their usual white uniforms and into the smart, formal wear the palace also provided. For the women, this was a dark, knee-length dress that was the least flattering thing Milly owned. A few days before Christmas, she stood in her short-sleeve dress feeling dowdy and uncomfortably cold as the Household staff lined up in the Quadrangle to see the royal family depart for Sandringham where they'd celebrate Christmas together.

Standing in a line, with the winter wind whipping around, Milly's teeth chattered horribly.

'Why didn't you wear your cardigan?' Caroline whispered, earning a reproachful stare from Mrs Fernsby, the Chief Housekeeper.

'Because it's stretched out of shape and looks terrible.'

'So's mine. Look. You could get two of us in here.' She held it out and they both tried not to laugh.

'Show me your curtseys, ladies,' Mrs Fernsby demanded. Though wiry and thin, she didn't seem to feel the cold at all. Caroline went first and Milly followed.

'Lovely job, Milly.'

'Thank you, Mrs Fernsby.'

'Just don't bend your front knee so deeply. You're not trying to shrink, simply to show respect for your betters.'

She moved on and a moment later, the King and Queen walked down the line, wishing everyone a Merry Christmas and thanking them for all the hard work they'd done over the last year. The Princesses followed, shaking hands and repeating their father's sentiments. The awkward dinner seemed to be forgotten. Or at least the public mask had come down again.

When Princess Elizabeth stepped in front of her, Milly placed one foot behind, ready to dip, just as a fat little corgi decided to sniff around her feet sending her off balance. She fell forward swallowing a curse and Princess Elizabeth shot out a steadying hand.

'Are you all right? What a naughty boy.' She stifled a laugh. 'Come here, you little terror. I'm so sorry, Milly.'

Though her face was flaming, Milly forgot her embarrassment and Mrs Fernsby's furious glare under Princess Elizabeth's smile.

'At least he didn't bite you. He attempted to nip poor Charles the other day, didn't he, darling?' She looked at the Duke of Edinburgh, who was by her side. 'Luckily Charles jumped up on the furniture. Mr Parker—' She waved her hand at the older man who stood a few yards down. 'You may want to step away or you will find you have a rather wet leg.'

Milly stifled a laugh as another of the corgis cocked its hind leg and Mr Parker leapt out of the way to the great amusement of both Princess Margaret and Princess Elizabeth, who, with a final smile in Milly's direction, moved on to the next person. Milly caught Timothy's eye and he gave her a shy smile, clearly still embarrassed by the other night.

Finally dismissed, Milly and Caroline changed, meeting Helen in Oxford Street to buy their Christmas presents. The traffic was heavy, and the pavements packed with people. Given that they were all short of money, as most of Britain was, the trip involved a lot of traipsing backwards and forwards as they found the best price for the items they wanted. Milly was shopping for Edie and for something for her mum. She'd thought about buying Timothy and even Robert something but it felt too soon for Timothy and she had no idea what would be appropriate for Robert. Helen had only her father and the kindly neighbour who stopped in when she was at work, while Caroline had both her parents and a sister and brother to buy for. Milly envied the number of bags she was forced to carry. It meant she was loved by so many people.

'I gave my father his lunch early,' Helen said, 'so he'll probably just sleep this afternoon. It's important he eats a good meal to keep his strength up, but he does get ever so tired.'

'He's lucky he's got you,' Caroline said.

Unsure if that was a jibe at her behaviour towards Edie or if she was simply being paranoid, Milly kept her eyes on the shop windows. The Christmas displays were so much more vibrant than they had been in recent years. There was a time, during and just after the war, when you couldn't get anything for anyone. Presents had to be homemade: knitted, crocheted or stitched yourself. Milly much preferred going out and searching for a gift, for something special to give to someone.

'Do you think Edie will like these gloves?' She fished into the shopping bag hooked on her arm and pulled out a small box containing brown leather gloves. She opened it and showed them to Caroline and Helen. 'Her old pair are falling apart, and I don't really know what else to get her.'

'I think she'll love them, don't you, Caroline?'

'Yes. Yes, I do.'

'Are you all right? You're very quiet today,' Helen said. 'That's the first actual sentence you've said since you came out.'

Milly cast her eyes towards the youngest member of their group. It was true, she normally chatted away like a fishwife.

'Is everything all right?' Helen asked.

'I'm just knackered. Honestly, I'm absolutely done in this week. I saw Ma and Pa last Sunday which meant slogging off to Whitechapel and I'm back again the day after tomorrow. It's been hard at the palace too, ain't it, Milly? All those trees to clean up after and then this morning seeing the King and Queen off to Sandringham. Now we've gotta sort out our own Christmases and there's only a few days to go.' She leaned in to whisper conspiratorially. 'Did you see that Peter Townsend went with them? Mrs Barnes had a few choice things to say about that.'

Did she? She hadn't said anything to Milly about it, but their conversations were strained and difficult at the best of times.

'The telephone exchange has been busier too,' Helen said. 'There's so much going on. Calls are flying in and out all the time. I'm just glad Sandringham can take over now.

You've been here the longest, Milly. Please tell us it gets better from here!'

Milly shrugged. 'It does calm down a bit. Not that we get time off, mind.'

'Do we get a Christmas bonus?' asked Caroline. 'My sister did, and it don't half come in handy.'

'It would be very helpful,' Helen added.

'Afraid not,' Milly replied. 'But we get a Christmas pudding.' Caroline and Helen both stared at her, and she giggled at their comical expressions. 'You both look like fish out of water.'

'A pudding?' scoffed Caroline. 'A Christmas pudding?'

'What other type would you expect?'

'Why?' asked Helen incredulously. 'I can make one of those myself. It wouldn't be very nice but that's not the point. What would be more useful would be an extra bob or two.'

'Ma and Pa have been fair cooing over Nancy's bonus,' Caroline lamented. 'Can't imagine what they'd say if I turned up with a Christmas pudding. Ma might think I didn't like hers no more. Why give us all a Christmas pudding?'

'It's an old family tradition started by King George V,' Milly explained. 'He gave out Christmas puddings one year to people in need and the royal family have done the same ever since.'

Helen shook her head. 'It's not quite what I had in mind, but better than nothing, I suppose. And the money I would have spent on one I can spend on something else. I could get another Christmas present for Dad.'

'I dunno what to get my sister,' Caroline said. 'She's so fussy.'

'What about one of those *Royal Family Picture Annual*s?' Milly asked teasingly.

'Crikey, no. That'd be a waste of money and no mistake. She'd throw it on the fire.'

'How are things between you and your aunt, Milly?' Helen asked. 'Are they calming down?'

Before Milly could say anything, Caroline leaned forward to speak to Helen, as if Milly weren't standing right between them. 'She had an awful row with Edie yesterday, didn'tcha?'

'Another one?'

'She got told off for not cleaning properly.'

'Caroline!' Milly exclaimed.

'What? Don't you wanna talk about it?'

'No, I don't.'

'Oh, sorry.'

Edie had spotted Milly had missed one of the side tables. She hadn't done it on purpose, but she'd ended up with another dressing-down and her cheeks burned with embarrassment even now. That Caroline was talking about it so glibly annoyed her, but she pressed the feeling down. Seeing her chance to find out if what Timothy had been saying was true, she said, 'What were you and my aunt talking about last week, Caroline? Timothy said he saw you whispering together but you stopped when he went by.'

Caroline's eyes were wide, like a rabbit caught in headlights, her pale skin pink and flustered. 'You was talking to Timothy? When?'

'Doesn't matter.' She lightened her tone, trying not to sound as frustrated as she felt. 'What were you talking about?'

'Nothing.' She looked everywhere except at Milly.

If it was nothing, why not just tell her what it was? She had no reason to be defensive unless she had something to hide. Milly couldn't help but worry that Timothy was right. Other shoppers bumped past them, laughing and enjoying themselves. That was how Milly had hoped the day would be, but she was feeling increasingly isolated from her friends. 'It doesn't sound like it was nothing.'

'Why was Timothy talking to you anyway? You said there was nothing going on between you.'

'We're friends,' Milly replied coolly.

'Friends?'

Helen kept her eyes down, caught in the middle by Milly's lies. The atmosphere thickened between them.

'Yes.' Milly tried to laugh to lighten the tone, but it came out cold. 'We work at the same place, after all. He just mentioned it in passing. Can't you tell me what you were talking about?'

'It was . . . it was nothing, really. Just something private.'

'I don't believe you,' Milly replied, adding another fake chuckle to give the impression she was curious rather than angry. 'Was it about me?'

Caroline's gaze shot to Milly, then she dropped her eyes back down. She'd given herself away.

'It was, wasn't it?' Milly, under attack and surrounded, felt her temper rise. All the people she loved and liked were either lying to her or working against her. Her throat tightened as she controlled the frustration building inside. 'Was Edie telling you then that she wanted you to keep an eye on me? I know you've been trying to get above me.'

'Above you? Whatever do you mean?'

Helen spoke up, drawing them to the side of the road. They'd stopped outside a clothing shop, the windows full of mannequins dressed in their finery. 'I'm sure Caroline was just talking to Edie like she normally does. She wouldn't be trying to make you look bad, Milly.'

'Of course I'm not,' Caroline replied, her eyes shining with welling tears. 'I thought we were in it together after the handkerchief thing. I didn't like that she asked me to check your work the other day. It was horrible. I hated it.'

'Then what were you talking about?'

Caroline hesitated; then her shoulders slumped. 'She was asking about your mum. Asking when you were seeing her next and what she was like.'

'You've been spying on me?'

'No! I only told her what you'd told us to say.'

'Really? You can't help putting your foot in it, Caroline. You always do. I bet that's why Edie asked you.'

'Milly!' Helen chided.

She hadn't meant to sound so cruel. It was just that she knew Caroline. Knew she couldn't help but blurt the truth out sometimes and that she had a habit of saying the wrong thing. The tears that had been welling in Caroline's eyes burst forth, spilling down her cheeks.

'She was only asking 'cause she cares.' Her voice was small and quiet. 'She's worried about you. You've changed since you met your mum. We can all see it. You're the only one who doesn't.'

'I haven't changed,' Milly protested. Just as in the park when Edie and her mum were rowing, she was horribly aware of people listening as they passed. She was fed up of being the subject of gossip, of being at the centre of scenes. 'I really don't know what you're talking about, Caroline.'

'You're different, Milly. It's like you're not really with us any more. Like you don't care as much.'

It was as if she'd been slapped: a cold hand had smacked her cheek. Her face stung. She had no option but to defend herself, but Caroline's words were drifting into her head, making her think about everything she'd said and done. 'I really haven't.'

'Yes, you have. You even let your mum take the mickey out of Edie and you joined in. You told us what she said when you met in the park. You would never have done that before. Not in a million years. You'd have been the first one defending her. Even Helen thought that was wrong, didn'tcha?'

Helen finally lifted her eyes, clearly wishing Caroline hadn't said anything.

'Were you two talking about me behind my back?'

'I was just surprised when you told us about it. It wasn't like you.' Helen reached out and placed a hand on Milly's arm. 'We were both worried that Jean might be . . . might be—'

'What?'

'Leading you astray.' Helen's expression was suddenly defiant as it met her own.

'I'm a grown woman, Helen, making my own choices. How is she possibly leading me astray?'

'She's just—'

'What?'

'I'm just not sure I trust her.'

'Then it's a good job you don't have to,' Milly replied. 'She's not your mum, she's mine. You have no idea what's it like. Either of you.'

'We do actually,' Caroline replied. 'We've been with you through all of it, ain't we? I don't know exactly what you're feeling and I'm not pretending to, but—'

'No. You've no idea, Caroline. Your mum and dad have always been there. You've got your whole family around you. I know you miss them but they're still here in London. You can visit them any time you like. And you, Helen, have always had your dad. I thought my mum was dead but she's *alive*. Now Mum's back I have the *right* to get to know her, and find out the truth about my childhood. I don't like being torn between Mum and Edie but Edie's the one putting me in this situation. If she'd get to know Mum, she'd see she's sorry.'

'She *has* started to change you,' Caroline insisted. 'You'd never have been late before, and you'd always be the one telling me the bits I'd missed. And you're hiding things from Edie—'

'For her own good!'

'It's like none of it's as important to you any more. Work, the palace—'

'Of course it is. I love my job, but I've enjoyed seeing a

190

different side to London too. Haven't you? There's more to life than just that place.'

'We're your friends,' Helen said quietly, reaching out for Milly's hand. Milly let her friend take it, but the anger pulsing inside acted like a shield, refusing to let her feel anything. 'And friends sometimes have to speak the truth even when it's hard to hear.'

'I was late once,' Milly replied. '*Once*. And my job is important to me. But – but—' She didn't know what else to say. Her own thoughts were such a jumble she couldn't make head or tail of them.

'Please, Milly,' Helen said. 'Maybe you should take a break from seeing your mum for a while. Just until things have calmed—'

'I've had enough of this.' Milly turned and started to walk in the opposite direction. How could Helen suggest such a thing? If only they could understand.

'Milly,' Helen called. 'Where are you going?'

'I'd prefer to be on my own, thank you.'

All she was doing was trying to get to know the mum who'd been forced to leave her behind. And maybe she was changing, but that didn't mean she wasn't changing for the better. The world felt bigger than it ever had before, and she felt more a part of it. Buckingham Palace had kept her locked inside it for most of her life and she was finally breaking free, seeing the city outside the one she'd been brought up in, living like all young ladies did. This was the fifties, for heaven's sake. They weren't living in fear of their lives any more. Edie must have known she'd spread her wings sooner or later.

Chapter Eighteen

That evening, Milly arrived at the Sunrise Club and hurried down the black staircase. This time, she hadn't told her aunt she was going out or asked any of her friends to join her. She wasn't entirely sure they were her friends any more. The darkened streets of London had felt so much more intimidating on her own, but that was nothing compared to walking into the club.

As she arrived, she saw her mum, sitting at the bar in another exquisite off-the-shoulder gown, her thin shoulder blades flexing as she moved. The man she was with ran his hand slowly up her back until his fingers brushed her bare skin. Milly waited for her mum to wriggle away, to tell him to stop being so impertinent, but, trapped by her responsibility as hostess, she didn't move. Milly went to call out but she wouldn't be heard above the deafening music.

Jean laughed, tossing her head back, but as she did something or someone caught her eye. She stood, whispered something to the man and began to make her way through the crowd towards the door at the side of the stage. Jack was there and he leered as she came towards him. His arm reached around her waist as he guided her through the doorway and they both disappeared from sight.

Milly stepped further into the club. She glanced at the

bar, thinking of asking permission to go backstage and speak to Jean, but it was crammed full of people all shouting at the bartenders for a drink. What good would it do and what would she do if they said no? She'd simply ignore them and so, with that thought in mind, she weaved her way through a sea of writhing bodies, the high, brassy notes of the trumpet and saxophone piercing her ears while the thumping double bass echoed through her muscles.

After checking behind her, Milly opened the door and slid through. A smell of perfume, cigarette smoke and dank air met her. She hadn't exactly pictured the backstage world of the West End – quick changes, chorus girls flitting here and there, stagehands getting props in place – but she had imagined something more glamorous than this. It reminded her of old, dirty underpasses. Empty, litter-strewn tube stations. The walls were painted black like the stairs down from the road. The floor was dirty with a fine layer of grit embedding into the cracks. It was seedy. Sordid. The music still pounded through the walls and chatter from the bar and cheers from the mob dancing out front seeped in.

She shouldn't be here, and had a sudden feeling that if she were caught, she'd receive more than just a telling-off. The door back into the club was just behind her, and she contemplated sneaking back through it, but she needed to see her mum. She needed to talk to someone. She crept further along the corridor, edging slowly, pinning herself to the sides to make herself as small and inconspicuous as possible.

A few small rooms ran off it and she assumed one had to be Jean's dressing room. One was a sort of bathroom-cum-kitchen where a young boy was washing glass after glass in a sink of murky water. Her stomach vaulted and she vowed never to drink here again. She was just about to ask if he'd seen Jean when another door opened and Jack, the club owner, came out. She hid behind the beer barrels stacked high at one side as he swaggered away from her. He opened the furthest door, leaning against it as he lit a cigarette, his silver lighter reflecting in the moonlight. It swung shut behind him as he stepped into the night. Milly released a breath. At least he wouldn't find her.

Voices sounded from another room, and she edged her way towards it. Cigarette smoke thickened the air over the heads of a group of men all seated around a small wooden table. Suit jackets were thrown over chairs, shirtsleeves were rolled up, cigars or cigarettes hung from their mouths and, in the centre of the table, poker chips mounted. Was this legal? She was pretty sure gambling like this wasn't, and there was something shady about all the men at the table. Something about the way they conducted themselves. Their posturing and bravado. She couldn't imagine them working in an office.

An overweight man, whose buttons were straining across his stomach, said something to another, who leapt to his feet, his chair hitting the ground with a crack. Within seconds they were at each other's throats, pulling each other across the table, snarling faces pressed together. She heard movement outside and ran back behind the barrels as Jack threw open the door and charged in.

'What's all this then, eh, fellas? Where's that gentlemanly

behaviour we talked about?' He was cool, clearly in charge, and the voices calmed in his presence. But it was enough for Milly.

She ran back to the club door and tugged it open, throwing herself into the crowd. At the very end of the room, the doorway leading up to the stairs was blocked by incoming guests, so she made her way to the bar. She had no intention of buying a drink, not after what she'd seen, but it gave a good view of the stage door and she still desperately wanted to speak to her mum. She had so much to tell her. Milly waited for what seemed like hours but was only about fifteen minutes. Her mum still hadn't emerged from backstage, and she wasn't prepared to venture there again. She'd have to write to her, but she still didn't know her home address. Yet what other choice did she have? She moved away from the bar, about to force her way through the heaving crowd, when a voice from behind stopped her, sending a cold shiver down her spine.

'Goin' somewhere?' asked Jack. He too was in his shirt-sleeves; tattoos covered his forearms. 'Surely I can buy yer a drink before yer go.'

There was an air of power about him that made his long, rodent-like features sharper. Too much power, too much confidence, Milly thought. 'That's very kind, but I really should be going.'

'Does Jean know you're 'ere? She's your friend, ain't she?'

'I haven't seen her yet. She's probably busy. I can come back another time.' She went to walk away and with a slight movement he blocked her path.

'Just one drink? Come on. Please?' His smile showed crooked but still-white teeth. 'I wanna ask you about 'er.' He took her arm, turning her back around to face the bar. She searched for her mum, but Jean still wasn't there. Where had she got to?

Fear gripped her muscles, but she wrenched her arm free. 'Do you mind?'

'Not at all,' he replied coolly. 'Now, what can I get yer?'

'Nothing, thank you. I was just leaving.'

'Nonsense.' He lengthened the word and turned his attention to the barman. It was Robert's friend. 'George, what does this young lady usually drink?'

'Gin fizz, I think. That's right, isn't it?'

'It is,' Milly said. 'But I don't want one, thank you, I was just leaving.' She went to step around Jack, but he moved again, closing the gap between him and the crowd.

'So tell me.' He leaned on the bar as though they were friends. It didn't matter that there wasn't much room, people parted for him, his self-assurance pushing them aside, his manner saying don't mess with me. 'Whereabouts in Southampton does your friend come from?'

'Why do you want to know so badly?'

'I'm interested. I like to know all about my employees. I'm nice like that.'

Milly swallowed down her fear. She hadn't met a man like him before, but somehow, she knew that showing him how scared she was would only make him happier. 'Just because she's your employee doesn't give you the right to go prying into her life.'

'If she's got nothin' to hide, she's got nothin' to worry about.'

'I—' Milly struggled. Until recently lies had never come easy to her. Under Edie's guidance she'd soon learned that the truth will out. Always. But it couldn't in this case and she worried about giving too much away or saying the wrong thing. Although this man couldn't be the loan shark Jean and Billy had run away from during the Blitz, she didn't trust him. Just standing in front of him sent ripples of fear through her body. 'I don't know why you're asking me. We only met recently.'

''Ow?'

George put two gin fizzes on the bar, giving Milly a fleeting but apologetic smile. Clearly whatever the boss said was more important than anything else. Milly left hers untouched as Jack slugged his back in one large mouthful, all the while still watching her.

'We just sort of ran into each other.'

'When?'

'A few weeks ago.'

'Where?'

'Mind your own business,' she spat. He was backing her into a corner with his questions.

Anger darkened his eyes, but he laughed. 'So yer can't tell me much about 'er then?'

'No. Not really.'

'You see, I'm not sure I believe yer – what did yer say your name was?'

'I didn't.'

197

He waited for more and when she didn't offer it, added, 'Ain't yer goin' to tell me?'

She didn't want him to know, but it was possible Jean had already said, and as the barman had recognised her and knew about her friendship with Robert, there didn't seem much point in lying. With the way this man intimidated her, Milly truly believed any lie could land her in more than just trouble.

'Milly. My name's Milly.

'Milly. Nice to meet yer. Yer see, at first, I thought she was your sister.' He reached out and touched a strand of hair that had fallen beside Milly's face. She leaned away from him, repressing the urge to shudder.

'My sister?' She tried to laugh it off, to pretend she was at ease, because she could see he was enjoying how nervous she was. 'I don't have any sisters, or brothers. We're just friends.'

'And where does she live?'

He'd never believe that she honestly didn't know and didn't want to contemplate how he might try and get the truth from her. He picked up Milly's drink as if to slug that back too, but before she could answer, a couple dancing bashed into him, sending the drink from his hand, the clear liquid spilling down his fingers and soaking his trousers. The glass smashed on the floor and as the couple turned to apologise, he grabbed the man by the lapels, shouting at him. The burly man who had whispered in his ear on their first visit to the club appeared from nowhere, grabbing the poor, apologetic customer and hitting him. Without a second's hesitation, Milly took the opportunity to get away.

Her heart hammered in her chest as she pushed her way through the crowd and up the stairs. She stumbled as a familiar face came into view. Robert was climbing down the steps.

'Milly! Are you here on your own? W-what are you doing here?' He seemed so surprised to see her his stammer was hardly noticeable.

'I just came to see my mum but I'm going now. I need to get out of this place.'

'Are you OK?'

She studied the room again, her eyes roving over the scene, but there was no sign of Jack. 'Yes. Yes, I'm fine.'

'What happened this afternoon? You seemed upset when you got back from wherever you'd been.'

She'd run into him only moments after returning alone from the disastrous shopping trip with Helen and Caroline and was so eager to get away she'd been snappy and short with him, coming across as rude.

The man behind Robert nudged him forwards. 'Come on, Rob, get moving. I'm stuck between stairs here.'

'Sorry, Jim.' Milly took a step back and Robert moved aside with her so the others could pass. 'Are you l-leaving?'

'I was. There's just been a bit of a fight and I'd quite like to get out of here.'

'There's been a couple here before. Let's go outside.'

He led her up the stairs and they emerged into the darkened city. The street was quiet with only the shrouded noise of the music and the faint footsteps of those still around. Only the Sunrise Club seemed to be open. The pubs had all shut for the night, the last few customers wearily making their way back to their homes. The theatres were closed, and the streets were all but empty.

'Shall I walk you back?' he asked. 'I can't let you go on your own at this time of night.'

After facing Jack, Milly wanted to get as far away from the club as possible. She tried not to let the relief at his offer show on her face. 'I don't want to ruin your evening. You've only just arrived.'

'I don't mind. It's not far. Come on. I insist.'

With each step away from the club she felt safer, but her worries mounted for her mum. Why was Jack so interested in Jean? Did he like her? He hadn't seemed enamoured when she'd spoken to him. It was sinister.

'Are there many fights at the club?' she asked.

'Unfortunately, yes, but they get broken up pretty quickly. Are you OK? You're not hurt?'

'No, I'm fine. But I'm glad I've seen you.' She paused, not wanting to let this opportunity pass her by. 'I wanted to speak to you. To apologise for earlier. I was rude to you, and it wasn't fair. It wasn't even you I was angry at.'

In the light of the streetlamps, she became aware of Robert's dark hair and pale green eyes, wishing she'd bought him something for Christmas after all. She liked the way his freckles peppered his nose, his endearing shyness, and he was proving a true friend.

'So who w-were you angry at?'

'Can't you guess? I was upset because Aunt Edie's asked Caroline to spy on me. I was so cross I was horribly rude to Caroline earlier, and I feel terrible about it. It isn't her fault she's caught up in all this.'

'Are you sure spying's the right word? Maybe it's just concern. I'm sure you can apologise and move on. She's a nice girl is Caroline.'

Milly felt a stab of jealousy but pushed it away. It was only because she was feeling so cross with her. 'I will. I felt so bad after I'd left her and Helen in the street, I got her a present for Christmas. Nothing big, just a little treat to say I'm sorry.'

'That's n-nice of you. And Edie is p-probably just trying to look out for you.'

'She has a funny way of showing it.'

'I think she's just hurt because of . . . you know.' Milly knew Edie was hurting but she didn't feel it excused her actions.

'Robert, do you think I've changed?'

'Changed? Changed how?'

'I don't know exactly. It was something Caroline said. Helen too. They said they think I've changed. Do you?'

'You are a bit different, but a lot's happened to you. It would be strange if you didn't change.'

'Thank you.' He always knew what to say to make her feel better. 'Are you working tomorrow?'

He shook his head, grinning mischievously. 'Day off.'

'Lucky thing.'

'W-what about you?'

'Up early and I dare not be late again. It's a good thing we're heading back.'

A part of her wished they were back at the club. She'd have loved to dance with him again. She'd loved how he'd given her time to gain some confidence and how his hand had been there to catch her. Then her mind wandered to all she'd seen tonight both in public and backstage.

'Does the Sunrise Club break the law?' she asked. 'By opening late?'

'I guess so. Some of the clubs around here pay people to look the other way. And some are owned by people you and I w-wouldn't like to get on the wrong side of.'

That summed up Jack. 'I'm surprised to find you there then, Robert. You've always seemed a – a—'

'A what?'

'A bit of a goody two-shoes. Like me,' she added, so he knew she meant it kindly.

'No one can be that good all the time, can they?'

'I suppose not.'

'Anyway, maybe you don't know me as w-well as you think.'

'You mean you have hidden depths?'

He hummed his agreement. 'There's more to me than meets the eye.' Robert's eyes sparkled with mischief as they turned towards the servants' entrance of Buckingham Palace.

'Thanks for bringing me home, Robert, and for forgiving me. I didn't mean to be rude to you earlier. You're a true friend.'

He paused, his eyes darting to the ground and then back to her face. 'A f-friend? Is th-that all I am?'

Despite the cold, heat built in Milly's chest, shooting over her. 'Robert, I—'

'Milly, I think you're the kindest, nicest, prettiest girl in the w-world.'

'Robert, no. Stop.' She held her hands up and though she wasn't touching him, he recoiled, stepping backwards. 'I'm sorry, Robert. Really. But I just don't think of you like that. We're friends.' His face flamed and he turned away, scuffing his shoe along the gravel. 'You're lovely, but—'

'D–don't say it,' he pleaded. 'I get it. I should have known.' He began to walk away.

'Should have known what?'

'That you could never love someone like m-me.'

'Robert.' She hated seeing him hurting but she couldn't change her feelings. 'Robert, please.'

But he never turned back.

Chapter Nineteen

Christmas Day

The fire burned brightly in Edie's small room, adding an orange glow far stronger than that the little electric light bulb gave off, and the warmth permeated Milly's bones as Edie sighed contentedly.

The icy tension between them had thawed. Milly had thought long and hard about what Caroline had said and had decided it was time to forgive her aunt and let the anger inside her subside. She just hoped her heart would follow the decision her head had made.

Christmas Day had dawned with a pale grey sky and the sun, lemon-coloured, lighting it as best it could. London was unusually quiet. It wasn't often the bustling city stopped dead in its tracks but today was one of those days. Without buses and cars on the roads, the hum of traffic, usually an ever-present background noise, had vanished completely, leaving in its place a quiet stillness, a feeling of otherworldliness.

Every year, since Milly had moved into her own room from the camp bed squeezed at the foot of Edie's bed, she'd come into Edie's room as soon as she woke, dressed in her dressing gown and slippers. Today more than ever, Milly was grateful that all those years ago, Edie had pleaded with the Chief Housekeeper to let her stay. Edie had often recounted the story of how, unable to make the decision herself, the Chief Housekeeper had taken it to the Deputy Master of the Household, who had referred it to the Master of the Household, who had spoken to the King, and all had been agreed. It was one of the reasons Edie and Milly were so loyal to him. When Milly had turned fifteen, finished her schooling and was working at the palace in her own right, she was allowed her own room, but had continued to celebrate Christmas morning in her aunt's room, often snuggled on the end of her bed.

Every Christmas Day they turned on the wireless and listened to the Light Programme while they unwrapped their presents. They had never followed the tradition of the royal family and exchanged gifts on Christmas Eve. It just hadn't seemed right. Then it would be down to the Household Breakfast Room for breakfast. Later, they might take a walk through the palace gardens, and it always felt particularly freeing knowing you weren't going to run into a member of the royal family in the rose garden or by the lake. She remembered the first time Edie had shown her Victoria and Albert, the two enormous plane trees that had been planted by them and now stood watch over a covered walkway. Maybe she and Edie could take a stroll through there later if the rain stayed off.

'This is for you.' Milly handed over the small box containing the gloves she'd bought with Caroline and Helen. 'I hope you like it.'

'I'm sure I will,' Edie replied with a smile. She carefully

untied the ribbon, unwrapped the brown paper and opened the box. Her eyes glowed, her cheeks lifting in a genuine smile as she took the top glove, studying the stitching and the quality of the leather. 'Oh, Milly, they're lovely. They must've cost a fortune.'

'Not a fortune, no. I know you don't like me spending too much on things like gloves, but I wanted to get you something special and your old ones are falling apart. Do you really like them?'

'I do.' She placed them carefully back in the box and moved to Milly. Milly stood as she approached, and they hugged with such strong, genuine affection, Milly wondered how they could ever have argued. The love they'd always had for one another came rushing back. Edie seemed to hold her tighter than ever and Milly allowed her head to rest on her shoulder, her heart full. 'Merry Christmas, my girl.'

'Merry Christmas, Aunty.'

Edie planted a kiss on her cheek and moved away without looking at her. The slight snuffling indicated she was tearful, and Milly allowed her a moment to compose herself, studying the flames in the fire to dry her own eyes.

'Here's yours then.' Edie placed a much larger box, held closed with a wide pink ribbon, on the table between them.

Clearly Edie hadn't taken her own advice as whatever it was it must have cost a pretty penny. Milly untied the ribbon carefully, keeping it flat so she could use it again. The make-do-and-mend mentality still hadn't left them all and she couldn't bring herself to ruin something so beautiful. She lifted the lid to reveal the folded neck of a coat. Raising it out of the box, the thick burgundy fabric unfurled to reveal a double-breasted coat with a tie waist. It was the most beautiful thing Milly had ever owned. As she stared at it, her brain placed the swallow-shaped Bakelite brooch Robert had bought her on the lapel, once again wishing she'd bought him a present, and sorry she hadn't been able to return his affections.

'Do you like it?'

'It's wonderful, Aunt Edie. So, so beautiful.' Milly placed it on the table and ran her hands over the seams, pulling the bottom out to study it all again. 'However did you afford it?'

'Oh, that don't matter.'

'It does. I don't like to think of you going without.'

'I haven't had to, have I? You've replaced my gloves for me, and I don't want for much anyway. Now shall we go to breakfast? I don't know about you, but I'm starvin'. It's this blimmin' cold weather: it always makes me hungry. My stomach thinks my throat's been cut.'

Milly began to move towards the door, then faltered. 'Aunt Edie?'

'Yes?'

Edie looked at Milly. Milly wanted to tell her about the handkerchief and their visit to the Master of the Household. She wanted to tell her about Timothy and be rid of all the secrets forcing themselves between the two of them. But as a gentle peace filled the room, she found she couldn't. They'd had the nicest morning possible and there was still time for them to spend together before she left to meet her mum.

After missing her at the Sunrise Club she'd written a short note asking when they could meet again and sent it to the club. Though she'd wanted to pour her heart into the letter she couldn't risk it being read by anyone else and had kept the details short. Jean had written back asking Milly to meet her at a hotel tonight. She still wished they could meet at her flat and was determined to get the address out of her later. It was just so odd that Jean wouldn't give it to her. She hadn't told Edie they were meeting for fear of ruining her Christmas and as she studied her face, Edie's eyes still shining, her nose a little red, she realised she couldn't do it now.

'Nothing. It doesn't matter. I just wanted to say thank you again for my lovely coat.' She hugged her aunt once more.

'You're welcome. Now, what's that?' Edie signalled towards another small gift Milly had with her.

'This is for someone else.'

'Not that Timothy, I hope. I know you've seen him a couple of times. I'm not stupid, you know.'

It was the first time she'd mentioned the subject and Milly's cheeks grew hot. 'No, it's for someone else.'

'Good. I'm glad to hear it.'

They dressed and made their way to the Household Breakfast Room where a breakfast spread was laid out in silver dishes. The staff could help themselves and Milly took a plate, taking as much as she could get away with without compromising someone else's ration. It smelled delicious. There wasn't a lot of bacon and barely any sausages, but the cooks had made a huge batch of kedgeree and though she hadn't loved it at first, it had become one of her favourite dishes. The King had given them a tree and it stood proudly in the corner, decorated with lights, and red and gold baubles.

She and Edie settled themselves to drink strong tea and enjoy the lively chatter and cheerful Merry Christmases shouted across the room. Mr Newington had just wished Edie a very happy Christmas, departing before he turned any pinker, as Robert came out from behind the serving area.

'Merry Christmas, Mrs Barnes. Merry Christmas, Milly.'

'You too, Robert. Did you get anythin' nice?' Edie asked.

'My d-dad sent me a jumper. It's pretty smart.' Robert's family lived somewhere in Kent. She got the impression his family life had been strained after the death of his mum and that his relationship with his dad was somewhat difficult. 'What did you get, Milly?'

It was the first time he'd spoken to her since she'd refused his advances. That he was speaking to her at all almost broke her heart. He was such a thoroughly decent chap. She answered, describing the coat in detail.

'I'm sure you'll look beautiful,' he replied.

'Happy Christmas, Milly,' Timothy said, striding over. 'Season's greetings, Mrs B.' He was in the suit he'd worn on their first night out together and Milly was aware of how close he was standing, of the smell of his aftershave.

Edie returned the greeting politely, if somewhat begrudgingly, and Robert too turned away without saying any more, going back to the kitchen.

'Nice to have a day off, isn't it?'

'Definitely,' Milly replied, and unspoken words floated between them. She was looking forward to seeing him later that night and could tell he was too.

Always polite, Edie asked, 'Did your family send you anythin' nice, Timothy?'

'Bits and bobs, Mrs B., thanks for asking. Now' – he rubbed his hands together – 'I need some grub. I'm starving.' He moved to the food set out on the counter and began helping himself. 'Any chance of some more bacon?' he asked cheekily and one of the cooks shouted back, telling him to be grateful for what he had. The kitchen staff laughed, and Timothy joined in too, taking the ribbing on the chin, though a slight pinkness crept over the collar of his shirt.

About half an hour later, a sleepy Caroline joined them. She saw Timothy as she passed and turned away, dropping her eyes to the floor. Timothy hadn't noticed, busy eating his breakfast and reading a newspaper. This time Milly wondered if she was angry that he'd told Milly about her secret conversation with Edie, but as Caroline spotted them she brightened.

'Good mornin', young lady,' Edie trilled. 'Merry Christmas to you.'

'And you, Mrs Barnes. Happy Christmas, Milly.'

Though they'd worked together and seen each other around the palace, neither had really spoken to the other since their row a few days before. Milly was determined to put that right by starting a conversation. 'You look like you haven't quite woken up yet.'

'I ain't—'

'Haven't,' Edie corrected gently.

'Haven't,' Caroline echoed. 'We don't often get to lie in 'til whenever we like. My body don't quite know what to do with itself.'

A male voice from the table next to them interrupted. 'I know what to do with your body.' The young chap laughed, as did his companion, and as Caroline shrunk down, a blush rising up her face, Milly reached out and grabbed her friend's hand. Knowing what she did, it was clear the throw-away comment had upset her deeply. Edie spun to face them.

'I'll have none of that talk, Mr Harris. If I have to, I'll report you to the senior footmen.'

'Sorry, Mrs Barnes,' he replied immediately.

'You best show some manners and apologise to Caroline right now.' Edie could be quite terrifying when she was in full swing and young Mr Harris was realising that himself. 'Terrible behaviour. I'll not have it, Mr Harris.'

'Really sorry, Mrs Barnes,' he repeated.

'Don't apologise to me. Apologise to her.' She pointed at Caroline.

'Sorry, Caroline. It was just a silly joke. I – I didn't mean to upset you.'

'Still drunk from whatever shenanigans you was at last night, I expect. When the cat's away the mice will play. Any more silliness and I shall have your guts for garters.' Edie turned back. 'Right, another cup of tea for me, I think. Milly, do you want anythin'? Oh, there's Mrs Chadwick, I must just take her her gift.'

Before Milly could confirm she didn't want another cup of tea, Edie had left the table and Milly pulled the small parcel she'd brought with her out from under it. 'I'm really sorry about what I said on Friday, Caroline. I shouldn't have reacted the way I did, and I wish I hadn't ruined our shopping trip.'

A smile spread across Caroline's face as she instantly forgave Milly. It was the most wonderful thing about Caroline's nature. She had an ability to forgive and forget without holding a grudge. 'It's all right. I've got a narky brother and bossy sister so I know all about silly squabbles. Let's just forget it.'

'Thank you. This is for you.' She handed over the package.

'For me? But I ain't got you anything.'

'That's all right. I knew you'd be missing your family today and I wanted to apologise again for being so beastly to you when we went shopping. I felt so bad I got it that day before I came home.'

Caroline's eyes were glassy with tears. 'Oh, Milly!'

'Now don't cry. Come on, open it. You might not like it anyway.'

'I bet I do.' Unlike Milly and Edie, Caroline tore the paper apart, eager to see what was inside. Her eyes and mouth widened with glee as she pulled it out of the scraps on the table. 'Oh, I've wanted to read this for ages.' She hugged the book to her chest melodramatically. 'How did you know?'

'You haven't got it then?'

'No.'

Nancy Mitford's *Love in a Cold Climate* had been so popular that Milly had worried Caroline might already own a copy, but she was already turning the pages, reading every single word, even the publisher's details.

'Don't forget your breakfast, Caroline. You don't want to miss out.'

'I won't.' She lowered the book. 'Do you know, after the King's speech I'm gonna curl up on my bed and read this.'

The notice had gone out from Buckingham Palace on 23 December that the King had recorded his Christmas Day address to the nation because his voice was still a little uncertain and the long speech would tire him out. Though Milly had never seen him herself, a man from the BBC had come to the palace and recorded the speech in small sections; then it had been edited together by some clever person. It was a tradition that everyone gathered together in the Household Lounge to listen to it, but it would be the first time it wasn't broadcast live.

Caroline wiped her eyes. 'That'll stop me thinking about Ma and Pa and what they're up to.'

With the bus and train services reduced it was going to be difficult for Caroline to reach them safely and stay for any decent amount of time. It would be her first Christmas away from her family and Milly wished she could invite her to visit Jean that evening. She would have done so if she weren't going with Timothy, but they had managed to arrange to see each other tonight during snatched conversations in the palace corridors.

Milly had also been to see Helen at her station in the telephone exchange on Christmas Eve, but she'd been too busy to speak. Milly had handed her a Christmas card, hoping Helen could see the regret on her face. When Helen's expression had filled with warmth and she'd hurriedly mouthed the words 'Merry Christmas', Milly had felt a thousand times better.

'I'm sure your family will be missing you too. But when you've got a full belly from our lovely Christmas lunch, you'll be happy not to move. Do you really like it?'

'I do.'

'I'm glad.'

Caroline glanced over her shoulder. 'Before Edie comes back – have you told her about ... you know ... the handkerchief?'

'No. We've been sworn to secrecy, and I hate it, but what can we do?'

The weight of all the secrets she was keeping pressed down on her. Edie returned to the table as Caroline left, deep in her book again. She almost collided with a chair, she was so busy flipping pages. 'What did she have there?'

Milly told Edie it was a present from her but not why she'd felt the need to buy it.

'That's lovely of you, Milly. A wonderful thing to do. I knew she'd find Christmas Day hard. I got her a little somethin' too but I'll give it to her after breakfast. She's a family girl, that one. Sends most of her money home to her parents too. I'm sure she appreciated it. She really looks up to you, you know?' Edie took another drink of tea, relaxing into her chair and enjoying the slow start to the day. 'Shall we go for a walk later? We can go after the King's speech.'

'That'd be nice.' Milly stared out of the window at the clouds gathering and the wind whistling through the old windowpanes. 'Do you mind if we go between lunch and the King's speech?'

A slight stiffening of Edie's posture put Milly on her guard. 'Got plans, have you?'

'I'm going to see Jean. She's singing at a hotel in Kensington. I thought I could wear my new coat. Being Kensington it's probably fancy.'

'Right.'

Silence descended and Milly wished she could list all the reasons she needed to go. Not least because she had to tell her mum about Jack and the way he'd questioned her the other night.

'Please don't mind, Aunt Edie. I won't be back too late, I promise. It's the first Christmas I'll have got to see her in ten years.'

'I know. I didn't say anythin'.' Edie placed her cup on the table. When she next spoke, her voice was softer. 'Remember the tube is always a bit tricky on Christmas Day and we're back to work tomorrow so it'll be up and at it as normal.'

'Promise,' Edie replied with a smile, grateful for her support.

'But, Milly—'

'Yes?'

'Don't expect too much of her. For your own sake.'

'What do you mean?'

'Nothin'.' She shook her head. 'It doesn't matter.' She picked her cup back up, but it didn't reach her lips. 'Just don't hope for a present from her.'

'I won't.' It was a lie, but the need to defend her mum was strong on such a special day. Surely her mum would have got her a little something, knowing they were seeing each other?

215

'Anyway,' Edie said, brightening a little, trying to put the mention of Jean behind them. 'A walk will be lovely. We could head towards the summer house and that way, if it rains, we won't get soaked.'

'Good idea.'

She fanned her hands out in front of her studying them. 'Wherever we go I think I'll wear my new gloves.'

'And me my new coat.'

Edie and Milly shared a loving glance, but she wasn't blind to the way her aunt kept adjusting her dress and crossing and uncrossing her legs. It was clear there was more she wanted to say but wouldn't.

Chapter Twenty

The staff gathered together, squeezing into the Household Dining Room to share Christmas Day lunch. It was a jovial and raucous affair that they all enjoyed, and everyone pitched in with the clearing up so Mrs Chadwick, Robert and the rest of the cooks could have time to relax. Afterwards, everyone retired to the Household Lounge to enjoy the remains of the afternoon.

All the while Milly had listened to the King's address being broadcast, the handkerchief, which now sat in the Master's hands and had once been wrapped in paper and hidden in her underwear drawer, played on her mind.

The King had sounded much older than his fifty-six years. She'd wanted to believe it was just the crackling of the radio, the static on the line, but there was no denying the gravel in his voice, the weakness to his tone. When he'd opened the Festival of Britain earlier that year, his voice had been strong and certain; the change was unnerving, a moment tinged with sadness. Gracious as he always was, the King thanked his doctors and told the nation how much he appreciated their support as well as that of his family during his illness and recovery. Edie had swiped a tear from her cheek, as had so many others, but the question hung in the air as to how recovered he really was. Concern was written across each and every face though they all tried to hide it under nods of agreement as the King praised the troops still fighting and pleaded with everyone to take pride in their nation once more. Thinking of the blood-stained cloth, Milly was beginning to fear that, despite what everyone told her, his health wasn't returning, and the handkerchief they'd found had been more recent than she'd hoped.

Milly left at six o'clock, promising her she'd be home by nine and they could spend the rest of the evening together.

As she met Timothy at the palace gates, she tried to shake off the dark feelings lingering in her mind. Shortly, she would be seeing her mum on Christmas Day for the first time in ten years and that was something to celebrate. She gripped the short handle of her bag, knowing it contained the compact she'd bought and carefully wrapped as a present for her mum.

After a swift kiss on the cheek, she and Timothy agreed to get the tube to Kensington. Though the service was unpredictable, neither she nor Timothy minded waiting and it was too far to walk on such a drizzly evening. They could easily hop on the Piccadilly line and would be in Kensington in no time.

'Looking forward to meeting your mum,' Timothy said as they descended the steps to the Hyde Park Corner underpass and on to the tube station platform. 'Makes it kind of official, doesn't it?'

The air was always hotter down here and Milly loosened her scarf, easing it away with a hooked finger. 'Are we official then?' she asked, glancing towards him.

'Suppose so, but I still think we should wait to tell everyone at the palace 'til your aunt's OK with it.'

That wasn't quite the definite answer she'd been hoping for but then he gave her a mischievous wink.

'Caroline will be jealous, I think,' Milly said.

'Caroline? Why d'you say about her?'

'I just reckon she has a bit of a thing for you, that's all.'

'Really? Can't say I've noticed. And if we're talking about jealousy, what about Robert?'

Milly remembered the pained look on his face and her chest tightened. It haunted her. 'I've told you before, we're just friends.'

He swung her around, catching her in his arms. 'Just promise you'll be only mine,' he announced dramatically.

Milly laughed. 'Have you been reading some magazine or other on how to woo women? You don't sound like yourself at all. Is it one too many Christmas sherries?'

'Might have had a couple at lunch but I'm perfectly fine, thank you very much.' He winked and placed an arm around her as they waited for the tube.

Soon they were at Gloucester Road tube station, emerging into the cold, winter night. It was only a short walk to Harrington Gardens and the Majestic Hotel where Jean was performing. The buildings that remained here were grand. Not as grand as Buckingham Palace, nothing really could be, but it was clearly a rich area of London. Yet it hadn't escaped its fair share of damage during the war and some areas were still boarded up, what had been shops or houses turned into building sites.

'You look like a movie star in that coat.'

'It was my Christmas present from Edie.'

'See, she does love you after all.'

She knew Edie loved her and hoped that love would last as they navigated their way through this difficult time. She'd said goodbye when Milly left but there was such a note of sadness to her voice, Milly could have cried.

As she'd suspected, the hotel was far more upmarket than the one in Poland Street. The Victorian building of red brick above white stonework, punctuated by arched windows, had three flagpoles all displaying the Union Jack. They ascended a small set of stone steps to the glossy black front door, its gold handles shining almost as brightly as the gilding in the palace.

'Blimey,' Timothy said, gazing at the columned portico at the front of the building. 'Bit snazzy.'

'I'll say.' Milly was suddenly glad she'd worn her best dress and prettiest gloves.

They entered the glittering gold and white lobby. The polished parquet floor glistened underneath a dazzling chandelier, and they made their way past a small circular table covered by a festive floral display. A Christmas tree nestled in an alcove decorated with white and gold glass ornaments. At the end of the lobby, a curving staircase with ornamental ironwork led guests up to their rooms, and beside it, a sign above a set of doors directed Milly and Timothy to the lounge.

'I'm not sure we'll fit in here,' Milly said. 'This place is making me nervous.'

'Don't be silly!' Timothy chuckled. 'We live and work at Buckingham Palace. This place don't match that.'

'Yes, but we're servants there. It's not like it's our house, and the bit we live in is quite different to the actual palace. It's being here as a guest. It feels above my station.'

She could already hear her mum singing as they entered the hotel lounge. It was certainly a step up for Jean. The lounge was as grand as the lobby and reminded Milly of one of the palace's State Rooms – the 1844 Room in particular. The colour scheme was the same: bright blue and shining gold, with fancy plasterwork that covered the ceiling. Milly couldn't help but think about the cleaning staff and how they must work as hard as she, Edie and Caroline did, though probably for less pay and without accommodation.

'Pah!' Timothy exclaimed. 'No one thinks about class like that any more, Milly, and you're as good as any of them.'

'Don't they?' She didn't quite agree, and it didn't stop her feeling inferior amongst the guests in their fine clothes and plummy accents similar to the Royals. Not one person had Caroline's East End twang and she couldn't imagine any of them saying 'Gaw blimey' or 'bleedin' hell', as Edie did.

Jean was wearing the elegant black evening gown she'd worn the first time Milly had watched her and, as usual, her singing was beautiful. What she assumed to be the hotel's own band – a jazz quartet – provided the music. They were playing 'Too Young', made famous by Nat King Cole, and Jean's eyes skimmed over the busy crowd as she gently swayed her arms side to side.

'Blimey, this is nice. I'll get us some drinks. Back in a tick.' Timothy strode purposefully to the gleaming wooden bar as if he belonged there and Milly admired his courage.

He returned a few minutes later, after Milly had unbuttoned her coat and sat down. 'You're a right looker, Milly, and no mistake. 'Specially in that dress.'

She hadn't a new one to wear but had repurposed the large pink silk ribbon that had secured the coat box, tying it around her waist. It had given her old dusky pink dress a new lease of life.

'That can't be your mum.' Timothy's eyes widened as he sipped his martini.

'It is.'

'Got a cracking voice.'

'I thought you preferred beer,' Milly said as he tried to hide a grimace at the taste of virtually pure alcohol.

'Not a beer sort of place though, is it? Wouldn't want to show you up.'

She looked round at the other guests, wondering who they were. Nearly everyone was drinking cocktails of various shapes and sizes. Some even sipped champagne. The bottles sat in ice buckets, condensation pooling on the thick green glass and the thin champagne flutes were held in hands clad in the finest kidskin gloves. Over the music, she heard the table behind them muttering, a man's voice carrying louder than intended.

'She's very good. Just a shame about the platinum blonde.'

'She does look rather trashy,' a woman replied. 'I'm surprised the hotel hired her, but she does have a good voice, you have to give her that.'

Milly turned to glare at them, but the man didn't notice her over his thick handlebar moustache and the woman simply ignored her. Some rich people just couldn't bear to see a working-class person doing well for themselves. Whatever Timothy might think, that type of snobbery still abounded in London.

A few more songs followed. When Jean had finished, she flashed Milly a smile but didn't come straight to them; instead, she chatted first with the band before moving about the room. A man in a well-cut suit bought her a drink and offered her a cigarette and she smiled affectionately at him, gently touching his arm as she blew a ribbon of smoke into the air.

'Your mum seems busy. Think I'll get meself another drink. D'you want one?'

'No thanks,' she replied, cradling her still-full glass. He slugged back the rest of his drink, grimacing again. 'Why don't you get something else if you don't like it? You don't have to drink martinis.'

'It's fine. I can handle it. They're just an acquired taste that's all.'

A moment later, Timothy returned and Milly shuffled in her seat, her eyes following her mum around the room.

'What's wrong?' he asked.

'I promised Edie I wouldn't be late tonight. I wanted to be back before nine so we could spend some time together.'

He checked his watch, staring at his wrist for a second before answering. ''Fraid you won't make that now, Milly. We can say it's my fault then Edie won't be cross with you.'

'That's sweet,' she replied with a sigh. 'But I'll tell her the truth.'

She hadn't wanted to let Edie down but with the train

being late and Jean's set lasting longer than she'd antici-pated, there wouldn't be much evening left by the time she got back. She'd have to settle for giving her mum the Christ-mas present she'd bought and leaving straight after.

Eventually, Jean made her way over. 'Merry Christmas, darling.' She kissed her on each cheek.

'Mum—' Jean cleared her throat in warning. 'Sorry, Jean, this is Timothy. Timothy, this is Jean.' She leaned into him, whispering. 'She doesn't like me calling her mum when she's working.'

'It's silly, I know, but . . .'

Timothy bowed slightly. 'Pleasure, Jean.' When he took her hand, he raised it to his lips and kissed it.

Impressed, Jean giggled. 'Timothy, it's a pleasure to meet you.'

'Likewise. Can I get you a drink, or are you going to tap up an old fogey at the bar for one?'

Timothy and her mum seemed to stare at each other for a moment almost knowingly, as if they were sharing a joke Milly wasn't in on. Then Jean tossed her head back and laughed.

'No need to spend your hard-earned money on me when you should be spending it on Milly. When I need a refill, I shall ask Major Gormley over there.' She indicated an older man in military uniform at the bar, giving him a wave.

Only a few years ago men in uniform were everywhere but now it was much rarer to see them. It tended to be the older chaps, like this one, as the younger men opted for suits. He lifted his drink to her, and she did the same.

'We spoke earlier and he's a rather charming old dear. My favourite of the hotel guests so far.'

Milly pulled the carefully-wrapped compact from her bag. 'Here you are, Jean, I got you this for Christmas.' Milly had desperately wanted to say 'Mum' as she handed it over. She'd not been able to say the word for such a long time and it seemed important somehow that she did, today of all days.

'For me? You got me a Christmas present? If I'd known, I would've got you something . . .'

How could she not have known? It was Christmas. Milly couldn't hide the disappointment on her face or help but hear Edie's words echoing around her head. 'That's OK. Never mind.'

'Timothy, why don't you be a dear and fetch Milly another drink.'

'Sure you don't want one, Jean?'

'Such a gentleman! But no, thank you.' When he'd gone, she sat down, and Milly retook her seat. 'Now don't be disappointed, darling.' She reached out and took her hand. 'I didn't know if you'd want anything from me, and to be honest, you're not a little girl any more. I'd have no idea what to get you.' She sipped her drink. 'Also, I'm embarrassed to say money's a little tight at the moment. That's partly why I agreed to work tonight. Sometimes we're given good tips. People can be more generous on Christmas Day. But I'm not sure this lot are a tipping type. They look like they hold on to their money. Not that they need to.' Milly tried to decipher her tone as Jean picked up the gift. 'So what's this?' She opened the small package and checked her reflection in the compact. From her tiny evening bag, she pulled a new lipstick and reapplied. 'Thank you, darling. It's perfect. How sweet of you.'

This should have been the moment Jean gave her something in return. Milly told herself not to be ungrateful. She knew her mum didn't have a lot of money and at least she had been able to see her. She'd have given anything for that in the intervening years when she'd thought she was dead. Still, she had hoped for a small something. It didn't have to be fancy or expensive. It didn't have to be much at all. Milly didn't need a material gift, but it had felt like an important step in rebuilding their relationship. A sign that Jean really did love her as much as she had said in her letter.

'While Timothy's at the bar, Jean—'

'He's just coming back. Look.'

If only the barman had taken longer; she needed to tell Jean about Jack and his attempt at extracting information at the Sunrise Club.

'Here we are.' Timothy placed down a gin fizz for Milly and another martini for himself. She'd watched him sipping it as he walked towards them.

'So I take it you're stepping out with my Milly, are you?'

The familiarity made Milly bristle, but she smiled thinly.

'I am. Luckiest chap in the world, I reckon.'

'Marriage soon then,' Jean joked, and Timothy guffawed before turning a serious face on Milly.

'Yeah, why not.'

Was that a proposal of sorts? She was too surprised at his words to answer; besides, she worried they were driven by the martinis rather than any real feeling.

Jean leaned towards him as he offered her a cigarette and lit it. 'I think you could do worse than this young man, Milly.' Glassy-eyed, Timothy attempted to focus on her mum. The martinis combined with what Milly now suspected was more than just a couple of sherries at lunch were having an effect. 'Now, Timothy, Milly's been promising me a trip to the palace, but we haven't managed to sort anything out yet. Don't you think I should come?'

'Course you should. You should come tomorrow while the Royals are away.'

Jean laughed. 'I can't do tomorrow, but how about at New Year, Milly? I'd so love to see where you live, and Timothy's right, it might be easier before the royal family get back. I bet the atmosphere is wonderfully relaxed without them.'

'Too right. What a grand idea, ain't it, Milly?'

They both turned to Milly. 'Yes, yes, it's a great idea. I'd still like to come and see you at home some time too.'

'Oh, not this again, darling. I've already told you. As soon as I get somewhere else you'll be the first person I invite for tea. You really don't want to come to my little place right now.'

'When do you think that will be? It's getting difficult to keep meeting at the Sunrise Club and I can't write freely to you there.' She thought of the new hat, the new lipstick.

'Oh, I don't know. Soon, I should think.' Jean watched Timothy as he swallowed the last of his drink. 'Now, I have more work to do and hadn't you two better be going? Timothy, it's been delightful to meet you, but would you mind if I spoke to Milly alone for a second?'

'As long as you say nice things about me.'

Jean laughed again, her hair swinging back from her face to reveal pale, peachy skin. 'How could I not?'

Timothy left, swaying slightly. Milly had never seen him like that before but considering she'd had one too many gin fizzes not that long ago she was in no position to judge.

'I like him, Milly,' Jean continued. 'I like him a lot. Anyway, listen—'

'I have to talk to you about Jack, Mum—'

'Jean,' she said through gritted teeth. 'What about him?'

Milly swallowed her annoyance. 'I came to see you at the Sunrise Club the other night—'

'Did you? When?'

'Last Friday but you went backstage and—' She thought about telling her she'd followed but wasn't sure what response she'd get. 'While I was waiting for you to come back out, he cornered me, asking questions about you again.'

'What sort of questions?' She seemed irritated rather than worried and Milly wanted to shake her and wake her up to the fact something fishy was going on.

'Just questions. He wanted to know where in Southampton you came from and he was even asking me how long I'd known you.'

'And?'

'And I said not very long because it is sort of true.'

Jean's face hardened. 'I don't really see what the problem is, Milly. I think he likes me, that's all. He's been following me around like a lost puppy. Surely you're not too shocked someone could have a crush on me? I know I'm your mother' – she whispered the word – 'but it is known to happen.'

'But why is he asking so many questions?'

'One day, Milly, when you're more experienced with

men, you'll understand. Thank you for worrying, darling, but you don't need to. You really are more than I deserve. Now, I need to ask you a favour.' She lifted Milly's hands, holding them gently in hers. Milly suddenly realised that though they'd seen each other a few times, they very rarely made such close physical contact. It was something she took for granted with Edie, but as Jean's eyes met hers, the gesture meant a great deal. 'Do you think you could lend me a couple of bob just until the New Year? I'll pay it back when I come and visit the palace – oh, that sounds so grand! – but like I said, I'm not sure this is a tipping sort of crowd.'

'Oh, of course.' Milly reached into her bag and took out her purse; she found the money and handed it to Jean. 'Is it worth trying to find another job? You could work in a shop during the day or something and then you'd still get to sing at night.'

'Shop work?' Jean laughed at the idea. 'I'm not doing shop work, darling. I'm a singer. And I couldn't possibly work during the day, I'd be exhausted. Anyway, you're a lifesaver. But you won't miss it, will you? You can get Timothy to pay for everything, after all.'

At that moment the man in military uniform approached and Jean turned her attention to him. She tucked the money into her bag. 'Major! I was just on my way to see you. Goodnight, darling,' she said to Milly. 'Say goodbye to Timothy for me.' She hooked her arm around the major's, leading him towards the bar.

Milly had no intention of asking Timothy to pay for more than a few drinks as a gentleman should. She took up her coat and left the hotel, but the whole evening had unsettled her. Edie had been right about Jean not getting her a present – but what did that mean? And why did lending her money make Milly feel uneasy? It wasn't that she wasn't generous. She'd lend money to anyone who needed it. She was so lost in thought she almost passed Timothy leaning against a column, his hand cupped around the end of his cigarette as he tried to light it.

'Shall we go?' Milly asked. 'I really need to get back.'

'All right then. Nowhere's open anyway and it's too cold for a stroll.'

They walked down the steps in silence. As she reached the last one a man turned off the pavement and began to climb up them. His hands were in his pockets, and he pulled his elbows in to avoid hitting her. There was something familiar about him. He smelled strongly of cologne and cigarettes, which wasn't unusual, but his coat carried a musky scent reminiscent of something else. *Somewhere* else.

The Sunrise Club.

Could it have been Jack? She hadn't seen his face well enough to be sure but there'd been a certain rat-like shape to his features. Jean thought he fancied her and whilst it was possible she'd invited him there this evening, Milly couldn't help the disquiet growing inside her. Surely Jean would have said when they were talking about him? She wished her mum would heed her warnings. Milly didn't know much about men, but it was clear to her he was too interested in Jean's history. Asking too many questions to be trustworthy. And the way he'd grabbed the man who'd accidentally spilled his drink showed he had a temper.

Jack was a man clearly used to being respected, in control. Jean could only land herself in trouble with someone like him.

'Your mum's nice,' Timothy said as they continued away from the hotel. The fresh air seemed to have sobered him up and his speech was back to normal, his gaze clearer.

'Yes, she is.' If she allowed herself to be honest, Milly still got the feeling she didn't know the real Jean. She'd really only ever seen her at work, playing a role. She didn't yet know her favourite food, her favourite drink or who Jean Hendry actually was. Or Jean Beaumont as she now called herself.

'I was expecting someone a bit more like your aunt.'

'They are very different.'

'Least your mum likes me, hey?' He nudged her elbow and she laughed half-heartedly. She was too busy worrying the man she'd passed was Jack.

'I was proud as punch to have you on me arm tonight.'

'Were you?'

'Course. The best-looking woman in the room by far. And . . .' He dipped his head to catch her eye. 'What d'you reckon about the next step for us?'

She paused under the light of a streetlamp. 'Marriage?'

'Yeah, eventually. I can't afford to marry you at the moment, but we could later. If you wanted. What d'you say?'

'Is that a proposal? Because I thought you were supposed to get down on one knee with a ring or something?'

'I will.' He grinned, his eyes sparkling in the bright beam of light. 'If I know you're gonna say yes.'

She didn't know what to say. It was the next logical step for them, but something held her back.

'I love you, Milly.' It was the first time he'd said it and every nerve in her body fluttered.

He placed his fingers under her chin, gently tipping her head up so their lips could meet. The kiss was gentle but built in intensity. She felt momentarily apprehensive after their last encounter, but his hands stayed on her waist, only moving to wrap around her in a tight embrace. Passion stirred and grew within her as the kiss went on. She could feel it in Timothy too, in the tautness of his arms and shoulders. Still, he kept his hands around her, respecting her wishes.

One day she would give herself to him, but not now. Not until she was ready. Not until there was a ring on her finger. She didn't want a shotgun wedding as Jean and her dad had had. She didn't want to be tied into an unhappy marriage. If only Milly could remember what her mum and dad had been like together, but she didn't trust her memories any more. Were the smiles she recalled genuine or false? She allowed her thoughts to return to Timothy's kiss. The feel of his tongue in her mouth gently finding her own.

Finally, he pulled away. 'I could kiss you forever.' It started to rain: a fine light drizzle that settled on their hair and eyelashes. 'But we better move before this comes down even harder. Don't want you catching cold.'

Milly threaded her arm through Timothy's, allowing him to hold her closer, yet she couldn't help the disappointment inside. She hadn't expected to exchange gifts with her mum in front of a roaring log fire, like some Victorian scene, but she had hoped for something more than the night had given her. Coming back without a present from her mum, and a couple of bob lighter too, she thought that missing out on her evening with Edie and upsetting her even more just to see Jean on Christmas Day hadn't exactly been worth it. What's more, Edie had been right about the present. And if she'd been right about that, what else had she been right about?

January 1952

Chapter Twenty-One

The New Year dawned as grey and disobliging as every new year before. The first day of 1952 Milly spent with her palace family. They'd all stayed up and seen in the New Year together, she and Edie chinking glasses in toast as they always had. Mrs Chadwick had led them on a rendition of 'Auld Lang Syne' and the Household Lounge had been full of cheers and laughter.

For Milly, New Year had always felt muted, unable to match up to the excitement of Christmas Day, but it had been even more so this year despite her mum being due to visit her at the palace later that day. Perhaps it was the state of the King's health and the comments on his speech in the papers. They were kind, and reports were that it had been received well all over the world, but an undercurrent of worry continued to sweep the nation, and the cold, gloomy weather didn't help.

Today, after breakfasting together, they were back to work cleaning another area of the palace that could only be tackled while the King and Queen were away. With the King's rooms cleaned, it was Queen Elizabeth's turn, and returning to a normal routine was strangely reassuring for Milly. She had always loved Queen Elizabeth. There was something sturdy and matronly about her that made her feel like a mother to the entire palace staff, yet she also had a wicked sense of humour and a great sense of fun. A few times she'd passed down corridors in which Milly was working. The Queen had been very complimentary, saying she curtseyed better than some of her ladies-in-waiting, and the smile on Milly's face had hurt her cheeks as she'd told Edie the story. Edie too had beamed with pride.

The Queen's suite was just as opulent as the other palace rooms, though maybe a little more homely. Milly reached on to her tiptoes on top of the stool and dusted the curtain rails while Caroline polished the wooden dressing table and mirror. The Queen loved knick-knacks and it had taken almost as long to clear the thing as it was taking to clean it.

'I didn't know if I'd start the new year with a job,' Caroline muttered to Milly. 'Do you think the Master's still gonna sack us? I ain't told my parents anything, but they know summat's bothering me.'

'I don't know. I suppose he'd have to come up with an excuse – something we've both done wrong – to get away with it. And I'd like to think that Edie would fight him over it.'

'She definitely would. She wouldn't let him say we're bad workers or anything. No, you're right.' She let out a great sigh. 'I feel like a giant weight's gone now.'

'One at least,' Milly muttered, though she still wasn't convinced they were safe. Her thoughts ran to Timothy and his mention of marriage but knew better than to discuss it with Caroline. She wasn't even sure Timothy had meant it. As the year progressed, would Edie grow used to Milly going to see her mum to the point that it one day become a normal thing for them both? 'Just off to see Mum, Aunt Edie,' she'd be able to say. 'OK, love. See you later.' Somehow, she doubted it.

'Milly, Caroline, a word please.' Edie's tone was over formal as she marched into the room and both women immediately turned their attention to her. Milly climbed down from the stool, her chest constricting, and Caroline stood up. The other members of the team had the good sense to move away as Edie strode to the furthest corner, Milly and Caroline following. 'I've just heard from Mrs Morton that you two were seen goin' into the Master's office last month. Why? No one ever goes there unless it's trouble. What's goin' on? And more to the point, why don't I know about it?'

Caroline shot Milly a frightened look. She'd spoken too soon. The Master's warning rang around Milly's head. If the gossip reached his ears would he make good on his threat to sack them? Apprehension stalled her mind, her thoughts blank.

'One of you better say somethin' quick or I'll go and ask him myself.'

'No!' Caroline shot a hand out to stop her.

'It's about Jean,' Milly said, thinking rapidly. It was a flimsy excuse but the only one she could come up with. 'She's visiting today for the first time, and I needed to get permission. Like we normally do for visitors.'

Edie worked her jaw. Milly could see the slight movement of it as her teeth ground together. 'We don't normally go to the Master for that. He's a very busy man. Wasn't the Deputy Master around, or the Chief Housekeeper?'

Milly urged her mind to work quicker to find an excuse. She'd already got the required permissions from Mrs Fernsby but if she admitted that, Edie would know there would have been no need to see the Master. 'I don't think so. I was just in that part of the palace so I nipped in and asked him.'

'Nipped in and asked him?' Edie's incredulous tones echoed around the room. 'You just nipped in to ask the most senior member of staff somethin' triflin' like that?' Milly didn't answer. She was too busy praying Edie wouldn't mention any of this to the Chief Housekeeper. 'And when were you goin' to tell me Jean was visitin'?' Edie crossed her arms over her chest. 'Don't you think that's somethin' I should know?'

'Yes, of course, but ... Oh, I knew you wouldn't be pleased and I've been trying to find the right time to tell you. I just wanted us to have a nice Christmas first.' Though this line of questioning wasn't pleasant, it was at least better than the truth.

'And when's she comin'?'

'Today.'

'Today?'

'As it's my half-day I thought I could show her my room and then we'll probably go for a walk or something.'

'So why was Caroline with you?'

'We were just together, so she waited for me.'

Edie considered each of them in turn, taking in the information. She paid particular attention to Caroline, her eyes burning into her, and Milly willed Caroline to keep quiet. 'All right. Caroline, back to work with you.' Caroline shot

Milly an apologetic look before scurrying away. Edie stepped closer to Milly, speaking low. 'If you bring Jean here I'd appreciate it if you don't take her to the communal areas. We don't need any more gossip about us. I'll be civil if I see her but don't expect any big heart-to-hearts like you planned in the park.'

'She just wants to see where I live and then we'll be away. I swear.'

With a final glance up and down, Edie left. In the corner Caroline crumpled.

'Oh Milly, thank you. You're so clever to think of that. Is it true?'

'That Mum's visiting today? Yes. It was the only thing I could think of to cover ourselves.'

'D'you think we should've told her the truth?'

Milly shook her head. 'You heard what the Master said, and the gossip mill is already going. At least Mum arriving will give them something else to talk about.'

Caroline nodded, her features grey. 'You know that giant weight I said about earlier?'

'Yes.'

'It's back.'

Milly stroked Caroline's shoulder. It was weighing on her again too.

After they'd finished, Milly went to her room, tidying away magazines and remaking her bed while she waited for her mum to arrive. At five minutes to four she walked through the staff block and across the gravel to the guarded gate at the staff entrance.

'I've got a visitor coming. Here's my permission slip.'

She handed over the chit the Chief Housekeeper had given her, reminded again of her lies to Edie. They seemed to be piling on top of each other and even the strong winter wind couldn't blow away the guilt growing inside her.

'You should have worn a coat, Milly,' one of the soldiers on duty said. 'It's freezing today.'

Goosebumps were rising on her arms as she rubbed them, hopping from foot to foot. 'Silly of me really, wasn't it? But hopefully I won't be waiting long. I don't know how you lot don't freeze being out here day in day out.'

He pointed at his bearskin hat. 'These are pretty warm, and we get good coats.'

After a few minutes, she recognised the figure of her mum threading through the crowd that always lingered outside the palace. Milly stood on tiptoe and waved. 'Over here, Mum.'

Jean made her way towards the gate and, as she neared, the guard opened it, stepping aside so she could enter. 'Makes you feel like a film star, doesn't it, darling?'

'Yes, I suppose so.' Milly had never thought of it like that. 'Come on, let's get inside. I'm freezing.'

She led the way into the staff area and through the corridors towards her room. Seeing the almost disappointed look on her mum's face at the less than opulent surroundings, she said, 'Obviously, this part of the palace isn't as grand as the State Rooms or where the King and Queen live.'

'It's not, is it.'

'But it's perfectly nice and I'm very lucky.' She opened the door to her room and stepped inside. 'So here's my room.' She swept her arm across, showing off the space. She was quite proud of it really. It was neat and tidy and more than comfortable enough for her. In an ideal world she'd have her own bathroom but at least it was inside, at the end of the corridor. Caroline's parents still had an outside toilet.

'It's a little small, isn't it, darling? You couldn't have much of a party in here.'

Crestfallen, a sudden urge to defend herself reared up within Milly. 'We tend to use the communal areas for things like that. That's where I had my twenty-first birthday party.' Jean's face was impassive, the mention of her birthday failing to stir any response. 'There's the Household Dining and Breakfast Rooms for our meals and the Household Lounge for relaxing in the evenings. They're much larger.'

'Can we go and see them?'

'I'm not really supposed to show you around there.'

'Why not?' Jean asked, turning to face her. 'Let me guess, Edie doesn't want everyone seeing me and her getting embarrassed. She always cared far too much what the neighbours thought. I'm surprised you're going along with it, Milly.' Her mum hadn't even noticed the photograph of her with Milly's dad on their wedding day that sat staring at them from the windowsill. Perhaps he'd been so bad to her, she couldn't bear to look at him, but as Milly remembered her dad's smile, another flicker of doubt crept in.

'Don't you have a bathroom?' Jean asked, gazing around.

'There's one at the end of the corridor. We all have washbasins though.'

'Hmm. Can I see some of the State Rooms then? I've read they're very fine.'

'I'm sorry, they're very strict on what we're allowed to show visitors. It's for security. You understand, don't you?'

'Well, I suppose I do. But isn't there somewhere a bit more exciting I can see? There must be a room they don't use much. I mean, don't get me wrong, I'm so proud of you, sweetheart, but I may not get the chance to see any of this while the Royals are away again. I'd love to see just one of the finer rooms. Please? It would mean the world to me.'

'I suppose I could show you one of the guest bed-rooms. There are loads of those and they're all empty at the moment.' If they were quick and careful, no one need know.

Jean clapped her still-gloved hands together. 'That sounds marvellous. Oh, please do.'

Milly shut the door behind them and they made their way to the staff staircase that led to the guest rooms. This wasn't what she'd imagined, and disappointment lingered that her mum wasn't seeing the palace the same way she did. She reminded herself how fortunate she was to work here and to have a room of her own and fine food to eat.

'I only got that room when I started working here,' Milly said, hoping to stir a reaction. 'Before that I was in Edie's room on a camp bed. They must have had a high regard for Aunt Edie to let me stay. They don't normally let children live at the palace. I was very lucky.'

'Yes, it seems it,' Jean replied, missing Milly's point completely.

'Do you want to take your gloves off now we're inside?'

'No, thank you.' She pressed her hands together, making sure the gloves were firmly on. The small handbag looped over her wrist swung back and forth. 'I got quite cold making my way to you and I'm still warming up.'

Checking first, Milly exited the stairs and nipped across the corridor to ensure the room was unlocked. Most of the rooms were unless guests were staying. Turning the handle and feeling the door give easily, she signalled for her mum to join her. The thick carpet absorbed the noise of her heels.

'Now, you must be quiet, Mum. The Royals aren't here, but there are still footmen and senior staff around. I'll get into trouble if they catch us.' It suddenly dawned on Milly how stupid she was being showing Jean around this area of the palace. If the Master caught her, she'd be out on her ear before she had a chance to explain herself, not that the excuse of 'I just wanted to impress my mum' was likely to wash.

Jean held a finger to her lips, a gleam of excitement in her eyes. 'I'll be as quiet as a mouse.'

'OK. I'll open the door and you can poke your head in, all right?'

'Fine.' Milly opened the door and Jean darted through the gap before Milly could stop her. Her heart began to thud violently in her chest as panic mixed with anger. 'Mum, come back.' She followed her, softly inching the door closed behind herself. 'What are you doing? You're not supposed to be in here—'

'It's incredible. Just look at this place.'

As with all the palace rooms, this guest room was as sumptuous as a State Room, with a thick and luxurious carpet and an ornately carved four-poster bed littered with cushions. The mantelshelf above the Victorian fireplace was decorated with an enormous clock flanked by two tall silver candlesticks. A picture of the King sat in a small silver frame on the bedside.

Milly tried to control her growing frustration. 'Mum, I let you up, but you can't just do what you want. This is Buckingham Palace, not one of the hotels you work in.'

'I know, darling.' Jean ran to the window, deliberately ignoring her. 'I just want to see the view.'

The room was at the back of the house so at least none of the guards on the forecourt would see her but that didn't mean someone else wouldn't.

'Mum, come away.' Her voice was stronger than Jean would ever have heard it and it had the desired effect: she gave a final glance out of the window.

'All right. Gosh, I can really see Edie's influence on you. She never knew how to have fun either.'

'Fun? Mum, I could lose my job.' Jean's comment left her feeling sick. At least Edie wouldn't do something reckless that could cost her her livelihood.

'All right, I'm sorry.' She went to the bedside table and picked up the small, silver-framed photograph. Voices sounded from further up the corridor and panic flooded Milly's body, turning her cold.

'Be quiet, Mum.' She ran to the door, staring at the back of it, glad at least that she'd closed it behind her. Listening carefully, she waited for the voices to fade before turning back to her mum. 'We'd better go.'

Jean was retying the belt on her coat as Milly moved towards her, taking her arm and urging her from the room. 'Please, Mum. I'll lose my job if we're caught here. I can't risk it any more.'

'Fine then, let's go.'

Within minutes they were back in the safety of the staff area. It took a moment for Milly to hear the voice calling her name with the blood pounding in her ears, blocking all other sound.

'Milly,' Timothy said, hurrying towards her. 'You ignoring me?' he asked teasingly.

'Sorry. I didn't hear you. We were just—'

'Timothy,' Jean said, smiling. 'How lovely to see you again.'

Grateful for her mum's interruption, Milly used the time to steady herself.

'You too,' he replied. 'Enjoyed your visit?'

'Yes, very much, thank you. It's been as wonderful as I hoped.'

Wonderful? She hadn't given the impression she was enjoying it that much and Milly certainly wouldn't call it that.

'Might want to get going, Milly. The senior footman's on the warpath and he's headed this way.'

'Is he looking for you?' Jean taunted.

'Nah, not this time.'

'Come on, Mum. I'll show you out.'

Timothy held out his arm, directing Jean to the exit. His other hand touched the side of her body and his eyes widened in shock. Assuming he'd meant to touch Jean's arm and was embarrassed, Milly gave him a reassuring smile and led her mum away. When she glanced back, she was surprised to see Timothy still watching them, a quizzical look on his face.

'I think that was just an accident, Mum. I'm sure he didn't mean anything improper.'

'Of course.' Jean too looked back at him. 'And judging by his face he's more embarrassed than I am. Probably best not to mention it again.'

'I won't,' Milly replied. She didn't want to talk about anything that might lead on to questions over where she'd taken her mum. She seemed to be lying to everyone at the moment: she didn't want to add Timothy to that list.

'That was fun though, don't you think?'

'If we'd have got caught I'd have lost my job.'

'Oh now, don't be boring, darling.'

Milly didn't know what to say as annoyance rose and they remained in silence until they reached the guarded gate.

'I've enjoyed seeing where you live,' Jean said. The cold air whipped the hair around her face, but she kept her arms pinned to her sides.

'Hopefully I'll get to see where you live soon,' Milly replied. 'I don't care if it's not grand, Mum. You've seen my room isn't. It'd just be lovely not to see you at the club or in a hotel surrounded by other people.'

'Yes, hopefully soon, sweetheart.'

They parted with kisses on the cheek, Milly's smile hiding her relief that the visit was over. As she turned to head back inside, the unmistakable form of Edie hurried away from the open doorway.

Chapter Twenty-Two

Helen and Milly sat in the Lyons' Corner House on Tottenham Court Road surrounded by the art deco splendour. It was the first time they'd seen each other properly since their row before Christmas. Though Milly's Christmas card had gone some way to improving things, to begin with conversation had been a little too polite and stilted; but soon their initial reticence had been forgotten.

Once settled at a table, their order placed, Milly relaxed. The marble columns that surrounded them were topped with geometric designs and the lights on the walls radiated from behind fan-shaped sconces. The café bustled with colour and life, the black and white uniforms of the Nippies standing out against the brightly-coloured hats and coats of the crowd. Conversation carried towards them from different tables: some of it serious, political; some of it happy and convivial. Nights out were arranged, trips to museums planned, dinner dates confirmed. A band played quiet, gentle swing and Milly realised that her life suddenly seemed shrouded in song in a way it hadn't before her mum's arrival. She'd often listened to the wireless with her aunt but the tinny speaker of the radio was so different to the songs heard straight from the musician's mouth.

'It's a shame Caroline can't join us today,' Helen said. 'It would have been nice to see her.'

'Yes. She said she had to go and see her sister.' It was sad their friend couldn't join them, but Milly was also relieved. It meant she could talk about Timothy, about him hinting at marriage.

'How's your dad doing?' Milly asked, holding the backs of her fingers to the pot of tea to test its warmth.

Helen stubbed out her cigarette, releasing the last of the smoke in her lungs as she did so. When they'd met briefly in the corridors of the palace she'd mentioned that her Christmas and New Year had been somewhat lonely; her dad had been going through a bad spell which forced him to spend much of his time in bed. But no matter how Milly had pleaded, Helen couldn't be persuaded to leave him any more than she had to for work and their weekly shopping. 'He's getting better, thanks. Seems to be getting some strength back.'

'Good, I'm glad. It must be hard on you.'

'It is sometimes. It's the unbearable guilt that's the worst. I feel awful having to leave him to go to work, but if I don't work, we can't live. I'm just lucky I have my neighbour to stop in. She sometimes leaves us a pie or a stew on the doorstep. It's saved my bacon more times than I can count.'

'She sounds lovely. Our neighbours weren't like that.'

'When you lived with your parents, you mean?'

'Yes. I don't really remember much. I was only ten. Nine when I was sent away, actually. But I don't remember any kindness like that. It's very different at the palace. Normally if you're unwell everyone's checking on you every five minutes and bringing you cups of tea.'

'I never realised the palace would be so like a family. I thought it would be all backstabbing and one-upmanship.'

'That happens too, but mostly we're all on the same side. Is your colleague pulling their weight now? You mentioned before someone leaving the work to the rest of you.'

'At the moment she is, so I'm grateful. How was your mum's visit?'

'Great,' Milly replied, forcing enthusiasm into her voice. The truth was, her visit the week before had left her exhausted and upset. Her mum had been too busy to see her since and Milly, though she'd never have admitted it to Edie, was glad of the break. She wasn't normally one for breaking rules, as impulsive as she could be, and she still worried their little trip to the guest bedrooms would come back to haunt her. 'It was lovely to see her,' she said meekly.

'What did she think of the place? It is quite impressive. I was gobsmacked the day I came to visit.'

'She wasn't that impressed with my room but then the staff quarters are quite small and dowdy compared with the main part of the house.'

'Yes, but she can't expect the staff to live like the Royals. That would be silly.' She gazed at Milly from over her teacup, narrowing her eyes slightly. 'What else happened?'

'Nothing.'

'I can see from your face something did. Come on, out with it.'

'You have a horrid ability to see right through people.' Milly replaced her cup in its saucer as Helen grinned at the compliment. 'She was so bored I took her to one of the empty guest rooms, just to show her how different those areas of the palace are.'

'Oh, Milly, you didn't. You're lucky you didn't get caught.'

'We nearly did,' Milly replied, feeling heat rise in her cheeks. 'But it was all right in the end.'

'Do take care, won't you?' Helen added gently: 'Don't do anything silly again.'

'I won't.' Milly meant it with all her heart. She had realised how much she didn't want to lose her job.

'Anyway, let's talk about something more cheery. Something like . . . Timothy.' Helen smiled as Milly blushed. 'I've been meaning to ask what he thought of your mum. Did he like her?'

'He liked her a lot. He thought she was the bee's knees. And she liked him too.'

'Well, that's good.'

'Yes, it is, but . . . Oh, I don't know.'

'What?'

'I just wonder if my mum can't help but act as hostess sometimes. There were times when she was a little . . .' She didn't really want to admit the thought that had been circling in her head at night.

'A little what?'

'Well, flirty, I suppose. With Timothy.'

A flash of concern crossed Helen's face, the skin around her eyes tightening and a slight crease marring her smooth brow. Then it was gone, but the fact it had appeared at all made Milly nervous.

'Like you say, perhaps she's just so used to acting as a hostess that she naturally does it when she's with people.'

'I'm sure that's right. I must admit I was a little shocked at her. But not as shocked as when he started talking about marriage!'

'Marriage?' Helen's hands hovered an inch or two above the table. She'd just picked up her cup and saucer again and was holding them still. 'Marriage? He talked about getting married? To you?'

'Of course to me.' Milly feigned offence. 'You don't need to sound so surprised.'

Helen laughed. 'You know I didn't mean anything by it. Of course someone is going to want to marry you and I'm not surprised Timothy does. It's just it seems a bit sudden after only a couple of months and especially as no one else knows you've been seeing each other. Perhaps that's just my lack of experience. I've never got that far with anyone even when I've been seeing them for a while.' She set down her cup and lit another cigarette.

'He said it was the next logical step for us.'

'That doesn't sound very romantic. What did you say?'

'I didn't really say anything. I didn't know what to say. He'd had a few drinks and I think they'd got to him a little bit. I'll see if he mentions it again before I reply.'

'You're not really thinking about it, are you? I mean, he's very handsome, but you don't really know him and you're only just twenty-one, you don't need to rush.' A thread of tobacco had come loose from her cigarette and Helen picked it from the end of her tongue. 'Although having said that, a lot of my old school friends are married with children already. They only found jobs to give them something to do until they caught a husband and had houses to look after. I know that's how it is these days but I'm awfully glad I've got my work. Something I enjoy. Even though it means leaving Dad and I'm considered an old spinster at the grand age of twenty-four.'

'Terrible, isn't it? So unfair. Shall we have another pot of tea?' Helen agreed and Milly caught the waitress's attention. 'If we get married and have children, I won't be able to work at the palace any more. I'll be expected to leave, and Timothy will stay.'

'Is that what you want?'

'No. I like my job. I know being a cleaner isn't the most fabulous thing in the world, but I like it. And I like working at the palace.'

Helen stubbed out the end of her cigarette. 'I used to get proposals all the time before my father got sick.'

'Did you?'

'Yes. They weren't real ones of course. They normally happened when I was out with my friends.'

Milly could see why she might. Helen was striking with dark hair and plump red lips. The mascara on her lashes made the blue of her eyes appear brighter. 'Did you never say yes to anyone?'

'Of course not. Never accept a drunk proposal, Milly. You never quite know if they're saying it because they're tipsy or if their true feelings are coming to the surface. A marriage should be built on absolute certainties. If you're tying yourself to someone for life, I believe you have to be absolutely sure of them.'

A fresh teapot was delivered. 'Sage advice,' Milly replied, smiling as she poured two fresh cups for her and Helen. Timothy had sobered up somewhat, but he'd definitely had a few too many for her to take the proposal seriously. Her mind ran to Robert and she explained what had happened when he'd taken her home from the Sunrise Club.

'Poor Robert. I like him. He's sweet. But I suppose if you don't like him in that way then you don't. I can imagine Jack getting beastly like that. He seemed the type who likes to be in charge. Sounds like you had a lucky escape.'

If only her mum had seen it like that too. She'd have to prove it to her somehow. An idea struck her, but she instantly realised that, for it to work, she'd need Robert. She put the thought to one side and answered: 'You're right. I'll be happy never to go back to the Sunrise Club again. I do wish she could work in more hotels. The one in Kensington was lovely. I wish you could have seen it. I suppose I could give her some more money, so she doesn't have to sing at the club any longer, but I'd rather not.' She still hadn't been paid back from the last time.

'What do you mean *more* money?' Helen's head fell to the side in enquiry. 'Oh, Milly. You haven't, have you?'

'She asked me to lend her a little on Christmas Day. How could I say no?'

'Easily. You say, "I'm terribly sorry, Jean, but I don't really have enough to spare at the moment." It's very simple.'

'But I can spare it. Why shouldn't I help her if I can?' Milly sat back in her chair forcing herself to relax.

Helen fixed Milly with a grim stare. 'I'm going to say something now and I know you're not going to like it, but I need you to listen to me because I'm saying this as your friend.'

A slight chill ran over Milly's back as if her skin were hardening ready for the attack.

'I've been worried she might ask you for money sooner or later. There's something not quite right with all this. She's been back for a couple of months now, surely that's enough time to find a small flat. Have you asked her what she's spending all her money on?'

'I—' Milly automatically leapt to defend her, but the reality was, she didn't know and she admitted as much to Helen.

'Didn't you say she bought a new hat recently?' Milly nodded. 'And wasn't she wearing a shiny gold band too? From what you told me it didn't sound old. Unless it's regularly polished, gold tends to dull over time. Look here—' She held out her right hand to show a small gold band. 'This was my mother's wedding ring. See how the gold is a bit lacklustre. If it was as shiny as you say, I think it was probably new.'

Why would her mum lie? Yet, after the awkward meeting at Christmas and Jean's disappointing visit to the palace, Milly had to admit fears had been building and she worried the newly formed strands binding them together were already beginning to falter. If they fell apart then everything she'd been through, everything Edie had been through, would have been for nothing. A burning need to weave them back together made her defensive.

'So?'

'So where is she getting the money for all these things?'

'Are you implying men are buying them for her?' The other option was that she was buying them for herself – in which case, why wasn't she saving for a decent place to live?

'I don't know. But you have to admit it's a possibility. She is very flirty and you've told me before how she never seems to pay for a drink.'

Another option suddenly occurred to Milly. Could Helen be implying that she was receiving these gifts in exchange for something far more intimate? A wave of heat ran through her. No, she couldn't mean something like that. Not about her mum. 'Are you suggesting—' Her voice had risen so loudly that the next table tutted. Milly leaned forwards, glad she hadn't shouted the word out loud. 'Are you suggesting my mum's a – a—'

Helen thrust a hand out and held Milly's. 'No, I'm not saying that.' Though it was clear the thought had crossed her mind. Milly remembered Edie telling her there had been other men while Jean was still married to her dad, before she fell in love with Billy, but she hadn't believed it. Even if she had, that didn't mean Helen was right. 'I'm just saying that, if she's not happy with where she's living, why isn't she saving up instead of buying expensive things like that for herself? And if other people are buying them for her then what is she doing to deserve it? Either way, the question remains: what is she doing with her money? It just seems like she's not thinking about the future. The future she wants to have with you.'

Milly suddenly wondered what that future actually looked like. Two months on from receiving the letter and she still hadn't visited her mum's flat, she had no idea where she lived, only the various places she worked. Singing couldn't last forever and Jean had already admitted to lying about her age. What would she do when she couldn't do that any more?

'What does she do during the day?' Helen continued.

'She said she goes around different clubs and hotels trying to get an audition.'

'What? All day, every day?'

Milly had no answer. The idea of auditions and being independent like Jean had sounded so exotic, so exciting when she'd first heard of it. Now it sounded squalid, desperate. And Helen was right. She couldn't do that all day, every day.

Guilt suddenly ripped at Milly. This was her mum. The woman who had come back wanting to mend their relationship, to regain the time they'd lost. How could she sit there thinking such terrible things about her? How could Helen? Helen had even implied she might be a – a— She couldn't bring herself to say the word even in her mind. What sort of a daughter would Milly be if she let that insult go unanswered?

'Helen, I understand what you're saying and I do have some concerns, but you're wrong.' She sounded nothing like herself, overly formal and clipped. 'What my mum does with her money is her own business. She's a grown woman and so am I. I wouldn't like her sticking her nose into my financial affairs and I don't think it's right I do that to her either. And I don't appreciate you insinuating she might be a . . .' She leaned forwards and Helen mirrored her movement. 'How could you even think that?'

'I'm not judging her, Milly.'

'Yes, you are. Edie thinks she's good for nothing but—'

Helen lifted her chin and fidgeted with her jacket. 'Maybe, since she was there and saw it all happen, she *does* know her sister better than you do. I just get the feeling that—'

'She knows who her sister was ten years ago but I know who my mum is now. And even if Edie was right back then, Jean's changed. She's only got me now and—'

'I just don't want you getting hurt, Milly. I'm only thinking of you.'

'Everyone says that when what they really mean is they want to stick their noses in and tell you not to do things.'

'I'm not sticking my nose in.' Helen sat back in her chair, but her shoulders were high with tension. 'I told you I was saying it as your friend.'

'I thought friends were supposed to be supportive.'

'Friends must also tell you the truth.'

Their eyes met fiercely across the table, locked like two animals readying to fight, but Milly felt harassed enough already. She was falling out with everyone: first Edie, then Caroline and now Helen. She didn't have the strength for any more. She couldn't tell Caroline about Timothy, she couldn't speak to Edie about Jean, now she could no longer speak to Helen either. How could she when Helen thought such terrible things about her mum?

Milly felt suddenly isolated and stood, grabbing up her purse and taking out enough money to cover her share of the bill. She tossed the coins on the table. 'I should be getting back.'

'Milly—' Helen pleaded. 'Don't go.'

But Milly couldn't listen. Her head was spinning, her hands shaking as she retrieved her coat and attempted to do up the buttons. 'I think it's best I get going. You'll want to get back to your dad.' She left Helen sitting at the table, staring after her.

Her last ally gone.

Chapter Twenty-Three

Milly stopped in to see Edie when she returned to the palace. She'd been limping again that morning, her knee swollen, and Milly wanted to make sure she was all right before she made for the Household Lounge.

As she entered Edie's room, she found her aunt hobbling and, from the grimace on her face, her knee was exceedingly painful.

'Don't get old, Milly, that's my advice.' Edie lowered herself gingerly into her armchair and switched on the radio. 'Old age isn't for the faint of heart.'

'You're forty-eight, Aunty, you're not getting old. How bad is it?' She knelt down in front of her.

'I've had better days. My old bones don't like me today.'

'It's definitely swollen more since this morning. Perhaps I can take on some of your more difficult chores for a while.'

'Not on your life, Milly Hendry.'

'Why not?'

'Because what will the Chief Housekeeper think if I can't do my job? She'll think I'm over the hill and what do you think that means?'

'A decent rest,' Milly replied with a smile.

'Retirement,' Edie stated coldly. 'And not here neither. The apartments are for current staff only. I'll have to leave,

Milly, and where would I go? I know it's comin' sooner or later, but I'm not ready for it yet.'

Milly had never thought that her aunt might one day no longer be in the palace with her. It stabbed at her heart in a way nothing else had. 'Well, if we don't want that to happen, we need to get this swelling down which means rest. Have you any aspirin?'

'In the drawer over there.'

Milly went to check, rifling through until it was thoroughly searched. 'There's none here. I'll nip to the pharmacy now.'

When she returned, she unscrewed the bottle and handed two pills to Edie with a glass of water. 'Now, do you need anything else? A cup of tea? Some more water?'

'No, no. I'm fine.' She reached out and took Milly's hand. 'Thank you, my girl.'

'Do you want me to sit with you this evening? We can listen to the wireless or something?'

'No, no. You go. I'm fine here, honestly. I'll probably just doze a bit anyway. I'm worn out today.'

'If you're sure. I'll stop in later and see if you need anything before you settle for the night.'

In the dim lamplight, Milly could finally see how Edie's eyes were bruised with dark circles, and her mouth had turned down. She slumped with tiredness into the chair. Milly leaned forwards and placed a kiss on her aunt's head.

'I'll only be in the lounge if you need anything else. Someone can come and fetch me.'

'I'm sure I'll be all right after a good night's sleep. Oh,

how was your seein' Helen earlier? Did you have a nice time?'

Milly plastered on a smile, unable and unwilling to tell the truth. 'It was nice. Her dad's doing better.'

'I'm glad. You know, I wasn't sure about her when we first met. I think it was her lipstick. But I like her. She's a good friend to you.'

Milly bit her lip and bid her aunt goodnight, promising again to stop in, then closing the door behind her.

The air of the Household Lounge was opaque with cigarette smoke and, though windows had been opened, the fog was as dense as that which covered London. Familiar faces met her, and she waved a greeting in return. Most of them were like family, but there were always a few who preferred gossip and that gossip had abounded over the last few weeks, people speculating all sorts of things: that she was moving out of the palace to work with her mum in the clubs; that her mum and Edie had come to physical blows on more than one occasion. She hated feeling the whispers of it drifting over her and concentrated on the kind faces of the people she'd grown up with, carefully ignoring the normal culprits: the old Mrs Mortons and Mr Parkers of this world who garnered more delight from the goings-on in other people's lives than they did from their own.

Timothy was sitting on his own, reading the newspaper, and though she had planned to go straight to him, she needed to speak to Robert first. The idea that had struck her while she was having tea with Helen had developed into a plan.

'Hello, Robert.' He was playing cards with some friends

and blushed as he looked up. 'Can I speak to you for a minute, please?'

Robert placed his cards down and together they found a free table further away. From the corner of her eye, she noticed Timothy flick the paper down so he could see what she was doing.

The normal kindness that filled Robert's features was replaced with embarrassment and once more Milly wished she'd never hurt him. 'What c-can I do for you, Milly?'

'I need to ask a favour. I know I have no right to, and I know you probably hate me.'

'I don't hate you, Milly.' He gave a shy smile, and it melted her heart. He would have been too good for her anyway, even if she had returned his feelings. 'What do you need?'

'I need you to ask your barman friend about Jack, the owner of the Sunrise Club. There's something about him I don't trust.'

'He's not really a trustworthy sort. Most club owners aren't.'

'I know, but there's something else about him. Something dangerous. I can't put my finger on it exactly, but—'

'Why do you say that?'

She told him about the night he'd walked her home and the way Jack had grabbed her arm.

'I w-wish you'd told me. I would have gone back in there and punched him.'

'Then I'm glad I didn't. You might have got punched in return.' Concern shot through her body, stirring again that unnameable feeling deep inside. 'Please, Robert, will you ask him?'

'Of course.'

'Thank you. I know I don't deserve your friendship.' If there had been any other way of getting the information, she'd have taken it. She didn't want to use Robert or drag him into her mess of a life, but she couldn't face going back to the club. There was no telling what Jack might do this time around. Robert's friend was her only hope. They stood together in silence, the air thick between them. She wanted to apologise again but knew it would only drag up horrible feelings.

'I better get back to my game.'

Milly hoped he knew how much she appreciated his help but wasn't quite sure her words had shown it enough. She made her way to Timothy, aware that he'd been watching her. She hadn't spoken to him in front of anyone for a while and worried it would seem more suspicious if she blanked him, so she sat down in the empty chair opposite him.

As he'd met her mum and liked her, she was certain he'd reassure her Helen was wrong. He'd probably laugh when she told him what Helen had implied. That was if she could overcome her embarrassment at the idea of saying the word out loud. It wasn't something decent people spoke about.

'Hello.'

'Evening,' Timothy replied. He lowered his newspaper. 'What was all that about?'

'With Robert? Nothing. I just needed to speak to him, that's all.'

'What about?'

She shook her head. 'It doesn't matter.'

His brows pinched together but he didn't pursue it. 'Didn't think I'd see you this evening. Thought you'd be with Edie.'

'She's resting.'

Timothy folded his newspaper into a manageable size. 'I was hoping to see you today. Christmas Day seems a long time ago.'

'I know, but it's been so busy I haven't had a moment to myself. I went to tea with Helen this afternoon.' She longed to tell him everything that had been said but couldn't do it here and as their relationship was still a secret, she shouldn't be caught speaking to him for longer than was necessary. 'I haven't seen Helen since before Christmas. Apart from work she's stayed at home with her dad, so we've rather been ships that pass in the night. We went to a Lyons.'

'Sounds nice. Fancy a walk? Stroll around the gardens?'

'But it's getting dark out there.'

'Yeah, but it's not dark yet.' He leaned forwards. 'Come on. Live a little.'

'All right then. It always gets a bit stuffy in here anyway.' The cigarette smoke filling the air grated on her throat. 'I'll just go and fetch my coat and meet you outside.'

Milly headed back to her room and Timothy stayed where he was, nonchalantly picking up his paper again and reading. She was getting tired of this secrecy. It had been exciting at first, but now it was just an inconvenience.

A few moments later, coats buttoned up against the cold wind, they began their walk through Buckingham Palace gardens. The light was fading, the sky slate-grey and tinged with creeping darkness. They kept their hands in their pockets to keep their fingers warm, but she longed to take his hand in hers and feel the relief of being cared for.

It was hard to believe they were still in the centre of London. The sound of traffic, dimmed by the trees and bushes, was barely audible. Instead, the evening was filled with the sound of birdsong as they fluttered to their nests ready to hunker down for the night. They passed Victoria and Albert. The bare branches of the enormous trees entwined together. Milly preferred seeing it bare rather than covered in leaves. They obscured the way the boughs touched like lovers' hands. She glanced behind her to see if anyone was watching and though no one in particular stood there, the many windows of the palace, blinking as the departing sun washed over them, kept her hands from Timothy's.

'What have you been up to?' Milly asked.

'This and that. Just the normal stuff: opening doors, closing doors. I hate it when the Royals aren't here. I know it means we can be a little more relaxed, but with the Master around it does ruin the fun a bit.'

'I suppose that is his job. We should still make the most of the next few weeks.'

The royal family weren't due to come back from Sandringham until the end of January. Milly thought of the handkerchief. Was that part of the reason for the King's extended absence?

'Have a nice time with Helen?'

Milly hesitated, taking a hand from her pocket and

pushing her hair behind her ear. The breeze was picking up, whipping her hair across her face. 'It all got a bit heated actually.' She told him of Helen's suspicions.

Timothy gave such a hearty laugh she could see his teeth gleaming in the light. 'A lady of the night? Really?'

'Shh! I don't want anyone to hear me even say it out loud, let alone know I'm talking about my mum. Please, just lower your voice.'

'All right. I'm sorry.' He wiped his eyes, clearly finding the suggestion so amusing he'd almost cried with laughter. She supposed that was a good sign. It meant he couldn't think it was true either.

'After rowing with Edie these last couple of months and falling out with Caroline because she was spying on me, and now Helen too . . . I just feel so alone.'

'Don't feel alone,' he said gently, stopping and turning her towards him.

'Don't,' she replied with a thin laugh. 'Someone will see.'

With a mischievous glint in his eye, he slid his arms around her and pulled her behind a large bush into the darkness of a shadow.

'What are you doing?' Milly laughed, enjoying the naughtiness of it, the idea that at any moment they could be caught by one of their friends or even the Chief Housekeeper.

'Just want to make you feel better, that's all.' He kissed her gently, edging her ever further out of sight. 'Make you smile again.' Timothy pressed his lips to Milly's more passionately, so fiercely she was pushed backwards another step. She let herself be taken by his embrace and melted into his kiss. In the dark all was intensified, and she focused on how it felt to be wanted. He moaned into her ear, his hands beginning to wander from her waist around to her back, hugging her close. But then his hands moved again, brushing over the front of her coat. Had he realised what he'd done? She was suddenly taken back to the reality of where they were and what they were doing.

Timothy continued to kiss her neck and, though she wanted to enjoy it, it felt too much. His lips returned to hers as he pushed her back into the trunk of a tree. It was cold and hard, and her hair caught on the rough bark, tugging at her scalp. She tried to speak. 'Slow down, Timothy, please.'

But he didn't. He continued to kiss her neck. She could feel the warmth of his breath mixed with an uncomfortable wetness left behind by his kisses. His hands were fumbling with the buttons of her coat, and she tried to speak again but as soon as she made a noise, his mouth clamped down over hers. Deftly the buttons were undone, and his hand was cupping her breast, tightening then unfurling. In seconds he was pulling her blouse from the waistband of her skirt, his cold fingers reaching under her shirt.

Fear gripped her, almost rooting her to the spot, but summoning all her strength she pushed him away, wiping her mouth with the back of her hand, then her neck with her fingers. 'Timothy, stop it.'

'God, Milly, why are you such a prude?'

'I'm not a prude,' she replied fiercely. In the echoey darkness her voice seemed louder, reverberating through the trees and bouncing back from the far-off walls of the garden.

'Yeah, you are,' he fired back, adjusting himself. He'd clearly enjoyed it more than she had. 'You're a tease. How many times have we been out? I've even told you I'll marry you. What more d'you want? Ain't that enough?'

'Enough for what?' she asked, tucking her shirt back in and refastening her coat.

'A bit of fun, maybe.'

'Fun? You think that was *fun*?'

'It would have been if you weren't such a prude.'

'What did you think we were going to do? Make love behind the bushes?'

'No, but there's more you can do than just kissing. You'd know that if you weren't so bloody naive.'

Her heart throbbed and if she weren't so angry it would have broken completely. Who was this man standing in front of her? His features were cold, his eyes dark and hard. Yes, she was naive. Far more naive than she'd ever realised. She'd met country bumpkins who'd come to work at the palace and been enthralled by the lights and noise of the city but because she'd grown up here, and was used to the constant activity, the ever-present heartbeat of the capital, she'd thought herself worldly. Grimly, she realised there was so much she didn't know about the world and the people in it.

'I'm going back inside.' She pushed past Timothy and he attempted to catch hold of her.

'Milly, wait. I'm sorry. I'm sorry. I shouldn't have said that. I was just frustrated. You know how much I love you. I want to marry you. I can't help it that you drive me wild.'

'Don't tell me I should take it as a compliment,' she barked over her shoulder. 'That won't wash.'

'No, you're right. I was out of line.' His tone was warm once again. Entreating. 'You won't say anything, will you? Please?' He finally caught hold of her wrist, pulling her around to face him. 'Please?'

'Why? Because you'd most likely be sacked?'

'I just need to learn to control me – me passion. No one's ever made me feel the way you do, Milly. Honest. Let me make it up to you.'

Rage flared inside and her breathing became uneven. 'Are you mad? After all those horrible things you said, you just want to carry on as before?'

He ran a hand through his hair. 'Just words, Milly. Stupid words. I didn't mean 'em.'

Her expression, even in the fading light, must have shown how much she didn't believe him. 'Just leave me alone, Timothy.'

He adjusted his collar and slipped his hands into his pockets. They could have been having a chat about anything, his posture was so relaxed. 'If you say anything,' he said coldly, sounding more like Jack from the Sunrise Club than the man she'd known, 'I'd have to tell them what your mum does for a living – Helen's suspicions. Which might be right, by the way. I might even have to tell them that your mum stole from Buckingham Palace when you took her places she shouldn't have been. That wouldn't go down well, would it?'

Milly froze. 'What? How dare you! First of all, Helen's wrong.'

He gave a cold laugh. 'She ain't, Milly. Met her type before, ain't I? Could see it as soon as I walked into that snooty hotel in Kensington.'

She ignored him, though the words rang around her head. 'And my mum never took anything from the palace.'

'Oh Milly,' he replied, his voice dripping with sarcasm. 'Loyal little Milly. D'you not see she had something under her coat?'

'Of course she didn't. You're wrong.'

'Afraid I'm not. Felt it when I touched her side, didn't I?'

'Rubbish. What do you think she stole?'

He shrugged. 'Don't really matter, does it? But there was something small and hard under her coat and it wasn't part of her clothes, I can promise you that.'

'Well, you'd know all about getting under women's clothes. But I don't believe you. She wouldn't do something like that. And why would she need to?' There'd been nothing in that guest room to steal and if she'd taken one of the candlesticks or vases Milly would have seen. She drowned out Timothy's words with an accusation of her own. 'You're just saying anything you can think of so I don't report you.'

He chuckled, the cold hardness of it matching the freezing night air. 'Think that if you like, Milly. Truth is, if you report me, what'll they say? I don't want them to think badly of you but – well – you've already got a warning for being slack and if they thought you was the daughter of a stealing whore . . .' He let the sentence die and with it all her hopes he was wrong. 'The shame, Milly. You'd be out on your ear. Edie too. It'd kill her.'

A red-hot fire pushed out the freezing cold. How had she ever found him attractive? How had she ever have wished to be with this man? She'd confided in him, and he was using her words against her – and not just against her, against Edie too. Her aunt had been right about him all along. Right again.

She wrenched her arm away from Timothy's grasp. 'You're disgusting. I won't say anything, Timothy, but you'd better leave me alone. Do you understand? Don't speak to me, don't even look at me.'

She thought of Robert and his shyness, unable to imagine him ever treating someone so horribly. It wasn't in his nature.

He sighed and began speaking as if none of their previous conversation had happened. 'Don't say anything and I won't. It's that simple. I enjoyed taking you out, Milly, but maybe it's better we don't see each other again. I reckon we're not really suited.'

He strode ahead, back to the glittering lights of the palace, and she let him, glad to see him go. She made it back inside using the last of her energy and hurried to her room. She suddenly realised she'd forgotten her promise to Edie, but she couldn't see her now. Not in this state. All she wanted was to curl up in her bed. To snuggle into the pillows and forget the day had ever happened. Yet her familiar world was alien and she felt utterly friendless. Lost at sea.

Tonight, the palace didn't feel like home any more.

Nowhere did.

Chapter Twenty-Four

Timothy's words had burned within Milly's brain since the night they were spoken. For days she'd tried to ignore them and wanted to think him a liar, but, she realised now, something had happened when he'd touched her mum's side. She'd been a fool. His lingering looks at Jean had been admiring, which was a deceit in itself, and his touching her hadn't been an accident either, only he'd discovered more than he'd bargained for. Was there another explanation? Surely her mum wouldn't do that to her. If she'd needed more money, she would have asked for it, and if she'd wanted a souvenir, which Milly wasn't sure she had, she could have asked for one.

On Saturday evening, Milly found herself once more on her way to the Sunrise Club. She had to find out one way or another. She'd never wanted to set foot in the place again, especially alone, but she couldn't ask Robert to accompany her. Foreboding burned in her stomach, making her muscles twitch, but no matter how scared she was, she didn't want him to think she only used him when she needed something. Their friendship had been more than a little one-way of late and she was determined to prove that he meant more to her than that. So she was here alone, biting her lip to ensure the nerves didn't turn her feet around and march her back towards the palace.

Rain battered the pavement, and she hunkered down against the wind. She had no intention of stopping for a drink. She simply wanted to speak to Jean and hear her reassurance that Timothy was wrong. As soon as she'd heard that she could leave, go home, back to the palace and forget all about it.

The route was familiar to her now and she hurried down the dark staircase into the cellar bar grateful to be out of the gale. As usual, the place was alive with laughter and raised voices. Dancers were swinging both on and off stage and everywhere she turned she was surrounded by people dangerously close to one another. She peered around. There was no sign of Jack, and she relaxed a little as she wormed her way through the throng to her mum. She was with a man, and Milly searched for any signs that Timothy, and indeed Helen, could have been right.

'Mum?'

'Mum?' exclaimed the doughy man next to her.

Anger flew across Jean's face; then she tossed her head back and laughed. 'It's a nickname, darling, do calm down.' She placed a hand over her heart as the laugh subsided. 'You men are so literal. Honestly, you have no imagination.' Jean spun on the chair and hopped down, taking hold of Milly's arm and dragging her to the other side of the room. She tried to pull her arm free from Jean's vice-like grip.

'Mum, you're hurting me.'

'You can't call me that here, Milly. How many times?' She

let go, smoothing down her dress. 'Now, what're you doing here? I didn't expect to see you tonight.'

'I had to come. I really must speak with you.'

She laughed. 'You're very dramatic sometimes, darling, but then Edie always was too.'

Milly was so busy checking around that the words only registered a few seconds later. 'Edie isn't dramatic. She's the most down-to-earth person I know.'

'Really? Well, she was as a child.'

'Is Jack here tonight?' She peered around her again.

'Jack? No, I don't think so. Please don't start all that nonsense again, Milly. If it's Jack you wanted to speak to me about then—'

'It's not.' Though relief swept through her at his absence, Milly still wanted to be out of there as soon as possible. She came straight to the point. 'When I spoke to Timothy the other day, he accused you of stealing something from the palace. Something from the guest room we went into. You didn't, did you?'

Jean's face froze; another emotion, fleeting and vague, crossed her eyes before anger regained control. 'That nice young man of yours said that? Whyever would he think so?'

'He said he felt something underneath your coat when he touched your side, which I'm not sure was an accident.'

'You don't think he did it on purpose?'

'Possibly.'

'But he's your beau.'

'Not any more.'

Jean visibly relaxed. 'Ah, I see. You two have had a tiff

and he's hitting out like all men do when their pride is wounded. What happened?'

Milly took a breath and explained. Jean blew out a long trail of smoke. 'Well, I can partly understand. A man can only hold out for so long, Milly, and you shouldn't tease.'

That her mum would side with Timothy knocked the wind from her. 'I wasn't teasing him.'

'Clearly that's not what he thinks.'

Jean's words left Milly cold. She just wanted to get out. The air was cloying with alcohol and smoke, suffocating her.

Her mother continued: 'I can't believe he'd say something like that.'

'So you didn't take anything from the palace?'

'Of course I didn't, darling. How could you ask me that? It really is hurtful that you'd even think it possible. I mean, why would I? I'm not that much of a fan of the royal family. I – I am quite offended, Milly.' She wiped at the corner of her eye and guilt flooded Milly's body.

'I'm sorry, Mum. I knew you wouldn't have, but what could he have felt underneath your coat?'

'What did he say it felt like?'

'Something small and hard.'

'What a stupid boy.' Jean spat the words out. She looked around at the flock of people dancing, at the band, their bodies swaying with the rhythm as they played their instruments. She leaned into Milly so she could lower her voice. 'I hate having to admit this, but I can see I haven't a choice – and if you breathe a word to another living soul, I swear, Milly, I will never see you again.'

'What is it?' Milly asked, fear growing inside her. Jean

was almost as formidable as the Master of the Household. Or Edie.

'It was my girdle.'

'Your—'

'Yes,' Jean snapped.

'But why would it be small and hard?'

'He probably touched some of the boning. It's a rather old-fashioned design but as we get older a woman needs something . . . sturdy to help keep her shape. If the silly boy didn't know what it was it goes to show he isn't as experienced with women as he thinks he is.'

Though Milly had never really believed it could be true, a wave of relief – one so strong she could have drowned beneath it – hit her. Timothy was wrong, as she'd known he would be. He was cruel and hurtful and would say anything to try and excuse his own behaviour.

'I didn't think you needed anything like that. You're so slim.'

'That's so sweet of you, but life can be cruel sometimes and extra weight around the middle seems to be our curse. Just look at your Aunt Edie.'

'I didn't mean to embarrass you. I'm sorry, Mum.' She said the last word quietly.

'Can we forget about this awful subject now then?'

'Yes, of course.'

'Good. Now, it's lovely to see you, darling, but I really must get back to work.'

'I was going to head off anyway.' She leaned forwards and gave her mum a kiss on the cheek. Jean seemed shocked by such a display of affection.

'What was that for?'

'For trusting me with your secret. Good night, Jean.'

Her eyes wide at what had passed between them, Jean responded mechanically but Milly gave her a reassuring smile as she waved goodbye, climbing the stairs into the dark and rainy night, relieved that she could now put both the Sunrise Club and Timothy's horrible accusation behind her.

February 1952

Chapter Twenty-Five

The King was dead.

On 6 February, as Milly, Edie and Caroline began their day, news came that the King had died at Sandringham some time in the night.

As day broke, the Royal Household was in chaos. People were darting back and forth, unsure where to go or what to do until the Master of the Household gathered everyone in the ballroom to break the news. His eyes found Milly and Caroline in the throng, staying on them as if in warning. Her stomach churned, leaving her sickened and queasy.

As he said the words, Edie fell against Milly for support and nearly every single member of staff, both male and female, were either crying or holding back tears. Those that weren't were working their jaws hard to stop the emotion rising to the surface. Robert comforted Mrs Chadwick, Mr Newington slipped an arm around Edie's shoulders, drawing her to him, and Caroline and Milly clung tightly to each other.

The royal family had returned to Buckingham Palace at the end of January, and then promptly left again for Sandringham. Before they'd gone, Milly had seen the King and Queen walking in the gardens. He'd been gaunt, nothing but skin and bone, the angles of his face sharp, his cheeks sallow, flesh thin. The voice that had sounded so weak on the radio had been even weaker and a permanent grimace had marred his features.

Yet the reality of his death was still a shock. As if the foundation of their lives had vanished.

'How did Princess Elizabeth take it?' someone asked.

'You mean Her Majesty?' the Master corrected. From the moment the King passed she had become Queen at the age of only twenty-five, the burden of not only the country but of every nation in the Commonwealth on her shoulders. 'Her Majesty and, indeed, all the royal family, are of course, devastated by the news. However, Her Majesty is said to have reacted with her usual grace and composure. She was informed by the Duke of Edinburgh, and they are now travelling back from Kenya.'

'She'll be heartbroken she wasn't with him,' Edie whispered to Milly.

Queen Elizabeth, as she now was, and the Duke of Edinburgh had departed for Kenya a week before. The papers had commented then on how sick the King had looked as he'd seen them off. The night before their departure, he'd attended a performance of *South Pacific* at the Theatre Royal, Drury Lane, and the papers had been full of his frailty. Milly had yearned to tell Edie about the handkerchief as she'd grown ever more certain a miracle was what the King's ailing body needed. It hadn't arrived and now they were left with a gaping hole in the world they'd known.

'Poor love,' Edie said. 'She'll live here now.'

Of course, Milly thought, her mind visualising all the changes that lay ahead. Elizabeth didn't have the option of living anywhere else. Milly determined to ensure the palace was as beautiful as any of them could make it. It was going to be hard enough for her to step into her father's shoes.

'And poor Queen Mary,' Caroline said, wiping her nose. 'Losing her husband and her son. My ma and pa say a parent should never outlive their own child. It must fair break her heart.'

Milly's heart broke for them all. For Princess Elizabeth, now the Queen. For Princess Margaret, who probably wished she hadn't added to his stress, and for—

'The King's widow,' the Master continued. 'Will now be known as Queen Elizabeth The Queen Mother.'

They'd always been so in love. Such a close family even if they'd had their fair share of rows. 'She must be distraught,' Milly whispered.

'Do you know the hardest thing?' Edie said, turning to her. 'None of them are allowed to show it. It's all that stiff-upper-lip, no-cryin'-in-public nonsense. Why? Why shouldn't they be allowed to sob like the rest of us?' She wiped her eyes with a handkerchief. The royal family would all be expected to rein in their emotions and set a dignified example but there was nothing wrong with showing your feelings.

The Master gave them all the relevant information, confirming more would come over the coming hours, and sent them on their way. With the new Queen arriving the next day, work was to continue as normal and there'd be visits to the palace all day from politicians and ambassadors, people paying their respects, but shock filled them all as they attempted to go about their daily duties.

Outside the palace, as the news spread around the world, the busy metropolis was eerily quiet. Along the Mall cars stopped in the streets, and in the city theatres, cinemas, restaurants and clubs all closed as a mark of respect. Crowds gathered outside, as they had months before when news came that the King was seriously ill. Not only because King George VI had restored the nation's trust in the monarchy after the abdication, but because everyone knew what a kind, noble and generous man he was.

Milly, Caroline and Edie huddled at a window to watch the notice of His Majesty's passing be taken out by two footmen and pinned to the palace gate. A moment of history marked. A gun salute from Hyde Park could be heard and at just before one o'clock, the white blinds of the palace were pulled. The world had stopped and wouldn't start again for nine days.

They worked in a daze, barely speaking, and when their work was finished, Milly, Caroline and Edie went back to Edie's room and listened to the wireless. Tributes poured in from America, France, Canada: every nation wishing to pay their respects. Special editions of the newspapers were printed with updates on the country's national period of mourning and details of the King's funeral.

Later that night, at nine o'clock, everyone gathered in the Household Lounge to listen to Winston Churchill, the Prime Minister, make his address to the nation. Unable to hold back the tears at the moving and heartfelt tribute, Milly and Edie cried openly, holding hands and reassuring each other that after fifteen difficult years on the throne the King, who had been taken far too soon, was at least now at peace.

A few days after the King's death, on Milly's Saturday off, she walked down Piccadilly, buffeted by a winter wind cold and full of petrol fumes. The world was slowly returning to normal as the initial shock wore off. Businesses were beginning to open again and hectic morning commutes and evening returns home were framing the days once more. She was off to visit Hatchards to buy a book, something to take her mind off the uncertainty and strangeness of the world around her. She'd thought of asking Caroline if she could borrow *Love in a Cold Climate* but didn't want it to seem as though she'd only given her it so she could read it too.

She entered the shop, relieved the smell of cars and buses was replaced by that of paper and print. She began searching the shelves, reading the titles on the spines and examining the covers. The trouble was, she much preferred magazines and something like the latest *Tatler* or *Vogue* would be much more entertaining.

Just as she was leaving, a man attempted to enter the shop. With his head down and his hat low over his eyes, he almost bumped into her, muttering an apology as she leapt out of the way. Milly stepped back into the street and went further down towards the magazine seller on the corner. Something about the man had been familiar but she couldn't think what. Perhaps he'd crossed the road at the same time as her. She wasn't sure why anything about him should be noticeable. He'd worn a bowler hat and raincoat the same as every other businessman hurrying about, and yet she remembered his small, dark, darting eyes.

Dodging the briefcases and umbrellas, Milly wandered further down Piccadilly. Seeing women together chatting and joking, she missed Helen. It had been a month since she'd spoken to her. She missed her laughter, missed her confident outlook on the world, missed her kindness. She'd tried to see her after the news had come about the King, but the telephone exchange had been like a madhouse and Milly hadn't had any time to hang around. If the last few days had taught her anything, it was that friends and family should be cherished. She'd make another visit to the exchange tomorrow and if that didn't work, she'd write.

Milly stopped at the magazine stand and scanned the racks for an eye-catching cover. None of the titles or pictures took her interest and, sighing, she moved away, wondering where to go next. Despite the wind, the rain had stayed away, and Milly headed in the direction of Regent Street to stare at the shop windows and the dresses she couldn't afford. Rather than follow the busier road of Piccadilly, she escaped down the quieter side roads of Sackville Street and Vigo Street.

As she passed one of the smaller alleyways, a hand gripped her arm tightly, painfully, pulling her away from the crowds. Within seconds she was alone and as she tried to call out another hand clamped over her mouth, muffling any and all sound. Panic rose in her throat, compounded by her inability to shout for help. The world swam by, blurred by the pace with which she was being dragged and the tears that had sprung unbidden to her eyes. Her breathing came in short, interrupted gasps as she tried to free herself, twisting her body and arms, anything to get away from him.

In seconds she was pinned in a doorway by the man with the bowler hat who'd gone into Hatchards as she was leaving. He stared at her, his dark eyes no longer darting but full of menace. One hand was still clamped over her mouth but the other flew in front of her face, a single finger jabbing towards her. Its tip had yellowed with tobacco, as if someone had dipped it in varnish; his fingernails were black with dirt.

'Don't scream and I won't have to hit ya. Got it? *Got it?*' he repeated, his voice low and grave.

Milly tried to bob her head. Her eyes flashed left and right, searching for the end of the alley, hoping to land on someone who could help. This was London. Someone must be walking past. Where were the chittering people shopping, the shop workers on their way to work? He'd dragged her down a tiny alley away from them all. The buildings overhead seemed to close together, blocking the sky and with it any chance of being seen.

'Now,' he continued, 'I'm gonna ask ya a question and if ya answer it honestly then I won't need to ask it again. And believe me, ya don't want me to ask it again. Right?'

It was difficult to nod with his hand pressed to her mouth, pushing her head against the brick of the wall, but she managed a small movement. His cheeks were pitted with acne marks and much, much worse. Tiny silver threads of scar tissue ran over his neck and round, puffy face. He could have been wounded in the war, but Milly didn't think this man had seen service, or if he had, he'd turned to something darker since the war ended. His nose was bulbous and red, thread-veined. The nose of a drinker, Edie would have said.

Edie.

She'd give anything to run to her now. To be held by her, to bury her head on her lap as she listened to the wireless. To have Edie stroke her hair as she had when she was a child. Tears spilled from Milly's eyes and ran down her cheeks.

When the man released his hand, moving it to the collar of her coat and pressing down to keep her from moving, she noticed her tears glistening on his skin.

'There. That's better, ain't it? Now don't do anythin' silly and I won't have to get me knife or me gun. There's a good girl.'

The mention of weapons sent her legs trembling violently. If he hadn't been pressing so hard on her chest she'd have fallen to the ground. All she had to do was answer his question. But who was he? Was this something to do with Jack and the Sunrise Club? Something to do with the palace? They'd all been warned that people might try and get information from them but to her knowledge, apart from the odd journalist hanging about the gate, no one had ever been approached like this. Her body shook uncontrollably, her breath lost, returning only when she remembered to breathe in and out.

'Now, I wanna know where Jean Venables is. And you're gonna tell me.'

In her fear and panic the name was foreign. 'Who?' He balled his fist, pulling it back as if readying to strike. Milly put her hands up to defend herself. 'I don't know who that is. Honestly.'

'Jean. Jean Venables. She might be Jean somethin' else now. She looks like ya, just older. We know she came here.'

Her mum. He was after her mum. Her stomach knotted. What had Jean done? Who were these people?

'You're gonna tell me her address.'

'I don't know it.'

'Ah! So ya do know who she is then.' He tutted. 'I've already told ya not to lie to me, missy.'

'Yes, I do know who she is. We're – we're friends.'

He banged his fist hard against the wall. The knuckles came back red and bloodied but he didn't even flinch. 'Don't lie to me, girl. We found a letter. Or a try at one.'

It was then his accent penetrated her ears. In the blindness of panic, she hadn't heard it before. He was from Birmingham where that first letter from her mum had come from.

'It weren't finished, but ya name were in it.' He grinned menacingly. 'Buckingham Palace, eh? Seems ya tart of a mother did ya a favour leavin' ya behind. Ya've done all right, ain't ya? Now,' he demanded through gritted teeth. 'Tell me where she lives.'

'I swear to you, I don't know. I've asked but she wouldn't tell me.' More tears began to spill down her cheeks.

'We been lookin' for her everywhere, *Milly*. She ain't up there no more. This is the only place she could be. It's where she came from. She's here, hidin' from me, and I'm gonna find her.'

The sound of her name issuing from the man's mouth sent a chill down her spine. She didn't know if she'd ever be able to hear it the same way again, as if it had been tainted by his voice, tarnished by his throat.

'I'm not gonna keep asking ya, girl. Ya lucky me patience has lasted this long. Where is she?'

Milly shook her head and saw the anger grow in his eyes as he assumed she was refusing, not that she didn't know. Quickly, she added, 'I promise I don't know. I'm telling the truth. We've only ever met at—' Her mind began to work quickly. She couldn't mention the club. If he'd known about that he'd have gone straight there. If she told him about the

Sunrise Club, he might wait for Jean there and then what would he do to her? Milly thought of the knife, of the gun, and trembled. 'She won't tell me where she lives. We've only ever met at coffee houses or for walks in the park.' His fist rose again and once more her legs almost gave way. 'Please.'

His arm pulled back. 'Why wouldn't she tell her daughter where she lives?'

'I don't know. She's always been shady about it.'

'Didn't want ya involved, probably.' He seemed to be thinking out loud. He didn't strike her as the quickest of fellas. She could imagine him as a child reading aloud, fumbling over the words as they formed and then joining the sentence together. 'Can't have known she left that scrap of paper behind, I reckon. She'd cleared out everythin' else, after all. She was clever, though, goin' back to Birmingham. Chased her all around we did. Led us on a merry old dance. Coventry, Leicester. Then doubled back thinkin' we'd give up on her and old Billy the Swindler.' His eyes suddenly darted back to her face, losing the glazed look they'd had in thought. 'When ya seein' her next?'

'We haven't arranged anything yet. She said she'd drop a note into the palace.'

That wasn't true, but he wouldn't be able to do anything to her or her mum near the palace, there were too many guards, too many policemen, and they were there day and night.

'Look me in the eye and tell me ya don't know where she is.' He stared at her, widening his eyes so his heavy brow folded together. His eyes were almost black, dark with malevolence and like nothing she'd ever seen before. He leaned in, the pressure on her chest increasing as his weight pushed against it.

'I promise,' she replied, another tear falling down her cheek, her voice quivering. 'I don't know where she lives.' She prayed her sincerity would come through. He had to believe her.

He did nothing for a moment, then the strain eased from her breastbone as he straightened. 'All right, Milly. Here's what I'm gonna do. You're gonna wait till ya see ya mum and you're gonna tell her that Ray's looking for her. Ray Turnsell. And the boss wants his money back.'

Back? What did he mean *back*? Had Billy repeated his mistake and taken a loan from the wrong sort of person before he died? Had Jean? Or maybe Edie had been right after all. He'd called Billy the Swindler and he must have done something to deserve that name.

'You're gonna tell her', he continued, 'that she's to take what she and Billy owe to the Golden Hotel in Ganton Street and ask for Mr John Smith. D'ya know where Ganton Street is?' he asked almost civilly as if she were a tourist and he about to give her directions. 'Off Carnaby Street.'

Milly felt relief begin to loosen her terrified muscles. He was about to let her go. This would soon be over.

'And one last thing, Milly – and it's the important bit, so ya pay attention now. Ya gonna tell her that we know where ya live – her daughter – and ya can't stay in Buckingham Palace forever. Ya gotta leave sometime – to go to the pictures, step out with ya young man, go shoppin' for all those things ladies like to have. And if ya mum don't give us what

293

we're owed, we're gonna find ya and we're gonna make ya pay instead. Got it?'

As the words came tumbling from his mouth, his lips lifting on one side to form a terrifying, lopsided smile, her heart hammered against her ribcage. Vomit rose from her stomach, the acid liquid burning her throat. Her chest rose and fell with quickened breaths, the world spinning as she grew lightheaded.

'Ya got all that?'

She croaked an incoherent answer.

'Sure? Tell me the name and address again.'

He'd have done this before. Made other victims recite his words back to him to prove they'd understood. 'The Golden Hotel, Ganton Street, just off Carnaby. Mr John Smith.'

'And what's my real name?'

'Ray. Ray Turnsell.'

'Good girl. And don't go runnin' to the pigs, Milly. Like I said, ya gotta leave some time and if ya do, when I find ya or ya mum – and I will find ya *both* again – it'll be worse. Much, much worse than if she just gives us the money. Got it?'

'Yes. I understand.' Her voice was feeble. She didn't sound like herself; it was as if the words had come from another body, another mouth.

He stepped away, released his hand from her chest and put both in his pockets, pushing the trench coat back to find them. Then, as if in some grotesque parody of a gentleman, he tipped his hat and began to whistle as he walked away.

Chapter Twenty-Six

Milly didn't leave the alley straight away. Her heart was pounding so violently she thought it would give out. Now he'd gone, the queasiness subsided but the trembling in her legs remained. She dried her face, wiping the moisture away with her hand and willing the tears to stop. Noises emerged from her throat: gasps, sobs, strange exclamations of sound. She told herself to calm down and take slow, even breaths. A few moments later she felt more like herself and knew the next step had to be deciding what to do next.

Ray wasn't waiting at the end of the alley for her, she was sure. He'd turned left, out of sight and away. He knew she'd do what he asked. Knew the fear in her had been too strong and his threat too real: he would do whatever was necessary to get the money he was owed. She had to warn her mum. She had to find her before he did. He wouldn't stop looking just because he'd delivered his message to Milly. He wasn't a patient man, willing to wait. She had to find out what was going on.

Milly checked her watch. It was just after eleven. Her mum would most likely still be asleep if she'd worked the night before. Milly needed her home address and surely the Sunrise Club would have it. Taking another deep breath to calm her still racing heartbeat, she lurched to the end of the alley and regained her bearings. The world seemed to have turned on its axis. She made her way to the busy thorough-fare of Regent Street, eager to be near crowds, surrounded by the comfort of people, and stuck to the main roads until she made it to Soho and the Sunrise Club.

The black, heavy doorway reminded her instantly of the one she'd just been threatened in and fear rose once more. Would Jack be there? He'd scared her before but that was nothing compared to the terror Ray had instilled in her. She banged on the closed door and when no one answered, she hammered even harder.

'Hello? Hello? Is there anyone there?'

From somewhere beyond a noise emerged and she lis-tened closely as it grew louder. Someone was climbing the wooden staircase. A moment later, the door opened.

'Yes? We're not open yet, love. You'll have to come back later.' It was Robert's friend, the barman.

'No. I can't. I'm sorry but I need to talk to you now. It's important.'

'Is this about Robert? Is he OK?'

His concern for sweet, kind Robert made the faintest smile lift Milly's mouth. 'Robert's fine. I need to talk to you about something else. Please, please can I come in?'

She glanced around the street, looking for a bowler hat, a trench coat. How long had he been following her before he'd grabbed her? Hours? Days? No, it couldn't be. If it had, he'd have acted before now. If he'd been able to, she couldn't imagine him stopping himself. She'd been out with Jean only a day before. If he'd been in town then, he'd have found her already and wouldn't be bothering Milly. No, he must have just arrived and lucky for him it had been Milly's day off.

'You'd better come downstairs.'

The barman turned in the doorway and began his descent into the club. The crimson walls were gaudy in the daylight and Milly was grateful to reach the cellar bar to find no one there but the barman. He returned to the job he'd been doing before she arrived, stacking bottles behind the bar. The place hadn't been touched since the night before and the air smelled of spilled beer, the slightly medicinal aroma of spirits and unemptied ashtrays.

'What's your name?' she asked. She knew she'd heard it before but couldn't remember it in her panic.

'George.'

'That's right. I'm Milly.'

They shook hands over the counter. 'Yes, I know. Robert talks about you a lot.' How Milly wished he was with her now! 'What can I do for you?'

'I need to know where your singer, Jean Beaumont, lives.'

'Jean? You mean your mum?'

'Robert told you?'

'He mentioned it. He wasn't gossiping, mind. Just asking a few questions for you.' He peered at the door near the stage. 'He said you wanted to know some stuff about Jack.'

'I do, but right now, I really need to know where Jean lives. Is it on some paperwork somewhere?'

'Paperwork?' The preposterous idea made him laugh. 'This isn't the type of place that has paperwork.'

'Then how can I find her?'

'You don't know?'

'I wouldn't be asking if I did.' She hadn't meant to be sharp, but her nerves were frayed with no comfort in sight until she'd found and spoken to her mum. 'There's nothing you can tell me that might help?'

He stopped stacking bottles and leaned on the counter. 'She's said before that it's a boarding house. She's moaned about her room being tiny, barely large enough to swing a cat. And she said it's full of theatricals. It must be fairly nearby because once she was saying it only took her a few minutes to get to work so she could sleep in until the last minute. Oh, and I'm sure she's mentioned a barber's. Don't know if it's above one or next to one or just has one nearby but she definitely talked about that.'

That was more information than she could have hoped for. It was certainly far more than Jean had ever given her, even unwittingly, but at least she knew where to start looking. It had to be here in Soho, near one of the theatres. There were a lot of boarding houses around this area, many of them full of actors and actresses either looking for a job or working in one of the West End shows. She'd just have to make a start at the first one she came across and keep going.

'Thank you, George. That's very helpful.'

'Oh, and about Jack?'

'Yes, what can you tell me about him?'

'He comes from the East End originally.' The mention of that part of London sent a chill down her spine. 'His dad was quite a big gangster back in the day, during the war. Black-market stuff, lending money, all that sort of thing. He's dead now, but Jack's carrying on the family business. As soon as he was in charge, he started buying clubs here, said this was where the money was after the East End got bombed to bits. Don't worry though, you'll be all right as long as you stay on the right side of him.'

The right side. She was, but her mum certainly wasn't. If he was carrying on his father's legacy, that might mean he'd recognised Jean and would soon be making good on the threats they'd made all those years ago. And worse, Jean seemed to have no idea how close she'd come to paying for Billy's mistake. Milly's stomach dropped. If her encounter with Ray earlier had told her anything, it was that gangsters' debts weren't ever forgotten.

'Are you all right? You've gone really pale.'

'I'm fine.' She had to find Jean. Now.

'Will we see you later then? Robert won't be around, he's working, but Jean's due back tonight. Got herself a few admirers, she has, doesn't have to pay for a drink all night. She could teach some of these younger girls a few tricks.' He chuckled to himself, but his words left a sour taste in her mouth.

Had Edie been right about everything after all? Had Jean taken up with a conman? In love she may have been, but the evidence so far suggested Billy wasn't someone who'd taken a loan from the wrong sort. People didn't get the nickname 'the Swindler' for nothing. And if Jean had lied about him, how much more had she lied about? All the uneasiness Milly had buried in her desperation to build a relationship with her mum – her shock at her behaviour both at work and in the palace, the signs she'd refused to acknowledge, the warnings from the people who loved her – rose. She felt sick again.

'You won't see me later,' she replied. She'd said it before but this time she truly meant it. She had no intention of coming back to the Sunrise Club ever again.

Milly emerged into the daylight, the sky pale, covered in grey clouds. She hoped it wouldn't rain, but the gathering breeze signalled otherwise. At least it might blow away the traces of ash and ale clinging to her beautiful coat.

She spent the next hour scouring the streets of Soho, trying her best to work in an orderly fashion, avoiding doubling back on herself. The rain began to fall, heavily at first, soaking her coat and hat as she hid in doorways and under lintels. She swept her blonde hair, now almost brown from the rain, back from her face. Cigarette butts and empty packets surrounded her feet as she waited in the doorway of a tobacconist's but, unable to let any more minutes tick by, she brushed the rain from her face once more and stepped back into the road. It was only rain after all, she wouldn't die if she got wet, but she might die if she didn't deliver this message and find out what exactly was going on. Milly dashed along, the incessant drizzle dampening her already wet clothes.

Eventually she found a boarding house a few streets away from the Lyric Theatre, opposite a barber's, the red and white striped barber's pole bright against the blackened, smog-stained building. The rain had eased off to a mere dankness but she was soaked to the skin and shivering. Mrs Dean's boarding house, as the sign on the railings proclaimed, was squalid and dirty with a grimy, black front door and three storeys of soot-smeared red brick. A handwritten sign in a ground-floor window stated: 'No Blacks. No Irish.'

She didn't want to enter this horrid place. She couldn't believe her mum was living here. It was a far cry from Milly's own life in Buckingham Palace and she wondered how she could have ever, for one second, forgotten to be grateful. A prison it definitely wasn't. The only prison she was in was one of her own creation. She stepped forwards and lifted the heavy iron knocker, banging it down twice. The sound seemed to echo through the house and a matronly woman wearing a floral apron and with her hair tied in a headscarf answered the door.

'Can I 'elp yer? We've no rooms, I'm afraid. I'm all booked out. Couldn't squeeze anyone else in if I tried.' Her cockney accent was stronger than Caroline's and remnants of the pink lipstick she'd applied that morning clung to her yellowing teeth.

'I was looking for Jean Beaumont. Is this her lodgings?'

'Jean Beaumont?' She thought for a moment, tapping a raw, red finger against her lips. 'Don't think I've got a Jean Beaumont. Got a Jean Barnes but not a Beaumont.'

Barnes was Edie's surname, her mum's maiden name. She must have used a different name for her lodgings. Another measure to avoid being found. It had to be her. 'Oh, yes, sorry. I forgot. Beaumont is her stage name. Is she in? I'm her – a friend of hers.'

'She's asleep, I think, but yer welcome to go up if yer like. These theatrical types are like foxes. Sleep through the day and only come out at night. That's why I make 'em clean their own rooms. I'm not waitin' up till eleven o'clock at night just ter sweep the floors. Well, you comin' in or ain'tcha?'

Milly would if she stood aside and stopped talking. As the woman hadn't moved, she nodded in response.

'I'm Mrs Dean. Pleased ter meet yer.' She finally turned, allowing Milly just enough room to squeeze by.

'Milly. Milly Hendry.'

'It's up the stairs ter the second floor, third door on yer left.'

Milly thanked her and climbed the steep, precarious staircase, the treads creaking and moaning under her feet. She held tightly to the banister as the floor protested; she could almost hear it threatening to give way. At the top she counted the doors as she made her way along the tattered carpet covering the landing floor. She knocked and waited for an answer. Impatiently, she knocked again.

'All right, I'm coming.' It was her mum's voice and movement from behind the door signalled she was dressing. The door flung open as Jean exclaimed, 'If you're chasing your rent again, Mrs Dean, I've already told you that – Oh, Milly. It's you. What are you doing here? Who gave you my address?' She stepped out into the corridor, pulling the door closed behind her.

Milly caught the smell of stale alcohol on her breath while cigarettes and perfume carried from the air of the room. 'I need to talk to you, Mum.' Her teeth were beginning to chatter from her sodden clothes.

'You're soaked, Milly. You better get yourself home rather than hanging about here.'

'Can't I come in and dry off?' She pointed at the door. 'I need to speak with you. It's urgent.'

'I wish you could, but now's not a good time, darling. I

302

need to go back to bed. Who did you say gave you my address?'

'I didn't. I went to see George at the Sunrise Club, he told me what he knew and I found you.'

Jean looked up and down the corridor before stepping back towards the door. 'Well, I'm at the club tonight. You can come and see me there.'

'No,' Milly replied firmly, ignoring the chattering of her teeth. 'I need to speak to you now. I was attacked, in the street, this morning, by someone looking for you.'

At this Jean's face paled. The remnants of last night's make-up, the dark kohl around her eyes, gave her a ghostly appearance as she stood there in her nightdress. 'Well, it must be some mistake, Milly. Or a joke.'

'A joke? This man wasn't joking, Mum, and he had a Birmingham accent.'

She grabbed Milly's arm and hauled her into the room, slamming the door shut behind them and running immediately to the window. Milly noticed a view of the street below. Had Jean asked for that specifically?

'What happened?' Jean demanded.

She hadn't asked Milly to take off her wet coat. She hadn't offered her a towel to dry her hair. There was a hard wooden chair in one corner of the tiny room and Milly sat on it, the wet fabric of her clothes scratching the back of her legs. Milly's heart was racked with pain as she realised her mum might as well be a stranger for how much she knew her. It had all been an act.

'So you still think it's a joke or a mistake? Just like it was all those years ago with Billy and the loan shark?'

Jean's gaze darted between the window and Milly. 'Tell me what happened,' she snapped.

Her anger rising, Milly relayed the whole incident in as much detail as she could remember.

'Ray? He definitely said his name was Ray.'

'It's not something I'm likely to forget. Ray Turnsell. And his boss wants his money back.' Jean scoffed and Milly shot to standing, anger pulsing through her veins. She'd sacrificed her bond with Edie, the woman who'd been a true mother to her, for a mum she wasn't sure actually existed. Shame fuelled her anger. 'How can you scoff at a moment like this? I was threatened. He said he'd stab or shoot me. How can you be so selfish?'

'It's not selfishness, Milly. It's survival.'

'What is? What's going on, Mum?' Her use of the word Mum shocked Jean from her position at the window and she staggered forwards, collapsing on to the bed. 'What money is he talking about? Tell me the truth.'

Jean stared at Milly, searching her face. Milly could see the wheels turning in her mind as she tried to come up with a lie. Some reasonable explanation as to why gangsters were after her for money again. 'It's not what you think,' she began, but Milly cut her off.

'Excuse me, Jean, but I'm not stupid. The only reason that gangster doesn't know you work at the Sunrise Club is because I had the good sense not to tell him, but do you think it'll be long before he finds out? He's threatened my life, he's threatened yours, so don't give me the first load of guff you can think of. Tell me the truth. All of it.'

In her fury her body had warmed, but as she watched

Jean the freezing air of the unheated room swam around her causing her teeth to chatter again.

'All right. All right. Billy was a musician and a – a con-man.' She spat the words out venomously. 'This is all his fault.'

Milly shook her head. 'You need to start at the beginning. What happened when I was little? Were you cheating on Dad?'

'No!'

'Don't lie to me,' Milly yelled. 'I know you didn't love him. Edie was right, wasn't she?'

'No, I didn't love him. Your father was boring. All he wanted was to stay at home and raise a family.' The polished tones fell away as the real Jean came through. 'He wanted us to 'ave more children. Four he wanted in total. Four! I wished I'd never married 'im. I wish—' She broke off, but Milly finished the sentence for her.

'You wish you'd never had me.'

Jean turned away. 'Maybe I would've liked children one day, but I wasn't ready then and turns out I'm not ready now.'

'You're forty-three.'

'So?'

If she wasn't ready now, she never would be, but Milly bit back the words. 'So you cheated on him and ran off with your fancy man. Edie was right, wasn't she? That Billy got a doctor to sign a death certificate and they buried another body in your place all so you could run away with Billy the Swindler.' The pain in Milly's heart was so intense it almost took her breath away. 'What had he done? What had *you* done?'

305

'Me? I didn't do anything except fall in love with a scoundrel. Billy tried a con with some East End gangsters – a man called Walter Klink – and it didn't work. He got caught. They were going to kill him. We had to get away.'

'What's Jack's surname?'

'Jack? Why?'

'What is it?'

'I don't know. Why should I know that? He's just Jack.'

'Because he's Walter Klink's son,' Milly shouted, leaning forwards in her chair. 'I got George the barman to do some digging. Jack's the son of an East End gangster. His father's dead but he's taken on the family business and moved it out of the East End.'

'So? That doesn't mean he's Walter's son. There was more than one low life around during the war, I can tell you.'

'Don't be stupid, Mum. It can't be coincidence. He's been too interested in you from the start. He comes from the East End, his father was a gangster, and if you're that sure, why don't you ask him?' Jean didn't say anything, just crossed her arms over her chest. 'Can you really risk him figuring out who you really are? Leaving all those years ago, it wasn't about keeping me safe, was it? You left me behind because you didn't want me around. It was just an excuse to go back to being free.'

'I wasn't ready to be a mother,' she muttered, but the pathetic excuse wouldn't wash.

'You should have thought of that before you had me,' Milly snarled, watching as Jean pulled at the loose threads on the blanket covering the bed. 'And what happened when you went up north?'

'Nothing.' She shrugged. 'Not at first. We lived our lives, Billy playing piano, me singing. Everything was fine until the money ran out. He always did like the good life.'

'Sounds like you both did.'

Jean cast a hand out. 'Look at me now though, hey? Living in this squalid little hell hole. We had to move to a place like this in Birmingham. Living with God knows who, all of us in tiny rooms like mice in boxes. He couldn't take it. So he decided to rehash an old con. He'd done it hundreds of times, he said. It couldn't go wrong, but it did. I should've known it would. He'd always been arrogant. It was one of the things I loved about him at first, but Ray's boss ain't no fool. He saw through it all but by then Billy had gone. Left me in the middle of the night with no money.'

Milly shot to standing. 'He's not dead? You lied about that too?'

'I had to. You wouldn't have cared if I'd told you the truth. That I made another mistake. The man's like a cat with nine lives. Or a cockroach. When the world ends it'll just be him and them sitting in the ashes.'

Her hard, angry tone was mirrored in her face. Her mouth pursed. Refusing to allow tears to form, Milly swallowed. 'Has anything that's come out of your mouth these last few months been true?'

Jean kept her head down, unable to meet her eye. No, nothing had been true.

'When Billy left me, I panicked. I had no idea where he'd gone or with who, but I knew they'd be coming after us both. I tried to stay up there. I didn't know if it was even safe to come back to London, but eventually I ran out of options.

It'd been ten years. Walter was fifty when he was in charge down here. I figured he was probably dead now and even if he wasn't, as long as I stayed out of the East End I'd be fine.'

'And what about the money you owed up north?'

'I thought if I could make contact with you, I could get something from the palace and get some money that way.'

'You—' Her breath vanished. 'Timothy was right. You did steal from the palace, didn't you?'

'I had to.'

'It wasn't your girdle at all, was it? Do you even wear one?'

Jean didn't answer, but subconsciously her hand went to her slim stomach.

Milly's eyes skimmed the floor. A girdle wasn't among the clothes littered there. Another lie. 'What did you take?'

'That small photograph of the King on the bedside cabinet. Not that there was any point – it wasn't worth anything near what I thought it'd be. The man didn't even believe it had come from Buckingham Palace. I thought it would have something on it to show it was. Stupid old fool.'

Milly shook her head, unable to believe what she was hearing. After everything Jean had said, she still only cared about herself and how badly the world had treated her. 'What man? What did you do with it?'

'I sold it.'

'To who?'

'To a pawnbroker in Frith Street.'

'And what did you do with the money?' Seeing the opened packet of stockings on the floor, Milly already knew the answer. 'Is there any of it left?'

'A little. I had to buy those. For my job.'

'Your job? I could lose everything.' Pain, regret, guilt and anger seared across Milly's heart.

'If they find me and I've got nothing to give them, I'm looking at losing my life, Milly. What else was I supposed to do?' She twisted the gold bangle on her wrist.

'I don't know,' Milly replied. Any sympathy she had left for her mum faded as she recalled the new hat and lipstick, her fine nails and the jewellery on her wrist. Why wasn't she working as many jobs as possible to scrape together enough to pay them something? 'If you were that desperate you could have not bought yourself gold bracelets and fancy hats or stockings.'

'I deserve those things,' Jean insisted. 'I work hard. I always have. Do you think it's easy doing what I do?'

Milly saw the woman Edie had described clearly in front of her. The selfish, spoiled child who thought only of herself.

'You should be grateful,' Jean exclaimed. 'I could have taken something far more valuable, something that would have been missed.'

'Grateful? I should be *grateful* you stole from my employer?' Milly flung her hands in the air. All those months ago, anger and pain had battled inside when Edie had told her the truth about Jean, and now those emotions filled her again; but this time she could understand exactly why Edie had hidden that truth for so long. 'I could lose my job – my home. I've already received a warning because of you.'

'That was your own fault. I didn't make you oversleep.'

'I should never have doubted Edie,' Milly said, her voice

rising again. 'I should have trusted her, like I always had. The only lies she's ever told me have been to save me from you!'

'I may not be perfect, but neither is your aunt. She would have married my husband if she'd had the chance and she always hated me that he never looked at her twice. That's not my fault.'

'Don't insult Edie,' Milly shouted, her jaw set. Jean fell silent and Milly's mind began to move. Trading slurs wasn't going to get them anywhere. They had to find a way out of this. 'We need to decide what we're going to do because it's not only your life on the line now, Jean. Mine is too. If we don't take their money to the Golden Hotel soon, we're done for. It's only a matter of time until they find you or come back for me. How much do you owe Ray?'

'Two hundred and fifty pounds.'

'*Two hundred and fifty pounds?*' Milly repeated the amount incredulously. How were they ever going to gather that much money together? 'How much have you got?'

'Nothing near that. Nothing at all really.'

Milly fell back into the chair with a thump, her legs giving way. 'Then what are we going to do?'

Fear had weakened her voice and was written in every aspect of Jean's face. 'I don't know.'

Chapter Twenty-Seven

Milly returned to the palace, her heart used and empty. Her mum had lied about everything. About who she was, where she'd been and why. Her heart yearned for Edie. She wanted to beg her forgiveness. Edie would give it, she knew that already, but Milly also knew that deep down some things could never be forgotten. All those months ago, the shock of learning that Edie had lied to her had driven a wedge between them and she worried now that her blind belief in her mum, her refusal to acknowledge her own misgivings, had damaged their relationship beyond repair.

Back in the staff quarters, Milly made her way towards her room. She was still soaking wet, her body chilled through to the marrow in her bones. She couldn't believe that just a few short months ago a letter had changed her life beyond all recognition and now her life was once again undone. She'd wanted so badly to believe her mum couldn't really have abandoned her, that she'd been worth more to her than that, but she'd been wrong, and believing her mum had pushed her further and further away from the woman who'd actually raised her. Who'd loved her, always. She'd been so stupid. So naive. Just like Timothy said she was.

Cold and lonely, she wanted nothing more than to

change and climb into bed but as Milly passed Caroline's door, she halted. Noises were coming from the other side. Voices. She couldn't quite make them out at first but then something crashed on to the floor – a lamp or teacup. The voices rose. Not loud enough to make out words but there was the deep pitch of a man's followed swiftly by a shrill, panicked cry.

Immediately, Milly thumped her fist on the door. 'Caroline? Caroline, are you all right?'

The low voice mumbled incoherently, and Milly cursed the thick oak doors of the palace. But it was certainly a man's voice and they weren't allowed to have men in their rooms.

'Caroline?' she called again.

'Yeah?' Her voice was small, flustered.

'Caroline, open the door.'

'No! I – I'm all right, really. I knocked over a lamp, that's all.'

'I don't believe you. Open the door.'

Silence.

The low voice mumbled again. She could hear anger pulsing through it.

'If you don't open this door right now I'm getting Edie.'

There were more murmurs and scurrying about on the other side, then the door slowly opened an inch. Caroline's cheeks were flushed, untidy strands of hair fell about her face and her eyes were glassy as if she were about to cry but doing everything in her power to hold the tears back. Some of her shirt hung loosely from her waistband.

'Please, Milly. Just go. I'm all right, honest.'

She shook her head. 'Who's in there?'

'No one.'

She tried to see through the tiny gap. 'I know there is. Open the door.'

Caroline protested again, but Milly knew something was terribly wrong from the fearful glances she threw over her shoulder. She forced her way past Caroline, flinging the door open.

Milly's body stiffened. Timothy sat on the edge of the bed, his legs splayed, his hands clasped between them. Smug, triumphant.

'You!' Milly almost shouted, controlling her voice just in time. 'What did you do to her?' She stepped forwards, wrapping her arm around Caroline and pulling her close. Caroline was sobbing, covering her face with her hands, turning her back on him.

'Nothing to do with you, Milly. Best keep your nose out.'

'I bloody well won't. Caroline?' She inclined her head, trying to catch Caroline's eye.

'He – he followed me. I tried to run – to get to my room – but he put his foot in the door and—'

'Only wanted a chat.' Timothy added glibly, 'for old times' sake.'

Old times' sake? Milly's stomach dropped to the floor. She'd been so stupid. Timothy must have been the man who'd assaulted Caroline the first time. But she'd assumed the incident had happened before Caroline had started, believing something like that couldn't possibly happen at the palace. Her awkwardness whenever he was around wasn't a crush. It wasn't awkwardness either. It was fear.

'Get out,' Milly said coldly. 'Now.'

Timothy stood, adjusting his footman's jacket and giving a carefree shrug. 'Was leaving anyway.'

As Timothy reached the doorway, she added, 'You're disgusting. And if you come near Caroline again, I'll report you to the Master of the Household. I don't care what happens to me.'

'Think he's got his hands full with a dead king.'

Milly and Caroline both gasped. No one spoke of the King with such disrespect. He hadn't even been buried yet. Milly glared at Timothy. It was as if she was looking at a totally different man.

'How dare you. The Master will be furious when he finds out how you've used us. I could go to the police too.'

'Used you?' He laughed. 'You were happy to go to the pictures. I just wanted a little something for my trouble. Any bloke would.'

'A gentleman wouldn't.'

'And I wouldn't go to the police, Milly. With everything I know about you . . . ?' Timothy sauntered down the corridor. A few yards on, he turned back to face them. 'You might not care what happens to you, but don't forget about Edie. Be a shame if she lost her job 'cause of you.'

'Do you think this is what your brother would do, Timothy? Do you think your poor dead brother, who gave his life for this country, would be happy you're spending yours using people?'

She had no idea if her words had any effect as he continued to walk away, rounding the corner and disappearing from sight.

'What's he talking about, Milly?' Caroline asked, her voice small. 'What does he know?'

'Nothing. It doesn't matter. Let's get you inside and cleaned up.' After settling Caroline on the bed, she closed the door. A wash cloth stood by the small basin in the corner and Milly warmed it. Sitting beside Caroline, she gently brushed the hair away from her face and wiped the tears from her cheeks. 'There,' she said soothingly, as Caroline's breathing calmed. 'It was Timothy, wasn't it? The man who assaulted you before.'

Tears welled in her eyes, and she brushed them away, nodding. 'Not long after I started. I thought he was the bee's knees. I couldn't believe my luck. Thought what's this man wanting me for? He could have anyone. We went out a few times and he was lovely. A real gentleman. He told me to keep it quiet, didn't want me getting a reputation so soon after starting. I thought he was doing me a favour. Then . . .' Milly slipped her hand into Caroline's. 'Then one night after dinner here at the palace, he followed me to my room. I thought we was just gonna kiss but then he wanted more. He said I shouldn't be a prude. Other girls weren't.' A sob stole the next words.

'I think I can guess what happened next. You said before it could have been worse. I take he didn't . . .' The word made her feel sick. Caroline shook her head. 'What stopped him?'

'Someone came by. I don't know who it was. But it was long enough for me to get the door open. He had to go after that, but he told me not to bother telling anyone. He said no one would believe me. I'd only been here five minutes, and no one would believe a silly thing like me. I know I'm not the sharpest and it was taking me so long to remember all the rules and what I was supposed to call people I didn't wanna make trouble.'

'Oh, Caroline, I'm so sorry. You should have been able to tell us and we should have seen something had happened. I'm so sorry.'

'Sorry?' Caroline's eyes widened. 'You got nothing to be sorry about.'

A small, knitted rabbit sat on Caroline's bedside table. A thread had come loose from one of the eyes and it hung slightly low, giving the toy a forlorn expression. Milly had thought herself young and naive compared to Helen, but Caroline was younger still and she'd been through so much.

'I have,' Milly replied, loosening her grip on Caroline a little now she had calmed down. She took a deep breath. 'He did the same to me. Or similar. I have a feeling he was worse with you.'

Caroline stared with wide eyes. 'He . . . So, you *have* been seeing him?'

Guilt pricked her skin, raising the hairs like a chill wind. 'I kept it a secret because I thought you liked him. You blushed every time he came in the room, so I thought . . . I realise now how wrong I was. And all your questions. You suspected, didn't you?'

'I was gonna warn you. I hadn't told anyone who did it, but I was gonna tell you to keep you safe.'

Milly hugged Caroline closely despite her wet coat. She'd let Timothy's lies make her suspicious of Caroline.

She'd trusted all the wrong people, it seemed. 'He told me not to tell anyone about us too. He blamed Edie and the fact she didn't like him.'

'Well, she were right there, weren't she?'

Milly managed a chuckle though nothing about this was amusing. 'She was. I thought he was being kind and considerate but he's not. Timothy's not the man I thought he was.'

'No, he ain't.'

'We were in the garden and . . . he started going too far. When I pushed him away, he got angry and called me horrible names.'

'He did that to me too.' She sat up a little straighter. 'When did he . . . with you?'

'Almost a month ago. Why?'

'That's when he started being nice to me again. I told him to leave me alone. Then he started slipping notes under my door, telling me he was sorry and he'd learned his lesson.'

'And you believed him?'

'No! Course not. But today he followed me. He kept saying he just wanted to talk and . . . luckily you came along.' She threw her arms around Milly, holding her tight and Milly laid her head on her arm.

Timothy must have thought her worth another try after Milly had thrown him over. A sour taste filled Milly's dry mouth as her guilt surged again. She'd told him she thought Caroline had a crush on him – had that fuelled his trying a second time? She pressed a hand to her mouth. She should have said something. Then he wouldn't have been able to get near her friend again.

'What did Edie say when you told her?' Caroline asked.

'I haven't. Timothy threatened to tell the Chief House-keeper things about my mum and Edie. He said we'd probably get the sack for having such connections. And I think he's right.' Especially now she knew the truth about her mum. 'But I'm scared if we don't, he'll do it to some-one else and they might not be able to fight him off or he might not take no for an answer.'

Caroline's eyes widened as Milly silently urged her to understand.

'But . . . will I lose my job?'

'You? Why should you?'

'Because I did let him in my room the first time and that alone could get me sacked. He'll say I led him on and after the handkerchief . . . Milly, what if that week we kept quiet could have made a difference to the King's life?'

'Caroline, I think that's a bit of a leap.'

'But what if that's what the Master thinks? He might blame us for the King's death, and he could still be wanting an excuse to get rid of us.'

She had a point. Now she, Edie and Caroline were all in the firing line. 'I need to think about it.'

'Oh, please don't tell, Milly.' She grabbed Milly's hands tightly in hers. 'I can't afford to lose this job. Please?'

'Caroline—'

'Please, Milly.' The panic and fear in her voice cut Milly deeply. Her friend's breathing had quickened again, and her eyes were wild with panic.

'You need to rest, Caroline. Try and get some sleep. I'll come and check on you later.'

Caroline collapsed, falling sideways on to the bed,

sobbing anew. Milly stood and fetched her a glass of water before draping the blankets over her. Her mind was full with the events of the morning. A morning that seemed a lifetime ago. She desperately wanted to talk to someone, but who would listen to her after all the mistakes she'd made? 'It'll be all right, Caroline. We'll think of something.'

Milly stood and went to the door, Caroline was still begging, asking her to keep the events secret. Milly apologised again, tears trickling down her face. She hated seeing Caroline like this and wanted nothing more than to agree, to relieve her suffering, but she wanted to do the right thing. She wanted to protect the next girl Timothy set his sights on. She'd done the wrong thing so much lately, hurting people she cared about, she was determined to think this through and find the right course of action.

'Just try and rest, Caroline. You'll feel better after you've slept.'

She closed the door slowly behind her, aware of Caroline's muted sobs. Wiping her own eyes, she ran down the corridor towards the palace gardens, her heart never more broken than it was at that moment.

Chapter Twenty-Eight

Cold, fresh air assaulted Milly's senses. Her teeth chattered and she wrapped her arms over her damp coat for some additional warmth. When she'd returned to the palace all she'd wanted was to be closeted in the city within a city, the real world kept at bay. She'd hope to feel protected by the thick garden walls, by the space between her and a harsh, cruel world full of lies and betrayal, but she'd come home to find worse. Closing her eyes, she stalked along the paths, her mind churning with guilt and fear.

'Milly, th-there you are.'

She knew that voice, that sweet stutter, anywhere and slowed her pace. Turning, Milly watched as Robert jogged towards her, instantly relaxing. He was in his own clothes, trousers and a jumper with a slightly battered coat thrown over the top. He was still pushing one arm into it as he drew level.

'I saw you running out here. Are you all right?'

'No,' she replied with a laugh. How could she be? 'No. I really don't think I am.'

His brows pinched together, creating tiny lines on his forehead. 'W-what's happened? You're soaking wet. Here—' He began removing his coat but Milly refused it. 'Then at least take this.' He unwound the scarf from his neck and wrapped it around her. His familiar smell warmed her instantly, driving out some of the cold. Clean soap, nothing fancy but wonderfully calming. 'Are you ill?'

'No, I'm fine.' But where did she even begin? She was just about to speak when the voices of the Master and Deputy Master of the Household carried on the air towards her. They were hushed as if speaking confidentially, and, unsure whether to pass them, no doubt receiving strange looks at her wet coat, or try and avoid them, she whispered, 'Quick. Over here.' Grabbing Robert's hand, she darted behind a large rhododendron and they ducked out of sight.

'There really is so much to do,' said the Master of the Household. 'Operation Hyde Park Corner is taking longer to organise than anyone thought it would.'

'But I thought the plans were all in place. How bad is it?' asked Mr Townsend, the Deputy Master. 'And is there anything I can do?'

'Just carry on as you are. Be there for the family. Queen Elizabeth especially. We must lead by example.'

'Queen Elizabeth,' he said with a sigh. 'The address is the same but I'm still getting used to saying that to a different woman.'

'Same, old boy. The very same.'

They passed and Milly gave a silent prayer of thanks she and Robert hadn't been spotted.

What would life be like with a queen? Milly wondered. She'd only ever known a king. And he'd been a steadying presence through so many years of hardship she wasn't sure the world would accept young Princess Elizabeth as they had her father and grandfather.

321

Milly turned to see Robert's face close to hers and the strange something that had stirred within her on so many occasions flourished into a single, strong feeling. It was attraction, yearning, love and friendship combined in one. How had she ever thought he couldn't compare to Timothy? Robert's eyes were kind, gentle, and she held her breath as she remembered her hand in his as they danced, the trust and closeness between them.

The Master and Deputy Master were now out of sight and Milly and Robert stood. 'How long before you have to be at work?' she asked. 'I have so much to tell you. That's if you don't mind listening. I've made so many mistakes, Robert, and I don't know how to fix them all.'

They began walking and Robert listened as she recounted everything that had happened. She left nothing out: Jean and the gangster, her mum stealing from the palace, the cold, hurtful truth that Edie had been right all along, as well as her argument with Helen, Timothy's behaviour towards her and now, finding him with Caroline.

'I'll k-kill him,' Robert said, turning back to the palace as if to find him immediately.

'No.' Milly had held him back. 'I want to make sure it can't happen again but what if Timothy's right and the palace tosses me, Edie and Caroline out too?'

'I don't think they will. I'm sure they'll understand. Edie's part of the furniture here; Caroline and you have both been b-badly used. They might not even believe him.'

'But what about Mum stealing? He'll use that against us, and I was wrong to take her into a guest room.'

'What if we can get it back? No one would be any the wiser.'

She considered what he'd said. 'That's not a bad idea. She did tell me where she'd pawned it. But I have to tell Edie about Timothy – about what he did to me, anyway – I know that much. I can't speak for Caroline, but Edie might be able to have a word with the senior footmen so it can all be handled quietly. I don't want Caroline to lose her job for letting him into her room.'

'I don't see why she should. She's very young and n-naive and Timothy can be very persuasive.'

'I hate him.' The vehemence in her voice surprised them both but Robert's gaze held no judgement. 'I – I . . .' It was her turn to stutter. 'I'm sorry, Robert, that I . . .' What could she say? She'd chosen Timothy over Robert and she'd made another terrible mistake. She thought of her birthday gift and her fingers found the brooch pinned to the lapel of her coat. Now she hoped it wasn't too late for her to right another mistake. 'I'm sorry I thought more of Timothy than I should. I feel such a fool.'

'You're not a fool. He's no gentleman.'

They walked on a few paces, and a little of the peace she'd hoped for started to return.

'Is there anything else you need to tell me?'

'No. That's all.' As she uttered this last sentence, she was overcome with exhaustion and such a range of emotions she didn't know what to feel.

'You've b-been very busy, Milly,' Robert observed. She laughed and the release it gave rebalanced her feelings, like taking a lid off a pot and a cascade of steam pouring out. A load had lifted just by telling him. He continued, 'I can hardly believe it.'

'What do I do, Robert? This man's threatening to hurt me and Mum if he doesn't get his money. And he means it.'

He took her hand. 'I won't let that happen.'

She believed him, but what could they do? She didn't have £250. The only people she knew who had were the Royals and she wasn't about to ask them for a loan.

'How much does your mum have?'

'Nothing really was all she said. She was so panicked I don't think she knows what to do. It won't be long until Ray finds her at one of the clubs or hotels. He's not stupid, he'll be looking for her. We've just been lucky there are so many in London he hasn't tracked her down yet. I hate her for every single lie she's told me but' – she sniffed and wiped her cold nose with a handkerchief – 'that doesn't mean I want to see her hurt.'

'I understand,' he said kindly, squeezing her hand. 'For what it's worth, I think the first thing to do is to tell Edie everything. You can't k-keep this from her, Milly. It's time you two put the past behind you.'

He was right, and though he didn't seem to think his advice was worth much, to her it meant everything.

Chapter Twenty-Nine

The next day, Milly took the first step to mending the broken relationships in her life and undoing the damage she'd caused.

In the days that had followed the King's death and the proclaiming of the new Queen, Buckingham Palace had been a hive of activity. If people weren't coming in, Queen Elizabeth was rushing out. In comparison, in Edie's room, where Helen, Edie and Caroline all looked at each other, silence and stillness reigned.

Milly had asked Edie for permission to meet everyone there because it was marginally larger than her own bedroom and now Caroline and Helen were sitting at the small table, Edie had the armchair and Milly stood, waiting to begin. There was so much to say, so much to decide. It was time to wipe the slate clean of all the lies and half-truths she'd told to them all.

Robert was delivering a plate of freshly made biscuits straight from the kitchen, courtesy of Mrs Chapman. He placed it on the table, casting his eyes over their concerned faces before turning and heading for the door. Milly followed him outside, taking his hand as he began to walk away.

'Robert?' He turned to face her and her thoughts ran again to their dance at the Sunrise Club, to his handsome face close to hers, to his arms around her. 'Thank you.' She placed a kiss on his cheek, her heart thudding as she did so.

He didn't say anything, too shocked to respond, but his mouth curved in a grin before he left her.

Milly drew in a deep breath. She'd barely slept last night, worrying as to whether Jean was at the Sunrise Club and if Jack or Ray had discovered the truth. She'd called the boarding house this morning from the staff telephone and Mrs Dean had confirmed Jean was there, in bed. She'd asked if she should fetch her, but Milly had refused, telling her to let Jean sleep and saying that she'd call back later. She'd needed to know she was safe, that was all. Once they'd decided what to do, she would speak to her, even though the hurt was still great, the betrayal still raw.

Edie's chair squeaked as she adjusted her position. Caroline cleared her throat, keeping her eyes down, glancing at Milly from the corners of her eyes, clearly apprehensive over what she'd say about Timothy. Helen's smooth forehead was lined with concern. Whether it was over her dad or the meeting, Milly didn't know. She hadn't seen her to ask how her dad was doing, but she looked tired and drawn.

They were like strangers and Milly knew the responsibility for the chasms between them lay with her. She worried no amount of truth or apology would bridge the gaps, but she had to try.

'Thank you all for agreeing to meet,' she said, wringing her hands together. She didn't know what to do with herself and in the strange atmosphere every action seemed forced.

Edie's eyes darted over the girls in front of her and then

settled on the glass of water on the table, giving away her nervousness.

'I wanted you all here because I—' Milly took a deep breath praying the words alone would be enough. 'I need to apologise to you all.' All the nervous fidgeting stopped, and the three women stared at Milly. 'And I need to tell you all the truth. All of it.' She glanced at Edie, hoping she'd understand. Her aunt adjusted her position in the armchair, sitting a little straighter. 'I know you're worried about it all coming out, Edie, but I trust Helen and Caroline, and the rest of what I'm going to say will only make sense if we all know what happened before.'

Edie met Milly's gaze. 'Are you sure?'

The question lit the dark fear inside her like a beacon of hope. It showed she still trusted her. 'If I thought there was another way, I'd take it, but these last few months I haven't been myself because I've been holding things back from everyone around me. It's time for the truth because something happened yesterday and I need to tell you all about it.' Caroline's fearful eyes fixed on Milly, and she hurried on to allow her to relax for a while longer. 'A gangster from Birmingham attacked me.'

'What?' Edie screeched. 'When? Did he hurt you?'

Milly shook her head, her heart warming at Edie's concern. 'No, he didn't. Not really. He's after Mum.' She turned to Caroline and Helen. 'You need to know the truth about my mum and what happened ten years ago.' She told them the full story from start to finish: why Jean had left, where she'd been and the threats against her now, the picture she'd stolen. As she described Edie's part, her sympathies were with the aunt who had been put in a desperate position and wanted nothing more than to protect her niece.

'And now, she and Billy owe someone else money too. He's threatened me and her, saying if she doesn't pay up, he'll come after me. He said I can't stay in the palace forever. You were right about her, Aunt Edie. You were right about everything. She never wanted me. She never wanted to see me again either. Not to be a mum, anyway – she wanted to get money, that was all. I'm sorry I didn't believe you.'

As she said these last words, tears filled her eyes. The carpet became nothing more than a smear of colour as she dropped her gaze, her vision misted. With a speed she hadn't possessed of late, Edie pushed herself out of the chair and took hold of Milly's hands, grasping them firmly, lovingly.

'It's her who's losin' out, Milly, not you. She's never goin' to know what a brilliant and clever young lady you are. And all those years she missed out on, we did all right, didn't we?'

Milly's heart pulsed and the tears she'd been trying to hold back burst forth. 'I'm so sorry, Aunt Edie.' Edie's strong arms engulfed her, and she returned the embrace, drinking in the warmth of Edie's affection, her comforting love. 'You're more of a mum to me than she ever was. Or will be.'

'Shush now. It's all over and done with. We've all learned lessons the hard way. She's not worth your tears, my girl. Not at all. She's always been trouble.' She moved so she could look at Milly. 'But she was right about one thing and it's somethin' I'd like you to know now. There shouldn't be any more secrets between us.' Milly held her breath, unsure what was coming. 'I *was* in love with your dad, and for a while he liked me too. Jean wouldn't have told you this and

328

I didn't mention it before, but we'd started sort of seein' each other. But then, when I brought him home, your mum decided she wanted him for herself and, the stupid fool that he was, he was sucked in by her. I never forgave her for that. Or him, for that matter. It hurt like hell that he picked my sister over me. Broke my heart, in fact. So Jean was right that maybe I was a bit jealous back then, but I put all that behind me when they married. Of course, feelin's don't disappear overnight, but I never did anythin' to come between them, and when you were born, I thought I could forgive them anythin' as long as they took care of you. Then when he died and she left, it became about you and me and no one else.'

'I wish it had stayed that way.'

'So do I, but it hasn't, and we can't undo what's happened. We just have to deal with it. We've both made mistakes. I should've been more supportive about you gettin' to know her again. Maybe if I'd come with you that first time she wouldn't have been able to tell such lies. And maybe you should have trusted her less, but there you are. We're still here and that's what matters.'

Milly kissed Edie's cheek and they stayed huddled together, sharing the love of a mother and daughter in all but name until Milly pulled a handkerchief from her pocket and blew her nose. Then she spoke again.

'I need to get the picture back before it's missed and decide what to do about Jean. And that's why you're here, Helen. And why I want to apologise to you too. You weren't quite right about my mum – at least, I don't think you were – but some of the things you said were true. You tried to warn me to be more careful and I wasn't. I shouldn't have been so rude to you just because I didn't like what I was hearing. She has been spending all of her money on herself. She seems to think it's what the world owes her. She never cared about me or thought about the future we might have as a family.'

Edie tutted and rolled her eyes as if she'd expected nothing less from her sister.

A smile lit Helen's tired eyes. 'I'm so sorry, Milly, but thank you for apologising. I was only thinking of you. I know we haven't known each other very long but I thought we really hit it off and I—' She stumbled. 'Well, friends are important, aren't they?'

Milly knew how difficult it was for Helen to spend time with other people with her dad being so sick. She hadn't had to accept the apology and had every right to chastise Milly first, yet she'd been kind and graceful and Milly appreciated that.

'What will you do?' asked Caroline, her eyes wide at the drama of it all.

'I don't know.'

'If I were you,' Edie said. 'I'd leave her to it. She won't thank you if you help her and she won't thank you if you don't. You can't win with that woman.'

'I know,' Milly replied. 'I know that she's very selfish. The only reason she was always so desperate to visit here was to try and steal something to pay Ray.'

'I can't believe she's done that.' Edie shuffled in outrage. 'Treason, that is.'

'It's certainly something you can be arrested for,' Helen replied.

Milly began to pace. Standing still seemed so passive and

though pacing the room wasn't going to fix anything, it would at least stop her worries catching up with her. 'There's something else as well.' She took a deep breath, catching Caroline's eye. Caroline gave a tiny shake of the head, panic ripping through her features. 'Now, Aunt Edie, I need you to promise—'

'No.' Caroline violently shook her head and reached out for Milly's hand. 'Milly, no. Please. You said—'

'I said I'd think about it, Caroline, and I have.' She leaned down in front of Caroline and placed a hand on her shoulder. 'I'm going to tell them about what happened to *me*.' She emphasised the final word. 'I have to do this, so it doesn't happen to anyone else. If I'd been honest . . . well . . .' She turned to Edie. 'I have to tell you about Timothy.'

Quietly, Milly outlined what had happened between her and Timothy. Edie's face reddened with every passing second. Her cheeks blazed, and patches of red appeared on her chest.

'That good-for-nothing rascal. I knew he was a wrong 'un the second I laid eyes on him. If I get my hands on him I'll – I'll rip it off. I've known men like him before. Full of their own piss and importance, my old dad used to say. Think they're God's gift to women. And I don't buy all that guff about his dead brother. I'm not sure he even has one, to be honest, and even if he does, he's not the only person to have lost someone. It's good to make the most of life – we've all learned that – but you can't go around usin' and abusin' people.'

Helen's kind expression had hardened with anger, her jaw held tight. Caroline's eyes suddenly met Milly's.

'There's summat else,' she said shakily. Milly took her hand, encouraging her to go on. Her voice quivered as she

331

told Edie and Helen everything Milly now knew. By the time she'd finished, both Helen and Milly had their arms wrapped around her as Edie gripped the arms of the chair with white knuckles.

'Right, let's see how brave he is with me, shall we?'

'Aunty.' Milly pressed Edie back down into her chair. 'Calm down. You'll give yourself a heart attack. Caroline won't lose her job for having him in her room, will she?'

'After what that villain's done to both of you?' Edie's ire receded a little. 'I shouldn't think so. You broke the rules, Caroline, so you might get a warnin', but what's happened to you is far worse. He's taken advantage of you bein' young and innocent. Timothy'll lose his job. I'll see to that.'

'I was thinking', Milly continued, 'that because we found the handkerchief and haven't breathed a word to anyone, it might help Caroline's case.'

'Handkerchief?' Edie asked.

Milly swallowed hard. That was the trouble with secrets, you often forgot which ones you were keeping from who. Bravely, Caroline explained what she and Milly had found and how they'd been sworn to secrecy.

'So that was why you went to see the Master?'

'I can't tell you how much I wanted to tell you, Aunt Edie. When we found it, I didn't know what to do for the best. I didn't want to ruin your Christmas or get you in trouble for it not being found earlier.'

'You mean them thinkin' I wasn't doing my job properly? How am I supposed to clean a bed that he's always in?'

'And then when the Master told us we'd lose our jobs if we spoke about it or if anyone gossiped, I couldn't risk dragging you into it. Things were hard enough between us and I would have hated myself if you'd been blamed for something that wasn't your fault.'

'I understand,' Edie replied. 'I'm not happy about it, but I understand. Has anythin' more been said since the King . . .'

'No, nothing.'

'Then we better get that mess cleared up too. It's not fair to threaten your jobs when it's not your fault you found it. Gaw blimey, you two.'

'Sorry, Mrs Barnes,' Caroline said.

Edie took her hand. 'You're a blimmin' good worker, Caroline. You've never let me down yet. You'll be fine. I'll make sure.'

Caroline's body collapsed as relief flooded through her. 'Oh, thank you, Mrs Barnes. And I promise I won't never break the rules again.'

'You better not. Or if you do it should be with someone a damn sight better than Timothy Ranger.'

Laughter burst from the three younger woman.

'And you and me, Aunt Edie?' Milly said. 'Will we get into trouble because of Jean? Will we lose our jobs because of our connection with her?'

Edit sat back in her chair, her eyes narrowed in thought. 'What does Timothy *know*? Only that she sings in clubs and hotels. Well, everyone needs to earn a livin'. Did you tell him the real truth, like you've just told the girls?'

She hadn't. The only other person she'd told was Robert and she trusted him implicitly. 'No. I haven't. I only ever stuck to what we agreed.'

'Then he's got nothin'. He might suspect her of stealin'

333

but he can suspect anythin' he likes as long as he ain't got no proof. If you can get the picture back he's got nothin'. And a young man with a bad attitude bein' accused by two honest, hardworkin' young ladies like you . . . No. We'll be fine. As long as we can get the picture back first.'

'I don't want to go anywhere unless Robert can come with me,' Milly said.

'Robert?'

'I told him everything too. He said whenever I leave the palace, I should have someone with me in case that gangster tries to put the frighteners on me again.' Her friends all gazed at one another knowingly. 'What? Don't look at me like that.'

Caroline giggled. 'You're not gonna tell us he's just a friend, are you? We're not blind, Milly.'

'No, but she is,' Helen said, lighting a cigarette for the first time since the meeting began.

Her two friends chuckled and even Edie smiled.

'I'm not any more,' Milly replied, her fingertips finding the swallow brooch he'd given her for her birthday, now pinned on to her jumper. 'But that's enough of that. My private life has been the topic of conversation enough lately.'

'So what will you do about Jean?' Edie asked.

'I don't know yet. I can't go and see her for a few days. Not until my next half-day off. Robert said he'd come with me. But I've got the number of her boarding house so I'll ring later and tell her to stay hidden until we decide what best to do.'

'She'll do what she wants no matter what the consequences or who it hurts. You know that, don't you?'

'I do,' Milly replied. It had been the lesson she'd learned hardest, and the one that hurt more than any other.

Chapter Thirty

On Monday, the King's coffin had come from Sandringham to King's Cross Station and from there a solemn procession had led it to Westminster Hall where he was now lying in state. A gun carriage, drawn by the King's Troop, Royal Horse Artillery, had taken the coffin through streets lined with people. Though no such procession was happening today, London was busy with policemen.

It was now Wednesday, Milly's half-day off, and she made her way deftly through the crowds to the pawnbroker's and from there had planned to see her mum. They had a lot to discuss. Robert insisted on going with her and though she didn't think Ray would try anything given the heightened security in London, the thick crowds could provide him with an opportunity to grab her, or worse, if he wanted to. Robert's broad and muscular presence at her side gave her a feeling of protection and a sense of confidence she wouldn't have had alone.

'It's just down here,' Milly said as they turned into Frith Street. 'Do you think it'll still be there?'

'Only one way to f-find out.'

She pushed open the door and a bell jangled. The shop was small and grubby. Dust motes fell like silver snowflakes in the shafts of light that penetrated the thick air. The owner, a wizened old man with greasy hair and an ill-fitting demob suit, stood behind a glass counter that was full of jewellery and watches.

'Afternoon, miss, young man. What can I do for you?'

Milly scanned the room and her eyes fell on the photograph of the King in a small silver frame behind him. Relief flooded her. It was still here. She tried to sound like her whole future didn't depend on buying that stupid small thing. 'I'd like that photograph, please.'

'This one?' He reached up and took it down. 'Lovely frame, this is. And now of course our King is gone – God rest him – worth a lot more than it was a few days ago.'

'How much do you want for it?'

He sucked the air in through his teeth. 'Two pounds, I reckon. Come straight from grand old Buckingham Palace itself it has, so by rights I should be charging a lot more, but you look like a nice girl.' He gave a grin that, she assumed, was supposed to be fatherly.

'We'll give you one pound,' Milly said sternly. 'And don't give me any guff about Buckingham Palace. These types of photographs are ten a penny. Pictures of the King get sent to all and sundry every day, so I know they're not as rare as hen's teeth.'

'Lordy, she's a plucky one,' he said to Robert.

'Yes, and I wouldn't test her if I were you.'

'I'll not offer any more,' Milly said, gaining the man's attention once more. 'And I shouldn't think with all the pictures of the King in the papers anyone will want a photograph when they can just cut one out.'

He looked at the photograph now sitting on top of the

counter. Milly held her breath. 'All right then. A pound it is. Though I'm doing myself out of money 'ere, you know. But like I say, you seem a nice young couple and it is of the King.'

Milly handed over the money, thanking him and placing the photograph in her bag. At least that solved one problem. As long as she could get it back into the guest room unnoticed.

A few minutes later, they turned down the road leading to Mrs Dean's Boarding House. Robert was peering around him, as he had done since leaving the palace. 'I really don't think Ray's around, Robert. I've been looking and haven't spotted him.'

'Yes, but you didn't spot him before, did you?'

'That's true. But we'll be inside again soon.' She knocked and waited. 'I hate that sign.' She pointed to the weathered handwritten note declaring 'No Blacks. No Irish.' They could give their lives to fight the Nazis, but now they weren't deemed good enough to sleep in a shabby boarding house. It was nonsense.

'Me too. Do you think there'll ever be a time when people don't h-hate each other? It feels like we've had nothing but hate for decades.'

'Maybe one day the world will be better. I hope so.' The door finally swung open but rather than smile, Mrs Dean scowled.

'Oh, you. Jean Barnes's friend. Come ter give me the rent I'm owed, 'ave yer?' She held a tea towel in her hand, and waved it angrily at Milly as she spoke.

'No, sorry. I've come to see Jean. Is she behind?'

Mrs Dean assessed her for a moment as if deciding if

337

she was telling the truth. 'Done a runner on yer as well, 'as she?' Milly's stomach dropped to the dirty paving slabs at her feet. 'Yep, that's right. Gone. Done a bunk. And without payin' 'er rent. Didn't tell yer neither by the looks of it.'

'No, she didn't.' Milly's throat tightened and for a moment she stared unseeing at the woman in front of her, aware only of Robert gently touching her elbow.

'Have you rented her room again yet?' he asked.

'No, not yet,' Mrs Dean replied. She tossed the tea towel over her shoulder and crossed her arms over her chest. 'I still need ter clear it out. Left it a right tip, she did. Made the most of this hoo-ha over the King's death ter run off without payin' 'er dues.'

'Is there any chance we can have a look around?'

'Yes,' Milly said, looking from Robert to Mrs Dean. 'She might have left me a note or something.'

'I didn't find one, but yer welcome ter 'ave a shufty.' She stood aside and Milly led the way up to Jean's room. Mrs Dean trailed along behind them.

The key was in the lock and Milly opened the door, surprised to find clothes and rubbish scattered about the floor.

'Can we just have a m-moment, please, Mrs Dean? This has come as quite a shock to my friend.' Robert gave her a rather charming grin and the older woman visibly melted at his gentlemanly request.

'Course, deary. I'm sorry fer you, ducky,' she said to Milly. 'But if yer ask me, she weren't a friend worth 'avin' anyway. 'Er type always lets yer down in the end.'

Milly nodded to acknowledge Mrs Dean's words as she

closed the door behind her. The truth of them stung, but she'd already known her mum had never been trustworthy. Still, she hadn't expected this. Another betrayal that cut her to the bone. Eyeing the untidy room she said, 'She must have left in a hurry.'

'Perhaps it was a last-minute decision?'

'I think she only makes last-minute decisions. I don't think she's ever thought anything through in her life. Let's see if she's left anything for me. Do you mind starting over there? It's such a tiny room it won't take us long.'

'Of c-course.'

Milly took one side of the room and Robert the other. A couple of old, ripped stockings lay on the floor, an empty bottle of perfume had been left on the windowsill that was damp with condensation and black with mould, but apart from that there was nothing. Jean had gone without leaving so much as a note for her daughter. Something in Milly wanted desperately to believe it was to keep her safe, although she knew there really wasn't any hope. A half-written letter had led Ray to Milly in the first place, but Jean wasn't trying to protect her by not leaving one this time. Like the flame of a candle extinguished in the wind, the hope faded as quickly as it had begun. She had no idea where she'd gone and wherever it was, Jean didn't want Milly, or anyone else, to follow her.

'I'm sorry, Milly,' Robert said, placing a hand on her shoulder.

'It's all right.' She wiped her eyes. She'd cried more over her mum in these last few months than she had when she'd thought she'd died; it was more than a woman who hadn't cared a fig for her deserved. 'I don't suppose there's much chance she paid a visit to Ray before she left, do you think?'

He shook his head. 'Judging by the room and that she left without paying her rent, I don't think so.'

'No, neither do I.'

'What do you want to do?'

Rolling her shoulders back and with a heavy breath, she gave the room one last look around. 'There's no point staying here any longer. We might as well go.'

'Thank God you're back,' Edie said as Milly opened the door to her aunt's room and stepped inside. Edie rushed towards her, arms encircling her in a tight hug. 'I've been worried sick. What happened? What did Jean say? More lies and excuses, knowin' her, but still . . .'

Milly unwound the scarf from her neck and placed it on the table before unbuttoning her coat. She was pleased to see Edie had been given a small electric heater and the glowing orange bars gave a bright warmth to the room. Milly moved over to it and thawed her hands. The heat was strong, burning through her ice-cold fingers.

'Milly?' Edie prompted.

'She's gone,' Milly replied, unable to hold back the tears. In the comfort and safety of the palace, the effect of her mum's latest betrayal cut deeply. The pain was excruciating, and she failed under the weight of it. 'She's left me again, Edie.'

'Oh, my girl.' Edie rushed back towards her, limping slightly on her swollen knee. The arms were around her once more, hands rubbing small circles on her back. 'I'm so sorry. I worried she might, but I hoped – I don't know why – but I hoped she might stay, see this one through instead of runnin' away from her troubles again. I thought for your sake she might.'

'It's all right, Aunt Edie. I should've expected it really.'

'No, you shouldn't. You had every right to think your mum would do her job, her duty, and look after you, but she never could.'

Milly allowed the anger and hurt pent up inside her to flow out. By the time her tears had run dry, her chest ached and her throat was sore. 'Losing her once was horrible enough, but losing her twice is . . .' She didn't have the words and fell silent, letting her emotions dissipate in the heat of the room. She'd done enough crying. 'Now I can't even keep my happy memories. Now I know the truth about her, she's ruined those as well. She's left me to deal with Ray, Edie. All on my own.'

'You're not on your own,' she replied firmly. 'You've got me, Helen, Caroline . . . everyone here who ever kept an eye on you or slipped you treats when they thought I wasn't lookin'. Now, let's think. We could tell the police?'

'Then the palace would know all about Mum and we'd still face being sacked. At least I've got the picture back so it doesn't have to come out that she stole. I'll slip it back in the guest room tonight. But what about Ray, Aunt Edie? He's still out there.'

'Your mum doesn't deserve your loyalty.'

'But he still might come after me. That's what he said he'd do.'

'Whatever you're thinkin', tears won't help. We need to think about this calmly. There's got to be somethin' we can do.'

'Unless you've got two hundred and fifty pounds I can't see what.'

'You're just hurtin', my girl, and it's cloudin' your judgement. Now, let's dry your eyes and have a cuppa before dinner. You'll be calmer after you've eaten. Will Robert be joinin' us?'

Milly shook her head. 'He can't. He's working this evening but he's going to come to the funeral with us if that's OK.' No one was looking forward to it, but they, like most of the country, wanted to pay their respects to the kind and noble King who'd led their nation through some of the most troubled times in history.

'Course. We've got a busy few days ahead of us. The Queen'll be movin' into the palace proper now. There'll be special things of hers as well as the Duke's and then there's the children's toys. I have to say Prince Charles is a bonny little thing and Princess Anne such a beautiful baby. It'll be lovely to have them here at the palace, but I dare say there'll be finger marks to clean off the walls and mud everywhere soon enough. And more corgis no doubt. I just hope they don't take one of my fingers off like they did one of the gardeners'.'

Milly tried to laugh but the world seemed darker than it ever had before. Her mum had gone, and she knew she'd never see her again. Ray the gangster was still in London and there was no denying that Milly's own life was in danger as long as he was around. And he'd been right. She couldn't hide in the palace forever; she'd already made that mistake and didn't intend to repeat it.

Chapter Thirty-One

On 15 February, Milly and Edie, along with Caroline, Helen and Robert, made their way to the other side of Green Park and on to Piccadilly to watch the funeral procession of King George VI pass by.

Dressed in black, as many of the mourners were, they were lucky to find a place near the front. As the cortège's route wouldn't pass Buckingham Palace on its way from Westminster Hall to Paddington Station from where it would go on to Windsor, most of the Royal Household – the cleaners, cooks and those footmen and butlers who weren't on duty – waited in groups huddled together along Piccadilly. They could have watched the procession, televised for the first time by the BBC, on the small TV in the Household Lounge, but Milly and Edie had felt it wasn't quite the same as paying their respects in person, and the scratchy black and white image wasn't going to convey the atmosphere of actually being there. Timothy, standing with the other footmen, kept shooting looks at her but, although something inside her cowered, Milly wouldn't turn away. They were united in truth, she and Caroline, and his power had diminished.

Over three hundred thousand mourners had paid their respects to the King as he lay in state in Westminster Hall, some waiting for hours in the four-mile queue that had snaked around the streets of London. Queen Elizabeth The Queen Mother had thanked everyone for the floral tributes that had been sent to Buckingham Palace and now filled nearly every room.

Today, the King's people lined the route for his final journey: his funeral procession.

Milly had never seen anything like it and realised she probably never would again in her lifetime. The feeling they'd been watching history be made hadn't left since the news of the King's death had been made public. Some older people had already seen so much: the abdication, war declared, Buckingham Palace bombed, and now this. She had a feeling it would be something she told her children and grandchildren about and wanted to drink in every detail, commit every moment to memory.

A strange atmosphere pervaded the city. The capital was deathly quiet, all the normal sounds absent. No motor cars or buses chugged through the streets and the naturally loud chatter of strangers was subdued and quiet. Overhead, the weather mirrored the nation's feelings. It was icy and wet, gloomy and miserable. The rain pattered down, creating mirrored pools in the street that reflected the anxious and often tearful faces of the crowd. They waited expectantly, impatiently.

Milly still feared Ray was waiting for her, but she felt safe with the patrolling policemen, the army lining the road in front of her and the thousands of people who she hoped would jump in to help if something seemed amiss. Robert too was by her side and his presence was the most reassuring.

Before the cortège arrived, the sound of brass and drums carried on the solemn, sorrow-laden air. The marching of feet, perfectly in time, grew stronger as it approached. Guns were held upside down as a mark of respect. Big Ben tolled fifty-six times, once for each year of the King's life, and the rhythmic thud of a gun salute punctured the sombre music played by the military band.

Eventually, the King's coffin came into view. It was laid on an ancient gun carriage covered with purple cloth; an orb and sceptre rested on top, along with a wreath from the Queen Mother, his widow, of orchids and lily of the valley. The coffin, pulled by Royal Navy sailors, known as the Sovereign's Guard, their rhythmical steps forming another beat to the music, was followed by a coach carrying the new Queen, the Queen Mother, Princess Margaret and the Princess Royal. They wore long black veils and Milly wondered how hard it was for them not to cry. She was finding it quite hard herself. There was something so moving about the whole event. The young Queen sat stoically, dignified, but her normally bright skin paled under the darkness of her veil and the King's distraught widow, who normally had a bubbly, almost naughty personality that shone from her sparkling eyes, bowed her head. Behind them, the Dukes of Gloucester, Windsor, Edinburgh and Kent marched in time.

Edie wiped her eyes. 'I can't help thinkin' he wouldn't have died so young if the Duke of Windsor hadn't been so selfish. Havin' to deal with all that and then the war, poor man. His health was never the same after.'

The Duke of Windsor, the King's older brother Edward,

had abdicated the throne in 1936 in favour of marriage to divorcee Wallis Simpson and it was clear that the British public, who had loved him in his day, had still not forgiven him for shirking his duty. Old wounds had, it seemed, reopened with the King's untimely death.

'I agree,' said the woman next to Edie. Someone they'd never met before. 'I'm all for love but there's such a thing as duty and honour too. Look at all the people we lost during the war: men on the front fighting, women and children in the raids. We all did our duty, but he couldn't be bothered.' Edie nodded as the woman carried on. 'At least that dreadful woman isn't here. She'd have tried to steal the spotlight no doubt. Probably thinks herself more important than Princess – I mean Queen Elizabeth.'

They made no further comment as whispers flowed through the crowd that Queen Mary, who had now outlived most of her family, including three sons and a husband, watched from Marlborough House and stood, passing her hand over the window to wave goodbye to her son as the procession filed past.

'God rest his soul,' Edie murmured, wiping a tear from her rain-drizzled face, and Milly, Helen, Caroline and Robert all echoed her words.

The cortège proceeded through Hyde Park to Marble Arch and along Edgware Road towards Paddington Station as the silence of grief descended on the crowd.

'It's unbelievable,' Milly whispered to Robert, who had taken off his hat as a mark of respect and was now replacing it. 'I know I'll never see anything like that again in my life-time. And it was terribly moving.' She turned to Edie. 'Shall

346

we head back now, Aunty? That rain's not easing and there's nothing more to see except for other people.'

They began to make their way through Green Park back towards Buckingham Palace. 'We should get you back inside before that gangster decides to try anythin'. Do you think *she's* here somewhere?' Edie scanned the crowd. It was too wet to walk over the grass, so they stuck to the paths, side-stepping as people bustled to and fro.

'I don't think so, Aunt Edie. I think she's long gone. I have no idea where. Somewhere no one knows her, no doubt. Somewhere she can start again.'

Though Edie and Jean hadn't made up, losing Jean again had been as hard for Edie as it had for Milly. She seemed to have aged over these last three months and her knee today was just as swollen and sore, causing her to limp. It would be a long time before she returned to her old self. Robert offered her his arm and Edie gratefully took it.

'Have you thought what you're going to d-do about Ray?' he asked Milly, who had taken his other arm.

She'd been thinking about him since the moment they'd visited her mum's boarding house and found her gone. Even when her mind was occupied with other things the shadow of it lay over her thoughts. Milly glanced behind her. There was nothing of the procession left to see but she was still able to hear the trumpets and drums of the military band.

'I haven't stopped thinking about it,' she confided. 'And I still don't know what I'm going to do.'

The royal family arrived back at Buckingham Palace the next day and all the royal residences – the palace, Clarence

House and Marlborough House – were hives of activity with visitors coming to pay their respects.

'She shoulda been allowed a few days off to grieve,' Caroline mumbled as they fiercely polished a marble column in the grand entrance.

'I agree,' Milly said, her arms throbbing with the effort. 'She's seen all and sundry today.'

'That King Whatshisname was nice though, weren't he?'

'Haakon? The one from Norway?'

'Yeah, he said good morning to me earlier. Didn't think he would. Funny name though. Hang on, someone's coming.'

Caroline and Milly prepared to curtsey as Queen Elizabeth came into view. She was on her own for a change and carried a handkerchief that she dabbed at her nose. When she saw the two of them standing there, the handkerchief was hastily tucked in a pocket, the moment of weakness gone.

'Good morning, Milly. Caroline.'

'Good morning, Your Majesty,' they chorused.

The Queen walked on, paused and took a step back. 'Milly, I – Caroline, could you perhaps work next door for a few moments, please?'

Unable to speak, Caroline simply nodded and mechanically moved into the next room. Milly swallowed. The Queen could want to speak to her about any number of things: Timothy, the handkerchief, the row she'd witnessed at dinner, her mum . . . Her mind stumbled from one panicked thought to another as Queen Elizabeth began to speak.

'I understand that Mrs Barnes has been having some trouble with her knee lately.'

'Y-yes, ma'am but she's fine honestly. She just—'

'Oh come now, I'm not about to replace her. She has always been a very loyal member of staff. No, I wanted to suggest that she try elevating it to take the swelling down. It should be higher than her heart so lying with a pillow under her knee should do it. And perhaps wrapping a bandage tightly around it for some support when she's working.'

Milly blinked before gathering herself; relief had muddled her brain. 'Thank you, ma'am. I'll tell her. She'll be happy to know you thought of her.'

'Well, of course I have,' she said with the slightest of laughs. 'We must look after each other. We are family and loyalty should always be rewarded.' Sadness tinged her stoic expression, though no tears appeared in her eyes.

'Are you all right, ma'am?' Milly asked without thinking. The Queen's startled gaze settled on her. 'I – I'm sorry. I didn't mean to be impertinent. I just – We all feel for you, ma'am, and, well – we're all very sorry for your loss.'

She seemed touched and her hand reached out to rest gently on Milly's arm. From the corner of her eye, Milly spotted Caroline sneaking a look around the doorframe, her eyes wide at the contact between them.

'It always surprised me my father broke the rules and allowed you to stay, Milly. He was rather a stickler when it came to these things. But I think I can see now why he did. He was a very good judge of character, and he always did what he thought was right, no matter what other people said. A good lesson, don't you think?' She continued on

349

before Milly could respond. 'Now, do not forget to tell your aunt what I said. I have rather damaged myself on several occasions while out riding so I am something of an expert on these things.'

The Queen hurried away, and Milly dropped into a curtsey until she was out of sight.

Caroline was in front of her within seconds. 'Crikey, Milly, what was all that about? Are we in trouble? Does she know about the handkerchief?'

'She was asking after Edie,' Milly said, still dumbfounded by the exchange. 'She was so nice. Just like her father.'

'Course she was. She's gonna be just like him.' Caroline cocked her head. 'You don't look at all well, Milly. Do you need a breather?'

She answered without thinking that she was fine, and Caroline sank back into her normal comforting chatter. All the while, Milly's brain ran over the Queen's words. A tiny sentence, said without thinking, had triggered something within Milly. She'd spent days agonising over this decision and now, suddenly, she knew exactly what to do. She just hoped that come tomorrow she'd still feel brave enough to do it.

Chapter Thirty-Two

On Sunday morning, the streets of London were still eerily quiet after the King's funeral. Milly slipped her arm into Robert's as they made their way to the Golden Hotel.

'Are you sure about this, M-Milly? It could be dangerous.'

'I'm positive, Robert. Truly. And I know Ray might well decide to carry out his threat on me, but I need to at least try.' Milly raised her chin, pretending the fear knotting in her stomach wasn't growing stronger with every step. She stopped, taking Robert's hand and turning him to face her. 'If he tries anything, we run. OK? I don't want you getting hurt because of me.'

His eyes roved over her face, and she hoped her firm voice and set expression showed she'd brook no argument. He signalled for her to lead the way.

They walked down Carnaby Street and turned into Ganton Street, finding the squalid, grubby hotel a few premises down. Milly marched to the tiny, cluttered reception desk and pressed the bell. It made no noise, and she called out. A man appeared from a small side room, a cigarette hanging from his thin lips, his greasy hair parted arrow straight down the middle revealing a white line of scalp.

'Yes, miss? What can I do for you?'

'I'm looking for Mr Smith. I believe he's staying here.'

'And who shall I say it is?'

For some reason she didn't really want to give her name. 'His niece,' she replied, earning a confused glance from Robert, who thankfully understood her reticence quickly enough.

'Jimmy? Jimmy?' The man called a young boy from the small, cramped seating area that must be the hotel lounge. He'd been playing with marbles in the corner and gathered them up quickly before making his way over. 'Go and tell Mr Smith in room three his niece is here to see him.'

He ran up the narrow staircase to the rooms above. The man disappeared back into his cubbyhole and Milly gave Robert a nervous glance. She prayed things wouldn't turn nasty. She didn't want Robert to get hurt, never mind herself. Anger blazed all over again at Jean and her disregard for anyone but herself, and Milly used it to give her strength to see this through.

A few minutes later, the boy's light, fast tread was followed down the stairs by an irregular heavy, thump.

'Me niece!' Ray declared, arms outstretched, the scarred and puckered skin on his face pulling into a smile. 'How lovely to see ya. And who's this?'

'This is my friend . . . Archibald.'

Robert quirked an eyebrow.

'Archibald, eh?' Ray shook Robert's hand, clenching it hard. 'Come up to me room and we can talk.' He led Robert towards the stairs, his hand still clamped in Ray's vice-like grip.

'Can't we talk down here, Uncle?' Milly's voice wavered, dread piercing through. If they followed him to his room, they'd be trapped and if things turned nasty where would they run?

Ray turned a terrifying glare on them. 'Ah, but then we can't talk like family, can we? And if we sit down here, dirty little ears'll be listenin'.' The young boy ran back to the corner of the room as Ray glowered at him. 'Come on,' he said, still holding on to Robert, who had tried and failed to release his hand. 'It'll be cosy. Just me niece and me and Archibald here.'

With no other option, Milly followed them both, praying she hadn't made an even worse mistake.

In his room, Ray all but tossed Robert towards the bed, finally letting go of his hand as he stumbled into a seated position. 'Sit down then, Archibald. And you—' he demanded of Milly, pronouncing the word properly and pointing to a hard wooden chair in front of an empty, tattered desk. 'There.'

Milly's eyes skittered over the room. She didn't know where the gun he'd mentioned to her in the alleyway was, but the knife he'd threatened to use lay on the windowsill beside where he now perched. He picked it up, studying the blade, turning it over in his large, tobacco-stained hands. Framed by thin, almost see-through, red curtains, he resembled a stage villain as the silver scars on his face were lit by the faint sun penetrating the grimy glass.

Robert shot a glance towards Milly. Neither of them knew what would happen now and though fear was rising from her belly forcing sickness with it, she swallowed it down.

'I have to say,' Ray began, his voice calm. 'I'm disappointed it's not ya mum come to see me.'

'She can't,' Milly replied, finding an unknown strength

deep down inside. Talking helped to keep the vomit from rising further into her throat. 'She's gone.'

Ray launched himself upright and flecks of paint sprang from the peeling sill, fluttering on to the carpet.

'I told her what you said, and we were going to find you the money somehow, but with all the upheaval since the King died—'

'God rest his soul,' Ray added solemnly, and the farcical nature of the comment almost made Milly laugh. She hadn't thought gangsters would be ardent fans of the monarchy.

'When I went to see her again, she'd run away. She's gone and I've no idea where.' It hurt to say the words, as if speaking them in front of Ray suddenly made them truer. 'She didn't leave a note this time.' Milly lifted her eyes to see him studying her.

'It's the t-truth,' Robert added.

'Is it n-now?' Ray mocked. Robert's face hardened but he didn't react. 'I thought ya didn't know where she lived?'

'I didn't when we spoke, but I managed to find out.'

'And ya didn't tell me?' His tone was almost teasing. She didn't know how to respond. Anger flared behind Ray's eyes as he tutted. He was toying with her, enjoying the fear radiating off her and Robert. 'Well, that's a shame, ain't it?'

'But I have something for you.' Milly stood and reached into her coat pocket, handing over all the money she had in the world. Robert stood too and Ray commanded him to sit down again. The tip of the knife danced towards Robert's face as Ray spoke.

'Ya don't wanna make any sudden moves when an angry man's holdin' a knife, sunshine.'

'It's not enough,' Milly said matter of factly. She'd already decided the best thing to do was be brutally honest. There was nothing else to be done. She wasn't about to borrow money from her friends and family to make it up. 'I wish it was, but it's not. But it is all I have.'

Ray transferred his angry glare back to Milly, lifting his chin. 'How much?'

'Just short of a hundred and ten pounds.' She held the small brown envelope out to him, and he eyed it warily. 'Could this be enough for you to leave me and my mum alone?'

He laughed, the deep, echoing sound bouncing around the room, resounding off the peeling walls. 'Ya want us to just forget about the rest of the debt? When she's run off and left ya to face it? To face me?'

'Yes. I want you to guarantee you'll leave my mum alone. That you won't go looking for her. You'll forget about it.'

Robert stared at Milly. He'd had no idea she'd been planning this but rather than fear it was pride that exuded from his eyes, giving her strength.

Ray put the knife down and took the envelope, opening it and counting the money inside. 'Ya got balls, girl, I'll give ya that. But it's less than half what she owes.'

'I know. If I could pay it all, I would. I work at Buckingham Palace but I'm only a cleaner. I'm not one of the Royals. This is everything I've saved over the last five years. It's every penny I own.'

'Ya could steal somethin', let me fence it and keep the cash.'

That had been her mum's plan, but Milly wouldn't do it.

No matter what Ray threatened her with. The palace was her home, the people there her family.

'No,' she replied firmly. 'I won't do that. Especially not now. They're going through enough. The King's just died, and I don't see why I should risk my livelihood for a mum who doesn't love me. I'm a victim in all of this too. I know it doesn't matter to you. There's no reason why you should care, but it's the truth. This' – she gestured towards the envelope –'will have to be enough.'

Ray cocked his head. 'Ya quite like her, ya know. Ya mum. Feisty. I always did have a soft spot for her.'

'So you agree?' Robert asked.

'Reckon I do, as long as she don't cross me path again.'

Milly dropped her eyes to the thin carpet. The swirling pattern hid most, but not all of the stains. It, like everything in the room, was covered in dust. She wanted to get out of there. To return to her palace life. The clean, safe walls. The friends and family that waited for her there. All the while she'd been planning what to say and how she'd say it, she hadn't thought beyond the next moment. It had seemed too much to hope they'd get to leave this squalid, awful place, but with the prospect now before her, she wanted to run outside and breathe in the smoggy air of London.

'She won't,' Milly confirmed. 'I have a feeling neither of us will ever see her again.' She willed the tears back from her eyes. It pained her how deeply she knew that was true.

Ray placed the envelope in his jacket pocket and picked up the knife again, using it to gesture towards the door. 'If ya see her again, ya tell her to stay away. If me boss sees her—' He shook his head. 'Let's just say there won't be anythin' I can do then.' Milly nodded her understanding. 'Ya better leave then. Nice to meet ya, Archibald. And goodbye, niece.'

They didn't shake hands. Robert led Milly from the room, his hand in the small of her back. It gave her comfort, but what she wanted was to fall into his arms and feel the safety of them wrap around her.

Outside, they hurried away from the hotel and back to Carnaby Street, neither speaking until they were a decent distance from Ray and sure that he hadn't followed them. When they reached Golden Square, they sat on a bench in the gardens. With the King's funeral over and the world waking up, the city had grown busier once more. Men and women filled the streets, children laughed, tourists strolled lazily.

Every limb shook as adrenaline pulsed through Milly's body. In the quiet of the small green square, she couldn't believe it had worked.

'We did it, Robert.' She turned to him, her hands resting in her lap, suddenly cold in the overcast February weather.

He slipped his hand into hers and warmth suffused her fingers. 'There's no we. You did it, Milly. Just you.'

'I'm not sure I'd have had the courage if you hadn't come with me.'

'You would have. You're far braver than you think.'

She shook her head. 'I don't know about that. Needs must when the devil drives.'

'C-can I ask you something?'

Milly turned to him. 'Anything.'

'How can you give up everything you've earned for her when she's left you again? Aren't you angry with her?'

'Yes!' Milly chuckled, hoping it would hide some of the

357

hurt springing from her words. 'I'm so angry I could scream. Losing her and Dad the first time, as a child, was so painful I thought I'd die. I never thought anything could be as painful as that but this – if anything it's even worse. She never loved me – not really – I know that now. And instead of facing this together, she's chosen to run away again, and to go without even saying goodbye. How could I mean so little to her?' Milly gasped in a breath and began to sob.

Robert pulled her close, wrapping his arm around her shoulder. 'She's the one who's losing out, Milly. If she can't see what a wonderful person you are, that's her loss. And you still have Edie and all of us.'

Milly squeezed her eyes shut. It was true. She had her palace family and Edie had been more of a mum to her than Jean ever had or ever could be.

'Do you want to go to the Sunrise Club too? See if we can throw Jack off the scent?'

She shook her head. 'I don't think so. I don't know for sure if Jack recognised her and he'll know she's gone by now. If he doesn't, he'll soon find out and I'd rather not be around when he does. She told him she'd come from Southampton so if he does look for her, it'll be there, and she definitely won't go there now.'

After a moment, Robert said, 'I want you to know, M-Milly, I was going to offer some money to that gangster too but I don't have any savings.'

Milly's spirits lifted. She knew he would have helped if he could. Knew it without even asking. Robert's cheeks coloured, and he dropped his eyes away to the pavement. 'You really should start saving, Robert. How else are you going to afford to take me out to the pictures? I don't have very expensive tastes and I'm happy to pay my share but there will be times when I expect – oh, I don't know – flowers, chocolates, another beautiful brooch like my swallow one.'

He lifted his gaze, meeting hers fully, and butterflies danced in her stomach. 'You mean we could – we could—'

She leaned forwards and kissed him, somehow knowing that after Timothy, he wouldn't dare make the first move unless he was absolutely sure it was what she wanted, and spelling it out would have rather killed the mood. His kiss fired the love deep inside she'd recognised the other day. A love that Timothy had been unable to reach. Perhaps deep down she had always known he wasn't right for her, or perhaps what she felt for Robert was something entirely different. Something more than just a crush based on appearance and charm. Robert's hand gently cupped her cheek as affection flooded her body. When he kissed her again, the feelings inside her were deep, as if some invisible force bound them together. A knot had been tied from her life to his. Like the branches of the Victoria and Albert trees wrapping around each other in the palace gardens.

When it ended, she laid her head on his shoulder and they sat in silence in the middle of the bustling city, no words required between them.

Chapter Thirty-Three

'Where've you been?' asked Edie when Milly knocked on her door later that day.

'To see Ray.'

'Oh, my girl, you could've been killed!'

'I don't think so, Aunt Edie. Hurt maybe.' The realisation of just how far Ray might have gone had he not been so reasonable dawned on Milly again and she shivered.

'You should've told me. I could've come with you.'

Though Edie would have been a force to be reckoned with, Milly was glad Robert had been the one by her side. 'I didn't tell you because I didn't want you to try and talk me out of it. I gave him as much money as I could.'

'You did what?' Edie's mouth hung slightly open. 'How much?'

'Everything I had. I paid off about half of what Jean owed, and he's promised to leave her alone as long as he never sees her again. I'm pretty certain he won't. I don't think we'll ever see her in London again. Please don't be angry at me, Aunt Edie.' She reached out and took her aunt's hand. 'I know it's a lot of money, but I couldn't just leave her at the mercy of these men. I needed to help. I know it seems silly given she's been a terrible mum but . . . The Queen said something to me yesterday, when she told me about your knee, about a matter

360

of conscience. About doing what you think is right no matter what anyone says and I thought, I can't let her carry on with this man after her. What if he never stopped looking? I couldn't live with myself thinking that one day they might find her and do goodness knows what. I just wish I could tell her she doesn't have to worry any more.'

Edie spoke softly. 'I understand, but you should've told me. Maybe I could've helped.'

'I was worried you might try and give me some money too. Not for Jean's sake, but to make sure he didn't do anything to me.'

Edie smiled knowingly and Milly knew she was right. Her aunt would have done anything, including paying Jean's debts, to make sure it kept her safe. 'I couldn't have given you the rest, but I do have a fair amount put by. I've been savin' for your weddin'.'

'My wedding? Well, that's not likely to happen anytime soon.'

'No? Is that what Robert thinks?' Milly's cheeks filled with heat. 'Put the kettle on, will you? I'm dyin' for a cuppa and we've got time before we see the senior footman.'

'I'd almost forgotten about that.' Milly did as asked and made up a tray. 'How's Caroline?'

'Scared, but I'm determined you won't be found at fault.'

Milly's stomach began to knot at this final hurdle. 'What if he mentions about Jean, Aunt?'

'I've already thought of that, don't you worry, my girl.'

Just as they finished their tea, Caroline knocked on the door.

'Come in,' Edie called out.

'All right, Mrs Barnes.' She stepped into the room and immediately began toying with her fingers.

'Now don't be nervous, lovey, we'll get this whole thing sorted out.' Edie drank the last of her tea and checked her watch. 'Come on. Better early than late.' She pushed herself up from the chair and together the three of them marched to find the senior footman. He didn't have an office of his own, so they had arranged to meet in the Household Dining Room. It wasn't yet dinnertime, and the room was empty. He sat alone at one of the tables.

'Mrs Barnes,' Mr Dankworth said, standing up. 'And some of your team, I see. You're making me nervous.' He had a kindly appearance with white hair and small glasses that perched on the bridge of his nose.

'I'm sorry to, Mr Dankworth, but I'm afraid there is somethin' serious we need to talk to you about.'

'Oh, dear. Well, do sit down and let's see what we can do about whatever this is.'

Caroline and Milly sat next to each other. Milly's nerves were spiking horribly and knowing Caroline's must be worse she reached out under the table and took her hand.

'You'd better begin, Milly,' Edie said.

She took a breath and turned to Mr Dankworth. 'I'm afraid we're here to complain about Timothy Ranger. I . . . We . . .'

'Take your time, my dear,' Mr Dankworth said gently.

She should have rehearsed what to say, found the words to talk about it plainly, but her mind had been so preoccupied with everything else she hadn't had time. 'We stepped out a few times and I'm afraid that one night he took things too far, if you know what I mean. I don't want to go into

362

details if I don't have to, but when I pushed him away, he didn't take it very kindly. He said some horrible things to me.' She looked at Edie, unsure what else to say, and Edie took over.

'And then he did the same to Caroline.'

Caroline bent over, her hands curled tightly around the cuffs of her cardigan.

'Is that right?' Mr Dankworth asked. She nodded.

'He'd done something like it before,' she said, raising her eyes and peering at them through her pale lashes. 'But I – oh, please don't make me talk about it again.' Stifled sobs could be heard through her fingers and the pain in Milly's heart intensified. She explained everything Caroline had told her before.

'I have a feelin' that these two aren't the only ones,' said Edie, 'and that he might be carryin' on with more than one woman at a time. He was certainly quick to try his luck with Caroline again once Milly had thrown him out on his ear.'

Mr Dankworth pushed his glasses up the bridge of his nose and clasped his hands in front of him. 'Well, this is very serious indeed. If this is true, he should really be dismissed.'

'I was hopin' you'd say that, and my girls wouldn't make this up.'

'Unfortunately, given the very serious nature of the accusations, I think I should defer to the Deputy Master.'

Milly's heart sank and she squeezed Caroline's hand under the table knowing this was the last thing she'd wanted.

'Can't we deal with this between ourselves, Mr

Dankworth?' Edie asked. 'You know my girls wouldn't lie about such a thing.'

'Oh, I know they're telling the truth, but Mr Ranger must be given a chance to put his side of the story, and I think it would be better if this was handled by the Deputy Master. He'll know just what to do. Let's go and see him now.'

He stood back from the table and Milly and Caroline followed automatically. Fear gripped Milly tightly. The convoy moved through the palace to the Deputy Master's office and knocked on the door. He called for them to enter and Mr Dankworth led the way inside.

'Goodness,' Group Captain Peter Townsend exclaimed as they entered. 'There's a lot of you. I'm not sure I've got enough chairs.' He had a kindly smile and bright, intelligent eyes.

'I don't mind standing, sir,' Mr Dankworth said.

'Me neither,' Milly replied.

With her sore knee, Edie sat down in the seat opposite and Mr Dankworth was convinced to take the second chair.

'Now, what can I do for you all?'

Mr Dankworth outlined the situation. The Deputy Master listened, asking questions about dates and times and making copious notes. When he spoke to Milly his gaze was so piercing, she had the distinct impression he could read her mind and would automatically know if she was lying. Eventually, he sat back in his chair, a forefinger tapping his chin.

'I see. Right. The first thing we need to do is speak to Mr Ranger. I'll have him summoned.' He lifted the receiver and rang through to someone. Within minutes, Timothy arrived, his eyes wary though his bearing was as confident as ever.

Milly swallowed, doing her best to control the shaking in her body, suddenly wishing she'd taken a seat as her legs trembled. She pressed her weight into her heels to stop it.

'Mr Ranger,' Mr Townsend began. 'Some serious accusations have been made against you.' He told him what Milly and Caroline had said. 'How do you respond?'

'Lies, sir. All of it. Both lying 'cause I broke it off with them. Caroline invited me to her room and Milly's unhappy I wasn't interested any more.' Milly bit her lip to stop from shouting out. Timothy glowered at her from the corner of his eye. 'She's upset her mum's back on the scene and – well, I don't think she's been a good influence on her. Sorry to say.'

Unable to control herself, Edie erupted. 'How dare you—'

'Mrs Barnes.' Mr Townsend's strong but calm voice stopped her. 'Please. I'll come back to you after Mr Ranger's had his say. Let's all try and stay calm. Mr Ranger, please continue.'

'Her mum's – well, I hate to say it out loud, sir – but her mum's a – a—' He turned his head this way and that. 'You know what I mean, sir.'

'No, I'm not sure I do.'

'A . . .' He leaned forward and whispered the word, though it was loud enough for everyone to hear. 'Prostitute.'

Mr Townsend sat back. 'And how do you know that, Mr Ranger?'

'Milly told me.'

'I did not,' Milly replied vehemently. She'd told him of Helen's suspicions but that was all. Timothy stared, his feelings of superiority clear in the way he lifted his chin and peered down his nose at her, but she wouldn't look away. She met his stare with one of her own.

'If I may,' Edie said, and Mr Townsend flicked his hand, gesturing for her to continue. 'My sister's no longer around to defend herself. Her visit's over and she's gone home. I think Mr Ranger's aware of that and is tryin' to cast shame on Milly, knowin' my sister isn't here to defend herself. She sings in hotels and clubs, Mr Townsend, but that's it. She earns a perfectly respectable livin' and I think it's terrible of Mr Ranger to say it's anythin' else.'

'I have to agree with you, Mrs Barnes. Casting aspersions like that without any proof is entirely inappropriate.'

Timothy's face froze under Peter Townsend's glower. 'She stole from the palace too, when Milly let her into one of the guest bedrooms.'

'Who did?'

'Milly's mum.'

Mr Townsend's eyes flicked towards Milly, who bit the inside of her cheek to stop her face from showing any fear.

'And what do you think she stole?' He checked some papers on his desk. 'I have a list of missing items here: let's see if it's on there.' He picked up a piece of paper, angling it so Timothy couldn't see it.

'I – I don't know exactly, but it was small and hard and . . . she hid it under her coat.'

'And how do you know that?'

Timothy stuttered but couldn't come up with a response. Admitting he'd deliberately touched her waist would only incriminate him further.

'There's nothing small and hard on my list. Nothing that

could be concealed under a coat without being noticed. A small photograph of the King was misplaced from one of the guest bedrooms but has now been found.' Timothy's head spun towards Milly. He was furious. 'If I were you, Mr Ranger, I'd stop making groundless accusations. Caroline, do you have anything you wish to say?'

Caroline finally lifted her eyes and to Milly's amazement found her strength. 'I didn't invite him to my room, Mr Townsend. Not the second time. The first time he asked to come, and I know I should have said no – I wish I had – but it wasn't me who asked. I made a terrible mistake that day.' With her right hand she pulled the neckline of her blouse closer together, an unconscious gesture that Mr Townsend obviously noticed, given the concern in his eyes. 'The second time he followed me. I tried to close the door on him, but . . .' Tears threatened and Milly hugged her, not caring who was watching.

Mr Townsend placed two hands on the edge of his desk and pushed his chair back. 'May I ask you to step outside for a few moments please?' The remark was directed at everyone except Caroline and Milly. They did as asked, and Edie closed the door behind them, her eyes meeting Milly's before it clicked shut.

'I'm aware, ladies, that you two found a handkerchief recently that belonged to the King and were sworn to secrecy.' He clasped his hands behind his back in a military fashion.

Milly thought she might be sick. Her throat closed over and she pushed the words out past a lump in her throat. 'Yes, sir.'

'And you've kept that promise?'

'Yes, sir. Neither of us has told a soul.' She'd told Edie and Helen, but they didn't count and she trusted them implicitly. 'Caroline hasn't even told her parents.'

'They knew summat was bothering me, but I never said a word, sir.'

He pursed his lips as he considered what to say. 'I think the Master was a little over-hasty in threatening your jobs the way he did. He told me of his conversation with you. I think he should have impressed upon you the importance of the secret for the nation. That you've both kept something so serious close to your chests is to your credit. It must have weighed on you both. Can you assure me that what you're saying about Mr Ranger is the absolute truth? No embellishments? No stretching the facts?'

'It is, sir,' Milly replied. 'I would never say anything against anyone who didn't deserve it. I never encouraged Mr Ranger in that way and neither did Caroline. He went too far and when we said no, he turned nasty. We've both spoken up because we couldn't live with ourselves if he did it to another girl.'

'Or did something worse,' Caroline added unexpectedly.

'I've had the misfortune to meet men like Mr Ranger before and I have a feeling you may not be the only ones. You've both been very brave coming forward. Another thing to your credit. Miss Stratton—' He looked directly at Caroline. 'We do have rules for a reason; please follow them in future.'

Relief brightened Caroline's features as the words sank in. 'I will, sir. I promise. I won't never let a man into my room again.'

368

'Good. Then you two had better get about your duties. Mr Ranger will be leaving the palace immediately and Mr Dankworth can see him out.' He pulled down his jacket. 'Off you go.' Milly bobbed a curtsey as she thanked him, and Mr Townsend laughed. 'I'm not the Queen, Milly, you don't need to do that.' He opened the door for them, and they walked out to see Edie, Mr Dankworth and Timothy in the corridor. 'Mr Ranger and Mr Dankworth, can you step back in, please?'

For the first time, concern darkened Timothy's eyes and the sly smile that had remained on his face fell away.

'So?' Edie asked after the door had closed and they'd reached the other end of the corridor.

'There you are!' Helen said breathily as she virtually ran towards them. 'I've been looking all over for you.'

'We had to go and see the Deputy Master,' Milly replied.

'Gosh. And—'

'What did he say?' Edie demanded.

Milly smiled, relief flooding her body. 'He believed us. Timothy will be leaving.'

'And right now, by the sound of it,' Caroline added.

Edie's smile was wide and unencumbered. 'Good. Timothy Ranger might think he's a bit of a jack the lad, but he didn't bank on us, did he?'

Helen reached out and hugged each of her friends. 'I'm so relieved. That'll teach him to try and take advantage. How are you feeling, Caroline?'

'She'll be fine, won't you?' Edie wrapped an arm around her shoulders.

'I will now. Oh, I could celebrate. At least I can tell Ma and Pa now. Pa'll probably threaten Timothy with summat

369

from the shed but at least they'll know. No doubt they'll tell me off for being naive.'

'Well, you're a little less so now. Let's go back to my room for a cuppa and a few minutes' rest. All this has frayed my nerves somethin' chronic. You're good workers,' Edie said. 'And they appreciate that here. Loyalty too. Loyalty's the most important thing.'

'That's what the Queen said,' Milly managed with a smile. 'You were right though, Aunt Edie. I was better off without Jean. I feel like none of this would've happened if we'd been pottering along as before.'

'Hmm,' Edie replied, thoughtfully.

'What?'

'I have to say I think these past few months have been good for you, in a way.'

'Good for me? How?'

'You've grown up a lot. I'm not sure you would've if you hadn't got that letter. You got out of the palace more. Out with friends. You're only young, Milly, and you live in London, you should be makin' the most of it rather than hidin' in these four walls, lovely as they are. One thing's for certain, these last few months have made you stronger and a bit more worldly – you too, Caroline – and that can only be a good thing.'

'A run-in with gangsters is likely to do that for you.'

'Well, just make sure you don't go back to stayin' locked behind the palace walls. Go out with Robert and Helen and Caroline. Enjoy life. We've all worked hard enough to get here after the war and if our poor King's death has shown us anythin', it's that we need to enjoy life while we can.'

'Robert and I are going to the National Gallery on our next day off,' Milly replied, her heart lifting at the idea.

'See!' Caroline said to Helen. 'I told you it was serious.' Everyone laughed.

'I remember takin' you there when you were little,' Edie replied, ignoring them.

'Really?' Milly didn't remember that trip, but then there was a lot she didn't remember Edie doing for her that she should have. 'Edie?' she began tentatively, tears once more stinging the back of her nose. 'You know I meant what I said the other day. You've been more of a mum to me than Jean ever was and I'm sorry I haven't told you that before. I took the love you always gave me for granted, but I realise now how lucky I've been. I didn't end up in an orphanage or left at the Harlows' farm when I was evacuated, and I wouldn't have ended up here at Buckingham Palace if it wasn't for you.'

'Well, all things worked out in the end, didn't they?' But Edie's eyes were glistening with tears. 'It's about time the world caught up with you young women.'

'Whatever do you mean, Mrs Barnes?' asked Caroline.

'You young girls don't just want husbands and kids, do you? Not till you're ready. In my day, you only got a job to tide you over 'til you got married and ran a house. I didn't, but then I wouldn't settle for anythin' less than true love. But now, women want to work like they did durin' the war. There needs to be more opportunities for young 'uns like you. If we can have a queen rulin' our country at twenty-five, then who's to say what you young ladies could achieve? And she wasn't even meant to be queen, was she? Her dad

371

was never meant to be king and only was because his brother didn't want the job, but look where life's taken her. Women can do anythin', if you ask me, and it's about time the world remembered that.'

'You keep saying "you women" like your life's over, Aunt Edie.' Milly chuckled. 'But you're only forty-eight. It's not like you're going off to the knacker's yard anytime soon.'

The compliment brought a stronger glow to Edie's rosy cheeks. 'I know. I'm just sayin'. A new era is startin' and I'm almost certain it's one you young ladies will make your own.'

Milly wasn't entirely convinced but she hoped so, and a small flicker of hope grew into something stronger. She'd been threatened and stood up to gangsters; she'd seen another side of London she hadn't known existed; and through their new young Queen she was seeing what was possible in this world. The spark wasn't yet a fire, and she had no idea what was in store for her next, but it was a flame growing ever stronger, and who knew how fierce that flame could become? Change was coming, and Milly, for one, was most certainly ready for it.

Their dearly loved King was gone, but now it was time to joyously declare long live the Queen as the new Elizabethan age dawned.

Acknowledgements

Writing this book was a wonderful journey and I'm extremely grateful to a number of people for making it happen.

Firstly, my thanks go to my agent Kate Nash of the Kate Nash Literary Agency, for everything she has done for me. I'm truly, truly grateful and this book wouldn't exist without her. She's an inspirational woman working tirelessly for her authors and I'm beyond grateful to have her in my corner.

Secondly, thank you to the entire team at Century, particularly my editor, Katie Loughnane, managing editor Katya Browne, designer Glenn O'Neill, and everyone else who has worked on the book. Thank you all so much for your enthusiasm for *The Palace Girls* and your efforts in making this novel the absolute best it could be. I'm truly indebted to you all.

The encouragement of friends goes a long way and my particular thanks go to Belinda Missen, the Writing Dream Team (Anita Faulkner, Lucy Keeling, Jaimie Admans, Leonie Mack, Emma Jackson and Kate Smith) and to one of the most amazing people I know: Jennifer Buchman.

Finally, my thanks go to my family for their endless support. To my mum and dad: thank you for delivering cake and making delicious dinners when I'm on a deadline.

And to all my in-laws: thank you for being so supportive! To my husband Phil: thank you for always believing in me, even when I find it hard to believe in myself, and to my children, Eleanore and Samuel: thank you for not minding when I miss football or ask for music to be turned down because I'm writing. Maybe you're not too bad after all!

And, of course, a final thank you has to go to the readers who have picked up a copy of this book. I wouldn't be able to do any of this without you and I cannot begin to tell you how grateful I am for your support.

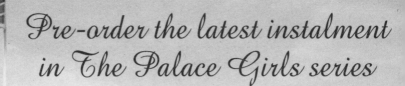

Pre-order the latest instalment
in The Palace Girls series

SECRETS
OF THE
PALACE
GIRLS

**COMING
AUGUST 2024**